THE FIRST ATOMIC
BOMB

THE FIRST ATOMIC BOMB

AN ALTERNATE HISTORY OF THE ENDING OF WW2

James Mangi

FRONTLINE
BOOKS

THE FIRST ATOMIC BOMB
An Alternate History to the Ending of WW2

First published in 2022 by Frontline Books,
an imprint of Pen & Sword Books Ltd, Yorkshire – Philadelphia

Typeset in by
Printed and bound by CPI Group (UK) Ltd, Croydon, CR0 4YY

Pen & Sword Books Ltd incorporates the imprints of Pen & Sword Archaeology,
Air World Books, Atlas, Aviation, Battleground, Discovery, Family History,
History, Maritime, Military, Naval, Politics, Social History, Transport,
True Crime, Claymore Press, Frontline Books, Praetorian Press, Seaforth
Publishing and White Owl

For a complete list of Pen & Sword titles please contact:

PEN & SWORD BOOKS LTD
47 Church Street, Barnsley, South Yorkshire, S70 2AS, UK.
E-mail: enquiries@pen-and-sword.co.uk
Website: www.pen-and-sword.co.uk

Or

PEN AND SWORD BOOKS,
1950 Lawrence Roadd, Havertown, PA 19083, USA
E-mail: Uspen-and-sword@casematepublishers.com
Website: www.penandswordbooks.com

Contents

List of Illustrations

10. North (Honshu) entrance to Kanmon railway tunnels connecting Honshu and Kyushu Islands.
    (https://commons.wikimedia.org/wiki/File:Kammon_railway_tunnel_Shimonoseki_portal.jpg)

11. Minesweeper *YMS-143* being transferred to Soviets as part of Project Hula, Cold Bay, Alaska.
    (US Navy Photo Public Domain. https://worldofwarships.com/en/news/history/usni-project-hula/)

12. Soviet paratroops dropped over Ishikari, Hokkaido, landed behind the Japanese forces that were deployed to defend against Soviet ground troops who were advancing down the Ishikari River valley.
    (Кадр кинохроники, Public domain, via Wikimedia Commons. https://commons.wikimedia.org/wiki/File:Paratroopers_jumping_from_Tupolev_TB-3.jpg)

13. Soviet troops advancing into occupation near the southern port of Pusan, Korea, 1945. (https://commons.wikimedia.org/wiki/File:Soviet_liberators_marching_through_the_Korean_county_road._October_1945.jpg)

14. Kim Il-sung (centre), with other Korean communists, and their Soviet sponsors, presiding at a 1946 meeting in Seoul establishing Kim's leadership of the Soviet-occupied Korean peninsula. (https://commons.wikimedia.org/wiki/File:28.08.1946_Labour_Party_North_Korea.jpg)

15. Kyuichi Tokuda, a communist member of the Japanese Diet, addresses the crowd at the May Day labour demonstration, 1946.
    (Unknown author, Public domain, via Wikimedia Commons https://upload.wikimedia.org/wikipedia/commons/0/09/Tokuda_Kyuichi_1946)

16. Tokyo police battle rioters on 'Bloody May Day, 1946'.
    (Unknown author, Public domain, via Wikimedia Commons https://upload.wikimedia.org/wikipedia/commons/0/0e/Bloody_May_Day_Incident3.JPG)

17. Japanese communist Sanzo Nosaka at a celebration, with his wife, of the declaration of his Ezo Democratic People's Republic of Japan in Sapporo, Hokkaido, 1947.
    (https://commons.wikimedia.org/wiki/File:Nosaka_Sanzo_and_Nosaka_Ryo.jpg)

18. Mao Zedong's People's Liberation Army enters Beijing, as the Soviet Red Army leaves, May 1946.
    (https://commons.wikimedia.org/wiki/File:PLA_Enters_Peking.jpg).

19. December 1947. In Beijing's Tiananmen Square, Mao Zedong proclaims the founding of the People's Republic of China (PRC).
(Hou Bo, Public domain, via Wikimedia Commons. https://upload.wikimedia.org/wikipedia/commons/3/3e/PRCFounding.jpg)
20. Campaign button for General Douglas MacArthur's short-lived bid for the Republican presidential nomination, 1948.
(Author's collection)
21. Bao Dai, last Emperor of Vietnam.
(https://commons.wikimedia.org/wiki/File:Baodai2.jpg)
22. Vietnamese Communist known as Ho Chi Minh.
(https://commons.wikimedia.org/wiki/File:Ho_Chi_Minh_1946.jpg)
23. USS *Belleau Wood* operating in the South China Sea during the Indochina War, 1952.
(US Navy Photo https://commons.wikimedia.org/wiki/File:USS_Belleau_Wood_(CVL-24)_underway_on_22_December_1943_(NH_97269).jpg)
24. Armoured bulldozers with heavy-duty ploughs were used by French motorized columns in Indochina to clear wide swathes of vegetation along roadways, denying the Viet Minh ambush hiding places during the Indochina War, 1949. (https://commons.wikimedia.org/wiki/File:Rome_Plow.jpg)
25. US President Harry Truman initiating US military involvement in the Indochina War, implementing the UN Resolution authorising member states to help the Bao Dai government repel Chinese Communist invasion, 1950. (Dept of Defense Photo https://commons.wikimedia.org/wiki/File:Truman_initiating_Korean_involvement.jpg)
26. US Marines land in Vietnam, 1950, to assist the Bao Dai government in its fight against Communist aggression.
(US Marine Corps Photo https://commons.wikimedia.org/wiki/File:DaNangMarch61965.jpg)
27. In Saigon, Vietnam, French General officer reviews Gurkha troops of the 32nd Indian Brigade, part of the British Empire's commitment to the UN Command in the Indochina War, 1950.
(Ministère de la Guerre, France https://upload.wikimedia.org/wikipedia/commons/9/9c/General_Leclerc_reviews_Indian_troops%2C_Saigon_1945.jpg)
28. US Senator Joseph McCarthy (left) confers with aide Roy Cohn, 1950.
(United Press International telephoto, Public domain, via Wikimedia Commons https://commons.wikimedia.org/wiki/File:McCarthy_Cohn.jpg)

29. At the UN Security Council, US delegate Warren Austin holds a Russian-made sub-machine gun captured by American troops in July 1950. (https://en.wikipedia.org/wiki/List_of_United_Nations_ Security_Council_resolutions_concerning_North_Korea#/media/ File:Warren_Austin_holds_up_Soviet_SMG_at_UN_HD-SN-99-03037.JPEG Public domain, via Wikimedia Commons)
30. Geneva Conference, 1953. (US Army Photograph. https://commons. wikimedia.org/wiki/File:Gen-commons.jpg)

List of Maps

Dedication

To the love of my life, Kathleen, who has smilingly accepted living in an alternate reality for so many years with Alzheimer's Disease.

The author's proceeds from this book will go to The Alzheimer's Society UK and the Alzheimer's Association US to help create a world where no one is forced by brain diseases to live in alternate realities.

Preface

This is a work of fictional history. It is not historical fiction. That rich and diverse genre consists of made-up tales placed in some actual or imagined historical setting. In contrast, fictional, or 'counterfactual', history is solidly based in reality and aims to be an accurate narrative of how history would have played out if a particular 'hinge event' had occurred differently. As with its predecessor, *Dropping the Atomic Bomb on Hitler and Hirohito*, the present work proceeds from the single counterfactual premise of a change in when the atomic bomb became available to the Allies. It describes a single, plausible hinge event or 'point of divergence' which would have changed that atomic timing. This is analogous to the point of divergence used in the previous work, but uses a different event to change the timing of the bomb. This is the author's only intervention. Everything else in the narrative – all the alterations in how the Second World War ends and how the post-war world develops – all flows logically from that single change in timing. No novel events 'just happen'. Rather, every altered event or development connects through a traceable chain of causes and effects all the way back to that fact-based, plausible counterfactual premise about the bomb's timing. This is not a sequel to *Dropping the Atomic Bomb on Hitler and Hirohito*, but rather a complementary companion work. They are separable, stand-alone works. While they are not mirror images, they do have some surprising parallels, such as in the post-war developments in Korea.

In this work, the hinge point is 'The Dud In The Desert', the July 1945 test of the first atomic device. Not a demonstration or rehearsal, it was a <u>test</u>, conducted because the world's best scientists weren't sure their bomb would work. The narrative identifies several plausible ways for it to fizzle, unintentionally or perhaps not. The Allied victory comes later, with widespread post-war consequences.

Events that would not have been affected by a changed course of history, such as flooding in Vietnam's Red River in 1945, are unchanged.

When the logical course of counterfactual history changes the dates of some events, their relative timing doesn't change. In this work, atom bombs fall on Japan three days apart, just as really happened, but the dates are shifted. Both narratives primarily feature actual leaders, generals, scientists and others; all major characters are real and they behave in accordance with the authentic historical record, but in response to the changed circumstances. For example, MacArthur presides over the Japanese surrender on the battleship *Missouri* in Tokyo Bay, but on a different date than really happened. He then serves as Supreme Allied Commander in Tokyo with the attitudes and aptitudes we know he had. The Occupation, however, plays out differently.

Cited references such as '(Frank 1999)' are all authentic sources. They show that Person A really did make quoted Statement B, or that an event in the narrative truly did occur. For example, the work describes unorthodox 'dentistry' by explosives expert George Kistiakowsky, and cites Richard Rhodes' authoritative book about the bomb. Including this citation means, 'Yes, Kistiakowsky really did that'. The full list of cited references is in the back, including several that substantiate some intriguing facts, like the Soviet Union's plans for the invasion of Japan. As syndicated columnist Dave Barry used to say: 'I'm not making this up.'

The 'What Really Happened' section is a timeline of authentic history. It serves as a quick reference for readers to double check their recall of various details of this period of history. In crafting the capsules of history in that table I tried to be accurate and objective; in a few cases, when these authentic events may be surprising, I cited references in the table entries as extra assurance that 'Yes, this is really what the record says did happen'. The 'What Really Happened' section is cross-referenced back and forth to the narratives: e.g. Presidential candidate Eisenhower promises to travel to the war zone to help end the war. A footnote link to 'What Really Happened' explains which war zone it really was. As with footnotes in conventional texts, go ahead and ignore them if you want.

Solidly rooted in the authentic record, this is a highly accurate historical account, except that it is fictional.

Everything is connected to everything else
Barry Commoner, *The Closing Circle* (1971).

PART I:
THE END OF
THE PACIFIC WAR

'The Dud In The Desert', the failure of the first atomic bomb test in July 1945, has fuelled conspiracy theories for over 75 years. 'The test was sabotaged by Soviet spy Klaus Fuchs,' goes one popular version, 'to help the Commies in the war against Japan.' 'That pinko, Oppenheimer' gets the blame in other versions. 'Leo Szilard sabotaged "the Gadget",' goes yet another version, 'because he hated the idea of actually using the weapon he had helped create.' As with most conspiracy theories, such claims are far more based on proponents' political predilections than on any factual evidence. Over the years, as more wartime records become declassified or simply get uncovered, a few previously hidden facts do come to light, and this fuels new rounds of conspiracy chatter. One such example is the very recent revelation, as discussed later, that there were more Soviet spies at Los Alamos than were discovered in the immediate post-war years. This includes at least one agent who had the knowledge and potential access to sabotage that first test device. Unlike Fuchs and Theodore Hall, Oscar Seborer not only worked at Los Alamos, but also helped develop the bomb's detonation mechanism, and was at the Trinity test site. Some conspiracy theories are like low-grade ore – there are ounces of fact deeply embedded in tons of garbage.

Of course to explain the Great Fizzle there are also the ever-popular 'extra-terrestrials'. A very confident group of conspiracists maintains that these ultimate illegal aliens intervened in the New Mexico desert. 'Using technology far beyond anything available on Earth,' the clichéd storyline goes, 'they remotely sabotaged the bomb to try to prevent humans from unlocking the Pandora's Box of atomic fission.' To these Believers it was no coincidence that the event which they consider to be bedrock certain, the crash of an alien spacecraft in Roswell, New Mexico occurred just two (earth) years later and a hundred miles away.

Notwithstanding these varied conspiracies, earthly and galactic, records now available show with a reasonable certainty that the cause of the Trinity test's fizzle was a relatively simple, human-caused flaw in a complicated device assembled on a rigid schedule. Once found, the flaw was not hard to remedy. But it was impossible to reverse the far-reaching consequences of the initial fizzle. Here is what happened:

Chapter 1

The Long Drive, 16 July 1945

After the atomic bomb fizzled, J. Robert Oppenheimer had a lot
to think about. It was a 250-mile drive from the desert test site
on New Mexico's Alamogordo Army Air Field back to the secret
bomb laboratory he directed at Los Alamos. There was plenty of time
to reflect, and to plan next steps. It was disappointing, yet not wholly
surprising, that the world's first nuclear explosive device had not
worked as intended.

As Oppenheimer well knew, atomic weapons had been talked about
for many years. They were key plot devices in numerous works of
fiction early in the twentieth century. In his 1914 novel *The World Set
Free*, H.G. Wells has scientists of 1956 devising immensely powerful
'atomic bombs'. In 1929, the popular play *Wings Over Europe* involved
the threatened use of 'atomic bombs', while *The Red Peril* in the same
year envisioned the use of atomic weapons to defend against airborne
invasion from the Soviet Union. The 1932 novel *Public Faces* foresaw
dropping an 'atomic bomb' off the US East Coast, while Eric Ambler in
1935's *The Dark Frontier* postulated atomic weapons emerging from the
Baltic nation of Ixania. The 1938 novel *The Doomsday Men* has a group
of religious fanatics using a cyclotron to detonate a nuclear explosion
in a target of radioactive material (Brians).[1] Winston Churchill also
speculated about such weapons in a 1931 magazine article 'Fifty
Years Hence' (Farmelo). But until the current war, no real person had
known how to create such weapons.

Now in July 1945, Oppenheimer and the other scientists of the
Manhattan Project (as the secret effort to build an atom bomb came
to be called) thought they had it figured out. They'd assembled a
complex device which they had believed would start a chain reaction of

---

1. All references are authentic; citing them means the preceding statements in the
narrative are also authentic. A full list of references is in the back matter.

radioactive atoms splitting apart, and releasing a huge amount of energy as they did so. But this hadn't happened in the morning's test. What had they gotten wrong? As an Army sergeant drove the government-issued sedan through the July heat of the New Mexico desert, 'Oppie' reviewed the science, the engineering, the fabrication, the assembly – all the factors that could have caused what he'd witnessed that morning – history's most expensive fizzle.[2]

The basic concept was simple: if you just put together a large enough amount of certain highly radioactive elements such as uranium, it will explode. Being 'radioactive' means that the nucleus at the centre of each atom is unstable. In any mass of radioactive material there are nuclei that break apart at seemingly random moments, usually flinging off small subatomic fragments of themselves. That's radiation. In the case of uranium, which has very heavy nuclei as these things go, instead of just shedding small bits, a nucleus will break into two large pieces. It will 'fission'. In the process it will fling off some small bits, too, along with releasing a considerable amount of energy. If those small flung-off bits, called neutrons, collide with other uranium nuclei, they will sometimes cause those nuclei to break, releasing more energy, and more neutrons to carry the process on. In uranium, fission occurs on its own only very very rarely, but scientists in recent years had discovered a way to force a lot more nuclear splits, with presumably a lot more energy released.

Therefore an atomic bomb was to be a contraption in which this was done. A sufficient number of nuclei were to be broken up in close enough proximity to more fissionable nuclei so that the neutrons released from one fission had a good chance of causing further fissions, with so much energy being released from so many fissions so quickly that the whole thing would yield an tremendous explosion. This energy released by nuclei breaking would be many times greater than what chemical explosives like TNT release when the bonds between whole atoms are broken.

Implementing this 'simple' concept was challenging. The Manhattan Project scientists had found two distinct ways to set off such a nuclear explosion and two 'fissionable' elements they could use. One way to start was to have two roughly 100lb pieces of (specially prepared) uranium and slam them together to 'assemble' a 'critical mass' in which spontaneously flung-off neutrons would smash into other nuclei often enough and soon enough to get an explosive chain reaction going.

---

2. See 'What Really Happened' (16 Jul 1945).

The other approach was to have a single ball of fissionable material sized so that most of its spontaneously flung-off neutrons never encounter any other fissionable nuclei. Then, quickly compress that ball so that it becomes much smaller and therefore more dense. Now, more of those neutrons zipping around will encounter other nuclei, splitting them, releasing more neutrons, and thereby blowing the whole thing up.

The morning's fizzle tested this more complicated compression method using the newly-discovered human-made element plutonium. The scientists had found that exposing some uranium to a stream of neutrons causes a few of the nuclei not to split or fling off small fragments but instead to absorb a neutron. This leads to formation of the new element, dubbed 'plutonium' after the planet even farther out than Uranus. However, plutonium is itself radioactive; it is so unstable that its 'critical mass' for a chain reaction is something like 20lbs, far less than the 100–200lbs needed for uranium.

Oppenheimer cringed a little as he reflected that the scientists' calculations about plutonium had caused the government to spend several hundred million dollars (which was a lot of money in the 1940s), and employ tens of thousands of workers to construct and operate several huge 'atomic piles'. These novel facilities, nowadays termed 'nuclear reactors', irradiated uranium and transformed it into plutonium. Then, complex chemical processing facilities extracted and purified the plutonium. The secret plutonium production installation sprawled in the high desert near Hanford, Washington was now, in mid-1945, beginning to produce several pounds of plutonium a month. But it had been believed that the investment would be worth it because a plutonium bomb would need much less nuclear material than a uranium one.

'Did we get the science wrong?' Oppenheimer asked himself. 'We didn't even have the concept of "nuclear fission" until a few years ago. Maybe the whole idea of a fission chain reaction is just wrong. Maybe that's what the Germans knew. Maybe that's why our guys following the Army into Germany found that the Nazis were nowhere close to developing a bomb. Did we let ourselves get snookered into wasting all this money and manpower trying to beat the Germans in a race they weren't even trying to run?' Oppenheimer reflected that it was a team in Germany, Otto Hahn and Fritz Strassmann, who had done key work leading to the discovery of nuclear fission back in 1938, and the Manhattan Project team included more than a few German refugee scientists, the likes of Hans Bethe, James Franck and Klaus Fuchs (the latter via the UK, but still . . .). And of course, the most prominent German genius, Einstein, had sent the letter that persuaded President Roosevelt to undertake this bomb programme, lest Germany developed one first. For a few moments, as his car passed through the desert landscape of dense creosote bushes and scraggly mesquite trees, Oppenheimer's mind raced and his stomach churned. 'Was this all a massive German deception?'

Former Berkeley physics professor Oppenheimer was a scientist who considered hard evidence before forming conclusions. This was especially so for anything that would involve an elaborate and prolonged conspiracy. 'No!' he said out loud, startling his driver. Oppenheimer shook his head to clear it, 'the Nazis were devious, fanatical and wicked,' he told himself, 'but we have far too much of our own data on nuclear fission, on uranium and on plutonium. It is not all a hoax . . . but we did get something wrong.'

Oppenheimer, now director of the bomb design lab, didn't think they had gotten the basic science wrong. He thought it more likely to be a flaw in the design, or a glitch in the fabrication and assembly of what they'd called the 'Gadget'. Perhaps they hadn't prepared the exotic plutonium fuel correctly. He glanced at the pencil he was taking notes with. Pure carbon can take the form of graphite like the pencil's 'lead', or of diamond, as in the ring he'd given his wife Kitty. Solid water can be fluffy snow or rock-hard ice. So too with plutonium: the pure element has several very different solid forms. Maybe they were using plutonium's 'graphite' when they needed to use its 'diamond'.

Or maybe they hadn't quite mastered how to set off the explosion. The plutonium device they'd tested was based on the 'squeeze one piece' approach. The simple idea of swiftly compressing a suitably sized radioactive sphere to make it dense enough to start a chain reaction nonetheless presented a major engineering challenge. As one of his colleagues had wryly described it in the lab's early days:

> It's a cinch. All we have to do is squeeze a solid ball of plutonium metal really really tightly to get the nuclear chain reaction going, and then, as it heats the hell up, keep squeezing the damn thing so the chain reaction multiplies and releases so much energy it blows the whole blessed thing apart, along with everything in the neighbourhood. Easy. Oh, and make sure that right when all this is happening, there are some fissions that just happen to happen at the right time. What could be easier?

The Los Alamos physicists had calculated that the nuclear chain reaction would take a matter of some microseconds (millionths of a second). So they had to design a way to compress the plutonium and keep the fissioning mass together for perhaps a hundred microseconds, which would be 'long enough' to get the desired energy release. The idea of severely compressing a solid ball of metal might itself seem impossible, but the scientists knew that at the atomic scale, metal is only a bit more 'solid' than foam rubber; its atoms can be crowded together much more closely. It's a harder squeeze, but a ball of plutonium can get considerably smaller, and more dense. The approach the scientists developed to accomplish this was an 'implosion', an inward-directed detonation of a conventional chemical explosive akin to TNT. They would surround a sphere of plutonium with a shell of carefully-shaped blocks of chemical explosives. Each block had carefully shaped layers of different explosives, which detonated at different speeds. (Although it seems instantaneous to human perception, some explosives release their energy less quickly than others.) With the right explosives shaped correctly, the resulting blast would be mostly focused inward, toward the sphere of plutonium. Setting off all these 'shaped charges' at exactly the same time would generate a spherical wave of intense pressure pushing inward uniformly. This would substantially compress the plutonium from all directions. Within a suitably designed 'containment' shell, the chemical explosives' pressure would then hold the compressed plutonium together for the microseconds needed for the nuclear chain reaction to build up force and produce the desired nuclear explosion, shattering the sphere, the container and a lot more.

So went the theory. In practice, this would work only if all roughly 100 explosive blocks worked as designed, creating a uniformly spherical compression wave. Perhaps some of the blocks they had used were faulty in some way, thought Oppenheimer; or maybe it was the newly-invented, highly specialised detonators. All of those dozens of electrical devices had to fire within about one millionth of a second or the compression would be lopsided. If the plutonium core were compressed unevenly, it would fly apart before a sustained chain reaction could produce the desired gigantic explosion. Recalling that morning's large but disappointing explosion, Oppenheimer suspected that something about the implosion mechanism hadn't worked as designed.

Perhaps the flaw was in the 'containment shell', the material surrounding the exploding components. This outer sphere had to hold together long enough (i.e. microseconds) to keep sufficient pressure on the fissioning mass of plutonium to prolong the chain reaction to achieve the desired devastating release of energy. The team had used the heaviest material they could find, indeed the heaviest natural material there was – uranium metal. In this use, the uranium was being relied on primarily for its physical density – far heavier than lead – and not for its own nuclear properties. In this implosion device, it was to be the plutonium's fission that was the main source of the explosive power, with the surrounding uranium being (not entirely, but largely) inert dead weight. But, what if this 'tamper' as they called it, hadn't tamped enough? Or had sprung a leak, releasing a portion of the plutonium's explosive force prematurely, in a lopsided fashion?

Or perhaps the problem was the 'initiator'; Oppenheimer recalled they'd had a lot of trouble designing that gizmo. Although plutonium is radioactive, and some its nuclei will spontaneously fission in a given period of time, the scientific team had to make sure a few nuclei would split at the right moment, just as the core was being compressed. So they embedded a neutron-emitting 'initiator' at the centre of the plutonium sphere. Called by some the 'Goldberg-Robinson Initiator' after the US and UK cartoonists who portrayed outrageously complicated machines, the device would jump-start the chain reaction. It contained the radioactive elements polonium and beryllium. Polonium spontaneously emits nuclear fragments called alpha particles, but these can knock neutrons out of nearby beryllium nuclei. Those neutrons in turn would enter the plutonium, ensuring a timely start to the chain reaction. However, the beryllium had to be shielded from the polonium's constant stream of alpha particles until it was time to trigger the bomb; then, just as the plutonium core was being compressed, the polonium's shielding would be breached, exposing the beryllium to alpha particles, prompting it to emit neutrons into the plutonium to start the chain reaction. Not for the first time this all reminded Oppenheimer of the nursery rhyme:

> This is the cow with the crumpled horn
> That tossed the dog that worried the cat
> That killed the rat that ate the malt
> That lay in the house that Jack built

Adding to the design difficulty was the odd behaviour of polonium: it tends to 'evaporate' from the solid state without melting (somewhat like solid carbon dioxide, dry ice, turning directly to vapour. Water ice can do that too, as a snowbank shrinks in cold dry air on a sunny day with no hint of meltwater). Designing a mechanism to maintain and contain a sufficient mass of polonium and ensure it would dislodge neutrons from the nearby beryllium exactly when they were needed, but not before, was itself a major undertaking. Only in May 1945 did the team

8

settle on a design they believed would meet these complex and exacting requirements (Rhodes).

'Maybe we got something wrong there,' thought Oppenheimer. If so, was it 'the cow with the crumpled horn', 'the dog that worried the cat', or 'the cat that ate the rat'?

As they passed through the desert community of Socorro he asked himself if they should have used the 'Jumbo'. This steel cask was a 200-ton reminder that the team was never sure the bomb would work. Jumbo was meant to contain the blast from the test device's chemical explosives if they failed to set off a nuclear explosion. The idea was that the cask would prevent the scarce plutonium from being scattered over the landscape by a failed test, as had now happened. But Oppenheimer also knew that after they had built Jumbo and transported it to the test site at considerable cost, the team had decided not to use the container after all. It would have made collecting data from the test much more difficult (Atomic Archive). So the precious plutonium was now lost, but they did get good readings from multiple instruments. These should enable the scientific team to figure out what went wrong. And even if they could not figure out the plutonium fizzle right away, there was always the backup, the uranium bomb.

Uranium was the other 'fissionable' element suitable for a bomb, and it was the element that had started the quest for an atomic bomb. Just as the war began in Europe, researchers had (accidentally) found they could cause uranium's unstable nuclei to split apart, releasing energy in the process. Previously used as a yellow pigment (such as in the popular Fiestaware dinner plates), uranium quickly became the focus of efforts to create an explosive nuclear chain reaction. But researchers found that only some uranium would work. Most uranium nuclei contain 238 subatomic particles; these nuclei are unstable and over any period of time, a very small proportion of the nuclei will spontaneously fission. However, in naturally-occurring uranium fewer than one in a hundred nuclei are somewhat more unstable, fissioning more readily. The nuclei in this variety, this 'isotope', of uranium have just 235 subatomic particles in them (neutrons and protons). It's only these 'U235' nuclei that are sufficiently fission-prone to sustain an explosive chain reaction. The nuclei of the much more common 'U238' isotope are not unstable enough to do the trick, and in natural uranium, there are too few of the highly unstable U235 nuclei to sustain a nuclear explosion. A uranium bomb therefore would require a larger proportion of the U235 isotope. Natural uranium had to be 'enriched'.

Yet isotopes of the same element (like U235 and U238) have the same chemical properties. They differ in the nucleus, but swarms of electrons surround each nucleus somewhat like miniature solar systems. The size and configuration of the electron swarm determines an element's chemistry, i.e. what it combines with, or dissolves or solidifies in. Isotopes of the same element all have the same size and configuration of these electron swarms, so the isotopes can't be distinguished by chemical properties. One can't separate U235 from U238 by adding some other chemical, like an acid, to make one dissolve and not the other, or by adding some kind of salt and causing one to solidify and the other not. In a chemistry lab, U238 behaves the same as U235. However, one can separate uranium's isotopes based on the very slight (about 1 per cent) difference in their weights (235 vs. 238 particles in their nuclei). The Manhattan Project used several different ways to exploit this subtle difference; all were difficult.

While atomic reactors to create plutonium and plants to process it took shape in Washington State in the Northwest, another series of unique factories came into being across the country in the Appalachian woodlands of Tennessee. This Oak Ridge site used abundant hydroelectric energy from the Tennessee Valley Authority to power several different technologies for extracting the rare U235 from the predominant U238. One technique separated the rare U235 atoms from those of very slightly heavier U238 based on the slight difference in how they moved in an electromagnetic field. Another exploited the gasified isotopes' slightly different rate of passing through an ultrafine filter. Yet another exploited the isotopes' different rates of movement from cold to hot ends of a container. In all these processes, the degree of enrichment of U235 versus U238 was very small with each pass through the process, so each technique repeated the separation step thousands of times before the resulting material reached the needed degree of U235 'enrichment'.

Some scientists had tried to perfect a method of spinning gasified uranium at very high speeds so that the slightly heavier U238 would be 'spun to the bottom'. Although all separation techniques were hard, during the war it was too hard to get this 'centrifuge' method to work reliably and efficiently (Kemp). (After the war, new technology so improved the reliability and efficiency of centrifuges that this later became the most commonly-used enrichment technique.)

By early 1945, Oak Ridge's multiple separation facilities were producing small amounts of enriched uranium. (The predominant U238 isotope had nevertheless proven extremely useful in another way: as noted above, when uranium is irradiated with the right stream of neutrons, it transmutes, in true alchemical fashion, into the new element, plutonium. It's the U238 isotope that does this magic trick, and large amounts of it in the reactors at Hanford Washington were producing the plutonium for the implosion device. As also noted, uranium was used as a 'tamper' to help briefly contain a plutonium explosion.)

Enriching U235 was frustratingly slow, especially considering that a uranium bomb was easier to build than the implosion device needed for plutonium. With sufficiently enriched uranium, the data showed that the 'slam two pieces together' technique to assemble a 'critical mass' would work to start an explosive chain reaction. The best way to slam together the pieces was with a gun: firing a correctly shaped uranium 'bullet' onto a uranium 'target'. Sure, the 'bullet' would shatter the 'target', but the speed of the nuclear chain reaction would be a thousand times faster, vaporising the entire gun device, and anything in the neighbourhood before the target shattered. And the Army knew how to build guns.

> DON'T WORRY ABOUT THAT
> The mechanical shattering vs. the nuclear vaporisation brings to mind the classic line in the movie *Butch Cassidy and the Sundance Kid* – the heroes are at the top of a cliff, chased by the security guys. Butch wants to jump into the river far below. Sundance balks: 'I can't swim' he says. 'Hell,' says Butch, 'don't worry about that, the fall's probably gonna kill you first.'

After calculating masses, shapes and bullet speeds, the scientists were confident that this relatively simple technique would work for uranium. There was no need to test this gun-type bomb, especially given that enriched uranium was in even shorter supply than plutonium. A uranium bomb would release as much energy as hundreds, or perhaps thousands, of tons of TNT, and it would only need 100 or 200lbs of the uranium. But the huge Oak Ridge facilities could only produce enriched uranium slowly. Thus, the 'easy to use' bomb fuel, uranium, was hard to get. The fuel they could get more readily, plutonium, was harder to use.

'Too bad plutonium won't work in a gun' thought Oppenheimer, as his sedan passed through Albuquerque. Initially, the team had thought they could load it into a gun just as they were planning to do with the uranium. Early measurements on tiny samples of plutonium created in the University of California's atom-smashing 'cyclotron' indicated that plutonium's propensity for fission would sustain an explosive chain reaction. This had been the basis for building those atomic piles at Hanford to create plutonium from the otherwise unusable U238. Very early in the bomb project, Oppenheimer and colleagues had settled on the 'slam two pieces together' gun mechanism as the simplest and best way to build a bomb. Richard Tolman, a Caltech physicist, had suggested using what he called an 'implosion mechanism', but that seemed very difficult to get right; his idea was not then taken up (Aspray). Work at Los Alamos focused on engineering the gun, refining its thickness, its length and so on. Already cast were several 17ft-long gun barrels for the plutonium gun device, known as 'Thin Man'. At that length, these were pushing the limit of what a B-29 could deliver, even if structural modifications were made to lengthen the bomb bay (Hoddeson).

In 1944, the scientists tested the first sample of Hanford-bred plutonium, and found it didn't match the plutonium from Berkeley's cyclotron. The Hanford material was so radioactive that it would not work in a gun after all (Baggott). As mentioned, the basically simple gun mechanism depended on precise relative timing: a nuclear chain reaction was many times faster than the bullet's shattering of the target. ('Hell, Sundance, the fall is gonna kill you first.') More challenging was making sure the chain reaction wasn't too fast. Instead of a conventionally shaped bullet fired at a flat target, the nuclear bullet and target were shaped somewhat like a blunt cylinder fitting tightly into a sheath; therefore it would take a miniscule fraction of a second for the two pieces of the critical mass to fully come together. When fully 'assembled' in this way the fuel would briefly have enough concentrated mass to sustain a hugely explosive chain reaction. However, the nuclear chain reaction would unavoidably start just when the cylinder began entering the sheath. If the reaction then proceeded too quickly, the energy first released would blow the device apart prematurely, before the cylinder was fully inserted, and therefore before the full energy release of the sustained chain reaction had been achieved.

Based on the early measurements on the Berkeley plutonium, the Los Alamos team had expected that the chain reaction in plutonium, as in uranium, would be fast enough for a chain reaction, yet slow enough to allow for complete 'assembly' of a critical mass. But now it seemed that the newly-available Hanford-bred plutonium would propagate a chain reaction far too rapidly (Rhodes). It would produce a premature, disappointing explosion, perhaps only as large as a conventional chemical explosive bomb (Baggott).

This realisation had been a monumental 'Aw shucks!' (or something similar). At first, Oppenheimer and his team thought there might be chemical impurities in the plutonium, as British scientist James Chadwick had warned about almost three years previous (Nichols). If that were the case, then perhaps improved chemical processing of the plutonium could solve the prematurity problem. However, the team had eventually realised the problem wasn't chemical impurities; it was a difference in isotopes. An atom smasher like Berkeley's briefly bombards U238 with neutrons, and some of these uranium nuclei absorb a neutron and then transform into plutonium 239. That's how this 'human-made' element had been discovered in 1940 (Atomic Heritage). The process is similar in a nuclear reactor except that the plutonium remains in the reactor for days or weeks, exposed to continuing streams of neutrons. Over that time some of the Pu239 will absorb still another neutron and become the even more unstable isotope, Pu240. That was the problem – the Hanford reactor plutonium, unlike the material rapidly created in and removed from the Berkeley cyclotron, had too much of the very unstable Pu240, which would propagate a chain reaction too quickly to be used in a gun mechanism. The planned gun could not assemble a critical mass of reactor-bred plutonium fast enough to avoid a premature chain reaction. No reshaping of the bullet and target for faster 'assembly' would solve this problem. It might have worked if they could get the bullet moving faster, assembling the critical mass faster, but that would require an even longer, 25ft gun barrel, and no existing aircraft could deliver a device that long (Hoddeson).

THE PREMATURE PROBLEM

One of the few women scientists at Los Alamos, Lili Hornig was a Harvard chemist involved in figuring out the Pu240 contamination (Hornig). Although certainly apocryphal, the story goes that in discussing the problem of the resulting too-fast explosion, Lili was heard to say, 'I'll bet every married woman here can relate to that problem.'

Nor was it feasible to separate Pu239 from Pu240 – the difference in their weights was only one-third the already slight difference between the U235 and U238 isotopes, and the separation of the latter already involved those enormous and enormously expensive facilities at Oak Ridge. Separating plutonium isotopes was just not practicable.

So in mid-1944 the Manhattan Project scientists had realised that a plutonium gun-type bomb was not feasible. This meant that unless they could find a way to use plutonium, the second path to a bomb was suddenly in question, not to mention the potential uselessness of the entire staggeringly expensive plutonium breeding enterprise at Hanford.

That's why in the summer of 1944, less than a year previous, Oppenheimer had shifted the lab's focus to Richard Tolman's long-ignored 'implosion' concept. Perhaps, Oppenheimer reflected as his car neared Los Alamos, if he had devoted more resources sooner to developing that more complicated mechanism, the morning's fizzle would not have occurred. He allowed himself a moment or two of regretful hindsight. But he'd leave most of that for what his boss, the General, called an 'After Action' report.

Nor did Oppenheimer allow himself to second guess the decision to do the test. He knew that the test of the plutonium bomb had been necessary, even though it had scattered into the desert a large fraction of all the plutonium on the planet (as far as anyone in the US knew). However, Hanford's output of plutonium was increasing; there would likely be enough plutonium for more bombs by the time the team figured out how to make them work.

'Wish Groves had given us a few more days to prepare the test,' Oppenheimer thought, referring to General Leslie Groves, his boss, 'we really had to rush things to meet his deadline.' But Oppenheimer was also aware that the bomb's availability date had already slipped significantly. In August 1944, with Oppenheimer's input, Groves had projected to his Pentagon superiors that one plutonium device would be ready in April 1945 and one uranium weapon in July 1945. The schedule then slipped several times. In June 1945, Groves had told Washington that neither type of bomb could be available until August, and the plutonium device depended on a test sometime in July (Frank 1999). For that test, the scientific team initially targeted 4 July 1945, but difficulties with the production of the explosive blocks prompted a slip to 10 July, then to 14 July.

Oppenheimer had requested yet a further delay beyond 14 July, but Groves refused (Rhodes). In the nearly three years they had worked together, Oppenheimer had seen Groves ramrod the swift creation of the immense facilities at Hanford, Oak Ridge, Los Alamos and elsewhere. Groves' previous feat of managing the design and construction of the Pentagon in 18 months was thus a prelude to his Manhattan Project leadership (Vogel). Initially, Oppenheimer knew, the urgency to develop the bomb stemmed from concern that the Nazis might do so first. Now, in mid-1945, the Nazi regime was gone, and the victors knew that the Germans' nuclear research programme had never gotten close to having an atomic bomb (J. Bernstein 1992). But the terrible war in the Pacific continued. Japan's defeat was a certainty, but the appallingly costly battles for Iwo Jima, Okinawa, the Philippines and elsewhere likely foreshadowed the horrendous casualties that an invasion of Japan would bring. Atomic bombs would very likely make a difference in how soon the Pacific war ended. Oppenheimer understood that the longer it took to field this new weapon, the more American and Allied soldiers, and civilians in various Asia Pacific nations, would die.

So he did not fault the General for refusing to let the test schedule slip any more. But the requirement to test the bomb by 14 July had caused concern. There were actually two tests planned: one test was of the full assembly of explosive blocks without a plutonium core, to check the effectiveness of the spherical implosion. A day or two later the other test, with the plutonium core installed, would see if the whole thing worked as planned. The pair of tests therefore required about 200 blocks of explosive, each with multiple layers of different explosives in complex configurations. Just creating all the moulds into which the batter-like, molten explosives would be cast was a very time-consuming task, and was not finished until late June (Rhodes). Then, casting about 200 perfect blocks into those moulds, and allowing them to cool slowly, with no irregularities, was another lengthy process. Indeed it was so time-consuming that it was never done: to meet Groves' deadline, the two implosion tests in mid-July had to proceed with the best available blocks, including some imperfect ones (Baggott).

Oppenheimer regretted that they'd had to compromise on the ideal test conditions, but he also knew that the deadline had originated not from Groves, or even from the Pentagon, but from the White House. This was far more than a scientific enterprise.

Chapter 2

Wartime Nuclear Geopolitics

The July 1945 timing of the bomb test traced back to the Yalta Conference. When Roosevelt, Churchill and Stalin had met there in February 1945, the defeat of Germany was clearly imminent. The defeat of Japan, although equally certain, seemed a much more distant and bloody prospect, not likely to happen before 1946 or 1947 (Hastings 2009). At the time of the conference President Roosevelt could not be sure how soon the atomic bomb would be available – the projections kept slipping – or how decisive it might prove to be. He told Churchill he did not expect the bomb to be ready even for testing until September. Therefore at Yalta FDR was pleased to hear Stalin reiterate his intent to join the Pacific War 'two or three months' after Germany was defeated. As far back as December 1941 Stalin had told Britain's Anthony Eden that he would make war on Japan 'several months' after the defeat of Germany; in October 1943 he had made a similar statement to Cordell Hull and Averill Harriman of the US (Hasegawa). In evidence of his plan, Stalin had by then ordered improvements to the transcontinental railway lines the Red Army would need for shifting troops from Europe to the Far East (Hasegawa). In November 1944 Stalin again affirmed his plan to fight Japan, but said he needed fuel, food and aircraft from the US to do so. The US then shipped such materiel from the American West Coast to Soviet Far Eastern ports. The dwindling Japanese Imperial Fleet let this traffic proceed unmolested, in part because of the Neutrality Treaty between the USSR and Japan (Frank 1999).

To be sure, Josef Stalin would not be entering the Pacific War as a favour to the Western Allies. It was more a matter of Soviet payback in the long-running competition with Japan. In the late 1800s, Russia had wrested valuable economic and military concessions in Manchuria from the Chinese government. (As shown in Map 1 page 56, 'Manchuria' is the north-east extension of China, 'protruding' into the Soviet Union's Far East.) Among the concessions, Russia had funded and maintained control of the South Manchurian Railway (Hasegawa), which connected Russia's Trans-Siberian Railway with ice-free ports in south Manchuria. Then in 1895, Japan defeated China in the Sino-Japanese War, and gained concessions in Manchuria at Russia's expense. At that time, the Russian minister for the Trans-Siberian Railway observed that 'The hostile actions of Japan [against China] are directed mainly against us'. In turn, Japan's minister to Russia observed that 'Russia hopes ultimately to bring the entire area (of Manchuria) under her influence' (Paine). After the 1900 Boxer Rebellion in China, Russia stationed 100,000 troops in Manchuria and Korea, to 'maintain stability', but also to shield these areas from increasing Japanese influence.

This Russian-Japanese rivalry in Manchuria and nearby Korea became war in 1905. Aided by a surprise attack on the Russian naval base at Port Arthur in Manchuria, the Japanese rapidly defeated Russia. In this embarrassing war, the Russian Empire lost international prestige, as well as its concessions in Manchuria and its sphere of influence in Korea. Russia also lost the southern portion of resource-rich, West Virginia-sized Sakhalin Island, north of Japan. Later, during the Russian Civil War following the 1917 Revolution, Japan sent 70,000 troops into the Russian Far East. They penetrated as much as 1,400 miles into Siberia and occupied many of the key cities and ports in the Russian Far East and northern Sakhalin Island and stayed for several years (Brooks). More recently, in the late 1930s, Soviet troops clashed several times with the Japanese along the border with Manchuria, or 'Manchukuo' as the Japanese called their puppet state in occupied north-eastern China.

Therefore the April 1941 Neutrality Pact between the USSR and Japan was something of a strategic aberration for these historic enemies. Yet it freed each party to concentrate their attentions elsewhere, however uneasily. Indeed, after Germany attacked the USSR just two months later, in June 1941, the Nazis pressed their Japanese allies to violate their promised neutrality and attack Soviet Siberia. For several months, as the Wehrmacht drove into European Russia, Soviet spy Richard Sorge in the German embassy in Tokyo told Moscow that Japan might attack from Manchuria. This forced Stalin to keep a very large army in Siberia. But late in 1941, Sorge informed Moscow that the Japanese had decided to move south instead, toward the resources of Southeast Asia (Hasegawa). Along with intelligence from other sources, this let Stalin safely pull several dozen army divisions out of Siberia and send them west to fight the Nazis (Andrew and Gordievsky). The influx of several hundred thousand fresh Soviet troops and their 1,700 tanks in the winter of 1941/42 made a major difference in the fight against the German juggernaut. Still, an untold number of Russian soldiers and civilians had died at Nazi hands in the latter half of 1941 because so much of the Red Army was in the Far East guarding against (more) Japanese perfidy. Even after this critical winter, Stalin still kept about 40 divisions (around 700,000 troops) in the Far East, just in case. These additional divisions would also have been valuable in pushing back the Germans, and saving Russian lives.

Theodore Roosevelt had won the Nobel Peace Prize for helping settle the 1905 Russo-Japanese War, so his cousin Franklin was likely aware that the Soviet Union had historic scores to settle with the Japanese Empire. He and Churchill knew that Stalin's promise to fight Japan was anything but altruistic. Moreover, the Soviet pledge came with a price. In addition to the war supplies flowing from America across the north Pacific, Stalin also required post-war economic and military concessions in Manchuria, such as access for the Soviet Far Eastern Fleet to ice-free ports in southern Manchuria, possession of the entire Sakhalin Island, and all of the several dozen Kuril Islands in the north Pacific. This was more than FDR's State Department had recommended he accede to, although none of these were America's to give (Dobbs). Nonetheless, at the Yalta Conference FDR 'accepted' the promise of Soviet assistance in defeating Japan, and did not balk at the price.

Indeed, through late 1944 and into the early months of 1945, Army leaders such as Generals George C. Marshall and Douglas MacArthur Jr. were positively inclined toward Soviet involvement in the defeat of Japan. In Europe, the Red Army had engaged a large part of the German army, and had likely thereby made the Normandy invasion substantially less difficult than it would otherwise have been. (From the Soviets' perspective, the Red Army was playing by far the greatest role in the defeat of Germany, while the Western Allies' Normandy invasion and advance on Germany through France was proceeding with 'minimal resistance' (Lyons).)

In Asia, MacArthur wanted the Soviets to play a similar role: tie down the large Japanese army in Manchuria so those troops could not reinforce the armies defending the Home Islands whenever MacArthur launched his invasion (Hastings 2009; Weinberg). MacArthur considered Soviet seizure of Manchuria, Northern China and Korea as inevitable consequences of Soviet involvement (Hasegawa). As of spring 1945, Secretary of War Stimson also thought the Soviets would be able to take whatever East Asian territory they chose to (Hasegawa), whether the US 'approved' or not.

19

By mid-1945, however, several things were different. The war against Germany was over and the US had a new President. Harry Truman was now concerned about Soviet misbehaviour in Eastern Europe. Stalin was reneging on promises he'd made at Yalta about elections in Poland and governance elsewhere in liberated Europe. Given the strength of the current US military situation, the Truman administration was viewing Soviet participation in the Pacific War as less beneficial and more strategically costly than it had seemed earlier in the year at Yalta. Maybe it would not be a bad thing if Stalin broke his promise about joining the Pacific War. Or if the new bomb ended the war before the Soviets could get in.

Truman only learned about that bomb project some days after he became President in April 1945 upon Roosevelt's death. He then learned that Groves expected to have a uranium-type weapon available in August. Although it was an untested device, the project team was confident it would produce an explosion many times more powerful than any previous bomb. A problem, they told the President, was that because of the limited production of the uranium they could not put together another such bomb until December.

As to plutonium, the Pentagon told Truman that the bomb makers expected to have enough of that reactor-bred fuel for perhaps half a dozen similarly powerful bombs in the August–October timeframe. But these weapons worked differently, and the team did not have the same confidence in them as in the uranium weapon. So the scientists planned a test of a plutonium device in early July in New Mexico.

TRUSTFUL TRUMAN

Truman probably recognised the irony of the Manhattan Project's role in his becoming President. As a US senator during the early part of the war, Truman gained prominence chairing the Senate Committee to Investigate the National Defense Program, known as the Truman Committee. He earned a reputation for thoroughness and fairness in rooting out inefficient, wasteful Pentagon spending. (In those days, critical inquiries of an administration were not automatically treated with derision.) In 1943 he phoned Secretary of War

Stimson about the many millions of dollars being spent at secret facilities in Oak Ridge and Hanford. Assured by the Secretary himself that the monies were going to a very important and very secret project, Senator Truman said, 'You won't have to say another word to me . . . that's all I want to hear' (NuclearFiles.org). Truman dropped the matter, and thereby burnished his image within the Administration. The next year, to the surprise of many, including Truman, he was on the ticket with FDR (Ferrell).

After the war with Germany ended in early May, Truman wanted to meet right away with Churchill and Stalin in Potsdam, near Berlin, to discuss issues regarding post-war Europe. But based on the planned bomb test in early July, Truman pushed the date for that Big Three conference back to mid-July. He chose the timing partly so that he would have good information on how soon he could bring atomic weapons into the war against Japan. Neither he nor anyone else knew how important such weapons might prove to be, but he wanted to know how strong his position was before he met, and likely had to haggle with, Stalin (Maddox; Rhodes).

It was therefore the timing of the already-deferred Potsdam Conference that drove the timing of the Trinity test. That's why Groves would not allow Oppenheimer any further slippage beyond 16 July. As Oppenheimer later wrote, 'We were under incredible pressure to get the test done before Potsdam' (Takaki). So he pushed the team assembling the test device. He knew they were careful, dedicated professionals, but even so . . .

Chapter 3

The Trinity Test, 16 July 1945

As Oppenheimer's sedan began climbing into the Sangre De Cristo Mountains north of Albuquerque, he reviewed the events surrounding the test. He knew that to meet the mandated test schedule, his colleague George Kistiakowsky had taken extraordinary measures. Before the war Kistiakowsky had been a chemistry professor at Harvard, where he was an expert in explosives. He had invented new types of explosives and explosive configurations such as 'shaped' charges that worked more like knives than hammers. Before coming to Los Alamos, he had worked with the Navy's first Underwater Demolition Teams (forerunners of Navy SEALs) inventing explosive devices to clear paths through coral reefs and human-made obstacles in advance of amphibious landings (Hornfischer). At the Los Alamos lab, Kistiakowsky directed the complicated process of fabricating the precisely-shaped, multi-layered explosive blocks surrounding the plutonium core.

Just days before the test, X-rays of the several hundred explosive blocks showed that some had unplanned voids within them, as in Swiss cheese. These came from bubbles in the pancake batter-like molten explosive as it flowed into the moulds. Bubble voids are fine in pancakes, but in these carefully designed blocks of explosive such irregularities would have disrupted the required perfectly spherical 'implosion'. Yet given the mandate to 'test the device before Potsdam', there wasn't sufficient time to cast more blocks, hoping to get enough perfect ones. So the ever-inventive Kistiakowsky got a fine dentist-type drill, and worked through the night to drill into the cavities in the defective blocks and give them fillings of fresh molten explosive (Baggott). Then he and his team selected the best blocks for the actual implosion bomb and the next best ones for the dummy implosion test that would precede it. This latter set of blocks specifically also included some with small imperfections such as chips off their outer corners (Rhodes). The team assembled the sets of explosive blocks into two spheres, one of which would get a plutonium core just before the last block was fitted into place.

In an amazingly brief time the Manhattan Project had designed and built from scratch several enormous industrial complexes using newly-invented techniques and machines to produce materials that had never existed before. Yet for all that advanced technology, the scientists putting together these first implosion devices used tissue paper and Scotch tape to help fit the explosive blocks together without jostling against one another, and perhaps denting or chipping them (Rhodes).

On 14 July 1945 they tested the dummy implosion device at Los Alamos. It had multiple instruments to measure whether the compression wave from the simultaneous detonation of all the sphere's blocks was perfectly spherical. Disappointingly, the data suggested a very uneven compression (Baggott; Rhodes). Had there been a plutonium core inside that test sphere, it appeared that it would have been squeezed into a distorted shape. If a chain reaction had gotten started, it would have blown the device apart prematurely. It would have been a nuclear fizzle.

Groves and his superiors 'expressed their concern' and Oppenheimer recalled that he felt about as much pressure that evening as the plutonium core was supposed to experience in the full test device. He and others had exchanged words with George Kistiakowsky. At one point there were blunt questions about the Harvard professor's basic scientific competence (which, in the circles of high-powered scientists, is akin to questioning the manhood of the burly guy next to you at the bar (Baggott; Rhodes)). With the full-up test of the plutonium device slated for the morning of the 16th, Oppenheimer had been frustrated because there was virtually no time for a full analysis of the dummy test results, much less time to make any changes in the test device, the 'Gadget'.

Overnight, however, physicist Hans Bethe re-examined the data from the dummy test. He found that the data determined – nothing. He realised that the improvised instrumentation for this novel test could not distinguish between a successfully spherical implosion and an uneven one. The data were inconclusive. It was like an eyewitness saying, 'Oh, yeah, that's the guy, yeah. I kinda think.' The dummy implosion may have been uneven, or it may have worked just right. No one could be sure (Baggott).

The political pressure from on high overpowered the scientists' inclination to do another, better instrumented, dummy test because that would have delayed the full test for some time until a whole new set of explosive blocks could be fabricated. Therefore the test of the world's first atomic explosive device went ahead in the New Mexico desert in the early hours of 16 July 1945.

It fizzled.

Members of the world's greatest assemblage of scientific expertise were in several observation posts there in the *Jornada del Muerto* desert basin, there to witness what physicist James Chadwick called 'The most expensive experiment in scientific history' (Farmelo). The several vantage points were at least 5 miles away and all eyes were on the Gadget atop a 100ft tower. Observers were told to protect their eyes from the damaging blast of light. At 5:30am the device exploded. There was a brief bright flash, some flying debris, some smoke. About 25 seconds later, they heard the bang. It was the largest explosion most of the observers had ever seen, and those who had worked just two days earlier on the dummy test with conventional explosives knew this blast was somewhat more than the previous one. Yet this flash-bang was nothing like the expected earth-shaking monster blast equivalent to hundreds or thousands of tons of TNT.

Several observers had memorable lines they had planned to use upon seeing the hoped-for event. They were left unsaid. History does not record who said it aloud first, but 'fizzle' was what Oppenheimer and many of his team were thinking right away. It appeared that the implosion design had perhaps worked well enough to initiate some nuclear-powered explosive force, but not well enough to keep the core together until the force could fully develop. Just as the inconclusive results from the dummy test suggested, the compression of the core might have been uneven.

The psychological shock of the fizzle lasted only moments before Groves turned to Oppenheimer: 'I am pretty sure that was far more than our Jumbo cask could have contained, and I think this was a partial success; you have just demonstrated that a nuclear bomb is possible. Let's find and fix the problem as soon as possible.' If Oppenheimer was tempted to remark that pressure from Groves (and the White House) to conduct the test on the 16th might have led to the disappointing test, there is no record of it.

Groves dispatched a brief message to Secretary of War Stimson: 'Doctor reports operation partially successful; patient will need further treatment, but prognosis good. Updates soonest.'[1] Groves also cancelled a local press release. The plan had been to explain to the public that the unusual explosion they'd heard out in the desert that morning was a massive accident at a military munitions facility in a remote area of the

1. See 'What Really Happened' (17 Jul 1945).

Alamogordo Army Air Field. Groves' press officer had heard the blast from the his viewing station 10 miles away, but he was doubtful anyone in the nearest town, Socorro 35 miles away, could have heard or seen the explosion much less be particularly curious about it.

As Oppenheimer's car passed through Santa Fe, he wondered how the sample collection was going. He'd left physicist Herbert Anderson at the test site to lead a team using a modified, lead-shielded Army tank to collect samples of the debris and soil from the bomb site (Rhodes). Perhaps the analysis of those samples would provide an 'Aha' moment that would reveal the problem.

The Manhattan Project, Oppenheimer recalled, had indeed experienced a series of 'Aha!' (or 'Aw shucks') moments over the years. In April 1943, for example, a weapons engineer had found an error in the scientists' thinking about the gun barrel: they had modelled it from the barrels of comparably-sized artillery pieces. But the weapons engineer pointed out that the thickness of such barrels is needed to withstand the intense wear and tear from firing many rounds. The atomic bomb's gun barrel would ever fire just that one bullet. So the 17ft barrel need not be nearly so thick and heavy (Baggott). This obvious-in-retrospect 'Aha!' let the bomb designers use a thinner barrel, substantially reducing the weight of the gun mechanism, which in turn improved its deliverability by aircraft.

Another 'Aha' came later in 1943 soon after physicist Emilio Segre came to Los Alamos. There he repeated measurements on uranium he'd made in Berkeley, near San Francisco. He was measuring the rate of 'spontaneous fission' – how many nuclei in a sample split apart 'on their own' in a given period of time. He found a higher rate of spontaneous fission in uranium at Los Alamos than at Berkeley. He then realised that Los Alamos was higher than Berkeley precisely because it was higher: that is, Los Alamos was at an elevation of 7,300ft, whereas Berkeley was at sea level. That elevation difference exposed his Los Alamos uranium to more of the fission-inducing neutrons that are generated in the upper atmosphere by cosmic rays from outer space. At Berkeley, fewer cosmic ray-derived neutrons penetrate the 'shielding' of the additional 7,300ft of atmosphere. Uranium at sea level gets hit by fewer fission-inducing outside particles. This turned out to be more than a laboratory curiosity: it shortened the gun barrel.

As noted, bomb design is about timing. The two pieces of the uranium critical mass (the bullet and the target) must be put together quickly so the nuclear chain reaction can fully build up before the first energy releases tear the device apart. But if the start of that nuclear chain reaction were delayed a little, this would allow a little more time for the uranium cylinder to fully enter the uranium sheath. Once the team understood that cosmic rays help prompt 'spontaneous' fissions, they realised they could prevent some of those fissions and thereby delay the start of the chain reaction. A neutron-absorbing material could shield the uranium from some of the cosmic ray neutrons. Then the two pieces of uranium would not have to be fitted into one another quite so quickly. So the bullet didn't need to be going so fast as it mated with the target. Therefore the bullet didn't need such a long gun barrel (Sublette 2007). ('This is the man all tattered and torn, who kissed the maiden all forlorn, that milked the cow with the crumpled horn, that tossed the dog' and so on.) These were seemingly inconsequential differences of millionths of a second, but the 'slower bullet', traveling at 1,000 vs. 3,000 feet per second (Cully), needed only a 6ft barrel, instead of the planned 17-footer. As noted, the engineers had lightened the barrel, now Emilio Segre had shortened it too. The bomb would be a lot easier to carry in an aircraft (Baggott).

As he passed the Pojoaque Pueblo, his driver turning west for the final climb into Los Alamos, Oppenheimer recalled another 'Aha!' moment, concerning the nuclear reactors at Hanford. Physicist Eugene Wigner designed these reactors to 'breed' plutonium from uranium, but he did not account for the self-poisoning problem: as neutrons bombard uranium in a reactor, a few nuclei absorb the neutrons and transform into plutonium as intended, but some of the other uranium nuclei just split apart and become the nuclei of lighter elements such as barium and krypton and others. As they accumulate, some of these fission products 'get in the way' by absorbing neutrons, thereby slowing the production of plutonium (which forms when U238 absorbs neutrons). But another member of the team, John Wheeler, figured out this might happen. Although construction was underway, he convinced the builders to drill more channels through the reactors' cores of graphite bricks. These would accommodate more uranium fuel rods. This delayed completion of the reactors, but would allow the operators to add 'fresh' fuel as the initial fuel rods accumulated the troublesome fission products. So when the production reactors came on line in December 1944 their plutonium output was greater than would have been the case with the original reactor design (Rhodes).

And about that dummy test two days earlier. Was there another 'Aw shucks' in the ambiguous data from that test-before-the-test? Oppenheimer was too good a scientist to spend much energy beating himself up about the inadequate test design. Instead, working with his initial observation that the 'fizzle' of the Gadget had been much more of a blast than conventional explosives alone could have generated, he made the preliminary hypothesis that they had achieved a small nuclear explosion. This, he surmised, had ripped the plutonium core apart before a chain reaction could fully propagate through it. He then mentally listed the possible ways the uneven compression could have happened. He then devised lines of data gathering and testing to determine which flaw had caused the imperfect detonation. By the time he arrived back at Los Alamos late on the 16th, he had worked out instructions for multiple task forces to find and fix the problem.

WHAT IF?

The 'overbuilding' of the Hanford reactors to accommodate extra fuel rods caused a delay of several months in the production of plutonium. But if John Wheeler had not seen the problem during the early construction, or had not convinced the builder to add capacity for more fresh fuel, then the self-poisoning in the reactors would have severely reduced plutonium production in 1945. Consequently the US would not have had more than one atomic bomb until the last months of 1945. By then, there would have been that much more conventional and incendiary bombing, and naval interdiction, mining and bombardment of Japan – strategies which some believed would eventually force Japanese surrender without the need for the massive US invasion slated for November. Moreover, if the atomic bombs had not been available until the late autumn, the Soviets' surprisingly successful onslaught against the Japanese Imperial armies that began on 8 August would have continued with that much more effect. For those who like that sort of thing, it would therefore be an interesting so-called 'counterfactual' speculation to look at the possibility of Japan surrendering without the atomic bomb ever being used, but after bloody fighting with Soviet troops approaching Tokyo.

Chapter 4

Potsdam, 17–19 July

On 17 July, Groves' brief report reached Secretary of War Stimson and President Truman at Potsdam, Germany. This was the day of the formal start of the conference. The message ('operation partially successful . . .') was not the clear-cut good news Truman may have hoped for, but it was not wholly surprising. In his diary in the run-up to the Potsdam conference, Truman had noted the possibility that the bomb test would not be successful (Hasegawa). If it took a little longer to perfect the plutonium weapon, so be it. Besides, they also had the other, the uranium weapon, albeit in very short supply.

While Stimson sought further information from Groves about the Trinity test, Truman had his introduction to Stalin, in an informal session the next day, 17 July. During this meeting, Stalin confirmed his February promise to Roosevelt to enter the war against Japan. He indicated he would move his armies into Manchuria, Korea, southern Sakhalin and the Kuril Islands, and even eventually into the northernmost Japanese Home Island, Hokkaido (Hastings 2009). He would commence in mid-August, he told Truman, which the President recorded in his diary of that day as: 'He will be in the Jap war on August 15th. Fini Japs when that comes about' (Truman 1945). Truman also noted that he was happy the Soviets had not called for any further 'gimme's', such as a Soviet occupation zone in Japan (Hastings 2009).

Presumably, Truman knew that many of the vehicles and much of the materiel the Red Army would use was stamped 'Made in the USA' (See the 'Under Japanese Noses' textbox following). He may or may not also have been familiar with Operation Hula. That was a large transfer of ships and landing craft and a training programme in how to use them, which the US Navy had been conducting with the Soviet Navy. (More on that later.) It was therefore credible that the Soviets would attempt to land on Hokkaido. But evidently the question of whether that would have given them a claim to occupation rights in Japan was not discussed at Potsdam.

UNDER JAPANESE NOSES

Shipping Lend-Lease material from the US to the USSR used several routes: across the north Atlantic to Archangel and Murmansk, across the south Atlantic and then to and across Iran, and the Pacific route from the US west coast to Kamchatka and Vladivostok. The first two were dangerous because of the German submarine threat. The last faced little threat from the Japanese because of the Soviet-Japanese Neutrality Pact. To be sure, the Pacific shipments had to be made in Soviet-flagged ships, but many of them also were US built. Thus, some of the 'deuce and a half' trucks and other materials the Red Army would use in their attacks on Japanese forces in Manchuria had sailed through the Soya Strait, just a few miles from Hokkaido (Saxe).

During the Potsdam conference Stalin also disclosed to Truman that the Japanese had approached the Soviet Union – still officially neutral in the Pacific War – and asked for their assistance in negotiating terms to end the war. Stalin assured the President that he had no intention of rendering such assistance to the Japanese, but that in order to maintain military surprise he had not clearly rebuffed their approach. Stalin also assured Truman of his commitment to demanding unconditional surrender from Japan as had the Western Allies. This satisfied Truman. The exchange can be read as Stalin assuring his ally that he was not dealing behind his back and planning to renege on his promise to enter the war. However, Stalin's 'stringing the Japanese along' can also be read as his attempt to ensure that the Japanese did not quit the war before the Red Army had their chance to join the fight, and claim the spoils thereof (Hastings, 2009; Hasegawa).

The first days of the formal Potsdam Conference focused on the aftermath of the European war such as borders and reparations. Truman was annoyed by Soviet infringements of agreements made at Yalta in February about the future of Eastern Europe. Unlike the ailing FDR at Yalta, Truman bargained hard on issues such as German reparations. Disappointed though he may have been at the Trinity fizzle, Truman was nonetheless confident that the US would in the coming months possess at least one if not two new, strategically significant types of weapon. He wasn't inclined to go easy on the Soviets, and certainly not in the expectation of getting their 'help' in the Pacific War.

Chapter 5

Los Alamos, 17–23 July

The Los Alamos team was working hard to determine the cause of the fizzle. Analysis of the soil retrieved from the Trinity site showed a ratio of plutonium and its fission products strontium and ruthenium that could only have come from a nuclear explosion. That is, just as the splitting of a uranium nucleus produces nuclei of the lighter elements barium and radium, the fissioning of plutonium produces strontium and ruthenium. Comparisons with other soil samples showed that these elements had been produced in the fizzle. From the relative amounts found, the scientists calculated that a small fraction of the plutonium had undergone an explosive chain reaction, with a force equivalent to about 50–60 tons of TNT.

The scientists compared photographic and noise measurements from the Trinity test to data from a 7 May test explosion of 100 tons of TNT, which had been a practice run of instrumentation and procedures (Nuclear Weapon Archive). Comparison of these data also indicated that Trinity had been on the order of 50–100 of tons of TNT. This confirmed the on-the-spot judgment by Oppenheimer and others that a small, 'inefficient' nuclear explosion had occurred. They had demonstrated the principle of a nuclear explosion. But determining what they needed to do to achieve more 'efficient', i.e. much more powerful, results would take some time.

Instrument data suggested that the core of the Gadget experienced high but uneven compression, deforming into a somewhat oblong shape. This was sufficient to initiate a nuclear chain reaction, but the energy from the initial fission events blew the deformed core apart before the fission chain reaction could spread throughout the condensed core. The designers had always known that a successful detonation would be what the Brits called 'a close run thing' – the critical mass of plutonium needed to stay compressed long enough for more and more fragmenting nuclei to demolish others, but the more such fissions

---

TIMELY PERSPECTIVE

'Sustained' may seem an inapt description of a chain reaction occurring in a fraction of a second, but that perception reflects our limited temporal 'comfort zone'. For most people, a century is a very long time while to a geologist it is an instant in the four-billion-year history of Earth. In the other direction, we cannot perceive events at a pace faster than tenths of a second. But events at the atomic level occur in microseconds (millionths of a second). So a nuclear chain reaction lasting one microsecond instead of a 'sustained' hundred microseconds, while totally imperceptible to us, is actually akin to the difference between one year and a century.

---

occurred, the more energy was released, blasting the core apart. Thus, although they had not gotten it exactly right, Oppenheimer and his colleagues knew they had successfully demonstrated an explosive nuclear fission chain reaction. There was every reason to believe that if they could get the spherical compression of the core right, they would get the sustained chain reaction and the devastating release of energy they sought. As Oppenheimer told an interviewer from *Life* magazine several years after the war, 'We had hoped the Gadget would work perfectly the first time, but given that nothing anything like this had ever been attempted by anyone, we were not really surprised that it was only a partial success. That was after all, why we had felt it necessary to test the thing.'

The Los Alamos team knew they were close. The question was whether the problem was inherent in the design, or was a matter of flawed manufacture or assembly of the device. There was rapid consensus that the design was sound – if every component (e.g. detonators, explosive lenses, neutron initiator, etc.) had worked as intended a properly sustained explosive chain reaction would have occurred.

Oppenheimer promptly set up several task forces at Los Alamos to systematically investigate each of the major component systems, looking at all conceivable ways in which they could have failed to perform correctly. As scientists, they were long accustomed to questioning their own and each other's findings. But Oppenheimer reminded them anyway to challenge assumptions and look for the kind of logic flaws that had led to their previous 'Aw Shucks' moments, like the over-designed gun barrel. Look too, he told them, for possible ways that simple things could have been done wrong, like wires attached to the wrong terminals. (More about faulty wiring later.)

To help ensure thoroughness, Oppenheimer salted each task force with 'cold eyes', i.e. personnel from other groups. Thus, scientists and engineers who had focused on the uranium gun device worked on the several plutonium task forces, personnel who'd worked on the initiator joined the group working on the detonators and so on. Partly to meet Groves' urgent demands for further information, but mainly to further ensure that all glitches were detected by someone on the team, Oppenheimer called progress meetings over dinner every evening. Called 'Beef and Briefs', these sessions ensured that as soon as one task force found something of interest it was shared with the others in case that finding had a bearing on others' work. This mechanism also provided for more 'cold eyes' to look at every facet of the investigation.

Attention focused on four components: the electrical devices detonating the explosive lenses, the lenses themselves, the plutonium core, and the complex polonium-beryllium neutron initiator within the bomb's core. One group developed improved instrumentation to test a set of electrical detonators, to ensure their virtually perfectly simultaneous firing. This determined that the detonators operated in synchrony well within the very tight allowable time tolerances of billionths of a second, even accounting for any slight differences in the lengths of cable connecting the initiators all over the outside of the device.

Similarly, the initiator task force came up with a way to test how well a sudden compressive implosion would quickly unshield the polonium from the beryllium in the initiator so that fragments from the unstable polonium nuclei would crash into beryllium nuclei, releasing neutrons into the surrounding plutonium and thereby initiating the chain reaction. This new 'House That Jack Built' test used small explosive lenses but no plutonium. It was an imperfect surrogate for the real thing, but analysis of the resulting nuclear isotopes in the debris indicated that the initiator had worked properly.

The third task force looked at problems with the plutonium core. This metal was new to science, and all data on its metallic and chemical properties was only a few years old. Plutonium can assume a whole series of crystal structures, with somewhat different densities and other properties (think snow vs. ice). The metallurgists had found that by alloying it with a small amount of another metal, gallium, the result was a stable yet malleable (shape-able) material (Coster-Mullen). Plutonium also readily oxidises (tarnishes), which had prompted the bomb metallurgists to coat the surface of the core with nickel, which doesn't. But shortly before the test, they found that the heat generated by plutonium's radioactivity had blistered the nickel coating. So they smoothed off the blisters and patched them with gold (Rhodes) (the dog that chased the cat that killed the rat . . .') The 'core' task force ran numerous calculations and verified that neither the gallium admixture, nor the nickel plating, nor the gold patching should have interfered with the chain reaction.

The fourth task force addressed the explosive blocks, or lenses. In those days before computer-based calculations and simulations, the Los Alamos team used hand-powered desk calculators and very early IBM punch-card machines, so the calculations verifying the lens design took some time. But the results showed that the complex design of the lenses, with explosives of differing detonation speeds in different parts of each lens, was sound. When fired at the same moment, a shell of these lenses would indeed focus their force into a spherical compression of the core.

Then, investigation of the fabrication process brought to light the late-night dentistry – George Kistiakowsky's filling of cavities in the explosive lenses. Laboratory tests replicated those efforts and examined the resulting explosive blocks. X-rays showed that even when explosive of identical composition was used to fill 'cavities', there were detectable boundaries between the original explosive and the fillings. 'Like with pancakes,' said one scientist, 'if you pour a pancake's worth of batter onto the griddle, wait a few moments, then add a little more of the identical batter to the cake, there will nevertheless be a permanently detectable boundary.' Even though the density irregularities of the bubble voids had been remedied, there remained small irregularities at the boundaries of the patches. In these precisely-designed explosive lenses, the investigators concluded, these could have distorted the perfectly spherical compression wave that was essential for the success of the implosion, especially if some of the 'patched' blocks happened to be clustered in one region of the spherical shell around the core.

Furthermore, the task force reviewed the fitting together of the lenses with the 'high tech' tools of tissue paper and adhesive tape. These protected the blocks of explosive from jiggling against one another, potentially leading to broken chips or fissures, which then could have disrupted the uniformity of the implosive force. The task force concluded that these precautions may not have been sufficient to maintain the integrity of the lenses, especially considering how the Gadget had been transported. The bomb builders had carefully assembled the lenses into a hollow sphere at Los Alamos, leaving out only the plutonium core assembly and one lens they would put into place after inserting the core. They packed this assembly onto a padded pallet, loaded it onto an Army truck and drove through the night nearly 250 miles from Los Alamos to the Trinity site, much of it on low-quality roads. The driver and the convoy commander reported no incidents on the drive, no sharp swerves to avoid wildlife. Nevertheless, Army trucks were not built for a smooth ride. Almost 250 miles in the back of a truck, padding or no, could have vibrated the explosive blocks enough to turn small imperfections in density into small, invisible fissures, perhaps at corners rubbing against one another. That would create even greater irregularities in the implosive compression wave. Although several scientists had visually inspected the Gadget atop the test tower at the Trinity site, there had been no way to know whether any of the explosive lenses harboured any internal fissures.

Because the actual bomb device for use against Japan was going to travel overland, across an ocean and finally by air, the separate weaponisation team at Los Alamos had long since developed a structural design that would protect all of the components from all manner of jostling and bruising, without tissue or tape. The team concluded that the unsophisticated procedures used for the test device may have caused lens imperfections that contributed to the fizzle. They also concluded that the more robust structure already developed for the weapon version would avoid any such problems.

While the plutonium groups were determining what caused the fizzle, a separate group was re-evaluating the uranium gun weapon. Was that design really as sound as they believed, and had they anticipated all the potential fabrication and assembly glitches involving that device? Were there any tissue and scotch tape issues? Were there quality assurance procedures in place to guard against or correct them? There could be no more 'Aw Shucks'.

This group was shortly able to verify the underlying calculations and the soundness of the design of the uranium gun weapon. They reviewed the earlier tests on the several components. The gun mechanism had successfully fired dummy bullets onto dummy targets at the correct speed. Researchers had measured fission rates in uranium assemblies that were not quite explosive, a highly dangerous test called 'tickling the dragon's tail' (Rhodes; Baggott). Ready since early May, the gun mechanism was carefully re-inspected. The reviewers presented their results and there was solid consensus that the gun design and assembly were sound. Being scientists and engineers, they could not

---

Knowing The Odds

That visit, and the discussion about the odds of the bomb working apparently had made an impression on Tibbets. When he judged that his unit was sufficiently prepared, he took the initiative, without going through the chain of command, to move his 509th Composite Group of specially-modified 'Silverplate' B-29s to Tinian Island, the launch point for the atomic missions. Although it was not his sole intent, the move he later realised had the effect of 'putting pressure on the scientists to quit quibbling about the odds and finish the job' (Hornfischer)

'guarantee' it would work, but assessed there was only a 1 in 10,000 chance it would fail to work. Oppenheimer recalled a comment by a visitor to Los Alamos early in the year. It was Colonel Paul Tibbets, the highly experienced bomber pilot now commanding the B-29 squadron slated to drop the weapon: 'The odds are 10,000 to 1?' he'd said. 'Hell nothing's certain, but that's a thousand times better odds than we had on bombing runs over Europe' (Hornfischer).

Chapter 6

Washington, 17–25 July

While Oppenheimer's task forces were searching for the cause of the fizzle, General Groves had his own task force going, looking at the possibility of sabotage. Security throughout the Manhattan Project's sprawling complex of facilities had been a critical concern from the beginning, both to guard against espionage leaks to German, Japanese or Soviet agents, and to prevent sabotage by agents of any of the above. Groves had a policy of constant vigilance to detect any hint of sabotage, and his security personnel 'investigated every instance of mechanical failure, equipment breakdown, fire, accident, or similar occurrence not readily attributable to normal causes, and kept under constant observation all processes and activities that might attract the efforts of saboteurs' (Rafalko). Could someone have done something that slipped through this surveillance? Groves needed to know.

Indeed, it may well have been a nightmare thought for Groves to consider whether Oppenheimer himself was a saboteur. The scientific director of Los Alamos, a man whom Groves had considered 'irreplaceable', was also a 'security nightmare' with known 'leftward wanderings' (Baggott). There was an FBI file on Robert Oppenheimer as early as March 1941, when FBI surveillance of suspected Soviet agents noticed him in their company. The FBI also suspected Oppenheimer to be the source of a leak they picked up on a wiretap about an 'important new weapon under development' (Baggott). Army Security, in the person of Lieutenant Colonel Boris Pash, interviewed Oppenheimer in 1943 and questioned him about his ongoing contacts with suspected Soviet agents. Pash then recommended Oppenheimer's removal from the programme. Pash's boss at the time, Lieutenant Colonel John Lansdale, instead recommended that Groves counsel Oppenheimer about the importance of security in light of the known Soviet efforts to penetrate the project. Groves had done so, believing that Oppenheimer was loyal and that he was too ambitious in regard to his career and reputation to jeopardise it by compromising security (Baggott).

Groves knew there was also the matter of Dr Frank Oppenheimer, Robert's younger brother. He too worked on the project; he was a key member of the Trinity site team, and he too had an FBI and an Army Security file documenting suspected contacts with Soviet agents (Bird and Sherwin). But the Oppenheimer brothers were far from the only potential security risks among the diverse Los Alamos team, as many of them hailed from all over Europe. Groves needed to conduct a large but rapid security review. If the fizzle came from sabotage, he needed to know how it was done, how to prevent it from happening again, and if possible to find who was responsible. All this had to be carried out with no delay in the use of the new weapons.

If the Japanese or the Germans had agents at Los Alamos, the motivation for sabotage was obvious. But by 1945, US security agencies believed those threats to have been largely neutralised (Department of Energy (2)). The mass internment of Japanese-Americans was seen to have addressed the Japanese problem, while the attempts by Germany at espionage had been quickly foiled. For example, Germany's Operation Pastorious landed saboteurs by submarine near the Hamptons on New York's Long Island. They were swiftly found, arrested, and most were executed before they could cause any harm (D. Taylor). And the Duquesne Spy Ring, named for the leader of over thirty German-American spies, was rolled up within a few months after Pearl Harbor (FBI).

However, espionage by the Soviet Union was still a concern. Although the USSR and US had both fought Germany, the Communist power was widely seen as a potential enemy after the war. 'The enemy of my enemy' may be a friend, but not necessarily best friends forever. The US wanted to keep the technology of the atomic bomb out of Stalin's hands. But even if 'Uncle Joe' had agents at Los Alamos, why would he have instructed them to sabotage a test?

Although Groves and security chief Pash may not have known about Stalin's specific commitment to the US and the UK to join the war against Japan after the defeat of Germany, the concept of the Soviet Union doing so had been discussed even in the news media at least since the beginning of the year (Hornfischer). If the Russians were planning to attack Japan, they could have a motive to delay the (clearly inevitable) Allied victory. It would give the Communists time to get in on the act, and get in on the spoils of the Pacific War.

Therefore it was essential to look into the possibility that the Trinity test had been sabotaged. Groves tasked security officer Lieutenant Colonel William Parsons to lead a two-pronged inquiry that mirrored Oppenheimer's. Was there sabotage of the design? Was there sabotage of the device? Bill Parsons had access to over 200 military and civilian personnel in the Manhattan District's security organisation (Rafalko). He organised many of them to review records and interview Los Alamos personnel. Just as Oppenheimer's technical personnel had determined that the design was sound, the security investigators determined that the design process had been far too collaborative for it to have been sabotaged. As any number of the Los Alamos scientists explained more or less patiently to the security types, if any scientists had tried to introduce a design flaw, at least several other scientists, reviewing and re-reviewing the work, would have detected and corrected it. That was the way modern science was done, with essentially everything any scientist does subject to being checked and challenged by the rest of the scientific community. Security agents asked several of the senior scientists whether Robert Oppenheimer had had any specific inputs to any aspects of the design, and if his colleagues had accepted such inputs without question. 'This isn't the Army, guys,' said one of the Nobel laureates, 'we don't just take anyone's input at face value, even Oppie's.'

So sabotage of the design was extremely unlikely, unless a large number of scientists had participated in a conspiracy. 'Conspiracy' was of course part of security agents' vocabulary. But they also understood that, as one of the Los Alamos team had expressed it, 'The probability of a successful conspiracy is an inverse function of the square of the number of participants' (as the number of people involved goes up, the likelihood of a conspiracy succeeding and staying hidden very rapidly goes down).

But in regard to sabotaging the assembly of the Gadget, there were a few possibilities. The security team reviewed the procedures surrounding each of the components (lenses, detonators, etc.) looking for points at which one person was alone with the item or could have tampered with it without others noticing. For example, they interviewed George Kistiakowsky, who was in charge of the truck convoy transporting the Gadget to the Trinity site. No, he told them, there was no time during that nine-hour trip when one person was or could have been alone on the bomb truck. As to Kistiakowsky's 'repair' of the explosive lenses, he had not done that work surreptitiously and it was clearly intended to improve, not lessen, the chances of success. Still, Kistiakowsky was Ukrainian-born and German-educated, which raised a few security agents' eyebrows. Agents re-contacted the physicists' faculty colleagues from Princeton and Harvard, and found no hint of disloyalty.

The security investigators did find two 'oversight gaps', when single individuals had access to the device with no witnesses. The first was on 13 July: the assembly team was finalising the device within a tent at the base of the test tower. After they put the plutonium core into the incomplete sphere of explosive lenses, Dr Norris Bradbury had worked on precisely emplacing and aligning the remaining lenses. There were several other people in the enclosure at the time, and even a movie record of the process, but there were times when Bradbury's arms were deep inside the well of the bomb, ostensibly scotch-taping the pieces into perfect alignment or making other adjustments. While Oppenheimer and others watched him, but not his hands, could Bradbury have done some intentional damage to the inside surfaces of one or more of the lenses? That possibility could not be ruled out, and there had been no independent inspection of the interior of the assembly after Bradbury had finished. Yet Bradbury was a commissioned naval officer and there had never been a whiff of doubt about his loyalty. None of the security team considered Bradbury a potential saboteur.

The second oversight gap occurred the night before the test. The assembled bomb was at the top of the 100ft tower. The thirty-two detonators each with two firing cables were connected to the intricate electrical firing mechanism (Borad). Everything was ready, and Robert Oppenheimer became nervous about leaving the bomb alone. He turned to Dr Don Hornig, the explosives expert who had helped develop the firing mechanism, and husband to Lili, who'd worked on the Pu240 problem. He asked Hornig to return to the tower and babysit the bomb, in case of sabotage. And so he did, sitting alone for several hours right there at the tower, reading, and shuddering as a thunderstorm raged nearby. The storm passed, dawn approached, and Don Hornig was the last man to see the first bomb (*New York Times*).

He was also the last man to touch the bomb, and he had more than adequate opportunity to tamper with it, perhaps somehow disabling one of the detonators so as to distort the required symmetry of the implosion. As an explosives expert, he would have known how to do that, and he'd know that there was probably not going to be anyone to check the device after him.

But as with Bradbury, there had never been any concerns about Dr Hornig's loyalty. The lead security investigator dealing with this issue had been an experienced and highly successful NYPD detective before the war. After participating in several intensive interviews of Dr Hornig, the investigator was highly confident that he was no saboteur. But because that solitary vigil at the top of the tower had been such a perfect opportunity for sabotage, the security team believed that further investigation was warranted. They concluded that if the fizzle had been an act of sabotage, the logical culprit would be Hornig.

Meanwhile, investigators ruled out Frank Oppenheimer, Robert's brother. He had helped prepare the facilities at the Trinity site and had been there continuously in the days leading up to the test. But there was no time at which Frank had access to the device in any situation in which he could have in any way tampered with it.

Parsons reported to General Groves on 24 July and asked for another week to make further inquiries about Don Hornig, just to be completely sure. 'We don't have the time "just to be completely sure", Bill' said Groves,

> the White House wants these things raining down on the Japs soonest. I know I told you guys to be thorough and you have been, but we can't afford the time you'd need to perfectly cover our backsides if it means diverting these guys from getting the device ready. You don't really think Hornig is a spy, and neither do I or anyone else. Besides, we've nailed down a technical problem that we are pretty sure caused the fizzle, not the long arm of Joe Stalin. Go ahead and do some more background research if you think it is warranted. Let me know if you find anything that smells bad. But don't do anything that will interfere with getting this thing ready.

There is no record of any further action concerning Dr Hornig, or of anyone having any doubts about him. He went on to a distinguished academic career, and a stint as White House science advisor (Boffey). Nor did anyone have any concerns about Norris Bradbury, the navy commander who did the final bomb assembly. He became director of the Los Alamos Lab after the war (Agnew and Schreiber).

General Groves might have thought, and acted, differently if he had known some information that has only come to light more than 70 years after the war: the Soviets had a spy at Los Alamos who had specific knowledge of the bomb's timing and detonation device. In the years shortly after the war, the presence of Soviet spies David Greenglass and Klaus Fuchs in the Manhattan Project was revealed. Much later, in the 1990s, information on another spy, Ted Hall, was revealed. All three gave the Kremlin valuable information about the atomic bomb project. But only after 2010 did a fourth, and perhaps the most valuable, spy publicly come to light: he was Oscar Seborer (Broad). Drafted in 1942, Oscar was an Army Technician/4, an enlisted man, with training as an electrical engineer. His technical expertise got him assigned to Los Alamos and he (unlike the other Soviet spies) had been involved in

41

the development and testing of the intricate mechanism for detonating the explosive shell in near-perfect synchrony (Dickson). Seborer was present at the Trinity site for the test (Klehr and Haynes).

In 1945 Groves and his security officer Parsons apparently did not know what is now known about Seborer's family: several siblings and in-laws were members of the Communist Party USA, and engaged in espionage for the USSR – so much that the Soviets dubbed their spy ring 'The Relatives' (Broad). If the General had known, he might have ordered a closer look at Seborer's activities and whereabouts at the time of the test. They might have looked into whether Seborer could have had an assignment that gave him an opportunity to subtly modify and thus sabotage the firing mechanism at Los Alamos or at the test site.

But the Manhattan Engineer District did not have that backstory about Seborer, so whether Oscar somehow did cause the fizzle may never be known. Even in the modern day, the full story has not come to light. Most, but not all, of the material the FBI compiled on the Seborer family has been declassified, and the Kremlin's side of the story remains hidden. We do know that Oscar and his brother defected to the Soviet Union in the early 1950s, and that when Oscar died in Moscow in 2015 he was posthumously awarded the Order of the Red Star (Klehr and Haynes).

Whether the Kremlin ordered the test to be sabotaged is unknown, but it would have had advantages for the Soviets and their desire for payback against the Japanese. Delaying the Americans' potentially war-ending weapon gave the Red Army more time to wreak havoc against the Japanese, and to gain a stronger position in East Asia after the war. So perhaps Oscar Seborer, on orders from Moscow, or perhaps even on his own traitorous initiative, tampered with the Gadget and redirected the course of history. Or maybe for the Soviets it was just a fortuitous fizzle.

As all effective decision makers know, absolute certainty is almost always an unavailable luxury, whether in regard to military, scientific, or other matters. On 23 July, Oppenheimer presented his several task forces' findings to Groves, who summed it up as: the weight of evidence says the uranium gun will work as is; we're confident we found the flaw in the plutonium implosion device, so with more careful manufacturing, it will work too. Groves himself was not absolutely certain about the sabotage question, but he too was persuaded by the weight of the evidence then available to him.

To Stimson, Groves then reported: 'Whole team of doctors agree on diagnosis; treatment underway and team confident of full recovery within a few weeks.' In a more detailed report the next day, Groves explained that Trinity had been the world's first nuclear explosive device, albeit an imperfectly functioning one with a fraction of the planned yield. He reported the team's confidence that they had found the problem, a relatively easily fixable fabrication flaw. He also reported his confidence that sabotage was not indicated. The team would be able to deliver a militarily significant plutonium bomb within a matter of a few weeks. Groves said that one uranium bomb would also be available at that time.

Chapter 7

Potsdam, 2–26 July

Truman was now confident that he would have a new super weapon soon enough to potentially make a major difference in ending the Pacific War. After conferring with his advisors and with Churchill, he decided to tell his ally Stalin about the bomb (Hasegawa). He believed that would be better than having Stalin find out about it only when it was first used. Truman chose a low-key approach. As a formal session of the Potsdam Conference was breaking up on the evening of 24 July, Truman 'casually' approached Stalin and mentioned to him in an almost offhand manner that the US was developing new weapons of unusual destructive power.[1] Stalin showed virtually no reaction, replying in an ostensibly similar offhand manner that he hoped the US would put them to good use against the Japanese, once they were perfected. Truman and his advisors were satisfied that they had done sufficient disclosure, although they felt that Stalin had not comprehended the significance of the new weapons.

We now realise that Stalin knew about the atom bomb project well before President Truman mentioned it to him. Indeed, Stalin knew about the project years before Senator Truman did. Soviet spies such as Klaus Fuchs and David Greenglass at Los Alamos had informed the Soviets regularly about the atomic bomb programme for years. Fuchs had told the Soviets that a test was slated for mid-July, but there had not been any further information since early in the month. Therefore, Stalin's security services chief, Lavrenti Beria, did not know of the test's specific outcome (Hasegawa; Dobbs). Given the impressive knowledge of the programme they already had, the Soviets concluded from Truman's 'offhand' disclosure that the test of the bomb had been at least partly successful and that it would soon be used against the Japanese. Accordingly,

---

1. See 'What Really Happened' (24 Jul 1945).

DISAPPEARING DEMONSTRATION

In the months prior to the Trinity test, a committee of prominent atomic scientists including Eugene Rabinowitch, Glenn T. Seaborg, J. C. Stearns, and Leó Szilárd approached the White House. They advocated that before the US used the new weapon in war, there should be a demonstration of it for the Japanese, perhaps on some uninhabited island or in a desert. Even before Trinity, the White House had not supported this idea; after the fizzle, no more was heard about it.

In a similar vein, a White House meeting in June had discussed issuing an advance warning to Japan about the atomic bomb. But that idea was dismissed out of concern that the bomb might not work (Hoyt).

Stalin proceeded with his plans to enter the war against Japan as soon as his forces were in place for a surprise attack into Japanese-held Manchuria. As discussed later, there is some indication that the apparent advent of atomic weapons prompted Stalin to accelerate these plans.

Meanwhile, the good-enough news from New Mexico also helped prompt Truman and Churchill to issue a formal call for Japan's unconditional surrender. What came to be termed the Potsdam Declaration went through many preliminary drafts among Truman's War and State Department staffers. There were suggestions that Japan's surrender might be hastened if the declaration included language clarifying that Japan's Imperial System would not necessarily be abolished (Hasegawa). But to others this sounded too much like a retreat from the unconditional surrender demand that had long been the core of Allied policy. As issued, the declaration called for the unconditional surrender of 'all Japanese armed forces', and made no direct mention of the Emperor. Absent the required surrender, the Allies promised 'the complete destruction of the Japanese armed forces and just as inevitably the utter devastation of the Japanese homeland' (Atomic Archive (b)).

The few experts knowledgeable of 'international law' could note that the specific call for surrender of Japan's armed forces was technically something less than a demand for absolute capitulation. What was demanded was a bit closer to 'We'll stop fighting' than to 'Come in and own our country'. But the niceties of international law were probably not foremost in Truman's mind, although he may have thought twice about the Potsdam provision that Japan 'provide proper and adequate assurances of their good faith in such (surrender) action.' 'Good faith my keyster you sneak-attacking bastards' he might have thought. But he kept it to himself.

The symbolism of sending out a call for Japan's surrender from amid the smoking ruins of their ally's capital was intentional. The text, however, was not symbolic. It could be read as a threat to continue or increase the highly destructive aerial bombing of Japan.

Once the new long-range B-29 bombers had become able to operate from the Marianas Islands (Saipan, Tinian and Guam), Tokyo and other cities were within their range. Beginning in November 1944, US Army Air Force planes routinely dropped tons of bombs on the Japanese homeland (although initially very inaccurately). Early the next year, the Home Islands also came within range of US Naval aviation. On 16 February, sixteen US aircraft carriers sailed to within 100 miles of Japan and launched their air wings toward the Tokyo area. There they destroyed critical aircraft engine factories, ten airfields and over 500 Japanese planes, plus a Japanese aircraft carrier (Hornfischer).

A few weeks later, on 9 March, the Air Force used new tactics in their raid on Tokyo, dropping not just high explosive bombs, but incendiaries. The resulting firestorm destroyed about a quarter of the city and may have killed 100,000 people (Strategic Bombing Survey).

So to Japanese ears, the 'utter devastation' Truman and Churchill were threatening from Potsdam might have meant a continuation of these sorts of raids with hundreds of planes dropping thousands of bombs. Neither the Japanese nor virtually anyone else knew that Truman was referring to just a few of the atomic bombs that would be available shortly.

In occupied China there were at the time about 1.5 million troops of the Japanese army and the armies of the Japanese puppet regimes in 'Manchukuo', 'Menjiang' (Inner Mongolia) and the 'Re-organised National Chinese Government' (Occupied China). Accordingly, Truman and Churchill obtained concurrence from the Chinese Nationalist leader Chiang Kai-shek before issuing the Potsdam Declaration. Chiang's Guomindang (GMD) army had ostensibly been fighting the Japanese for control of vast portions of China for several years even before the start of the European war.

But Truman and Churchill issued their 26 July declaration from Potsdam without consulting Stalin. Officially this was because the USSR was not then at war with Japan (Dobbs). However, at least part of the reason for excluding the Soviets was the US and UK desire to minimise the Soviet role in the Japanese war. As had been the case for some time, there were still mixed views among senior Americans on this. Joseph Grew at the State Department adamantly sought to exclude or lessen the role of the Soviets in the defeat of Japan, so as to minimise their role in post-war East Asia (Hasegawa). Secretary of War Stimson was more receptive to including the Soviets, whose involvement would save American GIs' lives. Indeed, ten months earlier, at the Quebec Conference, the US Joint Chiefs had expressed the position that 'every effort should be made to bring the USSR into the war against Japan at the earliest practicable date' (Combined Chiefs). Stimson had even opined that a Soviet occupation role, perhaps on the northern island of Hokkaido, would ease the burden on US troops in post-war Japan (Hasegawa).

But now, with the advent of the new bombs, the value of Soviet participation in the now-imminent defeat of Japan looked far lower, likely not worth the high cost of post-war Soviet influence in the Far East. That is, if the atom bombs became available in time.

Truman recognised that Soviet entry into the Pacific War was likely to make a strategic difference, not so much in the short term but definitely in the post-war period. He also recognised that while he might not now be inclined to urge Stalin to enter the war as quickly and forcefully as he could, neither could the Western Allies prevent the Soviets from entering the war against Japan. There was too much history between those two Asian powers. All Truman could perhaps influence is how quickly the war ended in relation to when the Soviets entered it.

Given the dominance of American land, naval and air power by July 1945, there was no doubt that the US would prevail against the Japanese, with British Empire forces also playing an important role, along with Free French and Dutch Empire forces. From intercepted cables between Tokyo and their ambassador to Moscow, the US even had evidence that as of mid-1945 the Japanese Emperor wanted to end the war, although on terms clearly unacceptable to the Allies (Brooks).

Victory was certain, based on the overall military situation, not merely on the promise of the products of the Manhattan Project. Even among the few senior personnel who knew about that project, such as Army chief General George Marshall, there was no assumption that these new weapons alone would end the war (Hastings 2012). Marshall thought the new bombs might be used as part of the land invasion of Japan (Hornfischer). Admiral Leahy, Roosevelt's Chief of Staff, had earlier expressed his opinion – as a munitions expert – that the atomic bomb would not even work (Hoyt).

Nor had the long-running war planning efforts in Washington and London been premised on the timely arrival of the atom bomb. There had been debate, however, as to the best strategy to defeat Japan. Blockade, bombs and boots were the main available ingredients, with perhaps some

Bolsheviks. The arguments about emphasising one or another were in part a reflection of inter-service rivalries. Keeping all options open, Roosevelt, Churchill and their military chiefs had agreed at the 1944 Quebec conference on an 'all of the above' maximalist strategy to defeat Japan. The island-hopping campaign would continue approaching the Home Islands, and planning would be undertaken for a land invasion of them. The Allied navies would continue choking off Japan's maritime supply lines, with Allied air power destroying as much of Japan's war capacity as possible (Combined Chiefs). The agreed-upon strategy also called for flexibility to adapt to changing circumstances.

Begun in earnest in early 1945, the invasion planning envisioned 'Operation Downfall' to involve two major phases. There would first be an invasion of the southernmost Home Island, Kyushu, followed some months later by an invasion of the main island, Honshu, with landings near Tokyo. The operation would be larger, and in several ways more challenging, than Overlord, the 1944 invasion of northern France (Giangreco). Overlord had been the largest amphibious operation in history, involving over 6,000 ships and landing craft putting about 5 divisions ashore initially, with about 35 more to come (Tillman). Downfall's two major phases would together involve about 55 divisions. The cross-Channel invasion of France had the British Isles, less than 100 miles away, as a staging area, logistics hub and unsinkable aircraft carrier. In contrast, the invasion of Japan would have no such nearby support. The closest staging area for an invasion of Kyushu would have been Okinawa – over 500 miles away; the invasion of Honshu was to be staged out of the Marianas (Guam, Tinian, Saipan), 1,500 miles away. The ships to carry out these long-range invasions would have included many thousands of troop transports, landing craft and supply ships of various kinds, along with 63 aircraft carriers, 22 battleships, 50 cruisers, and 460 destroyers (Hornfischer). In comparison, the Normandy fleet had 7 battleships, 22 cruisers and 140 destroyers and escorts.

The forces landing in Normandy had faced stiff opposition from the Germans, but there had been so many possible landing locations that the German forces were relatively spread out. Because of highly effective Allied deception plans, even after the Normandy landings began the Germans were not sure if there were to be others. The geography of Japan, however, limited the possible landing sites for invaders, and made southern Kyushu an obvious first target. Concentrated defences could be expected there.

At the time of the Normandy invasion, Germany's reduced air power was largely focused on defending the homeland from Allied bombing, so the invaders in northern France had clear air superiority. They would also have clear superiority over Japan, but Allied intelligence was reporting that the Japanese might have on the order of 10,000 planes. Most would be no match for Allied aircraft, but the worry was that perhaps half of the Japanese planes would be used as suicide bombers in kamikaze attacks. With radar, anti-aircraft fire and aerial interdiction, the Navy was learning to counter this tactic, but could not yet achieve full effectiveness. In the conquest of Okinawa in April 1945, kamikazes had sunk 19 ships and damaged 181 others. A few months later, the Japanese sank a destroyer by using a stealth kamikaze, very hard to detect with the radar of the day. It was an obsolete biplane, made largely of plywood and fabric (Hornfischer).

Once they were clear of the beaches, the invaders at Normandy faced a relatively flat countryside, albeit initially presenting the obstacle of numerous dense hedgerows. But northern France did not have the mountainous terrain that Kyushu would force invaders to fight in.

In occupied France, the Western Allies were aided by the French Resistance, conducting sabotage of transportation assets and similar actions. Nor did the invaders face a hostile civilian population. That would not be the case in Japan. It was expected that a large portion of the civilian population would be mobilised to fight the first invasion of the Japanese home islands since 1281. Intercepted Japanese communications showed that the military were exhorting the entire Japanese population to give their lives to defend the honour of the Emperor (Hornfischer).

THE KAMIKAZE ('DIVINE WIND') WITH 90-KNOT GUSTS

In October 1945, Okinawa was hit by the powerful Typhoon Louise, which did not behave as predicted. The Navy was therefore unable to fully prepare for the storm, which sank 12 ships and damaged about 250 landing craft and other vessels (NHHC). This was after the war had ended, but it was at the time Okinawa would have been in use as a major staging area for the invasion of Kyushu if that had been needed. In that event, there would have been far more ships, planes and personnel at Okinawa when the unexpected storm hit. The Navy's history observes that if the war had not ended when it did, the storm 'would likely have seriously impacted the planned invasion of Japan' (Williams).

Given all this, the planners knew an invasion would have a high cost in casualties. There were widely divergent estimates, but data was accumulating. In the spring 1945 conquest of 900-square-mile Okinawa, more than one-third of the US Army and Marine Corps troops had been casualties, including 14,000 dead. Japan was 150 times the size of that bloody island. A conservative estimate was upwards of 100,000 Americans might die in this final campaign against the Japanese homeland (about 400,000 had died in the World War to that point). US planners assumed there would be intense, even fanatical resistance from the Japanese armed forces, including large numbers of the hastily mobilised and trained. Therefore even larger numbers of Japanese military personnel would also die, along with potentially still larger numbers of civilians. Thousands of civilians on Saipan, and perhaps 100,000 on Okinawa, had committed suicide during the American conquest of these islands (Bergamini; Seig). So it was highly possible that hundreds of thousands or perhaps millions more Japanese civilians would have vainly hurled themselves into battle or outright killed themselves during an invasion of the Home Islands.

To be sure, avoiding the deaths of enemy combatants was not a US objective. But the reports of masses of civilians throwing themselves, and their children, off cliffs in places like Saipan, and seeing the massed bodies of civilian suicides weighed on the minds of US commanders such as Admirals Spruance and Nimitz (Hornfischer).

Now in mid-1945 there were some senior military officers, largely from the Navy, who argued that the increasingly effective naval interdiction of the imported fuel and resources the Japanese war machine needed, plus the increased conventional bombing of transportation and other infrastructure within the Japanese homeland, would obviate the need for any boots on Japan's own ground. The Navy's chief, Admiral Ernest King wrote a memo to the other chiefs indicating that he did not believe an invasion was the best course of action (Frank 1999).

For their part, the Air Force was confident that aerial bombardment could deliver a knockout blow. Air Force chief Hap Arnold estimated that dropping tonnage on Japan similar to what the US had dropped on Germany 'would make possible the complete destruction of interior Japan', while Curtis LeMay, commander of the B-29s raiding Japan from the Marianas, believed that his incendiary raid tactic could end the war (Hornfischer). In addition, some of his B-29s were even then laying many thousands of mines in the waters around Japan, helping cut it off from Asian resources (Frank 1999).

Those who argued against the need for a land invasion pointed out the importance of the American home front. The United States had achieved and maintained a higher degree of military and industrial mobilisation than almost anyone anywhere had thought possible just a few years previously. Home front support for the war remained intense. Yet, with the end of the war in Europe, there was now some pressure building to bring the boys who'd fought there home, and not ship them halfway around the world to fight another enemy, and perhaps never see the US again (Heinrichs and Gallicchio). Americans can be determined, but patient they are often not, and the wartime restrictions on domestic production and consumption were now becoming irksome as the war was so obviously won, 'if only the blasted Japs would admit it'.

Yet as others pointed out a blockade could intensify Americans' incipient impatience. It would likely take longer than an invasion to force the Japanese to admit defeat. In the meantime Americans' resolve to force the unconditional surrender of the Japanese might soften (especially if cutting off food supplies to Japan meant the starvation of Allied POWs (Hornfischer).) Indeed, we now know that there were some in Japan, such as Army Minister Anami, who believed if Japan could hold out long enough, the Americans would decide the cost was too great, and would agree to a settlement far short of any unconditional Japanese surrender (Hornfischer). However, it was also true that a June 1945 Gallup poll of the American public had found nine out of ten Americans against accepting a peace offer from the Japanese that was anything less than unconditional (Hornfischer). It was also noted that this slower approach to the end of the war might give the Soviets more time to participate, and thereby enhance their claim to a post-war role in Northeast Asia.

Whichever strategy they used, US leaders were confident by July 1945 that there was no need for Soviet involvement against Japan. In addition to the imminent availability of atomic weapons, military planners believed that US and British Empire naval forces could interdict shipping, including troop transport, between the Asian mainland and Japan so effectively that the more than 1.5 million Japanese troops in Manchuria, China and Korea would not be able to return to the Home Islands and reinforce troops there. So any Russian attacks on Japanese forces on the mainland would not directly affect the pace of the US conquest of the Home Islands, costly as that might be (Frank 1999). The military value that MacArthur had previously envisioned in having the Red Army tie down Japanese forces on the mainland had apparently all but disappeared. The isolation of the Japanese homeland effected by the US Navy and the Army Air Forces had largely taken Japan's mainland forces out of the strategic equation (Allen and Polmar). It was

52

irrelevant whether they were tied down on the mainland. They couldn't have gotten back home in significant numbers.

On the other hand, the potential horrors of that planned Allied invasion of Japan by the US argued for the value of having the Soviets impose further pain on the Japanese by also bleeding their armies in Manchuria, North China and Korea as much as possible. To many US planners, Soviet troops killing and being killed by Japanese were preferable to Americans doing the same if it helped hasten the end of the bloodletting.

Regardless, US officials realised that the Soviets would likely enter the war against Japan for their own reasons, such as gaining access to Manchuria's ports, and there was no way now to prevent Soviet entry into the war even if the US and Britain had wanted to. With difficulties already developing with the Soviets on European issues such as reparations and governance, Truman wanted not only to end the war soonest but also to limit Soviet claims for occupation and reparations in East Asia. Having fought the Japanese since 1941, the US and the British Empire did not relish the prospect of the Soviet Union claiming to have won the war against Japan for them in the last few weeks or months.

The US was not all that cordial even toward the British Empire. By mid-1945, there were Royal Navy ships from the UK and from Australia interdicting Japanese shipping near Formosa (Taiwan), but their welcome

---

UNEASY NEUTRALITY

One interpretation of the 1941 Soviet-Japanese Neutrality Pact was that it was a shrewd device by Stalin. It may have helped steer Japan's war aims southward, away from Siberia. That way, by the time Stalin had settled things in Europe, Japan would be worn out by its war with the Western democracies. It would then be relatively easy for the USSR to take back from Japan what Russia had lost 40 years previously (Hoyt). Still, as mentioned previously, the potential that Japan might move against Soviet Siberia, a move Hitler pressured Japan to make, had forced Stalin to keep about forty divisions in the Far East, divisions he could well have used in the battle against Hitler's invasion. So even though Japan was officially neutral toward Russia, the potential Japanese threat had still cost Stalin dearly (Hasegawa).

---

from the US Navy had been underwhelming (Hastings 2009). The planners for the Downfall invasion had only somewhat begrudgingly included British and Australian forces in their plans (Combined Chiefs). Having spent so much blood and treasure, and having come so far, the US wanted to be the clearly decisive player in the defeat of Japan. Impressing the Soviets with the physical and strategic power of the new American weapons was an additional consideration (Takaki).

The sooner the atomic weapons could be deployed, the sooner the war was likely to end. And the clearer the role played by the new weapons, the clearer the US role would be in post-war East Asia. As Secretary of State Byrnes noted, 'We should get the Japanese affair over with before the Russians get in. Once they are in, it will not be easy to get them out' (Dobbs 2012).

Indeed, when would the Soviets enter the Pacific War? Stalin had told Roosevelt at Yalta in February that the USSR would enter the war against Japan within 'two or three months' after the defeat of Germany. If he had meant this as a precise deadline, this would fix about 8 August as the latest date for Soviet action. But there was no indication that Stalin meant this rough estimate as a date-certain commitment. As noted above, in Stalin's first meeting with Truman at Potsdam, the Soviet leader stated that he would enter the war in mid-August, which Truman recorded in his diary as 15 August. Also during the Potsdam Conference senior Soviet military personnel told their US counterparts that they would invade in the second half of August. The Soviets caveated their plans as subject not only to weather but also to their reaching an agreement with the Chinese Nationalist leader Chiang Kai-shek in regard to the concessions the Soviets sought in Manchuria.

At the time of Potsdam, negotiations in Moscow with the Chinese were still going on. On 10 July Foreign Minister Molotov told Chinese Nationalist (Guomindang) representative T.V. Soong that the Soviets planned to move into Manchuria in late August (Holloway). The US was by then in no hurry to have the Soviets enter the war, so Ambassador Averill Harriman encouraged Soong to hold firm and not concede too much to the Soviets (Holloway). The longer it took the Soviets and the Chinese to reach a deal, the later would likely be the Red Army's entry into Manchuria, and this was fine with the Americans. There were indeed several issues involved in the negotiations, not least of which was the assistance Stalin was giving to Uighurs and Kazakhs in China's western Xingiang province. In return for the economic and political concessions Stalin sought in Manchuria, Chiang wanted Stalin to stop aiding these rebellious minorities (Radchenko 2012). So the thinking among the

Americans at Potsdam was that the Soviets would not enter the war on 8 August (i.e. exactly three months after VE Day), but more likely would do so well after the 15th (Hastings 2009).

Once the Soviets did enter the war against Japan, how effective would they be? The Pentagon was not privy to the Soviets' battle plans, and the Chinese Nationalists were unable to provide reliable intelligence about the current battle readiness of Japan's Kwantung Army in Manchuria. However, by April 1945 US intercepts of Japanese communications indicated transfers of sixteen divisions from the Kwantung Army in Manchuria back to the Japanese homeland. The US shared this information with the Soviets (Hasegawa). Still, the US estimate was that Japan's Kwantung Army was a large, capable fighting force, and that the Soviets faced at least many weeks of hard fighting before they could reach their objectives inside Manchuria. After all, the several provinces forming China's north-east extension stretched well over 1,000 miles north-to-south and 700 miles east-to-west. Pentagon analysts acknowledged that the Red Army was formidable, but they did not believe the Soviets could quickly conquer a territory larger than France and Germany combined (Map 1)

On another aspect of ending the war, a high-level committee (Secretaries Byrnes and Stimson, Groves and others) had been meeting since the spring to determine how to use the atomic bombs. They considered events such as the Tokyo firebombing in March which killed perhaps 100,000 people, and saw that these had evidently not weakened Japanese resolve. The committee members were in general accord that the US would need to use multiple atomic bombs to bring the war to a close (Baggott; Maddox). So uncertain was the expected effectiveness of the new weapons in inducing a Japanese surrender that there were discussions at the Chief of Staff's level about the pace of their use. There would be two or perhaps three weapons available for use before the end of August or so (Frank 1999). Then, in September and October, the Los Alamos team could produce about one bomb every 10 days. The question was whether the Army should use these as they became available, or stockpile the bombs for use against Japanese troop concentrations during the scheduled November invasion (National Security Archives; Allen and Polmar). As a contingency, the ongoing planning for the US invasions of the Home Islands included developing an airbase on Okinawa capable of supporting continued atomic bombing missions well into the autumn or even later if needed (Maddox). Thus, US officials hoped the atomic weapons would hasten the end of the war, but few assumed they would bring it to an end promptly after their first use. Even with the Soviets

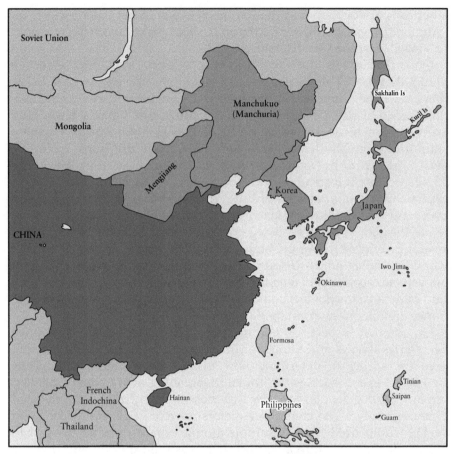

Map 1: East Asia Theatre of War

involved, and even with nuclear weapons in play, US officials recognised that there might be many more months of war (Hoyt; Allen and Polmar).

Or perhaps not. Atomic weapons might serve as the tipping point, forcing the Japanese to admit their long-obvious defeat. Indeed, Washington knew through its codebreaking success that Tokyo was considering ending the war. The intercepted traffic from Tokyo to its ambassador in Moscow discussing what terms to seek from the Allies told the US that while at least some in the Japanese government were still denying the obvious, there was peace sentiment there, even if they still hoped for 'favourable terms' (Weinberg). The US wanted to make sure the new weapons came into play and were seen as decisive before sustained

Red Army advances in Manchuria allowed the Soviets to claim much of the credit for prompting Japan to admit defeat.

If the Soviets entered the war after 15 August as the American delegation at Potsdam expected, the US use of atomic weapons at about the same time would preclude the Soviets' action from being seen as playing a decisive role in Japan's surrender, whenever it then occurred. Accordingly Stimson, in Potsdam with the President, sent the directive to Groves on 26 July to make every effort to drop one weapon as soon as operationally feasible but no later than a few days after 15 August. He directed that a second and a third bomb be ready to drop at intervals of a few days afterward, because the Japanese (and the Soviets) needed to know that the US had a continuing supply of these weapons.

Also on 26 July, the Soviet delegation at Potsdam sought to revise the 'draft' of the Potsdam Declaration which had been given to them. They proposed to become signatories to it, thereby using it as their declaration of war against Japan. But the US said their revisions were too late; the declaration had already been broadcast to the world (Dobbs 2012). Stalin may have felt snubbed. After all, he had (magnanimously!) promised Truman to join the war against Japan.

Chapter 8

Los Alamos, Late July–Early August

By the last week of July the Los Alamos team had developed and begun to implement more rigorous production procedures for the explosive lenses. But it would take some time to produce and thoroughly inspect the required number of flawless explosive lenses, with none of those pancake-batter bubbles. While that effort proceeded, Oppenheimer, Groves and their advisors debated whether they needed another implosion test, and also whether the uranium gun-type device should be tested. 'If we got one wrong,' ran the thinking, 'how can we be sure we have the other one right?'

In addition to the time pressure on the Manhattan Project to help end the war, save American lives (and minimise the Soviets' role), there were materiel limitations concerning testing. There would be only enough material for one plutonium and one uranium bomb by early August, with one more plutonium device by mid-to-late August. In September there would be enough plutonium for three bombs. As the new plutonium-breeding reactors at Hanford Washington increased their production the monthly supply would increase to about seven plutonium bombs in December (Maddox). Unfortunately the uranium isotope separation facilities at Oak Ridge were expected to be able to produce only enough enriched uranium for one more bomb by December (Frank 1999).

This scarcity of bomb-grade uranium precluded a test of the uranium bomb and its gun design. Moreover, as noted previously, Oppenheimer' task force had re-evaluated the design and fabrication of the uranium weapon. They had concluded, even in light of the plutonium fizzle, that the uranium weapon would deliver a devastating explosion. They were confident that a full test of the uranium bomb was still not warranted.

Given the team's confidence in the gun mechanism, General Groves asked them to consider whether the available plutonium should be used in a gun-type device rather than the implosion design that had fizzled at Trinity. As discussed above, use of the gun mechanism with plutonium was ruled out earlier because the fission rate of plutonium was so fast that there would be a premature detonation as the pieces began to come together in a gun device. But, Groves asked, would such a 'premature' detonation still yield enough explosive energy to make it militarily significant?

'No', was the answer. A plutonium gun-type bomb would be a wasted effort, very likely producing a yield of only a few tons of TNT, well within the range of some of the conventional bombs already in use. Moreover, because the gun mechanism used a far larger mass of fuel than the implosion mechanism did (Broad; Lallanilla), using plutonium in a gun would substantially decrease the number of bombs that could be produced.

Groves also asked about an approach he knew the Los Alamos crew had talked about some time ago: could uranium be imploded? (Groves 1945). The advantage was that implosion requires a smaller mass of fissionable fuel than a gun. So maybe they could make several uranium implosion bombs for the same amount of uranium they would need for a gun. Oppenheimer affirmed that a uranium-fuelled implosion device was possible and that it would use on the order of one-tenth as much uranium as the gun (Nichols). But the calculations they had done suggested its yield would be hundreds or perhaps a thousand tons of TNT (Sublette 2002). That is, they'd be similar to the fizzle they'd just had.[1]

If there were no other choice, Oppenheimer ventured, dropping a series of bombs with 500-ton yields might have had some utility. But would it make sense to repurpose the uranium from the gun device – with a very high chance of delivering thousands of tons of explosive power – to cobble together several smaller-yielding devices? No, it wouldn't, agreed Groves, after being assured again that the gun would work, and that now the scientists were confident that the plutonium implosion would work. Well, pretty confident.

So there would be no test of the uranium gun-type bomb, and the plutonium would be imploded. But was another implosion test warranted? Of course the scientists would have preferred another test. But the expenditure of more of the precious plutonium was hard to justify

---

1. See 'What Really Happened' (Mar–Apr 1953).

militarily when no one knew how many bombs the US would need in order to bring the war to an end, as many hoped they would do. Indeed, just prior to the Trinity test, some of the Los Alamos team had a betting pool on the yield, with bets ranging from 300 tons of TNT to 45,000 tons, revealing a startling degree of uncertainty among the very creators of the Gadget as to how potent an atom bomb would be (Rhodes).

There would be just a few bombs, and every additional one could possibly be important in hastening the end of the war. Given the White House's mandate to begin the atomic campaign by 15 August or very soon thereafter, it was not feasible to expend another plutonium device in another test.[2] Using several more kilograms of plutonium in a test would mean there would not be enough material for the three bombs the Secretary of War had wanted available for use in the latter part of August. Though it may have been a staffer's idea, General Groves is credited with the quote: 'Looks like we'll test the damn thing over a Jap city.'

The revised procedures for the more careful casting and milling of the explosive blocks added some days to the assembly of the plutonium weapon. Therefore, aware that a too-rushed schedule may have led to the Trinity fizzle, the Los Alamos team would not commit to having the first bomb before 19 August, about four days after the date the US officials assumed the Soviet campaign in Manchuria would start. Groves sought Pentagon concurrence for this bomb date.

Informed of this in Potsdam on 30 July, Truman recalled his 'Fini Japs when that happens' diary entry referring to the prospect of Soviet entry into the war. He asked General Marshall: 'I want this war over as fast as possible. But is there any chance the Japs will fold right away, a day or two after the Russians come in, before General Groves drops this new weapon?'

'Very little, Mr. President', replied Marshall.

No matter how hard the Soviets strike into Manchuria, it will take quite a while for the Russians to defeat the million or so Japanese troops in and around Manchuria. We believe the Japanese army in Manchuria is weaker than it once was, but it is still formidable, and we know they've had many years to develop defensive works. It will take at least some weeks for the Reds to take control of Manchuria – it is not obvious on the map, Mr. President, but Manchuria is much larger than Germany.

---

2. See 'What Really Happened' (6 Aug 1945).

Even when they do, that will not directly threaten the Jap Home Islands. Anyway, the Japanese still have maybe three million troops on the Home Islands. As you know, the Emperor issued a 'fight to the finish' edict to his people in June. So you and I know they are beaten, but they don't seem to. Even the loss of all of Manchuria maybe in late September, won't itself make Tokyo fold.

Truman seemed satisfied and indicated that the 19 August date for the first atomic bombing was acceptable, even though this could let the Soviets strike a powerful blow against the Japanese before the Americans introduced what could be their war-winning weapon.

The plan the scientists, General Groves and the Army Air Force worked out called for the first weapon employed to be a plutonium implosion device (dubbed Fat Man), even though the uranium gun device would be ready sooner, in the first few days of August. The plan was to use the Army Air Force's specially trained and equipped 509th Composite Group under Colonel Paul Tibbets to drop the plutonium implosion device on 19 August. If the weapon exploded as planned, the 509th's aircrews would observe and document the event. But if it were another fizzle, then about 100 additional B-29s from Curtis LeMay's XXI Bomber Command, flying a few minutes behind the 509th flight, would then conduct a conventional bombing raid over the target city. The Japanese were unlikely to note that a single unusual type of bomb fell from the 'lead' planes a few minutes before the main raid. Nor was it likely that the Japanese would detect the presence of radioactive debris amid the damage done by the conventional bombs. The Japanese would not know that they had been part of a high stakes weapons test.

Under this plan, if the Fat Man plutonium implosion weapon did perform as designed, then Tibbets' group would drop the reliable uranium weapon, dubbed Little Boy, as the second instalment of the atomic war a few days later, and if a third bomb were needed, it would be another plutonium device shortly after that. But if the Fat Man plutonium device became a second fizzle, then the military would meet Truman's mandate to initiate atomic warfare by dropping the Little Boy uranium bomb the next day. However, there was only that one uranium weapon available, so the mandate that there be at least one or two more bombs at intervals of several days could not be met with uranium devices. For this situation, the Los Alamos team had a contingency plan.

If two fizzles showed that the plutonium implosion design just did not work, the scientists would quickly modify the next device using an approach James Conant suggested in mid-1944. This was just after Los Alamos had discovered the plutonium isotope problem (Baggott 2010). Conant suggested using a mixed-fuel gun. Some amount of uranium mixed with plutonium would alter the fission rate such that there would be time enough for a limited chain reaction to occur in a gun assembly. Initially set aside as being too inefficient, the design was now revisited. Calculations showed that a mixed-fuel gun device could have a yield of about 500 tons (i.e. half a kiloton) of TNT – a 'weak' and very inefficient nuclear explosion, but still a potent blast. The Los Alamos team determined that there would be just enough uranium available to alloy with plutonium to make what they dubbed 'Tom Thumb' mixed-fuel gun devices. If needed, they could do this very quickly, but hoped they did not need to. Groves concurred in the contingency plan. He was prepared to trade off blast radius for reliability if he had to.

Chapter 9

The Japanese Empire, Mid-August

And so it was that on 19 August 1945 Colonel Paul Tibbets piloted the *Enola Gay*, a B-29 'Silverplate' version, modified to carry the oversized sphere that was the Fat Man.[1] He flew over Hiroshima, with two observation planes five miles behind. One hundred more B-29s were 20 miles behind them, ready to drop their loads of conventional bombs to obscure another atomic fizzle. But there was no need for the conventional raid. Fat Man's explosive lenses all worked as designed. They 'instantly' compressed the roughly softball-sized plutonium core evenly from all directions. The polonium/beryllium initiator spewed neutrons as planned and a sustained nuclear chain reaction occurred. The city was destroyed; the world was stunned.

But the war did not end. It was more than a full day before the Japanese Imperial General Headquarters recognised that what hit Hiroshima was not just another of the hugely destructive conventional or incendiary air raids which were becoming common. Observers along the flight path had seen a large formation of bombers approaching the city, so it took some time before surviving eyewitness accounts began to tell not of a rain of bombs and explosions all around, but of a single, unimaginably huge explosion. (Once it had occurred, the squadrons of B-29s behind the *Enola Gay* had promptly diverted and dropped their conventional bombs on Yahata.)

On the day Hiroshima was destroyed, 19 August, the Japanese General Staff paid it little attention, because they were more focused on the imminent loss of Manchuria, Korea and Sakhalin Island: after 10 days of fighting, an enormous Soviet offensive had pushed the Japanese out of much of Manchuria and Sakhalin Island. The Russian offensive began just after midnight on 9 August (8 August in Moscow).

---

1. See 'What Really Happened' (9 Aug 1945 (1)).

ANOTHER 'AW SHUCKS'

The night before the Fat Man device was loaded aboard the B-29 at Tinian, a member of the final assembly team, Bernard O'Keefe, found a problem. A cable was to be plugged in as part of arming the device during the long flight to Japan. It was backwards: the female end was where the male end needed to be. The cable itself snaked deep through the innards of the assembly, so removing it to fix it would have taken several days. With only the cable's two ends accessible, O'Keefe took remedial action contrary to all sorts of safety regulations. He cut off the male and female plugs and, working with a soldering iron not very far from the explosive lenses, he reattached the plugs at the correct ends. Phew! (Rhodes)

The timing of the Red Army's attack surprised the Japanese, and the Americans.[2]

The Japanese had known the Soviets were massing forces in eastern Siberia, but they had not believed they could be ready to move before much later in the year, or early in 1946 (Glantz 1983). Nor did the Japanese predict the size of the Soviet forces they would face. They had severely underestimated both the number of divisions garrisoned in Siberia along the Manchurian border, and the number of divisions Stalin shipped out there from Europe after the defeat of Germany. In August 1945 the Japanese believed they were facing about forty-five Soviet divisions; they would actually face eighty-nine (Teague). The Japanese noted that the Soviet preparations did not include winter gear, suggesting to them that perhaps the campaign would not occur until spring of 1946. This staff expectation ignored the July prediction from Japan's ambassador in Moscow that the Soviets would attack sometime after 1 August (Brooks). The irony of Japan being the target of a surprise attack was presumably not lost on the Russians, who had suffered a surprise naval attack from the Japanese 40 years previous at Port Arthur, and again in 1939 at Nomonhan, on the Siberian border. (Nor did many Americans miss the irony, incensed as they still were about Pearl Harbor.)

Surprise attacks were a well-established part of samurai thinking, but the timing of the Soviet move nevertheless caught the Japanese short.

---

2. See 'What Really Happened' (9 Aug 1945 (2)).

When the attack began on 9 August, the commander of the Kwantung Army was away from his post on leave, and several other senior commanders were away at a conference (Glantz 1983). On the western part of the front, over 600,000 Soviet and Mongolian troops attacked through the Grand Kinghan Mountains, terrain the Japanese considered impassable. In the east, another 500,000 troops attacked through 'impassable' marsh and forest, even through inundating thunderstorms (Glantz 1983). In the north, another force of 300,000 troops made amphibious landings across the Amur and Ussuri rivers, supported by gunboats (USMC). The Japanese had not anticipated either the locations or the scale of the Soviet attacks (Map 2).

On the first morning of war with the USSR, 9 August, the Japanese War Council had met. Known as the Big Six (Prime Minister Suzuki, Army

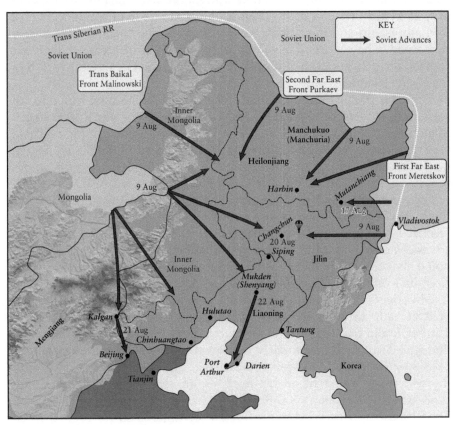

Map 2: Soviet Far Eastern Campaign

Minister Anami, Navy Minister Yonai, Army chief Umezu, Navy chief Toyoda and Foreign Minister Togo), they received initial reports from the General Staff. The estimates then were that the invading force was about one-fourth as large as it actually was, and the General Staff said they believed the superior numbers of Japanese and Manchukuo troops would be sufficient to defend against the Red Army (Frank 1999). The War Council still felt their planned all-out defence of the Homeland against a US invasion was feasible (Maddox). No matter how the situation might unfold in Manchuria, the Big Six knew there were strong defences and about 4,000,000 troops on the Home Islands (Brooks). This included over 900,000 troops on Kyushu ready to repel the anticipated initial US invasion that would start on the southernmost main island. (It is noteworthy that US planners were developing their invasion plans based on an estimate that there would be fewer than 400,000 Japanese troops facing them on Kyushu (Maddox).) But as the Soviets advanced over the next 10 days not only in Manchuria, but also in Korea, the Japanese-held southern half of Sakhalin Island and the Kurils, the Big Six in Tokyo became increasingly concerned. They worried not only about the loss of areas under their control, but also about their ability to defend against a Soviet invasion of the Home Islands.

For their part, US officials had not expected the Soviet move for at least another week or two – the 15th at the earliest. The day Russia struck Manchuria, 9 August, US Secretary of War Stimson was getting ready to take vacation leave (Maddox). When Truman heard of the Soviet action, he said to his aide, Admiral Leahy, 'They're jumping the gun, aren't they?'

'Yes, dammit,' said the Admiral, 'the prospect of the bomb did it. I think they wanted to get in before it's all over' (Dobbs 2012). It is not recorded whether Truman, at that moment, regretted giving Stalin that advance notice about the imminent availability of the atom bomb. But as noted above, Stalin hadn't heard about it first from Truman, thanks to the Kremlin's outpost in Los Alamos.

Moreover, the 9 August date matched Stalin's February pledge to FDR at Yalta to enter the war within three months of Hitler's defeat. Further, Stalin had told Truman's envoy Harry Hopkins in late May that 'the Red Army will be properly deployed on the Manchurian positions by 8 August' (Hoyt). However, Stalin had also said that his entry into the war was contingent on his reaching an agreement on Manchurian concessions with Chiang Kai-Shek. This had not happened by 9 August. The Chinese only acceded to the Soviets' conditions on 14 August, when the Red Army was already deep in Manchurian territory (Holloway).

Even with some recent access to Soviet records, the history of the date for the Soviet attack on Japan is still uncertain. One account has Stalin issuing orders before Potsdam for the attack to be ready by the first week of August or even the last week of July. In another account, it was during the Potsdam Conference, perhaps before or perhaps after Truman's disclosure about the bomb, that Stalin sought to get his commander of the Far Eastern Command, Marshal Aleksandr Vasilevsky, to advance the then planned attack date by 10 days from 11 August (Hasegawa; Holloway). Vasilevsky reportedly responded that, at that point, such a foreshortening of the plan was not feasible.

Still another account has Stalin changing the schedule right after Potsdam, perhaps in response to learning about the imminent arrival of atom bombs on the battlefield. In this account, Stalin directed Vasilevsky to move up the attack into Manchuria by 10 days from its planned late August date. In this account, Vasilevsky told Stalin on 3 August that the campaign could begin on 9 or 10 August (Holloway).

Regardless of who did what when, geopolitical considerations and the anticipated arrival of the atom bomb may not have had as much effect on the specific timing of the attack as did the military and logistical realities involved. Assembling 1.6 million troops and their equipment, fuel, ammunition and supplies was a daunting organisational task. The attack was to be along a 2,600-mile front, about the length of the US/Canada border. In addition to its length, the front encompassed mountains, river crossings, desert and marsh. It is not likely that the schedule for the offensive could have been significantly foreshortened in the last weeks. The Manchurian campaign was to be by far the largest land engagement of the Pacific War, and one of the largest in history, exceeded only by some of the Red Army's battles against Germany. An American military professional's detailed analysis of the Soviets' campaign found that they had accomplished the movement of forty or more Soviet divisions, and their armour, artillery, vehicles and supplies, from Europe to the Manchurian theatre by 25 July. This had mostly been accomplished since the defeat of Germany in early May (Glantz 1983). Colonel Glantz also found that on 2 August the Soviet's Far Eastern Command had ordered all units to be ready to attack by 9 August.

It may be that the reported 'second half of August' timeframe for the attack, and the notion that Soviet action would not occur until after Moscow had reached an agreement with the Nationalist Chinese, represented intentional Soviet disinformation. This would have been an ingredient in maintaining surprise, always a powerful military tool. In Manchuria, North China, Korea, Sakhalin and the Kuril Islands, the Soviets expected to face a potentially formidable force of Japanese, Manchukuo and other puppet-regime troops. The attack was to occur simultaneously from three directions around the great thumb-shaped bulge of Manchurian territory jutting into Siberia and Mongolia. There would be more than one and a half million Soviet and Mongolian troops attacking Manchuria from Mongolia in the west, and from the USSR in the east and north. Soviet planners considered that achieving surprise in the timing of the attack was critically important.

Once launched, the boldness and the swift success of the Soviet campaign were also surprising to the Americans. Application of massive force of arms was consistent with Red Army practice in Europe, where prolonged, grinding land battles against the Nazis had been the norm. The 1943 Battle of Kursk, for example, had spanned seven weeks on a battlefield measured in thousands of square miles. The Americans had no doubt that Red Army soldiers could fight long and hard against the Japanese. But what the Americans had not expected was the audacity of the Soviet commanders in launching a simultaneous double pincer attack into Manchuria from the east and from the west, along with a substantial closing attack from the north. This Soviet strategy aimed to 'pinch off' virtually all of Manchuria and trap or destroy the entire Kwantung Army.

In one sense, the map made the strategy obvious: the Manchurian 'thumb' sticking up into the Soviet Far East seemed well suited for amputation. But the Mongolian desert and the Greater Khingan Mountains on the western edge, marshy terrain and the Lesser Khingans on the eastern side, and the Amur River on the northern border all seemed to lessen Manchuria's geographic vulnerability.

Pentagon officials knew that the Soviets had been planning carefully for this campaign, including calling for massive materiel supplies through America's Lend-Lease effort since at least the previous October (Russell). US analysts inferred, and were later proven correct, that the Soviets had achieved a high degree of integration of the efforts of their infantry, their armour and mechanised units, their artillery and their air force support (Glantz 1983). This 'combined arms coordination', painfully developed on the battlefields of Eastern Europe in the previous four years, now proved highly effective on the expansive battlefields of Manchuria. It was a key ingredient in enabling the Soviets to advance faster not only than the Americans had anticipated, but also than the Soviets themselves had planned.

The Soviets anticipated doing battle with an enemy that had been impressive in clashes in the late 1930s along the Mongolian-Manchurian border. They also knew, however, that the Japanese Kwantung Army of mid-1945 was reduced in troop strength and equipment and in the quality of the troops' training and experience. In part from US sources, the Soviets knew that many of the best Japanese units had been moved to the Home Islands, or to Japanese-held Pacific islands, and replaced with newly-formed and reserve units. (The victors learned after the war that more than one-fourth of the Kwantung Army's entire combat force had been mobilised only 10 days prior to the Soviet offensive (USMC). Most of its armoured vehicles had been redeployed elsewhere (Teague).) Despite these indications of some weakening of Japanese strength, the Soviets were nevertheless determined not to underestimate their adversary. The Soviets believed they would be facing perhaps 1.2 million troops, including several hundred thousand Chinese and Mongolian troops of the Manchukuo, and Inner Mongolian (Menjiang) puppet regimes.

To ensure decisive defeat of that adversary, Stalin supplemented the forty divisions that remained in the Far East throughout the war with another forty divisions (about 750,000 troops) from the European theatre. With them came many of the highly experienced commanders and staffs who had directed the massive land campaigns that had rolled back the Nazis from deep inside the Soviet Union all the way to Berlin. In addition to these experienced troops and their commanders, the Trans-Siberian Railway had also brought equipment (some from the European theatre, some from Detroit via Vladivostok): over 5,600 tanks, 28,000 artillery pieces and 5,000 aircraft, overmatching corresponding Japanese numbers several-fold in each case. Including Outer Mongolian units, the Soviet attack force was about 1.6 million troops.

The ambitious Soviet plan called for wresting control of all of Manchuria (an area larger than modern Germany, or larger than the US states of Texas, New Mexico and Arizona combined), within 30 days. In the 10 days between the Soviet initiation of war with Japan, and the US destruction of Hiroshima on 19 August, the Red Army nearly achieved its 30-day goals. Incurring comparatively light casualties, Soviet troops advanced hundreds of miles along each of their three axes of advance. In heavily-fortified eastern Manchuria, elements of the Soviet Fifth Army penetrated by the fourth day as far as they had planned to reach by the seventeenth (Glantz 1983). In western Manchuria, some Red Army armour units advanced eastward across 'impassable' desert and mountain terrain so quickly they outran their fuel supplies. Hundreds of aircraft had to airlift fuel to the waiting armour units. In northern Manchuria, airborne troops took the major city of Harbin, with ground forces then moving in to hold it. By 20 August, as the eastern and western arms of the Soviet pincers closed, the city of Changchun fell, again with airborne troops' assistance. Soon thereafter, the southern city and rail hub of Shenyang (then often referred to as Mukden) came under Soviet occupation (Map 2). The Soviet advances were so swift that many Japanese units had neither time nor room to retreat. There were over 600,000 Japanese troops already or soon to be Soviet prisoners (Glantz 1983). The Soviets had captured in less than two weeks more Japanese troops than all the other Allies had captured since the beginning of the war (La Forte).

Nor was the action confined to Manchuria. From the Soviet Far East, elements of the First Far Eastern Front were advancing south-westward into Korea. Ahead of those land forces, on 12 August, the 393rd Rifle Division assisted a Soviet Navy task force in capturing the north-east Korean seaport of Unggi, just 100 miles from the Russian naval base at Vladivostok (Grey). These troops moved on to the Korean ports of Najin by 14 August, and Chongin on the 16th, linking up there with an amphibious landing force of the 355th Rifle Division (Glantz 1983). Also on 14 August, advance Soviet forces made an amphibious landing at Wonsan, a port and oil refinery centre located further down the Korean east coast (Grey). These moves into Korean ports were not merely exploitative land grabs, but were intended to interfere with the logistical support of the Kwantung Army from the Japanese homeland (Chandler). By 19 August, the day of the Hiroshima bombing, the 40th and 384th Rifle Divisions and the 259th Tank Brigade had also landed at Wonsan, and had begun to expand their holdings on some of the only flat terrain along the entire Korean east coast. (Map 3)

Of course, Soviet naval and amphibious capabilities were limited as compared to those of the US, but so were the distances involved: the Korean ports were less than 200 miles from the major Soviet base at Vladivostok. Besides, the Soviet Navy faced very little threat from the Japanese fleet, which the US Navy had by mid-1945 effectively cleared from these waters (Frank 1999).

Meanwhile, on Sakhalin Island north of the Japanese Home Islands, the Soviets re-established possession of the southern half of the island, which Japan had controlled since the 1905 Russo-Japanese War. On 11 August, several Soviet divisions began advancing overland from the northern, Soviet-controlled portion of the island. On 16 August, amphibious landings on the island's west coast overcame the relatively thin Japanese coastal defences, which were more strongly focused on the island's east coast against a possible US invasion (Hastings 2009; Hasegawa). Sakhalin would shortly be fully under Soviet control. (Map 4)

72

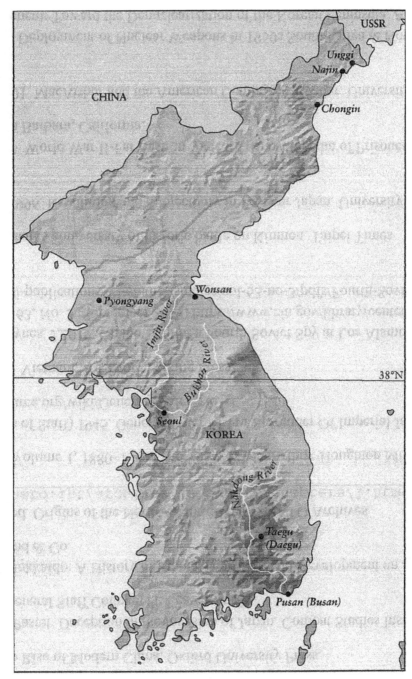

Map 3: Korea

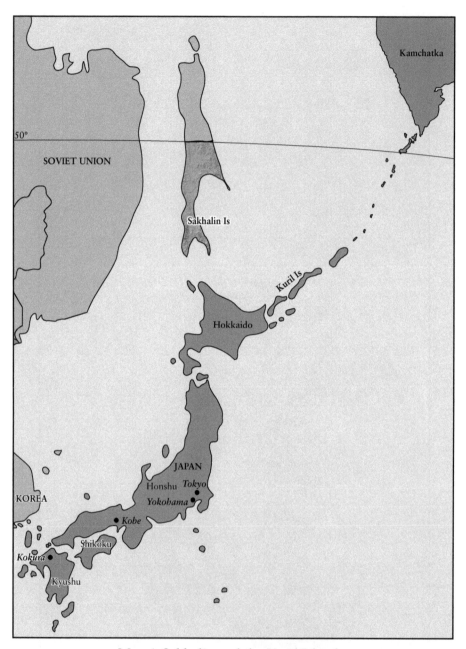

Map 4: Sakhalin and the Kuril Islands

A CHILLY HULA

The US helped make the Soviet amphibious operations in Korea possible. Earlier in 1945, the US had augmented the Russians' limited naval capabilities through 'the largest and most ambitious transfer programme of World War II', Project Hula. This was a secret US Navy programme operated out of Cold Bay in Alaska's Aleutian Islands. Starting in April 1945, the US Navy transferred 149 vessels to the Soviet Navy. These included patrol frigates, minesweepers and large infantry landing craft, among others. The project also trained 12,000 Soviet Navy personnel in the operation of these vessels (Russell). The intent of the programme was to assist the Soviets, once they entered the war, in their efforts to capture southern Sakhalin Island and the Kuril Islands. This was in keeping with FDR's agreement with Stalin at the February 1945 Yalta Conference, that the Soviets would have a post-war sphere of influence on these islands as well as in Manchuria (Department of State undated (2)). The US may not have anticipated the other locations where the Soviets would employ their newly-acquired amphibious capabilities.

On 18 August, the day before the first atomic attack, Soviet troops began landings on Shumshu, the northernmost of the Japanese-owned Kuril Islands, and the one closest to the Soviet Kamchatka peninsula to the north (Russell). Tokyo had reduced the defences of the Kurils in June when it was thought a US invasion of the southern Home Island Kyushu was imminent (Huber). The small, remote island's remaining garrison of infantry and coastal artillery nevertheless put up dogged resistance against the Red Army. The Soviets were still inexpert at amphibious operations, despite Project Hula's help (see text box). There were shore-to-ship communications problems and a lack of naval gun power. The Soviets suffered substantial casualties in their initial landings, but with the help of coastal artillery firing from the nearby Kamchatka peninsula, they maintained and then enlarged their beachhead. Hard fighting continued but the last Japanese resistance on the island ended several days later (Russell; Hastings 2009).

Chapter 10

Japan, Mid-August

By 19 August, the day the US dropped the first atomic bomb, the Japanese had, in 10 days, essentially lost Manchuria, most of southern Sakhalin Island, parts of Korea, part of the Kuril Islands, and perhaps three-quarters of a million soldiers. This, not the sudden arrival of a single new bomb, was the unfolding story that held most of the attention of the Imperial General Staff that day and well into the second half of August. Over the next several days reports reached Tokyo that tens of thousands of people had died and five square miles of Hiroshima had ceased to exist in what eyewitnesses claimed to have been a single blast. Few believed that a single bomb could have done the damage that was reported. There were indeed reports from the vicinity that multiple bombs had been dropped. This perhaps reflected sightings of several parachute-borne instrument packages which the observation planes dropped just before the bomb went off (Strategic Bombing Survey).

Eventually, Tokyo recognised that something major had happened in Hiroshima. Terrible as violent death is, and appalling as are death tolls in the tens of thousands, by that point in the war the bombing of Hiroshima did not reflect anything new in regard to mass death. The Japanese had already endured widespread bombing and destruction of most of their major cities, with a combined death toll in excess of 300,000 (Selden). This included the March 1945 firebombing of Tokyo, which, as mentioned above, had killed on the order of 100,000 people in one night and levelled 16 square miles of that city.

More recently, on 14 August, 800 bombers had taken to the skies in the largest air raid of the war, and conducted incendiary and conventional bombing of Tokyo and surrounding areas (Strategic Bombing Survey; Hastings 2012). That was just the largest of a continuing campaign of conventional and incendiary bombing of Japanese cities: on 7 August 23 B-24s raided the Mitsui Coal Liquefaction Plant at Omuta; that same day, 130 US Army Air Forces bombers attacked Tokokawa, and there was a 420-plane incendiary attack against Yawata on the 8th. On 9 August, there was a 109-plane mission, 114 bombers flew against Kumamoto on the 10th, and 53 B-24s burned Kurume the same day (Strategic Bombing Survey). Many thousands of Japanese perished in these attacks, as had many thousands of Chinese when Japan used the same tactic against Shanghai in 1932 (Hoyt). Nor was the US Navy idle. Since early in the year, its carriers had been able to sail close enough to Japan to launch air strikes against Tokyo and other locations. This positioning was possible because, thanks to America's Pacific Fleet, most of Japan's Combined Fleet was positioned on the bottom of various seas. Of Japan's 12 battleships, only one was afloat, accompanied only by five of her 25 carriers, two of her 18 heavy cruisers, two of 22 light cruisers, and just five of her 177 destroyers (Hornfischer).

Facing little risk from these remnants the US Navy's battleships could operate almost with impunity and get within gun range of the Home Islands. On 8 August for example, three US battleships fired on and heavily damaged industrial works at Kamaishi on northern Honshu (Cressman).

In addition to the current cataclysm, Japan's leaders and many of her people could still remember the Great Kanto Earthquake of 1923. The quake and resulting firestorms killed over 100,000 people in Tokyo (Takemura and Moroi). In the context of all this other death and destruction, the reports from Hiroshima did not have much effect on the General Staff in the days immediately following. Thus, however many thousands or tens of thousands had died in that city, they were but an increment to the death tolls the Japanese had been enduring for years. The apparent death of perhaps 20,000 troops of the Second General Army headquartered in Hiroshima was of course militarily regrettable.

The day after Hiroshima, President Truman announced the atomic bombing to the world and threatened the Japanese:

> If they do not now accept our terms, they may expect a rain of ruin from the air, the like of which has never been seen on this earth. Behind this air attack will follow sea and land forces in such numbers and power as they have not yet seen and with the fighting skill of which they are already well aware (Truman).

Truman's message made relatively little impression in Japan. As the evidence accumulated that the Hiroshima event had indeed been something new, General Staff senior personnel claimed to have consulted

Japanese nuclear scientists. Based on this, Navy chief Admiral Toyoda argued that the US could not have another such bomb any time soon (Frank 1999). Even if they did, the Admiral said with no evident concern for the hypocrisy, 'the world would not stand for the continued use of such an inhuman weapon' (Brooks).

Of perhaps greater concern to the Imperial General Staff than the 'unreliable' reports of huge new weapons was the recently increased effectiveness of the US Army Air Forces' conventional bombs. These were now falling in precision strikes on key transportation facilities and related infrastructure. One of the most damaging airstrikes of the war destroyed the Aomori-Hokodate rail ferry terminal in July, interdicting 80 per cent of the coal supply from the northern island of Hokkaido to Honshu (Frank 1999). Now in August, another key transportation link was broken: in southern Honshu, the undersea Kanmon railway tunnels to Kyushu Island were vital for shipment of coal, materiel and troops, all the more so since the US Navy had severely damaged inter-island and coastal shipping. The US Army Air Forces developed a plan to destroy these inter-island tunnels with 12,000lb earth-penetrator bombs similar to those used in Europe against railway tunnels and submarine pens. Along with bombing raids on nearby railway yards at Moji, Shimonoseki, Ilatabu and Tobata, the closing of the inter-island tunnels would badly disrupt transportation of coal and other items between Honshu and Kyushu (Strategic Bombing Survey).[1] On 15 August, the Air Force carried out these missions as planned. Battle damage assessment showed that the bombs had closed the entrances to both tunnels at the Kyushu end and one tunnel on the Honshu end.

---

1. See 'What Really Happened' (Mid-Aug 1945).

Chapter 11

Japan, Late August

Of even greater concern to the Japanese General Staff in the days after Hiroshima was the continuing advance of Soviet forces. On 21 August, after a brief pause to resupply, the Soviet Twenty-fifth Army advanced in force out of north-east Korea with armour and motorised infantry divisions. Their objective was to link up with the amphibious forces that had landed further south on the Korean east coast several days earlier.

On Sakhalin Island, with Soviet divisions pushing south, the Japanese Fifth Area Army HQ on nearby Hokkaido Island ordered its 88th Division to defend Sakhalin in a fight to the death (Glantz 1983). Fifth Army wanted to prevent the Soviets from using southern Sakhalin as a launch point for an attack on Hokkaido, only 30 miles to the south across the Soya strait. Civilians were fleeing, trying to return to Japan proper. On 22 August, Soviet naval forces attacked refugee-laden boats fleeing Sakhalin toward Hokkaido. Seventeen hundred civilians died (Ealey). Three days later Soviet control extended to the southern tip of Sakhalin (Hasegawa).

August 22nd was the day Soviet ground forces completed the capture of Shumshu Island in the Kurils and all of Sakhalin Island. It was also the day B-29s of the US Air Force's 509th Composite Group flew over Kokura and dropped Little Boy, the uranium gun-type bomb. Kokura was a major support base for the Japanese forces preparing to defend Kyushu from US invasion (Allen and Polmar). Unlike the raid on Hiroshima, there was no following wave of conventional bombers, ready to mask a plutonium implosion fizzle. Oppenheimer and Groves had always been confident that the gun-type weapon would detonate successfully. It did, with a force later estimated at about 15,000–20,000 thousand tons of TNT.

In the three days between the two atomic bombings, Tokyo still had not fully recognised the significance of the first. Army headquarters had sent a nuclear scientist, Professor Yoshio Nishina, to Hiroshima. Trained in Europe, Nishina had led the Imperial Army's own rudimentary atomic bomb project since 1941. Based on his reading of the scientific literature before then, and his own work since then, Nishina and his colleagues understood that a bomb could be made with perhaps 100–200lbs of U235, but they had not been successful in preparing any uranium enriched in that isotope. By 1944 he had concluded that doing so was not likely to be possible even for the US for many years to come (Rhodes). He reported two days after the bombing that the unlikely had happened. The US had used an atomic explosive. But that same day the Army general whose headquarters had been in Hiroshima reported that the city had been hit with conventional bombs; the widespread fire damage and burns on the victims resulted not from an atom bomb but largely from residential fires started when the early-morning conventional bombing caught residents cooking breakfast (Brooks).

The Navy sent another nuclear scientist, Professor Asada, to Hiroshima. Four days after the blast, he too reported that it had been an atomic bomb and estimated that the US might have 'five or six' more such bombs (Brooks). But when he briefed Navy HQ a few days later, their response was that all they needed to do was to round up a lot of Japanese physicists, sequester them in the military redoubt in the mountains of Nagano and have them hurry up and build some atom bombs for the Navy to drop on the US (Brooks). Home Ministry officials, when briefed on the bomb, planned to have the public wear white clothing (made from bedsheets if need be) to protect them from the radiation of any additional atom bombs (Brooks). (In every age it seems there are people who choose to disregard scientific reality and instead spew obvious nonsense. Many times, they are in positions of power.)

If the Japanese did not understand the nature and magnitude of what had been done, President Truman did. After the first two detonations, he directed that the Air Force use no additional atomic weapons until he gave his explicit authorisation. However, anticipating that the moratorium might be lifted, the 509th Composite Group personnel readied a third bomb, using the plutonium core that had arrived on Tinian on 19 August (National Security Archive). The primary target for that weapon was to be Nagasaki, but some sources maintain that the White House might have inserted itself into the choice of the next target (Frank 1999). A frustrated Truman is said to have told the Duke of Windsor during this time that it looked like he would have to drop the next one on Tokyo. But both Nagasaki and Tokyo escaped atomic destruction because, after two atomic bombings, continued conventional bombing of Tokyo and many other cities and transportation hubs, frequent and essentially unopposed naval shelling of coastal targets, interdiction of coastal transport and the loss to the Soviets of Manchuria, Korea, Sakhalin Island and the Kurils, Japanese resolve at last faltered.

The Emperor had wanted to bring the war to an end for months, as had some of his government ministers. Along with Foreign Minister Togo, the Emperor hoped to extract from the Allies acceptable terms for ending the war. The Emperor had noted the sullen, indifferent, irreverent, almost hostile attitude of the Tokyo populace he would pass on his recent forays outside the Imperial Palace. Former Prime Minister Prince Konoe told the Emperor of his concern that the deteriorating domestic situation could lead to a Communist revolution (Buruma 2003). The Prince had written to the Emperor as early as February, saying 'I believe Japan's defeat is inevitable. What should be the gravest concern to us is not the defeat but rather its subsequent Communist revolution. It appears to me that every condition for the achievement of Communist revolution is being daily fulfilled . . . continuation of this futile war will play into the hands of the Communists. I am convinced we should take measures to end the war as soon as possible' (Hornfischer).

For their part, the Army and Navy chiefs and others maintained that defeat was not at all inevitable. A horrific all-out fight defending the Home Islands from Allied invasion would at least cost the invaders so many casualties that they would be forced to grant the (perhaps few) surviving Japanese reasonable terms. The General Staff had reported to the Emperor earlier in 1945 that, 'It is characteristic of Americans to hold human lives so dear, it is necessary that we take advantage of this weakness and inflict tremendous losses on the enemy' (Allen and Polmar). The July Potsdam Declaration's call for unconditional surrender only hardened the already firm resolve of the military leadership to sacrifice, not themselves, but as many millions of their fellow Japanese as necessary to make the Allies come to terms. The military's April orders for Operation Ketsu-go (Decisive) called for, among other things, the mobilisation of all males 15–60 years old and all females 17–40 years old. They were to be trained with hand grenades, swords, sickles, knives, fire hooks and bamboo spears. As Prime Minister Suzuki had said in June, 'If the whole people will march forward with death-defying determination,' Suzuki said, 'devoting their entire efforts to their own duties and to refreshing their fighting spirit, I believe that we will be able to overcome all difficulties' (Bartlit and Yalman). In the press there was 'increasingly hysterical rhetoric exhorting the 'hundred million' to die gloriously in defence of the nation and its emperor-centered "national polity"' (Dower).

Shortly after the bombing of Hiroshima, the Emperor, hearing of the unprecedented devastation of the city and of his subjects, spoke to his trusted advisor Marquis Kido. 'Under these circumstances,' he said, 'we must bow to the inevitable. No matter what happens to my safety we must put an end to this war as speedily as possible so that this tragedy will not be repeated' (Brooks). The 124th Emperor of Japan, the embodiment of a 2,500-year unbroken lineage, was a divine descendant of the Sun Goddess Amaterasu (Chandler); he held the title of Commander-in-Chief of all of Japan's seven million military personnel; yet his practical control of the Japanese war machine was far from absolute. As Japanese historian Akira Namamuri has written, 'No one person in Japan had authority remotely resembling that of a US President' (Hastings 2012). The Emperor was supposed to approve decisions and actions taken by his government, not initiate them. Under the Japanese constitution, the Emperor had to heed the wishes of the military and civilian components of his government. Any 'decisions' he made were to be at the request of his government; they were not to be issued on his own (Hastings, 2012). And his government's several major councils (the Cabinet, the Supreme Council for the Direction of the War, the Privy Council) functioned primarily by consensus, which was seldom easily achieved. Meetings of top government officials often went through hours of ambiguous circumlocutions and ended with no resolution. (Such characteristically Japanese deliberations would have maddened American business executives, and likely would have frustrated even experienced Washington bureaucrats.) So it was one thing for the Emperor to conclude that the atomic devastation of a Japanese city must not happen again. Getting the disparate factions within the government if not to agree with, then to comply with, the Emperor's wishes was another. In this distinctive cultural context, it is not surprising that this took more than a week of manoeuvring, manipulating and haggling, even while many more Japanese died. Even then, the decision to end the war was more of a process than an event.

The day after the destruction of Hiroshima, Foreign Minister Togo told the Cabinet that the new weapon of revolutionary power 'drastically alters the whole military situation and offers the military ample grounds for ending the war' (Brooks). He was trying to show the military that they had an honourable way out. But War Minister Anami maintained that they should take no 'impetuous action' until the completion of the investigation he had ordered into the nature of the bomb. He asserted this despite the information already available and reported by Home Minister Abe to the Cabinet. Abe had informed them that, whatever it was, the bomb which had killed a tremendous number of citizens and destroyed almost all the buildings in Hiroshima was completely different from any known type of bomb. Yet the Cabinet was nowhere near the necessary unanimous sentiment for ending the war, so they adjourned for the day (Brooks). The reported Soviet advances in Manchuria, Korea, Sakhalin and the Kurils represented regrettable losses of outlying possessions (and personnel) but not yet an existential threat to the nation.

The next day Togo met with the Emperor, who told him that the nation could not continue the struggle in the face of this new weapon. It was useless, the Emperor said, to hope for better terms. He directed Togo to convey to Prime Minister Admiral Suzuki that the government should concentrate all efforts on ending the fighting quickly. Hearing this, Suzuki called a meeting of the War Council, but the military chiefs were 'too busy' and could not make themselves available until the next day (Brooks).

In this way it took three days after the first atomic bombing for the War Council to hold a meeting; while they were meeting, news arrived of the second (Brooks). The Prime Minister then told the Council, 'This, added to the previous barbaric attack on Hiroshima, compounds the impact of the Russian attack on Japan. I wish the Foreign Minister to introduce the discussion of the Potsdam terms' (Brooks).

In the several hours of discussion that followed, the military chiefs argued that Japan should not agree to the unconditional surrender demanded by the Potsdam Declaration, but should only end the fighting with a series of conditions. The Allies would have to agree, they said, to let the Japanese disarm themselves, and allow them the right to control any war crimes trials, and also to be free of any occupation of the Home Islands. The military said they were prepared to continue fighting, to impose a terrible cost for the Allies in blood and treasure until they agreed to Japan's terms. In contrast, the Prime Minister and the Foreign Minister were equally adamant that Japan could only hope to extract one condition from the Allies, i.e. that the Emperor and his power be protected (Frank 1999).

The War Council could reach no agreement. The full Cabinet convened later that day, for more arguing about what conditions to demand. They too deadlocked. Late in the evening, there was an Imperial Conference. The proponents of One Condition and those of Multiple Conditions presented their arguments before the Emperor. Then, in an unprecedented move, the Prime Minister asked the Emperor for his opinion. He was clear. End the war, now, he told them. Seek no other conditions but the preservation of the Imperial System (Frank 1999; Brooks).

Later that day the Japanese government used neutral Swiss and Swedish intermediaries to contact the US, Great Britain and the USSR. The Japanese indicated their acceptance – almost – of the Potsdam declaration. The message included the understanding that 'the said declaration does not comprise any demand which prejudices the prerogatives of His Majesty as a Sovereign Ruler' (Department of the Army).

Chapter 12

Washington, Late August

Welcome as it was, Japan's conditional offer to surrender caught many in Washington by surprise on 23 August. There had never been a unanimous expectation that the atomic bomb, or bombs, would themselves end the war. Most politicians and generals saw the new bombs as merely a dramatic increase in the efficiency of the air attacks already being carried out by LeMay's B-29s (Hastings 2012). Nor did Washington leaders expect that the Soviet involvement would yield prompt results. The Pentagon's planning assumption was still that a US invasion of the Home Islands would be necessary. In regard to this, earlier in the month (on 8 August), Secretary of the Navy Forrestal had sought to replace General MacArthur with either Admiral Nimitz or General Eisenhower as leader of the invasion (Frank 2007). No immediate decision on that matter was made since Secretary of War Stimson had taken vacation leave for health reasons starting on 10 August (Maddox). But fragmentary intercepts of some of the Japanese communications were enough to indicate by mid-August that the Soviets were advancing surprisingly rapidly. This, and the silence from the Japanese in the first days after the atomic bombings, prompted General Marshall to direct MacArthur to analyse and report to him the feasibility of launching some variant of Operation Olympic, the Kyushu invasion, substantially sooner than the planned 1 November date. Neither Marshall nor Truman intended to needlessly sacrifice the lives of American servicemen just to 'beat the Soviets to Tokyo'. Yet neither did they want Moscow to be able to say, 'After we finished the Nazis, we beat the Japanese for you, too'.

Now, on 23 August, considerations of moving up the planned date for Olympic were set aside in light of the apparently impending Japanese capitulation. The same day they received the provisional Japanese surrender message, Truman and Secretaries Byrnes, Forrestal and Stimson formulated a reply to the Japanese. Earlier, the US and

UK had not included deposing Emperor Hirohito in the terms laid out in the Potsdam Declaration. It had made no mention of the Emperor. Some senior officials thought at the time it would be helpful to retain the Emperor, at least for a while, to ensure the central government's control of the several million Japanese troops still active in China, Southeast Asia and on various Pacific Islands (Frank 1999). But now the Japanese had explicitly raised the issue on which the Potsdam Declaration had been silent. Now, if the Allies were to accede to the Japanese message as it was, they would seem to be relinquishing their demand for an unconditional surrender. So Washington drafted a response which accepted – without accepting – the Japanese premise. It read in part:

> From the moment of surrender the authority of the Emperor and the Japanese Government to rule the state shall be subject to the Supreme Commander of the Allied Powers who will take such steps as he deems proper to effectuate the surrender terms.
>
> The ultimate form of government of Japan shall, in accordance with the Potsdam Declaration, be established by the freely expressed will of the Japanese people (Department of the Army).

Great Britain and Chiang Kai-Shek quickly concurred with this 'you can keep your Emperor, for now' reply. But the Soviets balked and tried to hold up the response. True to their communist principles, they wanted to insist on removal of the Emperor. They also wanted a role in selecting the Supreme Commander of the Allied Powers, a post that had just then been invented in the proposed Allied response (Hastings 2012). US Ambassador Harriman informed Soviet Foreign Minister Molotov that the US could not allow the USSR to have veto power over the choice of the Allied commander. The Soviets had fought the Japanese for less than two weeks, Harriman pointed out, while the US had fought them for four years. Molotov pointed out that the Soviet Union currently had over a million and a half troops battling the Japanese, and that Soviet ground forces were closer to the Home Islands than any US troops. Harriman replied that the US had effectively kept the Japanese off the Soviets' Siberian back for those years, and had then provided much of the equipment now being used in the very Manchurian fighting he spoke of. Molotov responded that he would refrain from discussing the Allies' relative roles in the European War (where, as both men knew, Russian armies had prevented the Nazis from stationing far more troops in France to repel the Allied invasions there).

It is not recorded whether the Soviets' delay of the response was also an effort to buy time for the Red Army to make further territorial gains against the Japanese. Ultimately, the Soviets backed down on both points, at least for the time and approved the response (Hasegawa). On 25 August Washington transmitted the Allies' reply to the Japanese as it was originally drafted. But the Soviets in the field had benefited from the two days the Allies spent in hammering out their response to the Japanese.

Chapter 13

Soviet Far Eastern Command, Late August

U nits of the Soviet Transbaikal Front advanced through Manchuria and achieved their primary territorial objective ahead of schedule. They traversed much of Manchuria from the west then continued their advance by turning to the south, into northern China proper. The Soviet-Mongolian Cavalry Mechanised Group under Colonel General Pliyev crossed the Great Wall near Kalgan, about 100 miles north-west of Beijing (or 'Peking' as the city was then called in the West) by 21 August. Proceeding toward Beijing, they were joined in their march by the Chinese Communist Eighth Route Army (Glantz 1983). True, Stalin had signed an agreement a week earlier in which he agreed to recognise Chiang Kai-Shek's Nationalist regime, not the Communists, as the legitimate government of China. But the nearest Nationalist troops were hundreds of miles to the south, and Mao Zedong's Chinese Communist troops had maintained their presence in these rural areas of North China throughout the war. Without formally incorporating the Chinese Communists into the Red Army's battle formations, General Pliyev nonetheless directed his field commanders to inform the Chinese Communist commanders of their actions and movements, ostensibly so that Russian and Chinese units would not accidentally engage one another. The effect of this was to enable both Communist armies to coordinate their actions to do maximum damage to their common Japanese enemy.

Chiang Kai-shek's government sent a message requesting that the Red Army and their Mongolian allies cease their advance toward Beijing. They replied that they had advanced beyond Manchuria because there were Japanese troops threatening the rear of Soviet formations and that this was militarily unacceptable. Therefore they would advance as needed to protect their own troops (Chang).

On 23 August, reinforcing Pliyev's Cavalry-Mechanised Group with units of the V Guards Tank Corps, Front Commander Marshal Malinovsky deployed troops to surround Beijing. He also acquiesced in the deployment of the Chinese Eighth Route Army around the port of Tianjin, 75 miles to the south-east of Beijing. The headquarters of the Japanese North China Area Army was in Beijing and mustered about 100,000 troops to defend Beijing and Tianjin. By 24 August, these Japanese forces were intact, but surrounded. The Soviets prepared for a Battle for Beijing, conducting resupply operations, and allowing the Chinese Communists access to substantial amounts of Japanese weapons and ammunition which the Soviets had captured in Manchuria (Map 5).[2]

While Tokyo and Washington considered surrender terms, units of Marshal Meretskov's 1st Far Eastern Front continued their advance in Korea. The Soviet Twenty-fifth Army largely bypassed much of the formidable mountain terrain of north-east Korea, and exploited their beachhead on the east coast port of Wonsan. With additional units and supplies flowing into that port, and some trickling down the coast road from the more northerly ports seized earlier, Soviet infantry and armoured units cut across the Korean peninsula to the south-west toward Seoul, largely following river valleys such as the Bukhan and Han (Map 6).[3]

Opposing them was the Japanese Seventeenth Area Army, nominally consisting of the equivalent of eight divisions. But this army actually consisted largely of newly called-up reservists, conscripts and home guard militia. Not all of the troops even had firearms, and instead wielded spears, clubs and knives (Frank 1999). On 23 August, the Japanese 120th Division took their stand at the Imjin River north of Seoul, the site of a key battle in the 1592 Imjin War between Korea and Japan. This time, it was the Japanese who were routed, and the Soviet forces were in control of Seoul the next day.

That day, 24 August, as the Allies were developing their response to Japan's conditional surrender message, Stalin followed through on his statement at Potsdam that Hokkaido would be in his sights. The Soviet Far Eastern Command began their invasion of the northernmost Japanese Home Island.[4] Back in June, the Soviet Politburo had discussed this planned move onto Hokkaido, knowing that it would annoy the US. But with the Japanese not quite yet submitting, Stalin's action

---

2. See 'What Really Happened' (Late Aug 1945).
3. See What Really Happened (16 August 1945)
4. See 'What Really Happened' (16-20 August 1945).

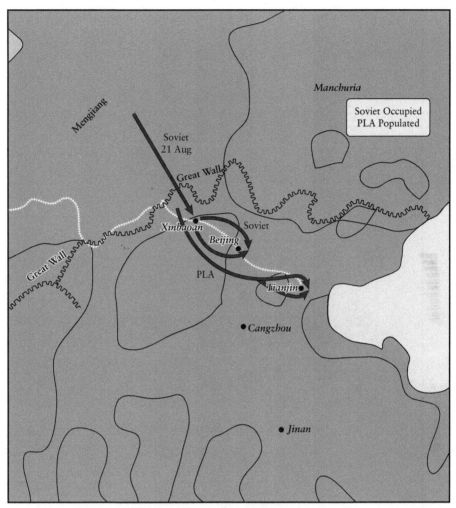

Map 5: Manchuria and North China

could be seen as entirely appropriate to hastening the war's end. It could also be argued that because control of Hokkaido would give the USSR control of the Soya Strait between Sakhalin and Hokkaido, ensuring unimpeded post-war Soviet naval access to the Pacific from Vladivostok, the value of this Pacific access outweighed the cost of the other Allies' irritation (Hasegawa; Hastings).

This least populated of the Japanese Home Islands is about the size of Ireland, or the US state of Indiana, and had relatively few defences in August 1945 (Frank 1999). What had been there earlier was thinned

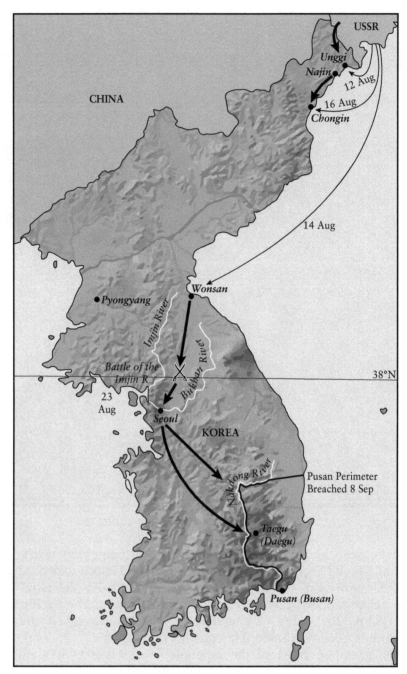

Map 6: Soviet Advances in Korea

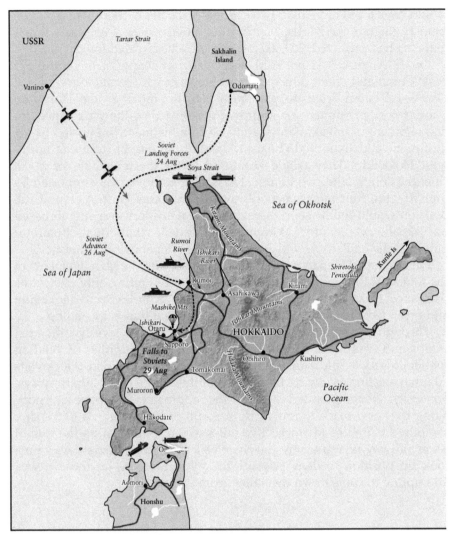

Map 7: The Hokkaido Campaign

out significantly in June when the Japanese General Staff moved troops
and equipment to hardened positions on Kyushu, the southernmost
Home Island, in the belief that a US invasion would occur there that
month (Huber). Whereas the Soviets estimated there were somewhat
more than three Japanese divisions defending Hokkaido, there were
only two (Frank 1999). (In part because of that June depletion of the
Hokkaido defences, the US forces slated to land on Kyushu in November

95

would have faced more than twice as many Japanese troops – redeployed from Hokkaido, the Kurils, Manchuria and elsewhere – as MacArthur's planners had projected: 900,000 rather than 400,000 (Maddox).)

On 18 August, Marshal A.M. Vasilevsky, in charge of the entire Far East Command, had directed Ivan Stepanovich, commander of the First Far Eastern Front, to prepare a plan for moving onto Hokkaido (Vasilevsky). Submitted for approval the next day, the plan called for one regiment of naval infantry and one rifle regiment, supported by six destroyers and six torpedo boats, to land at the port of Rumoi in north-west Hokkaido. They would secure areas for the remainder of a full rifle division to land two hours later, with that movement supported by four frigates, four minesweeper/trawlers and other craft. A second full division would follow soon thereafter. Naval artillery and aircraft based on Sakhalin would provide support as needed, while four submarines patrolled the La Perouse and Tsugaru straits (Stepanovich; Yumashev).

On 24 August Stepanovich began implementing the plan. Elements of the LXXXVII Rifle Corps landed at Rumoi, encountering only ineffective resistance (Map 7). Sakhalin Island is just 28 miles from Hokkaido and provided a base for air support and for naval transport staging.

Through the captured port of Rumoi the Soviets swiftly offloaded troops and equipment of the 264th Rifle Division. Supplies of aviation fuel followed as did construction machinery with which the Soviets adapted existing roadways in the delta of the Rumoi River into runways. Soviet gunboats guarded against the approach of Japanese troops along the coast roads to the north or south of Rumoi, and a Red Army armoured battalion advanced five miles to the south-east up the Rumoi River railway line to where the river valley narrows. Soviet tanks then took up position to deny passage to any reinforcing Japanese troops attempting to come down the valley from the interior.

Chapter 14

Washington – Occupation Planning

In the days after they received the first Japanese provisional surrender offer on 23 August, Pentagon officials learned from the Soviets that the Red Army was making substantial progress against the Kwantung Army. But the Americans had no confirmation or specifics as to what was going on in Manchuria and Korea; US code breakers did not have nearly as much access to the Japanese Army's codes as they did to the Japanese diplomatic and naval ciphers. Besides, much of the Kwantung Army relied on telephones, not military radio communication. As to Sakhalin, intercepted Japanese naval messages indicated to the Pentagon that the Soviets were making good on Stalin's intent to reclaim the southern half of the island, with the potential then to move on to Hokkaido. After the 24th, the Pentagon had unconfirmed reports that the Soviets had landed on Hokkaido.

So there was concern in Washington that any further delays in the Japanese surrender (and the likely delay in getting that word out to all Japanese forces) would give the Soviets time to gain even more ground and increase their claim to a role in the occupation of Japan. The rush of events was prompting some rethinking of earlier notions. In June, the Joint Chiefs had discussed with Truman their expectation that the USSR would deal with the Japanese in Korea (Hoyt). By 25 August, considering the Red Army's progress, the Pentagon sought to limit the Soviets' post-war leverage. Therefore, the same day the US sent its response to Japan's qualified offer to surrender, the Joint Chiefs directed MacArthur and Nimitz to prepare to occupy the Manchurian port of Dairen and a port in Korea immediately upon the Japanese surrender if these had not already been occupied by the Soviets (Maddox). At that time also Washington began developing General Order #1 establishing arrangements for Allied forces to accept surrender of the millions of Japanese forces throughout the theatre of war (Schnabel; Oberdorfer).

As part of that larger effort, Army staffers Colonel Charles Bonesteel and Lieutenant Colonel Dean Rusk received the task late that evening to develop surrender plans concerning Korea. The Yalta conferees in February, and the Potsdam conferees in July, had discussed a post-war joint Great Power trusteeship for Korea. But there had been no particulars discussed at either conference about battlefield arrangements. George Marshall had asked Truman for guidance on this at the time of Potsdam, but the President and Stalin discussed no specifics about end-of-war procedures. This silence somewhat alleviated the concern at the time of US officials such as Averill Harriman. He had thought that Russia, based on their historic interests, might insist on sole control of the Korea trusteeship (Hasegawa).

In August 1945, Korea was of far more interest to the USSR than it was to the US. Russia had coveted Korea, especially its ice-free ports, since at least the latter half of the previous century. In the late 1800s Russian Foreign Minister Lamsdorff had written, 'Korea's destiny as a component part of the Russian Empire had been foreordained' (Oberdorfer). Russia had sheltered the King of Korea in the 1890s as he fled a Japanese plot against him (Hoyt). In the early 1900s, Russia and Japan had argued over dividing Korea into spheres of influence to be demarcated at the 38th Parallel. The 1905 Russo-Japanese War stemmed in part from that disagreement (Oberdorfer). Then, Japan's stunning defeat of Russia in that war and their annexation of Korea a few years later stymied Russia's 'manifest destiny' in Korea for the next 40 years.

For its part the US had established friendly economic and supposedly military ties with Korea in the late 1800s. However, the US had not provided the military assistance which Korea then requested. After 1905, the US had even made an agreement with the Japanese not to interfere with the control of Korea which they had just wrested from Russia. In return, Japan would not interfere with American interests in the Philippines, recently seized from Spain in the Spanish-American War (Schnabel). In the modern era, the US still had little interest in Korea. As late as 1944, it is reported that Secretary of State Edward Stettinius had to ask one of his staff just where Korea was (Oberdorfer). Ignorance among senior government officials is not a new phenomenon.

While the Big Three leaders barely mentioned Korea at Potsdam, their military chiefs had discussed it. The chief of the Russian General Staff told General Marshall that Russia would attack Korea after declaring war on Japan. At this point he asked whether the US Navy could operate against Japanese forces on Korean shores in co-ordination with this Russian offensive. Marshall told him that the United States planned no amphibious operation into Korea until the US had brought Japan proper under control and Japanese strength in Korea was destroyed (Schnabel). In effect, the US told the Soviets that they would be happy to move in later, but they would not fight the Japanese in Korea nor help the Red Army in doing so, beyond the supplies and equipment the US had been providing to the Soviets for many months. The Americans gave Korea a priority consistent with their other strategic interests. So did the Soviets. That's why, as of late August, the Red Army was in control of Seoul.

However, with Japan's capitulation apparently imminent, the US now sought to limit the Soviets' control of real estate on the Korean peninsula, in accordance with the envisioned joint trusteeship. The working concept was to require Japanese units to surrender to US forces in the southern part of Korea, and to Red Army forces in the north. But where would that surrender demarcation be? Colonels Bonesteel and Rusk were told to take all the time they needed – up to 30 minutes – to develop an answer (Schnabel; Oberdorfer). Using a National Geographic map they had in their Pentagon office, they saw that there was no logical geographic feature, such as a river or ridgeline, to serve as a clear demarcation. The goal was for US forces to take the Japanese surrender as far north as they could get. Yet Rusk, the future US Secretary of State, selected the 38th Parallel, actually further north than the US forces could soon reach, because it put Seoul, Korea's largest city, in the southern area which US forces would (try to) occupy. Rusk said many years later that he had not known the 38th Parallel was the line of demarcation in Korea over which Japan and Russia had gone to war in 1905 (Rusk). Colonel Bonesteel submitted the 38th Parallel proposal up the chain of command for incorporation into the overall General Order #1 (Hasegawa). At the time he did not know how far the Soviets had already advanced into Korea: his 38th Parallel proposal was already overtaken by events. As will be discussed later, this was not the only aspect of the General Order's surrender procedures that was out of date by the time it was finally issued.

Chapter 15

Tokyo – Last Resistance

On 25 August, Tokyo received the Allied response to the Japanese conditional offer of surrender ('For now, you can keep your Emperor, and he'll be under our Supreme Commander'). This set off another series of meetings between the military chiefs, the Cabinet and the Emperor. The Army and Navy chiefs told the Emperor that the Allies' message about the Emperor being subject to the Allied commander, and about the Japanese people determining the future government, did not protect the Emperor and the Imperial System. The military chiefs maintained that they needed to continue the fight. The President of the Privy Council also balked at the Allied reply, maintaining that it threatened the Emperor's constitutional role.

To these members of the Cabinet and senior councils, the Imperial System was not only or perhaps even primarily a matter of continuing the reign of the Emperor. Rather it was the whole system by which those societal elites controlled the governance of the country, under the ostensible jurisdiction of the Emperor. The Meiji Restoration of 1868 had abolished the military dictatorship, the Shogunate, which had ruled Japan for most of the previous 700 years under token Emperors (Akamatsu). But while the Emperor's centrality was reaffirmed by that Restoration, he still was not an all-powerful figure. He was far more than a ceremonial Head of State as are some modern European monarchs, but he was also far short of the 'Decider-In-Chief' executive like a US President. Japan in 1945 was in effect an oligarchy. So preserving the 'Imperial System' also meant preserving the elites and their powers, and ideally keeping them off the gallows.

The Prime Minister was also concerned that the Allies' requirement for disarming all Japanese forces would be impossibly insulting to them, and could result in continued resistance on far-flung battlefields. The chief of the powerful military/secret police told the Cabinet Secretary: 'If Japan surrenders, the Army will rise. Tens of millions of lives may be sacrificed, but we must not surrender' (Brooks). Indeed, while the Cabinet was in its second day of debating the Allied response, a group of mid-level army officers almost succeeded in tricking the Japanese radio network to make a bogus broadcast. It would have announced that the Army and Navy were even then launching an all-out offensive. But for a timely inquiry from a radio reporter to the Cabinet Secretary, the message would have gone out announcing to the world that Japan had rejected surrender (Brooks).

Ostensibly to protect the Emperor and the Imperial System, the military chiefs and field commanders pledged to defend the Home Islands with every last civilian if need be (Hastings 2009). So while the Japanese government continued to deliberate, the Soviets continued to take them up on that pledge. On 26 August, the Soviets made their move out of Rumoi on the north-west coast of Hokkaido (Map 7, page 95). The 264th Rifle Division advanced virtually unopposed 20 miles to the south-east up the railway line to the head of the Rumoi River Valley. They then turned south-west to follow the Ishikari River Valley and railway line back down to the sea at the port in Ishikari Town. To block the oncoming Soviets, the Japanese Fifth Area Army's 7th Division was deploying north-eastward up the Ishikari Valley when they came under attack from elements of the Ninth Soviet Air Army flying from the newly-prepared airfields at Rumoi. Meanwhile Russian paratroopers flown in from Sakhalin began raining down on the flatlands around the port at Ishikari. A sharp, short fight between the Soviet airborne troops and the Japanese battalion guarding the port ended when Soviet (formerly American) Navy frigates fired on the Japanese defenders from behind.

The Red Army column poured down out of the Ishikari Valley and linked up with the paratroopers on the flats. The remaining Japanese troops retreated 20 miles south toward the island's largest city, Sapporo, where the Japanese 42nd Division had defensive positions. More Soviet troops, equipment and supplies soon began offloading at the newly-captured port of Ishikari. By 28 August, Sapporo was under attack.

The defending Japanese Fifth Area Army had the theoretical equivalent of two divisions on Hokkaido. These included some regulars, but were mostly ill-trained reservists, conscripted students and home guard militia, many lacking firearms, and even more lacking ammunition (Frank 1999). Supplementing the army, such as it was, were the newly-formed Patriotic Citizens Fighting Corps, essentially consisting of all the rest of the population, including women, except for the very young, very old or very sick. Bows and arrows and spears were common armaments for this fighting force. Yet the people fought

102

with the same tenacity the Americans had encountered on Okinawa, Iwo Jima and elsewhere. The effects of fanatical civilian resistance, however, were mitigated by the low population density of the island. The ragtag resistance barely slowed the veteran Soviet troops of the 87th Rifle Corps, backed by armour, artillery, aircraft and a willingness themselves to take casualties. They established control from Rumoi to Ishikari, and then, on the 29th, to Sapporo.

Beginning with the Soviet landings on 24 August, Army Headquarters in Tokyo began some hurried efforts to send more troops to Hokkaido. But reinforcement from Honshu was almost impossible because of the destruction of the port facilities at Hokodate in a US air raid in July, as noted earlier. The US Navy's mining of the waters between Honshu and Hokkaido also hampered troop transport (Frank 1999). Also, the 15 July bombardment of targets on Hokkaido by three US battleships had significantly disrupted railway and telephone systems on parts of the island (Chen 2008). Tokyo's reinforcement efforts were also limited by their concern that these Soviet landings in the north were really a diversion for the more massive US landings still expected imminently on Kyushu to the south.

Several 'kamikaze' attacks against Soviet naval vessels and cargo ships supporting the Hokkaido landings did some damage. However, there were few Japanese Army or Navy aircraft initially positioned within range of the battle in Hokkaido. So the weapon named for the 'divine wind' that had wrecked Kublai Khan's invasion fleet in the thirteenth century was little used on this twentieth-century fleet from mainland Asia.

Similarly, the Japanese were able to deploy only a few of their recently-developed 'kaitens,' human-guided suicide torpedoes (Weinberg). Kaitens sank two of the former US frigates the Soviets were using to support this operation, but by then, the landings were well established. In addition, lack of fuel limited the conventional operations of the few Japanese Navy vessels still afloat.

These Soviet landings in Hokkaido were the first successful foreign invasion of any of the Japanese Home Islands in the more than 2,000-year history of Japan as a nation. The last attempted invasion was that ill-fated effort by Kublai Khan 700 years ago, and the few Mongols who had reached the shore had never made it past the landing beaches of Kyushu (Allen and Polmar).

To Moscow, the occupation of Hokkaido was officially a militarily-appropriate operation intended to speed the end of the war. Unofficially it was payback for Russian defeat in 1905 and for Japanese incursions into Siberia in 1920. To the US, the Soviet move into Hokkaido was

> **TURNABOUT**
>
> Manifesting the bitterness of the action on Hokkaido in the last days of the war were post-war charges by the Tokyo government that Soviet troops committed atrocities against Japanese civilians on Hokkaido. Given that Tokyo in those last days had exhorted all of its citizens to take up swords, knives, bamboo spears or stones to fight the invading barbarians, it could be problematic to assume that any civilians killed were non-combatants. Regardless, to this day, the government of North Japan has steadfastly refused to investigate these charges.

blatant opportunism, an effort to grab more spoils in a war the US and the British Empire had all but won. It was also, the US believed, a move that might lengthen the war by hardening the Japanese militarists' resolve to oppose the pending surrender offer and instead fight on. President Truman is said to have wondered if he would soon be hearing about a Nipponese version of Churchill's 'we shall fight on the beaches, we shall fight on the landing grounds . . . we shall never surrender' speech.

For Japan, the landings were a profound shock and insult, but only for those who knew about them. Throughout the war, Tokyo tried to maintain tight control of the information available to the public. The government, speaking through the Domei News Agency and NHK Broadcasting, consistently told its citizens about the glorious victories of its forces, even when such reports had turned from truth to exaggeration to pure fiction (Brooks). Now, with almost the entire civilian population on the Home Islands ostensibly mobilised, and some of them armed, with cities all over the country in ruins and transportation barely functioning, the pretence of Japanese supremacy in battle could hardly be maintained. Still, the central government suppressed the news of the invasion of Hokkaido, blocking civilian telephone and telegraph communications. (In an age when all phones were landlines and were routed through a small number of switching offices, this was not very hard to do.) The Information Ministry directed Domei and NHK to ignore as Allied disinformation any reports they might receive alleging the presence of foreign troops on Hokkaido. The Kempeitai military/ secret police arrested for disloyalty anyone spreading rumours about any sort of fighting in Hokkaido. They made numerous arrests.

In the Cabinet meeting of the 26th – the second day of deliberations about the Allied response – War Minister Anami told his colleagues that the Allies' ambiguous reply about the future status of the Emperor and Japan's form of government was just their way to buy time to launch more invasions aimed at wiping out the Yamato race. He urged his colleagues to renounce their provisional offer to surrender and renew the commitment to fight the barbarians on every beach. (Had he read Churchill?) Foreign Minister Togo, in the polite circumlocutions that are hard-wired into Japanese, told him that was all nonsense. The US knows they have us beaten, he said, though not so directly. They know they don't have to shed any more of their blood. The Communists on the mainland and now on Hokkaido are just taking the opportunity to kick us when we're down. But they will keep doing so as long as we give them the opportunity. Ending this war right now will be terrible; prolonging it will be far more so. We will not get 'better' terms, only worse. He was also concerned, as Prince Konoe had warned several months earlier, that a Communist revolution would endanger the Imperial system. The loss of Hokkaido to the Soviets could be the spark for a general Japan-wide Communist uprising.

On 27 August, Japan's leaders continued to debate Imperial constitutional issues. Japanese troops continued dying from Manchuria and Korea to the Philippines and Southeast Asia. Japanese civilians all over the Home islands were dying in US air raids and naval shelling, and, on Hokkaido, at the hands of the Red Army. Also, while their seniors debated, the 'Young Tigers' – mid-level officers at Army headquarters who had tried to sabotage surrender talks with a broadcast on NHK – were not giving up. They continued plotting a full military coup. This was another long-established Japanese tradition: coup leaders would 'protect' the Imperial System from the mistaken and/or incompetent advisors surrounding the Emperor. The Tigers planned to enlist the Imperial Guards Division, plus other Tokyo-based troops, to arrest the peace faction and the traitorous advisors who were misleading the Emperor. To protect the Emperor, they would install the War Minister as a modern-day shogun, who would continue the war, and thereby protect the honour of (whatever was left of) Japan and the Imperial System (Brooks).

In US military command centres, after two days of waiting for Japan's capitulation, there was renewed discussion about dropping the third atomic bomb (Hastings 2009). According to a story that is possibly apocryphal, Air Force General Curtis LeMay inquired as to when the Okinawa airfield that was being adapted to handle atomic missions would be ready. 'We'll need that field to reach Hokkaido,' he said.

A staffer pointed out that the Russians were already on Hokkaido. 'I know,' the General is reported to have said.

Early on the third day of waiting for the Japanese to make good on their surrender offer, US B-29s took to the skies over Tokyo and other major cities once again in some of the most effective bombardment missions in history. This time, instead of destruction, they rained information: leaflets displaying the Japanese government's offer to the Allies to end the war, along with the Allies' reply (Hastings 2009). Reading one of these 3x5in slips of paper shortly after they had fallen all over the city, the Emperor, his top advisor Marquis Kido, and Prime Minister Suzuki believed that this 'propaganda' would cause unrest among the surprised public and might hasten the military coup they believed might be in the works (Buruma 2003).

In a rare move, an Imperial Conference convened later that morning at the Emperor's initiative. The conference included members of the War Council, the Cabinet and the Privy Council. Army Chief General Umezu told the Emperor that he knew they had lost the war, but if they could not be sure of preserving the Imperial System, he said, 'we must be ready to sacrifice the entire nation in a final battle' (Brooks). Navy Chief Admiral Toyoda echoed the potential for fighting 'a decisive battle on the homeland with the entire nation prepared for suicidal warfare'. He called for the government to seek further clarification from the Allies to safeguard the future status of the Emperor. Army Minister Anami maintained that there were still chances to win, or at least to get better terms (Brooks).

It is not recorded whether any of the ministers and advisors saw hypocrisy or perhaps just irony in the exhortations of the military chiefs. They were calling for the sacrifice of perhaps millions of lives ostensibly to protect the Emperor and the Imperial System, i.e. a system in which the Emperor's expected role was really just to approve the actions of these ministers and advisors. But on this day, the Emperor instead told the conference what he wanted his government to do. He reminded them that he had told them previously that he wanted the Potsdam Declaration to be accepted. He told them that he had studied the Allied response to their surrender offer and was convinced the Allies were not intent on destroying the Imperial System. He was also convinced that if the war continued, 'the nation would be devastated and reduced to ashes'. He then directed the Cabinet to immediately prepare an official Imperial announcement fully accepting the Potsdam Declaration. He would issue it that day, and broadcast it himself to ensure that Japan and the world knew its authenticity.

The Emperor further urged the military leaders not only to accept this surrender as reality, but also to ensure that their subordinates promptly did likewise. This was more than just a communications issue. Since the 1930s, the Japanese Army in China had often acted virtually independently from Tokyo (Dryburgh). As later events demonstrated, the Emperor's concerns were well founded.

As commanded, the Cabinet prepared the 'Imperial Rescript' and presented it to the Emperor, the evening of the 27th. He approved it, and all members of the Cabinet signed it. Then, with the help of NHK radio technicians summoned to the palace the Emperor recorded it for broadcast the next day.[1]

The Young Tigers now launched their coup. With no senior officers supporting them, several colonels and lower ranks nonetheless managed to mobilise some of the Imperial Guards Division to secure the palace grounds against 'traitors'. The plotters themselves ransacked much of the palace complex searching, futilely, for the recordings of the Emperor's planned broadcast. In the pre-dawn hours, loyal senior officers regained control of the situation, removed the machine-gun emplacements around the palace and put an end to the immediate crisis (Brooks).

At noon on the 28th, Japanese radio broadcast the Emperor's message. He told his people that 'the enemy has begun to employ a new and most cruel bomb, the power of which to do damage is indeed incalculable. Should we continue to fight, it would not only result in the ultimate collapse and obliteration of the Japanese nation, but also to the extinction of human civilisation' (Brooks). He informed his people that he had instructed his government to communicate to the Allies Japan's acceptance of the Potsdam Declaration.

Twenty-four hours after the Emperor spoke to his people, the Japanese government informed MacArthur's headquarters that the Emperor had issued an order that day commanding the entire armed forces of his nation to halt their fighting immediately. In that message to the millions of Japanese troops still in the field, the Emperor said: 'The Soviet Union has now entered the war and in view of the state of affairs both here and abroad, we feel that the prolongation of the struggle . . . may eventually result in the loss of the very foundation on which our Empire exists' (Brooks).

Prime Minister Suzuki resigned shortly after the Emperor's broadcast. In his last public message he cited both the atomic bombs and the Soviet

---

1. See 'What Really Happened' (15 Aug 1945 (1)).

attack as the two factors leading to the decision to end the war (Hasegawa). Thus Japan's leaders variously cited the bombs and/or the Soviets as prompting the surrender. What they did not cite was the Japanese public, their increasingly desperate situation, and their resentment. As Admiral Yonai put it, the external forces were like 'gifts of the gods. This way we don't have to say that we quit because of the domestic circumstances' (Buruma 2003).

The war was over, almost. Tokyo also told MacArthur's headquarters that the dispersion and the disrupted communications of the Japanese forces made the rapid and complete implementation of the ceasefire order exceedingly difficult. As the Japanese apologetically explained, the Imperial order would take anywhere from two to twelve days to reach Japanese forces throughout the Pacific and Asiatic areas, 'but whether and when the order will be received by the first line fighting forces it is difficult to foresee' they said (Department of the Army).

The day the Japanese notified his headquarters of their surrender, MacArthur ordered US forces under his command to cease offensive operations. He also issued an order to the Soviet Far Eastern Command to cease their offensive operations. There are no records available concerning Marshal Vasilevsky's reaction to receiving an order from an American general. We do know that the Soviets responded that only Generalissimo Stalin had the authority to issue such an order (Hasegawa). The next day, US intercepts of Japanese naval communications suggested that Soviet actions on Hokkaido were continuing.

'Let's make sure the commie bastards don't try to grab another island,' MacArthur is reported to have said, 'Get Nimitz to send a few battleships up into the Tsugaru Strait and keep the Russians off Honshu.' Nor was Admiral Nimitz under MacArthur's command, but at least they saluted the same flag. It has never been officially clear whether MacArthur would have tried to direct the *Iowa* or the *Wisconsin* to fire on Soviet troop transports crossing the Tsugaru Strait for a landing on northern Honshu. The situation never arose. After informing the Pentagon of MacArthur's directive, Nimitz's headquarters took no immediate action to detach any ships from their assignments elsewhere. Informed of MacArthur's initiative, Truman is reported to have said, 'We just ended the worst war the world has ever seen. That pompous legend-in-his-own-mind wants to start another! Sure glad we rescued his backside from Corregidor.' To be sure, there were some US leaders who foresaw war with the Soviets. Undersecretary of State Joseph Grew, for example said, 'a future war with Soviet Russia is about as certain as anything in the world can be' (Frank 1999). General George Patton, seemingly chafing at the bit in occupied Bavaria, is quoted as wanting to be let loose against the Red Army, and sooner rather than later (Hirshon). But Truman, the First World War veteran who was in charge, was certainly not ready for yet another war. At any rate, the Soviets made no effort to move onto the next island. They controlled all of Hokkaido.

Chapter 16

Asian Mainland, August–September

As Tokyo had predicted, far-flung Japanese forces in Manchuria, Northern China and Korea continued fighting the Soviets in some places for more than two weeks after the Emperor directed them to end hostilities (USMC; Hastings 2009). The Emperor's broadcast announcing the government's surrender used somewhat archaic formal language (think of Shakespeare's English compared to common usage today). Some army commanders did not understand it as a clear order for field units to lay down their arms. Moreover, it was not until two days after the broadcast that Imperial General Headquarters in Tokyo issued formal ceasefire orders to all units. Two days later came a clarification to all units telling soldiers that being taken by the enemy after laying down their own arms was not to be considered a combat 'surrender' mandating suicide under the Japanese warrior code (USMC). Citing disrupted communications, some Japanese commanders claimed not to have received these orders, or that they could not be sure they were authentic. For some time the Kwantung Army in Manchuria had not possessed military communications capabilities of its own, instead depending on public telephone lines. Because these were disrupted early in the Soviet advance, there was communications chaos among the Japanese forces in Manchuria (USMC). Soviet Marshal Vasilevsky met with General Yamada, commander of the Kwantung Army, four days after the Emperor's broadcast and agreed on a ceasefire, but that word did not reach Japanese field commanders in Manchuria for many days (Hasegawa). An initial attempt by General Yamada to countermand the Imperial HQ's surrender order contributed to the continued confusion (Glantz 1983).

South of the Great Wall, Lieutenant General Shimomura commanded the 75,000 troops of the North China Area Army. They were now surrounded by Soviet and Chinese Communist forces in Beijing and Tianjin respectively. (Map 5, page 93) Shimomura was under the command of the China Expeditionary Army in Nanjing, and that HQ issued unambiguous and direct orders to Shimomura to lay down his arms and surrender to the Soviets. He did so, to Colonel General Pliyev, on 30 August. With neither ceremony nor gunfire, troops of the Chinese Communist 115th Division commanded by Lin Biao, effectively took over the port city of Tianjin the next day. This was done without the official approval of or coordination with Pliyev's headquarters. The Soviets, assuming that they would not remain south of the Great Wall for long, were more focused on organising rail shipments out of Beijing, north through Manchuria and on to Siberia. Some trains carried Japanese POWs; many more carried unofficial reparations – industrial equipment and resources from Japanese-owned facilities in the city.[1]

The Japanese surrender came before the Pentagon's chain of command had finished reviewing and revising the proposed General Order regarding surrender procedures (Schnabel). Two days later, the Pentagon finalised that General Order: it called for the Soviets to take the surrender of Japanese forces in Manchuria and northern Korea, while the US would take the surrender of Japanese forces in Japan proper and in Korea south of the 38th Parallel (JCS). Japanese forces in China other than those in Manchuria would surrender to Chiang Kai-shek's Nationalist Army. By the time Truman had the Order sent to Great Britain and the USSR for their concurrence (Schnabel) it was already in part overtaken by events: the Soviets were in, and were cleaning out, Beijing.

Also by that time, the situation on the ground in Korea had changed further. After taking Seoul on the 24 August, units of the Soviet Twenty-fifth Army pushed south, primarily along the less mountainous western portion of the peninsula. By the time Moscow received the proposed General Order on 30 August, Soviet troops were south of Taejon, where they were fighting Japanese troops who had not received, or were ignoring, Tokyo's surrender message. Foreign Minister Molotov met that day with Ambassador Harriman in Moscow and informed him that the proposed General Order had been superseded by circumstances on the ground. The Red Army was already in control of 75 per cent of Korea, he said, and was 200km south of the 38th Parallel.[2] Harriman may or may not have realised the historical significance that the 38th Parallel had

---

1. See 'What Really Happened' (6–10 Oct 1945).
2. See 'What Really Happened' (26 Aug 1945).

The remains of 'The Dud In The Desert', July 1945. The first atomic device, tested in the New Mexico desert, produced an extremely limited explosion, a fizzle, only damaging the tower it was mounted on.

What It Really Shows: Test tower for the 1953 experimental RUTH uranium hydride bomb. The explosion of this uranium implosion device failed even to level the testing tower. (https://commons.wikimedia.org/w/index.php?curid=3160186)

Present-day stone marker at site of the world's first test of an atomic explosive. The marker explains that the device produced a relatively paltry explosion, but demonstrated that nuclear-powered explosions could be induced by improved detonation mechanisms.

What It Really Shows: The marker is at the site of the Trinity test, the first, and wholly successful, test of an atomic explosive. The area remains somewhat radioactive to the modern day, and visitors are allowed access to the site for a few hours on two days a year. Visitors are prohibited from collecting the radioactive nodules of Trinitite – glass fused from the desert sand by the blast heat. (https://www.wsmr.army.mil/Trinity/Pages/Home.aspx)

George Kistiakowsky's Los Alamos ID photo. After the explosives expert's unconventional dentistry work on the fizzled atomic bomb device came to light, he was briefly investigated as a potential saboteur.

What It Really Shows: Kistiakowsky's ID, and he was an explosives expert, and he did some unconventional dentistry work to fix flaws in the explosive blocks of the first atomic bomb device. But 'The Gadget worked as planned', likely because of that fix. Dr. Kistiakowsky was never under suspicion for anything and went on to a distinguished post-war career including as Chair of President Eisenhower's Science Advisory Committee. (https://commons.wikimedia.org/wiki/File:George_Kistiakowsky_ID_badge.png)

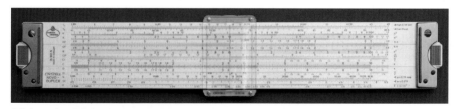

Slide rule. With these hand-operated 'slipsticks' scientists and engineers of the 1940s (and 1950s and 1960s) performed a wide variety of highly precise mathematical calculations.

What It Really Shows: As stated. In that era, 'computers' wore lipstick and skirts. (https://commons.wikimedia.org/wiki/File:Faber-Castell_2-83N-front.jpg)

'Jumbo' on its way to the Trinity test site, July 1945. The 120-ton steel vessel was designed to contain the explosion of the test bomb's high explosive and permit recovery of the plutonium material in case the weapon test was a failure. However, the Los Alamos team decided not to use it, not based on confidence in the test device, but because of the difficulty of obtaining data to determine the cause of a failure. When the test failed, its plutonium was regrettably lost to the desert, but the team's observational data allowed them to focus on the cause.

What It Really Shows: 'Jumbo' as stated, and it wasn't used, but there were no regrets because the Trinity test was successful. (Federal government of the United States, Public domain, via Wikimedia Commons https://commons.wikimedia. org/wiki/File:Trinity_-_Jumbo_brought_to_site.jpg)

The 17ft-long 'Aw shucks'. These gun casings were prepared for the 'Thin Man' device, the planned plutonium gun using a 17ft gun barrel. Subsequent tests on plutonium as it became available from the Hanford breeder reactors showed that it would not work effectively in a gun less than 25ft long, and that was not a feasible weapon for existing aircraft to carry. After the first bomb, the plutonium implosion device, fizzled, the use of these gun barrels was briefly considered, perhaps using a mixed plutonium+uranium fuel, even though this would have produced very low explosive yields.

What It Really Shows: As stated, except for the part about the fizzle. The Manhattan Project did have a few 'Aw shucks' events, but the Trinity test wasn't one of them. After the war, mixed fuel implosion devices, not gun types, were developed, and deployed, using composite plutonium+uranium fuel. (US Government employee. Public domain, via Wikimedia Commons. https://upload.wikimedia.org/ wikipedia/commons/c/ce/Thin_Man_plutonium_gun_bomb_casings.jpg)

The first of the Soviet spies at Los Alamos to be discovered, Klaus Fuchs, who began his espionage while working at the University of Edinburgh on the UK's 'Tube Alloys' nuclear weapon programme. His spying from Los Alamos is believed to have substantially assisted the Soviets' post-war weapons development. There is no image known of the last of the four Soviet spies at Los Alamos to be discovered, Oscar Seborer, and the one most likely to have been able to sabotage the Trinity nuclear weapons test, perhaps by some surreptitious alteration of the detonation circuitry essential for the success of the implosion.

What It Really Shows: As stated, but neither Seborer nor anyone else sabotaged the Trinity test. (The National Archives UK, Public domain, via Wikimedia. Commons https://commons.wikimedia.org/wiki/File:Klaus_Fuchs_-_police_photograph.jpg)

World's second atomic explosion, a uranium gun-type atomic bomb over Kokura, Japan, 22 August 1945. The first had occurred three days before when a plutonium implosion bomb was detonated over Hiroshima. The plutonium bomb was used first because of the lingering uncertainty about whether it would work, given the failure of that type of device in the New Mexico test in July. If the Hiroshima device had also failed, the Japanese would not have detected it amidst the firebombing that the USAAF would then have conducted. Atomic warfare would then have been initiated with the Kokura attack, using the more reliable uranium device.

What It Really Shows: The world's third atomic explosion; this was a plutonium bomb dropped on Nagaski, Japan, 9 August 1945, three days after the first bombing of a Japanese city, Hiroshima, with a uranium gun-type bomb. Based on the successful New Mexico test, the Allies were confident both types of atomic bomb would work. (George R. Caron, public domain, via Wikimedia Commons)

UK Prime Minister Winston Churchill (left), US President Harry Truman (centre) and Soviet leader Josef Stalin at Potsdam Conference July–August 1945. Upon receiving word of the disappointing test of the first atomic device, Truman, after conferring with Churchill, nevertheless informed Stalin that there would soon be available 'a new weapon of unusual destructive power'. Stalin barely reacted, perhaps because he already knew about the bomb project.

What It Really Shows: Potsdam Conference as stated, but Truman was able to inform Stalin that the US did have the new weapon. Nonetheless, Stalin actually did show little reaction – because the information was apparently no surprise to him. (US Navy Photo https://www.history.navy.mil/content/history/muse-ums/nmusn/explore/photography/wwii/wwii-conferences/potsdam-confer-ence/80-g-49958.html)

North (Honshu) entrance to Kanmon railway tunnels connecting Honshu and Kyushu Islands. Bombing by the US Army Air Force on 15 August 1945 with special British-designed 12,000lb Tallboy 'earth penetrator' bombs closed one northern and both southern tunnel entrances, imposing severe constraints on shipments of coal and other materials.

What It Really Shows: Tunnel entrance as stated. US planned an air attack for 15 August, but it was cancelled in light of the Japanese surrender. (https://commons.wikimedia.org/wiki/File:Kammon_railway_tunnel_Shimonoseki_portal.jpg)

Minesweeper *YMS-143* being transferred to the Soviets as part of Project Hula, Cold Bay, Alaska. As Soviet Navy *T-522*, this ship saw action against Japanese forces around Southern Sakhalin and Hokkaido, August 1945.

What It Really Shows: As stated, except for the Hokkaido part. (US Navy Photo Public Domain. https://worldofwarships.com/en/news/history/usni-project-hula/)

Soviet paratroops dropped over Ishikari, Hokkaido, landed behind the Japanese forces that were deployed to defend against Soviet ground troops who were advancing down the Ishikari River valley.

What It Really Shows: Soviet paratroops jump from a Tupolev TB 3 during a pre-Second World War exercise. The same type of aircraft was still in use during the war, and paratroopers were used in the fight against the Nazis, but not over Hokkaido. (Кадр кинохроники, Public domain, via Wikimedia Commons. https://commons.wikimedia.org/wiki/File:Paratroopers_jumping_from_Tupolev_TB-3.jpg)

Soviet troops advancing into occupation near the southern port of Pusan, Korea, 1945.

What It Really Shows: Soviets in Korea, but they only advanced to the 38th Parallel, about halfway down the Peninsula, to allow the US to occupy the southern portion. (https://commons.wikimedia.org/wiki/File:Soviet_liberators_marching_through_the_Korean_county_road._October_1945.jpg)

Kim Il-sung (centre), with other Korean communists, and their Soviet sponsors, presiding at a 1946 meeting in Seoul establishing Kim's leadership of the Soviet-occupied Korean peninsula.

What It Really Shows: Kim Il-sung (centre) at the joint meeting of the New People's Party and the Workers' Party of North Korea in Pyongyang, 28 August 1946. With the support of Soviet occupation authorities, Kim was installed as leader in the northern part of Korea, later becoming Premier, then President, of the People's Democratic Republic of Korea (North Korea). In 1950, Kim's forces invaded US- supported southern Korea, sparking the Korean War that resulted in almost no change in the demarcation between North and South Korea. (https://commons.wikimedia.org/wiki/File:28.08.1946_Labour_Party_North_Korea.jpg)

Kyuichi Tokuda, a communist member of the Japanese Diet, addresses the crowd at the May Day labour demonstration, 1946.

Tokyo police battle rioters on 'Bloody May Day, 1946'.

What They Really Show: Tokuda, as stated, but the 1946 May Day demonstration was peaceful. Bloody May Day was in 1952, when a peaceful labour demonstration was hijacked by Communist agitators and turned into a violent anti-American riot. (Unknown authors, Public domain, via Wikimedia Commons https://upload.wikimedia.org/wikipedia/commons/0/09/Tokuda_Kyuichi_1946.JPG https://upload.wikimedia.org/wikipedia/commons/0/0e/Bloody_May_Day_Incident3.JPG)

Japanese communist Sanzo Nosaka at a celebration, with his wife, of the declaration of his Ezo Democratic People's Republic of Japan in Sapporo, Hokkaido, 1947.

What It Really Shows: Mr Nosaka was a leader of the Japanese Communist Party from 1945 to 1982, elected to terms in the lower and the upper houses of Tokyo's legislature (Diet), but never able to achieve more than marginal political support from the Japanese public. (https://commons.wikimedia.org/wiki/File:Nosaka_Sanzo_and_Nosaka_Ryo.jpg)

Mao Zedong's People's Liberation Army enters Beijing, as the Soviet Red Army leaves, May 1946.

What It Really Shows: Mao Zedong's People's Liberation Army enters Beijing, after battling Chiang Kai-shek's Nationalists for control of the area, January 1949. (https://commons.wikimedia.org/wiki/File:PLA_Enters_Peking.jpg)

December 1947. In Beijing's Tiananmen Square, Mao Zedong proclaims the founding of the People's Republic of China (PRC). The Soviets' capture of Manchuria and much of north China including the Beijing and Tianjin region at the end of the Second World War had helped position Mao's Communists for a swift victory against Chiang Kai-shek's Nationalists.

What It Really Shows: Mao's Proclamation, but it was October 1949. The Soviets occupation of Manchuria at the end of the Second World War did assist Mao, but the Soviets had not penetrated the Beijing region and it took several years for Mao to do so. (Hou Bo, Public domain, via Wikimedia Commons. https://upload. wikimedia.org/wikipedia/commons/3/3e/PRCFounding.jpg)

Campaign button for General Douglas MacArthur's short-lived bid for the Republican presidential nomination, 1948. Having retired from military service gracefully in February, Mac campaigned and won the April primary in his home state, Wisconsin. But in response to a reporter's softball question about his role in dispersing the Depression-era Bonus Army, Mac called the First World War veterans 'disorderly slackers', and his campaign balloon deflated so much that even the General's puffery could not fix it.

What It Really Shows: The button is real, and from 1948, but at the time, MacArthur was still a serving officer overseeing the occupation in Japan. He did, however, make it known that he would magnanimously accept the Republican nomination if it were offered. Supporters entered his name in the Wisconsin primary and actively campaigned for him. But when he lost by a wide margin, in his home state, his electoral hopes faded away. (Photo, author's collection)

Bao Dai, last Emperor of Vietnam. Induced to abdicate by Ho Chi Minh and briefly become Ho's advisor, Bao Dai fled to China as French fought the Communists for control of Indochina. As a Communist victory loomed in China in 1947, he accepted a French deal to become head of state with substantial autonomy, thus helping make the struggle one against communism, not for colonialism.

What It Really Shows: Emperor Bao Dai abdicated as stated, but his re-installation by French as Head of State in 1949 brought no actual power, and did little to remove the colonialist stigma of the French Indochina War. Retained as Head of State of South Vietnam under the 1954 Geneva Accords, he was ousted in 1955 by his Prime Minister, Ngo Dinh Diem. (https://commons.wikimedia.org/wiki/File:Baodai2.jpg)

Vietnamese Communist known as Ho Chi Minh. After seizing control of northern Vietnam at the end of the Second World War, Ho fought the French and then, along with Chinese Communist troops, he fought UN forces for control of all Vietnam. The 1953 settlement of the stalemated Indochina War left him in charge of the People's Democratic Republic of Tonkin, based in Hanoi and encompassing only the Red River delta.

What It Really Shows: Ho Chi Minh led the Vietnamese Communists beginning during the Second World War. He served as Prime Minister, then President, of the People's Democratic Republic of Vietnam (North Vietnam) from 1945 to the time of his death in 1969. Helped by a communist spy in the French military headquarters, Ho and others barely escaped a French paratrooper assault in a remote area of northern Vietnam early in the French Indochina War. Ho went on to lead the communists' defeat of the French in 1954. Thus given control of the northern half of Vietnam, he then fought South Vietnam and the United States in the late 1960s and early 1970s, ending in reunification of Vietnam under Ho's communist successors. South Vietnam's capital, Saigon was renamed Ho Chi Minh City. (https://commons.wikimedia.org/wiki/File:Ho_Chi_Minh_1946.jpg)

USS *Belleau Wood* operating in the South China Sea during the Indochina War, 1952.

What It Really Shows: French aircraft carrier *Bois Belleau*, the former USS *Belleau Wood* transferred to France in support of the French Indochina War. (US Navy Photo https://commons.wikimedia.org/wiki/File:USS_Belleau_Wood_ (CVL-24)_underway_on_22_December_1943_(NH_97269).jpg)

Armoured bulldozers with heavy-duty ploughs were used by French motorized columns in Indochina to clear wide swathes of vegetation along roadways, denying the Viet Minh ambush hiding places during the Indochina War, 1949.

What It Really Shows: Dozers equipped with 'Rome Plows' (made by the Rome Plow Company), served the role as described, but with US forces during the Vietnam War, late 1960s. (https://commons.wikimedia.org/wiki/File:Rome_Plow.jpg)

US President Harry Truman initiating US military involvement in the Indochina War, implementing the UN Resolution authorising member states to help the Bao Dai government repel Chinese Communist invasion, 1950.

What It Really Shows: President Truman initiating US military involvement in the Korean War, implementing UN Resolution authorising member states to assist South Korea repel the North Korean invasion, 1950. (Dept of Defense Photo https://commons.wikimedia.org/wiki/File:Truman_initiating_Korean_involvement.jpg)

US Marines land in Vietnam, 1950, to assist the Bao Dai government in its fight against Communist aggression.

What It Really Shows: US Marines landing in Vietnam, March 1965, as US escalates war against the North Vietnamese Communists. (US Marine Corps Photo https://commons.wikimedia.org/wiki/File:DaNangMarch61965.jpg)

In Saigon, Vietnam, a French general officer reviews Gurkha troops of the 32nd Indian Brigade, part of the British Empire's commitment to the UN Command in the Indochina War, 1950.

What It Really Shows: In Saigon, Free French General Phillippe Leclerc reviews Gurkha troops, part of the British Empire troop contingent sent to southern Indochina to take the surrender of the Japanese. 24 December 1945. (Ministère de la Guerre, France https://upload.wikimedia.org/wikipedia/commons/9/9c/General_Leclerc_reviews_Indian_troops%2C_Saigon_1945.jpg)

US Senator Joseph McCarthy (left) confers with aide Roy Cohn, 1950, during the period when McCarthy was charging – without evidence – that thousands of communist subversives in the US government had helped Mao Zedong defeat Chiang Kai-shek, leading to the Chinese invasion of Vietnam.

What It Really Shows: As stated, but McCarthy's charge concerned the Chinese invasion of Korea. Years after working with McCarthy, Roy Cohn mentored a New York developer named Donald Trump. (United Press International telephoto, Public domain, via Wikimedia Commons https://commons.wikimedia.org/wiki/File:McCarthy_Cohn.jpg)

At the UN Security Council, US delegate Warren Austin holds a Russian-made sub-machine gun captured by American troops in July 1950. He charges that Russia was delivering arms to the North Vietnamese communists.

What It Really Shows: As stated, but the charge concerned weapons to North Korea. (https://en.wikipedia.org/wiki/List_of_United_Nations_Security_Council_resolutions_concerning_North_Korea#/media/File:Warren_Austin_holds_up_Soviet_SMG_at_UN_HD-SN-99-03037.JPEG Public domain, via Wikimedia Commons)

Geneva Conference, 1953. The conferees agreed to an end to the UN-led Indochina War, with a supposedly temporary division of Vietnam, at roughly the 20th Parallel, into the Democratic People's Republic of Tonkin, (the area around the Red River delta, and the Republic of Vietnam in all of the remainder of Vietnamese territory. The temporary demarcation became permanent.

What It Really Shows: The Geneva Conference – 1954 – produced Accords settling the French Indochina War, 'temporarily' dividing Vietnam roughly in half, at the 17th Parallel, calling for Vietnam-wide free and fair elections by 1956 to determine long-term control. Such elections did not occur and the northern People's Republic of Vietnam, based in Hanoi, and the southern Republic of Vietnam based in Saigon remained separate until the North's 1975 victory in the US-led Vietnam War. (US Army Photograph. https://commons.wikimedia.org/wiki/File:Gen-commons.jpg)

for the Russians. (As mentioned, their dispute with Japan over dividing Korea along that line was one of the causes of the 1905 Russo-Japanese War, which had been a humiliating defeat for Russia.) So the Soviets could have taken the US suggestion of the 38th Parallel for a demarcation line as an insult, if they thought the Americans knew the history of the issue (Oberdorfer). But the military facts on the Korean Peninsula made the history irrelevant, by at least 200km.

Molotov further noted to Harriman that the Red Army had advanced through almost all of Korea without the US naval assistance the Soviets had requested during the Potsdam Conference. He predicted that the valiant Red Army would reach Pusan at the southern tip of the peninsula in a few days. By contrast, Molotov said, with all of their other commitments and troop deployments, he doubted the US could land personnel in Korea in less than about a month. Molotov's speculation was right on the mark. MacArthur's staff had indeed projected being able to land troops in Korea about three weeks after the Japanese capitulation (Department of the Army). In light of this, Molotov maintained, it would be the Red Army which would either accept the surrender of the remaining Japanese forces throughout Korea, or defeat them if they kept fighting.

Harriman responded that while the current situation had altered the usefulness of the 38th Parallel in terms of the Japanese surrender, nonetheless that line would serve well to demarcate respective occupation zones during the planned joint trusteeship of Korea. Harriman noted that the situation would be analogous to that in Germany: by May 1945 US troops had fought their way eastward against the Nazis about 200km into the portion of Germany that the Allies had earlier agreed would be within the Soviet occupation zone. Accordingly, in July American forces had

---

HARDLY EMPTY-HANDED

Unbeknownst to the Soviets at the time, the US troops took with them out of the Soviet zone more than 1000 tons of uranium compounds they'd found at a German chemical plant (Groves 1962). This constituted almost all of the 1,200 tons of uranium ore the Germans were known to have seized from conquered Belgium in 1940. That ore, some of the richest ever found on the planet, was output from the Shinkolobwe mine in the Belgian Congo. After 1940, shipments from the mine continued – to the US.

withdrawn from about 16,000km² of Germany (40 per cent of the Soviet Zone), back to the designated American zone of occupation (Weinberg).

Harriman told Molotov that in Korea, the US would expect the Soviets to do likewise, withdrawing back up north to the 38th Parallel, when American occupation troops arrived in a few weeks.[3] Molotov pointed out that there had been explicit agreement at the Yalta Conference, months before the Nazi defeat, as to where the respective zones of occupation would be in Germany. No such agreement was even discussed in advance in regard to Korea, either at Yalta or at Potsdam. Moreover, continued Molotov, Korea was not like Germany. It was a victim, not a perpetrator of aggression, so this was not a matter of conquering forces occupying a vanquished foe, but rather of troops assisting the Korean people to return to independence. That was exactly what the Red Army intended to do. Molotov cited the Russians' sheltering the Korean king from the Japanese at the end of the previous century, and the Americans' refusal to assist Korea against Japan in that same era. The plain language translation of Molotov's message could have been: 'Korea, which you have never cared about, is now and historically has been in our sphere of influence. We told you we were going in there and we invited your assistance. You refused and now our troops have gotten as far as they have without your help. Now don't expect them to pull back to some line you have drawn on the map after the fact. And don't plan on landing your troops in Korea.'

Ostensibly as an aside, Molotov reminded the ambassador that the US and British POWs whom the Red Army had freed from a Manchurian prison camp were receiving excellent medical care from the Soviets. These 1,600 former POWs included US Lieutenant General Jonathan Wainwright, of Corregidor fame, as well as several UK generals and colonial governors (Spector). The Soviets had promptly undertaken to provide necessary medical care to the former prisoners, and were insistent that they would be handed over to their respective compatriots as soon as that was medically feasible. Molotov expressed his hope that in particular General Wainwright would be well enough to attend the surrender signing in Tokyo. Harriman seethed at the thinly veiled hostage-taking, but ended the discussion about US troops in Korea.[4]

Molotov also informed Harriman that the facts on the ground did not match the proposed General Order's provisions in regard to northern China, south of the Great Wall: the General Order called for the Japanese

3. See 'What Really Happened' (9 Sep 1945).
4. See 'What Really Happened' (18–20 Aug 1945).

in this area to surrender to Chiang Kai-shek's GMD forces, who were in south-east China. But Molotov noted that as of that day, 30 August, the Red Army had already taken the surrender of the Japanese forces in the major population and industrial corridor of Beijing-Tianjin.[5] Further, Molotov took exception to several other provisions of the General Order. Russian troops had already taken control of the Kuril Islands, so any remaining Japanese fighting formations in those islands would be surrendering to them, not to US forces, who were nowhere near the Kurils. Moreover, the Soviets expected Japanese forces on Hokkaido, already defeated, to formally surrender to the Red Army. This would be payback, Molotov said, telling Harriman that 'Comrade Stalin has asked me to convey to you that this 'holds special significance for the Russian public opinion. As is known, the Japanese in 1919-1921 had under occupation of their forces all of the Soviet Far East. The Russian public opinion would be seriously offended if the Russian forces did not have a region of occupation in some part of properly Japanese territory' (Hasegawa; Stalin).

Harriman reported his discussions with Molotov to Washington. Information from the Soviet battlefields was still incomplete, and unreliable. Truman the poker player decided he might as well call the Soviets' bluff: 'We don't know if the Reds really are where they say they are. I don't want to put any more real estate under their heavy hand than I have to. We'll issue General Order #1 as written and implement it as fully as we can.'

Truman was not sure if Molotov's assertion about the Red Army's progress into Korea was accurate. It was. In the days after Tokyo announced its surrender (and supposedly ordered its forces to ceasefire), three divisions of the Soviet LXXXVIII Rifle Corps and equivalent units of the X Mechanised Corps continued their rapid drive southward in Korea. The Soviets were fully aware that the war was supposed to be over, but the Japanese units firing on them were evidently of a different opinion. So as long as some of the Japanese units continued active resistance, the Soviets continued their offensive (Glantz 1983).

The Japanese 120th, 150th and 160th Divisions set up thin defensive positions along the Naktong River and in mountains to the north of the port of Pusan at the southern tip of the Korean peninsula. (Map 6, page 94) They were determined to make a stand until they could 'obtain authentic clarification' concerning surrender from Kwantung Army Headquarters. On 8 September, three Soviet rifle divisions provided clarification for

---

5. See 'What Really Happened' (21 Aug 1945).

them by breaching this 'Pusan Perimeter' at Taegu and capturing more than 30,000 stunned Japanese 'troops', many of whom had been farmers earlier in the summer. On 10 September, with the occupation of Pusan, Soviet control of Korea was complete. The residents, long expecting 'liberation' by the Red Army, had Soviet flags and welcome banners at the ready (Buruma 2013).[6]

In Sapporo, the largest city and the capital of Hokkaido Island, headquarters personnel of the Japanese Fifth Area Army listened to the Emperor's surrender broadcast – courtesy of their Soviet captors. The remnants of that army, mostly recently conscripted civilians, surrendered the next day, either under orders from Army HQ, or spontaneously. Soviet forces fanned out across the island, to Kushino on the eastern shore, and Hokodate, the southern port closest to Honshu (Map 7, page 95).

---

6. See What Really Happened (Jul 1950 (1)).

PART II:
PACIFIC WAR AFTERMATH –
NORTHEAST ASIA

Chapter 17

Occupied Japan

By 15 September, when the belligerents signed the instrument of surrender on the USS *Missouri* in Tokyo Bay,[1] Soviet troops were in firm control of Manchuria, portions of Northern China including the major industrial corridor of Tianjin-Beijing, all of Korea, Sakhalin Island, the Kurils and Hokkaido. These rapid accomplishments by the Soviets posed immediate and unexpected difficulties for the US. Planning for the occupation of Japan had assumed that the US would have the primary role for all of the Japanese Home Islands, with the British Commonwealth, China and the Soviet Union having responsibility for outlying islands and territories.[2]

MacArthur's planning staff was of course relieved that plans for the US invasions of Japanese Home Islands, Operations Olympic and Coronet, could go straight to the archives. But while the staffers had focused on the detailed and complex plans for the invasion, planning for the subsequent occupation did not receive much attention (a pattern the US military later vowed never to repeat, but did). MacArthur's planners had assumed that the occupation of Japan itself, termed Operation Blacklist, would be primarily a US operation, with some participation by British Empire troops (Department of the Army). But the presence of Soviet forces controlling one of the four major Home Islands suggested that the occupation would not be as unitary as the US planners had envisioned.

As if to underscore the point, Soviet Marshal Vasilevsky notified MacArthur's headquarters that he wanted to make a speech at the surrender ceremony in Tokyo. The plan had been for MacArthur, as Supreme Commander of the Allied Powers (SCAP) to be the only speaker, representing thereby the US, its British Empire allies, the Netherlands, France and China as well as the Soviet Union. But the

---

1. See 'What Really Happened' (2 Sep 1945 Japan).
2. See 'What Really Happened' (Sep 1945–Sep 1951).

Soviets pointed out that MacArthur had not commanded a single Soviet unit, that the Soviets had cleared Japanese control from over a million square kilometres of land (equivalent to the area of France and Germany combined) and that of all the Allies, only Soviets held any positions on Japanese Home Islands.

Aware of their boss's feeling about sharing any spotlight, MacArthur's staffers managed to persuade him to finesse the situation by allowing not only the Soviets to make their comments, but also the senior representatives of each of the other Allies. All were brief, and mostly forgettable. Vasilevsky said the Soviet Union looked forward to building constructive relations with the future government of the Japanese people. This sounded to some like an indication of future issues concerning the Emperor and the Occupation.

Well over a million of Stalin's troops had swept through Manchuria and parts of North China, but the disposition of those Soviet troops was primarily a matter between Stalin and Chiang Kai-shek, the recognised leader of China. What was of concern to the Americans was that the Soviets had 'liberated' the entire Korean peninsula (not incidentally securing their access to the warm-water port of Pusan among others). The Soviets also had forces holding Hokkaido, especially its ports, and they had let it be known that landing of US troops on that northern island would be 'unnecessary, and inappropriate'.

Moreover, General Derevyanko, Stalin's representative at MacArthur's HQ, sought to delineate a Soviet zone of occupation within Tokyo (Hasegawa). The Allies had carved up Germany's capital, the Soviets pointed out, even though Berlin was deep within Soviet-occupied eastern Germany. Austria's capital Vienna was a similarly-divided enclave within Soviet-occupied north-eastern Austria. Accordingly, the Soviets envisioned a Soviet occupation zone in Tokyo within the US-occupied island of Honshu. As with occupation zones in Korea, neither the Yalta nor Potsdam conferences had discussed joint occupation of Tokyo. The closest the Potsdam discussions came to this point was Stalin's suggestion that the next meeting of The Big Three be at Tokyo (Hastings, 2009).

MacArthur, a self-acknowledged expert on 'the Oriental mind', determined that the Russians were sufficiently Asiatic as to come within his area of expertise; therefore he knew how to deal with the Russkies. In late September he started to carry out the plan he had formulated in August, that of landing an American division at Pusan to begin the occupation of southern Korea. He directed the 25th Infantry Division to embark from Mindanao in the Philippines to Korea. He informed Vasilevsky that these troops would disembark at Pusan on 12 October and that he, as Supreme Commander of the Allied Powers, expected the Americans to be met with the utmost cooperation from Red Army troops. Vasilevsky replied that the assistance of US troops was not required in Korea. MacArthur, perhaps ready to issue the press release praising his brilliantly bold gambit, told Vasilevsky that the presence of US troops was an essential element of the joint trusteeship of Korea to which the USSR had agreed. He expected the USSR to live up to its agreements, he said. On receiving this, Vasilevsky's comment to his own staff referred to bovine excrement. In his return message he calmly informed MacArthur that also on 12 October the Soviet 92nd Rifle Division would be arriving at Tokyo Bay to take up their duties in the Soviet zone of occupation in Tokyo.

When the Pentagon learned of this exchange, several things happened rapidly: General Marshall checked and found that the unused third atomic bomb had not yet been shipped back to the US; it was still on Tinian. Marshall left nothing to chance. He directed General Groves to reaffirm to Colonel Tibbets at the 509th Composite Group on Tinian that only President Truman, not General MacArthur, nor General LeMay, had the authority to release an atomic bomb for use.

For his part, when Truman learned of the testy exchange between MacArthur and Vasilevsky, he is reported to have said something along the lines of,

Does he want to start another war? Does he think Uncle Joe is afraid of the prospect of the one atom bomb we could drop on Vladivostok? There are a hell of a lot more Communist troops within a day's march of Pusan than there are American boys; I sure as hell don't want any of our kids dying in a fight against a million or so Reds over a godawful little country we've never cared about and still don't. Dammit, I ought to fire that sonofabitch MacArthur.

With that guidance from the President, the Joint Chiefs informed MacArthur that effective until further notice all available US troops slated for occupation duties would be deployed to Japan and only to Japan. MacArthur diverted the 25th Division to Kyushu and of course made sure that the record showed that the change was a mandate from Washington. Secretary of State Byrnes informed Soviet Ambassador Gromyko that since no provision had been made for a divided Tokyo, the arrival of Soviet troops in Tokyo would be, as Molotov had said about US troops in Hokkaido, 'unnecessary, and inappropriate'. So the world's two superpowers backed down from the first near confrontation of the Cold War and began working out occupation dispositions.

Some US officials considered that allowing the Soviets to control a portion of Tokyo could be a price worth paying in exchange for gaining US occupation rights on a part of the Korean peninsula. But the prevailing American vision was that Korea was not of strategic value to the US, while the rebuilding of Japan as a democratic industrial power, with as little communist influence as possible, was of clear strategic importance. The Soviet presence on Hokkaido already positioned them to subvert US efforts to rebuild Japan; giving them a slice of Tokyo would make US efforts even more difficult. As to Korea, Washington figured that the Soviets were unlikely to soon give up either their ability to plunder and exploit Korean territory, or their warm water access at Pusan. Instead of holding Korean territory with US troops, it would have to suffice to have an American seat on a trusteeship council.

So after some mutual posturing, the US and USSR settled into the pattern that gave rise to the post-war political landscape: Soviet forces occupied the Korean peninsula in its entirety, as they did Hokkaido and all of Sakhalin and the Kuril Islands. The Soviets, however, obtained no occupation rights within Tokyo.

By the end of 1945, the US, USSR, UK and China agreed to set up a Far East Advisory Commission to advise and coordinate on fulfilling the conditions of the Potsdam Declaration (Dower). This commission also included the several combatant Allies (France, the Netherlands, Australia etc.). Under the aegis of the overall Far East Commission was to be an Allied Council for Japan to provide policy guidance on the occupation of Japan, and eventually its reconstruction and reintegration into the family of nations. The council had representatives of the US, USSR, UK and China, providing advice to the Supreme Commander of the Allied Powers, i.e. MacArthur (Hsu 1951).

Similarly, the Allies set up a four-power trusteeship council for Korea. This body was to provide advice to Marshal K.A. Meretskov, the Red Army commander in Korea, in helping the Koreans recover from the years of brutal Japanese occupation, and preparing them for full independence some years hence. Neither of these councils ever had any noticeable effect on the actions of the respective military commanders.

In Japan, MacArthur's vision had been that he would rule Japan as essentially a modern-day shogun. He would allow the Emperor to exercise nominal power, somewhat as had been the case for those 700 years before the Meiji Restoration in 1867. Retention of the 'national polity', the government structure led by the Emperor, had been a key component of the agreements under which the surrender of the armed forces of the Empire had been brought about. There were some voices on the US side calling for the prosecution of Emperor Hirohito as a war criminal, leaving open the possibility of Japan nevertheless retaining the Emperor system as a form of government. The Soviets went further, calling not only for prosecution of Hirohito but also for the abolition of Imperial government, with democratically-elected officials exercising power without deference to any sovereign but 'the people'. MacArthur's headquarters maintained that the form of government was for the Japanese people to decide, i.e. that they would be free to choose to retain an Emperor. MacArthur resisted calls to try Hirohito for war crimes, focusing instead on arresting and trying officials in the government (Buruma 2003).

The Allied Council for Japan met nominally every two weeks in Tokyo. At one of its earliest meetings in November the Soviet representative noted that MacArthur's staff had directed the Japanese government to issue rules to all prefectures concerning the looming problem of food distribution (Frank 2007). The Soviets demanded that all such nationwide policies had to be pre-approved by the Council. The US representative responded that General of the Army MacArthur was the Supreme Commander of the Allied Powers (SCAP), and had the sole responsibility for the conduct of the occupation of the nation of Japan. The Soviet pointed out that although 1945 had seen a poor harvest, on Hokkaido the food and fish supplies were more than adequate to feed its population; accordingly, SCAP HQ would do well to coordinate their actions with the Council, to ensure that such food was adequately distributed. Faced with the implied Soviet threat to hoard food on Hokkaido, now it was the Americans' turn to mutter about farmyard waste products.

Later, Secretary of State Byrnes discussed the Council proceedings with Truman and told him that Ambassador Gromyko had complained about MacArthur's 'superior attitude and non-responsiveness'. Truman had griped before about 'that five star primadonna' (AmEx), and 'that five star brass hat who tells God what to do' (Morris). Truman now grumbled, 'Don't the Russians know Mac is just as arrogant and unresponsive to us? I really ought to fire that sonafabitch someday. But in the meantime, tell him to try to be a little less rude when he tells the Russians to stick it.'

Chapter 18

Hokkaido, 1945–1946

In early December 1945, Sanzo Nosaka flew into Sapporo aboard a Soviet transport. He brought with him a small cadre of former Japanese Imperial Army troops turned communist. The 53-year-old Nosaka already had 26 years of international communist activity (Dower). After studying at London University, he had helped found the British Communist Party. The UK deported him in 1921. He worked briefly with the Communist Party in Moscow, and had returned to Japan and helped found the Japanese Communist Party in the early 1920s. Arrested and jailed several times, he returned to Moscow in 1931. In the mid-1930s he was on the West Coast of the US working as a Comintern agent spying against the Japanese government (Scalapino; Pace). In 1940, Moscow sent him to work with the Chinese Communists in Yenan, where he headed up a successful effort to re-educate Japanese soldiers captured by them. Japanese Army doctrine did not allow for its soldiers to be captured. They were to die fighting. Yet the Chinese did capture Japanese soldiers, often injured ones, whom they cared for, fed and treated decently. Nosaka found that his compatriots, surprised to be alive and more or less well, were then often amenable to accepting Marxist and anti-Imperial indoctrination.

Lin Biao, commander of the Chinese Communist Eighth Route Army, praised Nosaka's valuable role in the indoctrination of former Imperial Army soldiers and their transformation into capable, technically knowledgeable troops fighting for the Chinese Communists (Lin). So when Nosaka established himself on Hokkaido, he brought with him strong links to both the Communist Party of the Soviet Union and the Chinese Communist Party, links that were later transformed into formal international alliances. Courtesy of his Soviet patrons, Nosaka soon announced that he had become Chairman of the Hokkaido Communist Party, an affiliate of the Japanese Communist Party. From that position, he launched an increasing stream of criticism against MacArthur's 'protection' of Japanese war criminals and against the whole Imperial system. This was widely seen in Western capitals, and in Tokyo, as mostly a pretext to maintain communist control of the Soviet-occupied northern island. Washington further believed that the Communists intended such dominance to serve as a base for weakening US influence over the remainder of the Japanese homeland.

When Nosaka came to Sapporo, he found another prominent communist waiting for him. Kyuichi Tokuda had worked with Nosaka in the 1920s to establish the Japanese Communist Party. In Japan, Tokuda had resisted the war and had spent most of the war years in a prison located on Hokkaido (Koschmann). The two old comrades conferred for some time and determined that Tokuda should return to Tokyo and exploit the Occupation authorities' relaxation of the ban on left-wing dissent.

The portion of the Japanese homeland under Soviet control was significant in several ways. Hokkaido constituted about 20 per cent of the nation's land area, and 25 per cent of its arable land, but with four million people, it had just about 5 per cent of the Japanese population. Hokkaido's northerly location and lack of major targets had also limited the damage from American bombers. However, as previously noted, an American bombing raid in July 1945 had damaged the Hokodate port facilities that were key to shipping food, coal and other material to Honshu and the other Home Islands.

With substantial quantities of exportable resources – foodstuffs, fish, timber and coal – and a relatively undamaged infrastructure, Hokkaido had a potentially better-functioning economy in the months and years immediately after the war than the devastated south. Enhancing this was an infusion of technical assistance from Soviet advisors from Siberia and the Far East. The Hokkaido economy also benefited from the resettlement over the next several years of perhaps two million Japanese from Manchuria and Korea.

In the closing days of the war, the Red Army captured about 2.7 million Japanese soldiers and civilians in Manchuria (Frank 1999). When Stalin entered the war, the Soviet Union had acceded to the Potsdam Declaration and its commitment to allowing Japanese troops to return to their homes. But instead, the Red Army transported over 600,000 of these Japanese soldiers to Siberian POW camps (Dower). These soldiers endured many months of brutal confinement and forced labour in Siberia, along with a good deal of Nosaka-style communist indoctrination. Eventually the Soviets got around to honouring their Potsdam commitment and allowed the captured Japanese to return to their homeland.

These displaced Japanese were hardly averse to repatriation to the least densely populated, least damaged area of Japan. Hokkaido's relatively cold climate was tropical compared to Siberia. Furthermore, Hokkaido was an area with job opportunities available on the newly-organised collective farms, or in the coal mines, the steel mills and other expanding industries. Besides, as 'losers' in battle, these veterans were unwelcome in general Japanese society (Dower). During 1946, the ranks of the Hokkaido Communist Party swelled as former POWs released from Siberia resettled on the island. Many of these young men, disillusioned by their war experience and inculcated with communist teachings, made enthusiastic rank and file Party members. They were not above applying skills they had learned in the Imperial Army to help advance Party objectives, including organising workers in mines and steel mills, and ensuring general public discipline. Many former Imperial Army officers who had declined the honour of ritual suicide before they were captured were keen students of the Marxist-Leninist doctrines taught them in the POW camps. Upon their resettlement on Hokkaido, many took jobs with the Hokkaido Internal Security Agency.

Wherever they worked, residents of Hokkaido quickly found that they were never far from lectures, radio talks, pamphlets or newspaper diatribes against the sins of the Imperial government. In the previous century, Hokkaido had been Japan's frontier, so it was the island least imbued with 2,000 years of Imperial traditions. The island's culture was therefore the easiest to 'rewire', especially with the help of the returning 're-educated' POWs. The Emperor and the warmongers around him had caused the ruin of the nation, the people of Hokkaido learned. It was these militarists' misdeeds that were therefore responsible for the ill-treatment the former POWs had received from the (blameless) Soviets.

Under Soviet tutelage, propagandists began to emphasise the distinct history of Hokkaido. It was the least 'Japanese' and most recently settled of the Home Islands; it was originally populated by the indigenous Ainu people, whose distinct appearance, language and culture set them apart from the ethnically homogeneous Yamato Japanese. Ironically, in the 1800s a major factor prompting the Japanese people to develop 'remote' Hokkaido was the desire to forestall encroachment there by the Russians (Irish 2009). Hokkaido has a cold climate distinct from the other Japanese islands; it is Japan's Alaska. Yet this makes it similar to its Russian-controlled neighbours, such as Sakhalin and the Kurils, also originally peopled by Ainu. Soviet occupation authorities therefore emphasised

Hokkaido's cultural links with Sakhalin Island and its economic ties with the Soviet Far East. All this was to reinforce the distinct identity of Hokkaido, and not coincidentally to bring the occupied island more firmly into the Soviet sphere. The Soviets expelled indigenous Ainu people from Sakhalin (Ealey). They were resettled on Hokkaido.

Chapter 19

US-Occupied Japan, 1945–1946

In Tokyo, in the days after the surrender, MacArthur's occupation government faced the short-term problem of averting famine on the Home Islands under its jurisdiction. Typhoons and cold wet weather in September and October 1945 slashed the rice harvest by 20 per cent (Frank 2007).The bombing of rail and coastal transportation facilities in the last days of the war now made distribution of what harvest there was all the more difficult. This became yet more difficult when the Soviet authorities in late 1945 hampered timely shipment of foodstuffs from Hokkaido as they had implied they would do at the Allied Council meeting in November. (As it turned out, those surplus stores the Soviets held back on Hokkaido in 1945 became critically important in 1946 and 1947. That's when the newly collectivised farmlands of Hokkaido produced vastly diminished harvests.)

Meanwhile, the US provided huge imports of rice and other foodstuffs to the Japanese on Kyushu, Honshu, Shikoku and the many lesser islands of Japan proper. This prevented famine, although food shortages did cause some civil unrest in the major cities. High prices in the black market exacerbated discontent. In the final days of the war, Imperial General Headquarters ordered the release of huge military food stores, but much of it found its way onto the black market (Dower). The elites always had enough food, but it was the common people who were arrested for buying on the black market. Communist agitators tried to exploit the food shortages and inequalities to discredit the government. An investigation by the elected Diet in 1947 exposed scandalous hoarding by well-placed parties, but there were no prosecutions. This may have been because black market profits funded many politicians' campaigns (Dower). Still, most citizens noted and appreciated the role of the US in shipping in massive quantities of food to feed their former enemies in the first years of the occupation. Similarly, the role of the Soviets in limiting food supplies from Hokkaido was also long remembered in Tokyo.

MacArthur, functioning as the American shogun and expert on all things oriental, sought to dictate the remaking of Japan as a liberal democracy. This would keep it from returning to militarism, or to Communism. The hoped-for corollary was that the new Japan would emerge as a US ally. To that end in October 1945, SCAP rescinded the Japanese laws against dissent, ordered the vote for women and support for trade unions and land reform. He also ordered the breakup of the vast industrial conglomerates, the zaibatsu, which had benefited from and fostered Japan's militarism (Dower).

Nevertheless, the Soviets in 1946 continued to try to use Hokkaido's food and coal resources as a bargaining chip to influence the conduct of the Occupation. The Soviets wanted the US to put the Emperor on trial and abolish the entire Imperial form of government. But the Soviets underestimated US resolve both in terms of providing the needed food aid, and in terms of geopolitics. To be sure, there were some on the US side who themselves believed the Emperor was a war criminal. The US, however, was determined not to submit to Soviet blackmail or appear to do so. Nor was the US about to renege on the commitment it had made in accepting the surrender of the Japanese Imperial Armed Forces, i.e. that the Japanese would be free to determine their future form of government.

As had long been planned, therefore, the US brought Japan's top military leaders to trial in 1946. Seven top political and military leaders were hanged, with sixteen others sentenced to life imprisonment (Maga). But the Emperor and his family escaped virtually without blame, due in large part to efforts by SCAP staff to ensure that the indicted war criminals shouldered the blame themselves and shielded the Imperial family. As SCAP spun it, the story was that the militarists had exceeded the Emperor's wishes and had made war without his approval. As with so many myths, there was some truth to that; in the 1930s, the Kwantung Army made war in China without prior assent from Tokyo. But to say that the Emperor was anti-war as his armed forces conquered a huge Asia Pacific Empire was contrary to the demonstrable facts. Still, the American conquerors were merely following the well-established Japanese tradition of coup leaders: blame the Emperor's advisors for misleading him, and then remove the wicked advisors from the scene (Dower).

SCAP's protection of the Imperial war criminals was loudly criticised by Sanzo Nosaka in Sapporo, by Moscow not quite as loudly, relatively quietly by some in Washington, and not at all in Tokyo. At least, no criticism of MacArthur or SCAP's actions was allowed to be heard or read. SCAP censors protected the Shogun from criticism as diligently as any autocrat's loyal retainers (Dower). Kyuichi Tokuda, the formerly-imprisoned Japanese communist colleague of Hokkaido's Sanzo Nosaka, circulated a few leaflets critical of SCAP policies, but only on a limited basis.

By early 1946, Tokyo was ready to hold nationwide elections for representatives to the Diet. But the Soviet authorities in Sapporo refused to allow Hokkaido residents to participate in these elections, claiming that a legislature functioning under the purview of the Emperor was necessarily imperialist. Instead, over US protests, the Russians organised 'democratic' elections for a separate Hokkaido Assembly. These went forward in April 1946, coinciding with the elections for the national Diet in Tokyo. In Hokkaido, the Soviet authorities allowed only candidates with anti-imperial and/or socialist credentials to run. In the same election, and with strong assistance from General Meretskov's occupation authorities, Sanzo Nosaka won election as the Governor of Hokkaido. At the prefecture level, Soviet authorities in Sapporo oversaw establishment of people's committees to exercise local day-to-day management, always under the watchful eyes of Soviet commissars.

US analysts noted that it would have been quite feasible for the Soviet occupation authorities to allow the nationwide elections to proceed on Hokkaido, while ensuring the election of only left-leaning Diet representatives. (The Soviets indeed demonstrated mastery of election-rigging many times in Eastern Europe.) But with Hokkaido's relatively small population, the island was only allocated a few seats, and sending a relatively small number of Soviet-sympathising legislators to Tokyo was of little interest to the Soviets. They knew that the overall Diet was unlikely to be persuaded by Soviet-influenced sentiment against the Emperor. So the Soviets preferred to solidify their hold on a major piece of Japan, rather than have a small minority voice in a national government. They believed that Hokkaido would serve more effectively as a platform for subversion of the rest of Japan if it stood apart as a clearly communist entity (soon to be touted as a Workers' Paradise) than if it remained integrated with the other Home Islands.

The newly-elected 464-seat Diet did have a few communists, such as Kyuichi Tokuda, now in Tokyo, formerly of Hokkaido (Nohlen et al.). But they were far too few to prevent the Diet's declaration that Nosaka's administration on Hokkaido was not freely elected and that they would not recognise it. To the extent that the Tokyo administration had any dealings with Hokkaido, these were couched as working with the officials appointed by the Soviet occupation authorities. But there was a continuing sharp decline in trade or other dealings between Hokkaido and the other Home Islands. Hokodate, the war-damaged port on southern Hokkaido critical to shipments of coal, food, timber and other resources, remained crippled. Meanwhile, ports such as Rumoi and Ishikari, which faced the Soviet Far East and Sakhalin, expanded.

In Japan proper, the top-down liberal reforms commanded by SCAP in late 1945 and early 1946 unleashed social currents that were more powerful and more Marxist than the New Dealers on the SCAP staff had anticipated. There was a rapid emergence of a Marxist-leaning New Japanese Literature movement, along with increasing Marxist sentiment among Japanese intellectuals. Tokyo University, for example, was a hotbed of debates on theories of economics and history and even the application of science to the advancement of socialist goals (Dower).

Professionals familiar with Japan would not have been surprised by the resurgence of leftist sentiment among the intelligentsia. It had definitely been present in the 1920s, but it was suppressed in the 1930s and the war years. As noted earlier, senior advisors to the Emperor had feared a communist revolution if the war had gone on longer (Buruma 2003). The SCAP staff, however, were in large part complete neophytes in regard to Japan (Dower). This was perhaps to ensure that no expertise on 'the oriental mind' competed with that of MacArthur. As a result, the leftist foment in the universities, in literature and soon in the mass media, took the SCAP's staff by surprise. If Mac was surprised, he never would have admitted it.

Also coming as a surprise was the 'production control movement' in which workers all over (South) Japan took over mines, factories and offices and <u>increased</u> their production without management input. This 'soviet' sort of effort aimed in large part to demonstrate the managers' bad faith. The workers claimed that the managers of these enterprises had been dragging their feet to discredit the democratisation movement. It was the owners' intent, the workers claimed, to reverse the SCAP-directed breakup of the powerful business and industrial conglomerates, the zaibatsu (Dower).

'Law and order' concerns added to the problems of labour unrest. The black market created a widespread odour of illegality on the street, while disaffected former soldiers – 'losers' not very welcome in Japanese society – contributed to increased alcoholism, drug abuse and petty crime (Dower). Ordinary Japanese citizens also increasingly resented the priorities in housing, transportation and food availability accorded to the one million occupying troops, civilians and dependents (Dower).

May 1st 1946 was a watershed.[1] With support from the communist-led National Congress of Industrial Unions, huge demonstrations took place on May Day. In Tokyo, a large crowd protested food shortages, corrupt business practices and privileges for the elite (Dower). Kyuichi Tokuda, the Japanese communist just elected to the Japanese Diet, addressed the crowd (National Diet Library; Koschmann). The crowd swelled as the day wore on. Initially peaceful, the mood turned uglier. According to later police reports of unknown accuracy, the crowd became increasingly stirred up by 'a large number of communist trouble-makers', several of whom were known to have recently arrived from Hokkaido. Japanese police arrested several communist agitators, but others took this as provocation and intensified their efforts to rile the crowd. On the fringes of the mass of people, there was the sound of store windows shattering. First there was a little, then a lot of looting, the crowd railing against rich businessmen and the exploitation of the working class. Then a car, said to belong to a rich man, was set afire. Then another. Though some demonstrators (especially the known communist agitators) dispersed and disappeared, many others demonstrators morphed into rioters. The civilian police were unprepared and lost all control of the crowd as it surged toward the Imperial Palace. There, in a scene reminiscent of the attempted coup the previous August, demonstrators-turned-rioters rampaged through the Palace grounds and seemed intent on entering the Emperor's Residence itself and perhaps even harming the Emperor. (Imperial retainers had shepherded Hirohito to the wartime underground shelter.) More than one Molotov cocktail flew from the edges of the crowd.

Then there was gunfire, a lot of it, as US Army Military Police drove onto the Palace grounds. They fired their jeep-mounted machine guns in the air. The surging crowd halted. Then, two companies of well-armed infantry from the 1st Cavalry Division arrived in the Army's ubiquitous 'deuce-and-a-half' trucks. Several hundred soldiers quickly dismounted and formed lines confronting the crowd. They held their rifles pointed up, but ready. More armed jeeps took up flanking positions. There were megaphone warnings to the crowd to leave the Palace grounds and disperse. There was a moment. The rioters closest to the lines of troops looked uncertain. The American soldiers looked determined. A wave of complete quiet crept toward the back from the front lines of the now largely motionless crowd. Maybe it was all going to be okay. Army

---

1. See 'What Really Happened' (1 May 1946).

Lieutenant Colonel Mike Adams was just about to direct his Japanese liaison to repeat the call to disperse, when someone deep in the crowd shouted 'Tenno heika banzai'. There seemed to be movement of the front ranks. Then a moment later there was more gunfire, from the infantry's rifles and the jeeps' machine guns. Lieutenant Colonel Adams ordered 'cease-fire' immediately, and repeatedly. After a few moments, the firing stopped. The protesters were running away, except for about a hundred bodies on the ground.

The Japanese police arrested dozens of rioters. Ambulances took the fallen to hospitals. And investigators interviewed the US troops. Predictably, there were several equally sincere but radically divergent versions of events. From these interviews, the narrative emerged that some of the 1st Cavalry troops had heard 'something something banzai' from the crowd. As veterans of hard fighting in the Philippines, the troopers had heard Japanese soldiers yell 'Banzai' as they launched mass suicide charges against the Americans (Morton). So they figured the rioters were preparing to charge them. And so the firing began. No one could exactly remember whether they heard Adams, or one of his company officers give the 'open fire' order but they were sure they must have. Adams asserted that he had repeatedly cautioned his troops to 'hold your fire'. Investigators believed that in the tense, noisy situation, some of the troops might have misheard, or just heard the last word. Unsurprisingly, each trooper insisted that he had only opened fire after those around him had already done so.

For his part, Adams reported that he and his troops had moved in swiftly when the Japanese police lost control of the crowd. He understood that his orders authorised the use of deadly force to protect the lives of his own troops. But the movements of the crowd had not constituted such a threat, he said. He reported that he knew from his translator what 'Tenno heika banzai' meant: 'Long live the Emperor'. When he heard it that day, he had taken it as a perhaps ironic acquiescence, signalling that the crowd gathered on the Imperial Palace grounds would back off. No, he didn't see those in the front of the crowd beginning to charge his line; they were if anything just starting to turn themselves around.

In modern parlance, the spin control began immediately. Adams and his battalion were swiftly transferred out of Tokyo and away from civilian contact and were never heard from or about again. In Army doctrine, 'a commander is responsible for all that his unit does or fails to do' (US Army) and Adams therefore was responsible for failing to maintain control of his troops. But to court-martial him would be an admission that the US Army had erred. Such an admission was not allowed in

MacArthur's world. Lieutenant Colonel Adams was neither demoted nor ever promoted. After demobilisation, he sold linoleum flooring in Atlanta, where none of his neighbours ever knew of his role in the May Day Massacre.

The official account SCAP HQ published on 15 May 1946 was that Adams had seen the Molotov cocktails flying, and then heard gunfire emanating from the crowd of demonstrators. He had seen the crowd surge toward his line, and he judged that his troops were in danger. So he ordered them to fire. The incident was regrettable but the responsibility for the injuries and loss of life (forty-two dead, fifty-one wounded), rested upon the organisers of the demonstration, and perhaps with those who sent outside agitators, very likely illegally-armed agitators, to turn a peaceful, democratic demonstration into a violent confrontation with the authorities, which then descended into lawless deadly rioting. SCAP HQ sent a message to Marshal Meretskov's headquarters in Sapporo. It was couched as a request for assistance in the investigation of how armed Japanese citizens were able to travel from Hokkaido to Honshu. It was in effect an accusation of complicity by the Sapporo authorities in the attempt to destabilise the Tokyo government.

In Tokyo, police arrested protest organisers from the National Congress of Industrial Unions, along with hundreds of known and suspected communists and other left-leaning leaders, including Kyuichi Tokuda, the member of the Diet. They faced charges of conspiracy and inciting violence. Under Edict No. 109, crafted by SCAP and issued by the Emperor, Tokuda was 'purged' from his public office (National Diet Library). He was then convicted of conspiracy and incitement. MacArthur's censors ensured that only the 'correct' story reached the Japanese public, and that they came to the correct conclusion: communists and their sympathisers had gone too far. The disruptions they were causing were selfish (a most un-Japanese behaviour), sacrilegious and deeply damaging to the progress of rebuilding the nation and its economy.

The first post-war Diet was elected just three weeks prior to May Day, and gave the 'Liberal' party a large plurality of seats. Soon after, Yoshida Shigeru became Prime Minister and served in that role almost continuously for the next nine years. Despite the 'Liberal' moniker, Yoshida and his party were more nearly what modern Americans would call 'conservatives' of the stripe who supported big business and the use of big government to assist big business, all for the goal of fostering economic prosperity, especially for the owners of big business. Helped overtly and otherwise by the major business interests, Yoshida and his

Liberal Party sought to jump start the rebuilding of Japanese industry, and slow down or reverse the headlong democratisation (Dower).

In the wake of the May Day Massacre, the Diet's conservative legislative efforts met no resistance from SCAP HQ. In early 1946 the Americans in Tokyo had talked about the forced changes in land ownership and breakup of large business interests as being necessary to release the nation's full productivity. The newly-permitted free exchange of ideas in the public space, the Americans said, was a prerequisite to the flowering of democratic freedoms. But by late 1946, the more conservative-minded members of the SCAP staff, such as MacArthur's wartime intelligence chief Charles Willoughby, were in the ascendant (Buruma 2003). There was more emphasis on using proven economic structures to produce results (i.e. the oligopolies of the zaibatsu) and protecting the stability of the government from the corrosive influences of communism (i.e. cracking down on dissent and dissenters). Conservative-controlled media outlets sought to reinforce a swing to the right.

A comprehensive 'Red Purge' conducted by SCAP, Japanese government bureaucrats and conservative business managers removed over 10,000 'troublemakers' from government and business payrolls. At the same time, Occupation authorities reinstated some former government officials previously purged for nationalist and militarist activities during the war (Dower).

At the end of 1946 the Diet voted to accept the new constitution, which MacArthur's staff had drafted earlier that year (Dower). The new document provided for a wide range of rights for the people such as freedom of speech, writing, publication public meetings and associations and so on, but such rights were granted 'within the limits of law' (Dower). Even before the Constitution came into effect in 1947, there were many laws constraining individual rights to safeguard the common good, protect the stability of the government and ensure the future prosperity of the nation. Japan was moving to the right pushed by concern for internal security and progress, and by the actions of the Hokkaido breakaway entity.

Chapter 20

Hokkaido, 1947

The adoption of the new constitution by the Tokyo Diet in November 1946 became the excuse Nosaka's Hokkaido government sought. The new Tokyo constitution weakened but did not eliminate the role of the Emperor. In speeches seemingly written for him by his Soviet patrons, Nosaka claimed this was a formula for a potential return to 'hegemonism' (despite the new constitution's strong and unprecedented disavowal of the use of offensive war).

In January 1947 the Hokkaido Assembly declared the independence of the Ezo Democratic People's Republic of Japan, with its capital at Sapporo. Although actually exercising authority only on Hokkaido, Nosaka's new government nominally professed to seek the reunification of all of Japan under democratic socialist principles. The 'Ezo' in the official name was a reference to the Republic of Ezo, a short-lived 1869 effort at independence for Ezo, as Hokkaido was known to its original Ainu inhabitants (Irish 2009). At the time of the restoration of Imperial power under Emperor Meiji in 1868, forces loyal to the Tokugawa shogun fled to Hokkaido. There they set up a republic and held the first elections in Japanese history (Hillsborough). They succumbed a few years later to forces loyal to the Emperor. Thus the communist-dominated Hokkaido government was announcing its intent to oppose the Imperial form of government for Japan, and was prepared to maintain its own separate Japanese identity for as long as necessary.

Unsurprisingly, Moscow was the first to grant recognition to the Sapporo government. In the same diplomatic breath, the USSR and the EDPRJ (the official acronym for what most people today refer to as North Japan), announced a treaty of aid and friendship. The treaty declared the Soviet occupation to be at an end, while also announcing the stationing of Soviet land and naval forces on Hokkaido to protect against imperialist aggression.

The United Nations Security Council heard a challenge to the declaration of independence of North Japan. But the Soviet's predictable veto precluded that body from even passing any resolution critical of the action. And so, just as the post-war world watched two Germanys form and take diverging paths, a similar dichotomy played out in East Asia. North Japan collectivised farmland and claimed great gains in harvest volumes. But according to South Japan's PSIA (Public Security Intelligence Agency), the productivity per acre in North Japan soon fell below pre-war levels, while the size of the agricultural workforce increased. The agricultural and fishing industries were sufficient to feed the island nation's population, but shipments of food and fish to other parts of Japan, once a mainstay of Hokkaido's economy, all but disappeared by 1948. Exacerbating this were the 'protective restrictions' the Nosaka government placed on the fishing industry: during 1947, quite a number of fishing boats, full of crew and families, sailed off in search of snapper but found Honshu instead. After that, police in Hokkaido ports ensured that only crew members embarked. They warned the crews that they would imprison their families if the fishermen decided not to return.

Right after the war coal mines, now state enterprises, expanded rapidly for export as well as to provide energy for steel and other heavy industry, also now state enterprises. Some steel was exported, but much also went into new weapons. Nosaka, President of the EDPRJ, never tired of reminding his people of the imminent threat posed by the 'imperialistic hegemons' of South Japan, who were intent, he claimed, on reasserting their control of Hokkaido as just the first step in reconquering Korea and Manchuria, this time with the material aid of the anti-communist forces of the US. In late 1947, with rhetoric unencumbered by evidence, Nosaka began an ambitious re-armament effort for 'self-defence'. He nevertheless acquired a wide variety of weapons that could kill adversaries equally well on the offense as on the defence. Frequently 'discovering and thwarting' plans for invasion from the South, by 1950 Nosaka had built a sizable military of over 300,000 personnel, many of whom had served in the Kwantung Army in Manchuria. Based on an estimated Hokkaido population of about 6.5 million, this was one of the world's largest peacetime militaries in proportion to a nation's population. Despite Nosaka's emphasis on defending his people from 'imperialist aggression', his ten army divisions were all notably equipped for and trained in amphibious operations, which are not often needed as a defensive manoeuvre. His several hundred air force fighters and tactical bombers, and his several dozen frigates, cruisers, destroyers and submarines, constituted a further potential threat to South Japan. Also, under the terms of their treaty, the

USSR maintained on Hokkaido a similar number of army divisions, 'for the fraternal defence of the Peoples' Republic'. Overall, Hokkaido began to bristle with army bases and airfields. 'Rebuilt' ports such as Hakodate, 12 miles from Honshu, came to host numerous naval installations and fortifications. The narrow Tsugaru Strait between Hokkaido and Honshu was heavily mined on the Hokkaido side.

In addition to its relationship with the USSR, North Japan quickly established links with the two other People's Republics of East Asia. North Japan was one of the first governments to recognise the People's Republic of China after Mao Zedong established it in December 1947. Of course, the Japanese Imperial Army's brutal treatment of China and its people could not soon be forgotten, so the relations between those two People's Republics continue to this day to be correct, but chilly. What they shared, besides Marxism, was dislike for the still-Imperial government of South Japan. A similar formal but less-than-cordial relationship arose between Sapporo and Seoul, the intensely nationalistic People's Democratic Republic of Korea, which had suffered under decades of Japanese oppression.

Chapter 21

South Japan From 1948

The partition of Japan into North and South entities was not wholly unwelcome in the US, any more than was the analogous division of Germany. The fact that the North came under communist domination was geopolitically regrettable, but the US public had less sympathy for those former enemies than they did for former allies such as the Poles living under communist rule. The North/South split would hamper Japanese economic reconstruction, making any kind of threat from Japan to anyone a distant prospect. The southern Home Islands, still officially the State of Japan but commonly called South Japan, was initially even more dependent on US aid than it would have been if the foodstuffs and energy resources of Hokkaido had been available to it. The US committed to helping the Japanese rebuild their economy and eventually re-join the family of nations, presumably as a US ally.

Indeed, even as the Pacific War was coming to an end in 1945, it had been the US vision that America should help defeated Japan rebuild as a staunch US ally. It was to be a bulwark against the expansion of Soviet influence. To this end, amid the massive firebombing of Tokyo, the Army Air Forces had strict orders to avoid bombing the Emperor's Palace, on the belief that sparing the Emperor and his retinue would facilitate eventual good feelings on the part of the Japanese people toward their conquerors. The same thin logic led to the exclusion of the ancient capital of Kyoto from the list of cities to be wiped out by atomic weapons (Hasegawa). As events unfolded, if all of Japan could not be redeveloped as a bulwark against Communism, South Japan would have to do.

In the South, however, continuation of the formal occupation became increasingly untenable in light of the declared end of the Soviet occupation of the North. Accordingly, the January 1948 Treaty of San Francisco formally ended the war and the occupation government in the South.[1] The United States and its allies recognised the Tokyo government as the legitimate government of all of Japan. That was the easy part. What was more difficult and controversial was the accompanying US-Japan security treaty. It was generally agreed that South Japan could eventually be a bulwark against communism, but with the Soviet Union, Korea, China and even breakaway Hokkaido all part of the Red Tide, Tokyo would need some help ensuring its freedom. How much US help Tokyo would need and for how long was not clear in 1948.

The security treaty Tokyo and Washington negotiated at the end of the occupation called for the open-ended stationing of US military forces throughout Japan, at the discretion of the US (Buruma 2003). Yoshida's conservative government and the business interests supporting it welcomed the national security that came with continued US military presence. But as the terms of this agreement became known to the Japanese public, the protests were almost immediate. Ignoring the hypocrisy, Japanese communists and other groups on the left decried the 'new imperialism' of America (Buruma 2003).

In the US, where the Senate must vote to ratify treaties the President negotiates, there was also debate. The march of communism in East Asia was concerning, but there was disagreement as to the threat South Japan faced from its neighbours. The communist regime on Hokkaido was officially committed to reunification of Japan, under the leadership of the Communist Party. But most analysts believed the Sapporo government was unlikely to attempt a forcible reunification with South Japan, at least on its own. However, reports of the North Japanese Navy and Marine Infantry conducting training in amphibious operations were troubling. Their sponsor, the USSR, had formerly possessed little expertise in amphibious landings, but America's Operation Hula had given the Soviets excellent training by the world's experts. The Russians had applied that training in taking South Sakhalin, several of the Kuril Islands, and Hokkaido. They had apparently passed on their newly-acquired expertise to the North Japanese.

Across the Sea of Japan, the Seoul-based Democratic People's Republic of Korea (DPRK) had emerged from over 60 years of Japanese exploitation with no good regard for the Imperialist regime in Tokyo. Exploited by its neighbours for centuries, the DPRK was developing a strong military of its own, albeit with aid from its communist neighbours. The Soviet Army

---

1. See 'What Really Happened' (Sep 1951 (2)).

pulled out of Korea in 1948, but transferred not a few tanks, artillery pieces and other items to the Koreans (Seth). Would the Korean regime someday assist the Sapporo government in attempting a reunification of Japan as a People's Republic? Would the Koreans try to improve on Kublai Khan's thirteenth-century efforts to invade South Japan from Korea? Was the Koreans' thirst for retribution against the Japanese for their half century of oppression strong enough to get them to collaborate with the breakaway Japanese?

Probably not. But then again, the Japanese had in the latter years of the war attempted not ethnic cleansing, but a form of cultural cleansing of all things Korean. The Koreans had fresh memories of being forced to change their names to Japanese ones, of the suppression of the Korean language in schools and the theft of Korean cultural artefacts (Caprio). Post-war Korean nationalism was resurgent and the notion of Korea taking military action against (a part of) Japan could not be ruled out. As to capabilities, the Koreans had a long history of seafaring prowess (Paine). After all, the Mongol Kublai Khan had his invasion fleet built in Korea (Turnbull).

Then there was the 800lb gorilla in the neighbourhood, China. That nation had also suffered grievously at Japanese hands. As Mao Zedong established his control of China in 1947, Japanese Ministry of Defense analysts, and their Pentagon counterparts, contemplated defence of the Home Islands against a modern invasion from the Chinese mainland. Again, that was an unlikely event, but many unlikely things had happened in the last few years.

In the late 1940s, Washington's view of East Asia from the vantage point of Tokyo was an ostensibly peaceful region with potential for renewed war not far below the surface. So there was little question that the US needed to maintain a presence in Japan, to try to discourage adventurous neighbours. The debate in the US was about how to prepare for a failure of deterrence. If the US kept only enough forces in Japan to 'ring the fire bell' and call for reinforcements, the oceanic distances involved would prevent effective response. Although the US still had a monopoly on nuclear weapons, the Pentagon estimated that would not last far into the 1950s. (They were right; Stalin had the bomb in 1948.) Moreover, the usefulness of these weapons in a local struggle was already questionable.

If, however, the US kept enough forces in Japan to defeat any incursion, the cost in personnel and resources would be very high, too high for war-weary America to sustain. There was also the question of how acceptable it would be on Main Street USA for American troops to be used to fight and die to protect Japanese from other Japanese or from

Koreans or even Chinese who had been so recently and so badly abused by the Japanese.

The obvious solution was for the South Japanese to bear much of the responsibility and cost for their own defence. The new Japanese constitution's renunciation of war as a means of settling international disputes did not preclude South Japan from defending itself. Accordingly, Washington recommended that Tokyo develop a 300,000–350,000 man Ground Self Defense Force (Dower; Buruma 2003). MacArthur, who was responsible for the 'no war' provision in the Japanese constitution, voiced his strong objection to Washington's concept of a large, well-armed Japanese Self Defense Force. He declared 'It was against his principles' (Buruma 2003).

"HIS principles', my keyster!' said President Harry Truman when told about MacArthur's latest pronouncement. 'MY principles call for every blessed soldier in the US of A Army to do as his Commander in Chief directs. He may be the Supreme Muckety Muck over there, but I am his boss! I really ought to fire that arrogant sonofabitch. But I don't want to give him an excuse to come back here and get into politics.'

It was therefore in the domestic political interests of both the Yoshida and the Truman governments to revise the Japan-America Security Alliance as initially proposed. As ratified in mid-1948, it provided for a joint review of military dispositions in Japan every five years. These dispositions were to include the basing of US Army, Air Force, Navy and Marine personnel on the three Home Islands and Okinawa, with Japan making host nation payments to the US to offset the costs. The Treaty also called for the US to assist with the development of the Japanese Self Defense Force, which was to acquire defensive weapons, and capabilities to counter aggression from the potentially hostile neighbouring regimes.

So by the end of 1950, a Japanese Ground Self Defense Force of 350,000 thoroughly-trained personnel was equipped with excellent weapons capable of firing everything from defensive bullets to defensive heavy artillery shells. The 50,000-man Maritime Self Defense Force deployed coastal defence vessels (such as former US Navy defensive destroyers and anti-submarine ships), while the 40,000-man Air Self Defense Force flew hundreds of defensive combat aircraft, many also capable of dropping defensive bombs.[2] The continued presence of 75,000 US military personnel in South Japan, and the very existence of the Japanese Self

---

2. See 'What Really Happened' (Jul 1950 (2)).

Defense Forces led to strident, sometimes violent demonstrations from the Left. This militarisation jeopardised Japan's ability, they said, to live peacefully with her neighbours (Buruma 2003). The suspicion was that the South Japanese Left received substantial aid from the neighbours' communist parties.

For their part, business and other conservative interests inspired their own protests and demonstrations in the early 1950s. With Japan's sovereignty restored, there were many on the Right who called for revising the US-imposed constitution to delete the no-war clause and to restore the full role of the Emperor in the government (Buruma 2003). Although the Japanese conservatives were not monolithic, they were far less fragmented and fractious than those on the Left. By 1955 the business and government conservatives forged a coalition as the Liberal Democratic Party. The LDP, exploiting the splits among socialists and communists, gained control of the government and has held it almost continuously to the present day, with politicians from various wings of the party more or less alternating in power, so that everyone on the Right gets their turn (Buruma 2003).

As noted previously, the Occupation authorities initially targeted the business conglomerates of the war years for dissolution. But by the mid-1950s these zaibatsu had re-coalesced to a considerable degree and focused on rebuilding the Japanese economy in concert with the government's powerful central planning and policy agency, the Ministry of International Trade and Industry (MITI). They faced major challenges. National defence was a huge expense, in terms of the direct costs of the Self Defense Forces, and the host nation payments to the US. Until well into the 1960s, 'defence' took up, directly and indirectly, nearly 6 per cent of the Gross Domestic Product. That was comparable to that of the US, but far less sustainable for the rebuilding Japanese economy. There was also the opportunity cost of the diversion of resources such as steel and of personnel from civilian endeavours to the military and to military industries. How much more prosperous would the Japanese people (and the owners of the conglomerates) be if resources and personnel were focused on peaceful production? War reparations to the Philippines, Burma and other nations ravaged by the Imperial Army were also significant (Treaty). Of course, the separation of Hokkaido and its resources left a sizable hole in the Japanese Gross Domestic Product and forced South Japan to buy from other nations food and energy that would otherwise have been domestic products.

Despite South Japan's relative political stability, all this economic baggage slowed the redevelopment of South Japan in the 1950s. Early exports of simple consumer goods and things like tinny wind-up toys earned the moniker 'Cheap Jap Junk' (Elliot). Increased regional tensions after 1960 kept the direct and indirect costs of defence high. The gradually resurgent zaibatsu obtained some degree of labour peace and good productivity by promising workers essentially lifetime jobs and overall prosperity for the public. Eventually, by the 1980s, Japanese automakers began making minor inroads in the US car market, but the 'cheap junk' label was hard to overcome: the early Nissans and Datsuns were patently 'tinny', underpowered and repair-prone. Moreover, Japanese automakers faced stiff competition in the 1980s from the resurgent Detroit auto industry. Battered by the energy crises of the 1970s, the four major US automakers (General Motors, Ford, Chrysler, American Motors) had nevertheless grown stronger without serious foreign competition. They competed primarily with one another to sell the well-engineered, energy-efficient autos the American public began to demand. Nor did the Japanese automakers even do well in their domestic market. Despite some attempts by Tokyo to limit imports from the US, Ford and GM's compacts and mid-size vehicles were a hit in Japan, and soon accounted for large percentages of the US automakers' revenues. West Coast ports did a booming business in shipping American-made Saturns, Taurus and many others to Japan.

By the 1990s, Japanese TVs, music systems and other consumer electronics also began to acquire the reputation of being well made and reasonably priced. Slowly they enlarged their market share against US-made Phillips, Magnavox and other long-established brands. Then the upheavals of the 2000s hit Pause on the Japanese economy for years. The second decade of the new century saw the economy gradually absorbing the costs of reunification with bankrupt North Japan. Now as the world's twelfth largest economy, Japan has potential, but is not and may never be a major world economic player.[3]

---

3. See 'What Really Happened' (1968–2010).

Chapter 22

Korea From 1945

The establishment of People's Committees in Korean provinces followed on the heels of Soviet troops (Buzo). Such committees were populated, but not wholly dominated, by Korean communists; other left-leaning groups were also major players. In September in Pyongyang, prominent Christian leader Cho Man-sik set up a Committee To Prepare For Korean Independence. This group also included communists, such as Pak Hon-yong, who had survived the years of Japanese rule. Initially, the Soviets promised to work with this diverse group. However, in October the Soviet authorities set up an Interim Korean People's Committee, with non-communist Cho as its nominal head but with communists coming into a dominant role. To further help the locals run things, the Soviets in October repatriated several hundred Koreans who had spent the war in Manchuria and the Soviet Union as guerrillas fighting the Japanese. Among these was a native Korean named Kim Il-sung. The Soviets touted his exploits in Manchuria against the Japanese almost as soon as he arrived back in Korea (Seth). The Soviets began promoting Kim and his Siberian/ Manchurian wartime colleagues over the native communists, all the while sliding non-communist Cho Man-sik and even communist Pak Hon-yong to the side. In December, the Soviets made Kim head of the Korean Communist Party, replacing the provincial people's committees (Seth).

The Great Powers held a Foreign Ministers' Conference in Moscow in December 1945 (Leckie). The conferees agreed to a four-power (US, USSR, UK and China) trusteeship for Korea to last 4 or 5 years. The Soviets agreed to this trusteeship (Seth). It is likely they were confident that the multi-party but communist-dominated Korean governance structure would be readily responsive to the guidance of the Soviet Union, whose troops had lifted the yoke of Japanese oppression, and still walked the streets of Pyongyang, Seoul, Pusan and other cities throughout the peninsula. The Soviets further believed that they well understood Korea and its people through the help of a large number of Soviet citizens of Korean descent then living in the Soviet Far East (Spector).

The US made noises at the conference and later about the need for the other three powers overseeing the trusteeship to have a meaningful role in guiding that Korean government. With straight faces the Soviets promised to cooperate fully, indeed as fully as MacArthur's SCAP HQ in Tokyo cooperated with the four-power Allied Council for Japan. That is to say, as the US owned the occupation of South Japan, the USSR would own the Korean trusteeship.

But the feasibility of the trusteeship was challenged first and most strongly by the Koreans themselves. The 1943 Cairo Conference with US, UK and Chinese leaders had produced a declaration that 'in due course Korea shall become free and independent'. At the 1945 Yalta Conference the Big Three agreed to set up a Great Power trusteeship for Korea, but they did not specify a duration. FDR may well have been thinking in terms of 40–50 years, with America's long 'tutelage' of the Philippines as a model (Seth). But no one during the wartime conferences had apparently conferred with any Koreans.

When Koreans living in China and the US read about the Cairo Declaration's 'in due course', they certainly did not think in terms of 40–50 years. More like that many weeks. So even the much shorter 4–5-year duration the Moscow Conference now adopted was wholly unacceptable to the people who called Korea home. The reaction throughout the peninsula was immediate and strident. Opposition to a 'prolonged' trusteeship was politically and geographically broad. Korea's long history includes periods of independence, and of subjugation. It has stimulated a passionately strong nationalism. Now, with the hated Japanese gone, conservatives and communists, industrialists and farmers, northerners and southerners stood unified as Korean nationalists, opposed to a perceived continuation of their oppressed, humiliated condition.

Cho Man-sik, the non-communist who'd founded the Committee To Prepare For Korean Independence, voiced his opposition to the trusteeship. The Soviets booted him out (Buruma 2013). Korean communists too initially said they opposed the trusteeship, until Moscow told them that they didn't. This made them the only political group in Korea not opposed to the trusteeship, which in turn made them the only group that the Soviet Trustee would agree to work with. As one of the other Trustees, the US expressed willingness to discuss trusteeship governance with other

Korean factions, but the Soviets took the American advice about as well as MacArthur in Tokyo was taking Soviet advice.[1]

During 1946, the communist-dominated Interim People's Committee nationalised industries owned by Japanese or their collaborators (Seth). That is, those industrial facilities which had not been packed up by the Red Army and sent to the Soviet Union (Buruma 2013). The People's Committee also conducted land ownership reform, and widened workers' and women's rights (Seth).

In accordance with the Great Powers' stated goal that Korea would have its own independent government 'in due course', the Soviet occupation authority went ahead and set up national elections for a People's Assembly. Although the other powers had not been consulted, they could hardly object to the concept of Korean elections. By February 1947, Kim Il-sung was at the head of the Korean Workers Party, which dominated the Korean National Democratic Front. In the election, the Front won the overwhelming majority of the seats in the new People's Assembly (Seth). The US expressed some concern that the way the election had been conducted was not free and fair. In those times, such concerns were essentially formulaic, requiring only filling in the name of the specific country (Poland, Bulgaria, Romania, etc.). The Soviets and the newly elected Kim Il-sung ignored the complaint.

Compared to the problems of dealing with communists in North Japan and in China, and the more worrisome problems in Eastern Europe, the US saw the emerging communist domination of Korea as a relatively minor problem without inherent strategic significance for the US. Therefore, when Kim Il-sung in Seoul declared the establishment of the Democratic People's Republic of Korea (DPRK) in April 1947, and the USSR declared the trusteeship to be ended, the US noted its objections, but little more.[2] America hardly wanted to appear to be opposing the establishment of Korea as a free and independent nation, although they knew full well that the DPRK was neither, nor likely to be any time soon. A Treaty of Friendship called for the Red Army to pull out of Korea the next year, but there would remain Soviet military 'advisors' – several divisions' worth. A major naval base at the ice-free port of Pusan would also remain in Soviet hands, providing yet more advice.

For hundreds of years before the mid-nineteenth century Korea was quite closed off to the outside world, earning the moniker The Hermit

---

1. See 'What Really Happened' (1946–8).
2. See 'What Really Happened' (Oct 1948).

Kingdom (Strand 2004). Given that its opening up in the latter 1800s had resulted in occupation by the odious Japanese, it was not surprising to see the modern Korea once again withdrawing into hermitage.

In the early years of the DPRK, economic conditions were good. Initially, the 30 million people of the Korean peninsula were able to feed themselves, largely drawing on the agricultural south. Despite Japan's brutal treatment of the Korean people, there had been a good deal of industrialisation, and hydropower and transportation improvements. True, the Red Army then looted Japanese-owned facilities in Korea, but this 'liberation tax' left enough behind to sustain reasonable economic output. This was especially true in regard to the mining sector, which produced iron, tungsten, silver, zinc, copper, manganese, molybdenum, lead and uranium (Matray; Seth), largely from the mountainous north. The USSR was a ready and almost sole customer for much of this material. Moreover, the USSR initially assisted Korea in further development of hydroelectric power, ports and heavy industry (Seth).

The USSR may also have helped show Kim Il-sung how to deal with opposition. The long history of Korea is punctuated by periods of fractionating – often there have been multiple states co-existing on the Korean Peninsula, but seldom peacefully for long (D. Kim). The fractious habit persisted into the modern era: the Shanghai-based Korean Provisional Government that existed from 1919 to 1945 was a fusion of several separate provisional government groups, but it latter fissioned as its members once again decided to go their separate ways (Park 2009). There is no reason to believe that Korean sociopolitical DNA changed in 1945. Kim Il-sung, the long-time expatriate brought back to Korea by his Soviet mentors did have opponents, for a while. There was Kim Kyu-sik, for example, a leader in the Provisional Government. Despite being an ardent nationalist, he was far too centrist to be long tolerated. The details are unknown, but it is believed he died in the early years of the DPRK by order of Kim Il-sung (Nahm and Hoare). As mentioned above, Cho Man-sik and Pak Hon-yong were Korean leaders pushed out of their positions by the Soviets to make room for Kim Il-sung. Not much later, they were dead (Lankov 2002 and 2013). One potential opponent Kim never laid hands on was Syngman Rhee. A former member of the Korean Provisional Government, Rhee had spent much of his life in the United States where he lobbied frequently and sometimes stridently before and during the Second World War for Korea's liberation (Allen). He continued that role after the war, calling for his seldom-seen native country to be freed from the grasp of communism. The US State Department was weary of hearing from him, calling him 'acerbic', 'prickly' and a 'dangerous mischief maker' (Hastings 1988). Rhee had a PhD from Princeton in political science (Oliver 1954), so he was able to make a living as an educator, which led him to found a school focused on East Asian studies. But his autocratic tendencies did not work well for him in trying to build a new academy and it folded amid a corruption scandal. Rhee lived his final years in relative obscurity as a minister in a Korean Methodist church in the Korean American community in Annandale VA, 8 miles from Washington DC.[3]

With his mineral resources, Kim bought weapons and technical help from the Russians, building up a formidable military. His own intense nationalism reflected that of his fellow Koreans, to whom he promised that Korea would never again be under foreign domination. (The relationship with the domineering Soviets was of course one of socialist fraternity.) His treaty with Stalin attempted to keep the Russians friendly, but largely out of Korea (except for the naval base Stalin demanded at Pusan). Kim was primarily concerned with protection against an eventually resurgent Japan, which he foresaw as developing historically quickly, i.e. within 60–70 years. As the Cold War developed, Kim also told his compatriots about the threat American imperialism posed to Korea. By 1950, there were 300,000 Koreans under arms (Seth). That number grew several-fold in the next decade, even as Kim focused increased attention on the internal threat of dissent. As the Korean armed forces continued to swell into the millions, the military budget seriously sapped the economy.[4] Suppressing unrest with the help of many tens of thousands of police, Kim demonstrated how much he loved and cared for all Koreans and showed them how foolish it would be to doubt his benevolence.

One of the many ways he demonstrated his compassion was by collectivising the entire agricultural sector. Poor farmers who just a few years previous had struggled as tenants of big landlords now found themselves privileged to struggle for the biggest landlord of all, the State itself. Agricultural production shrank immediately and drastically.

Internally, Kim endlessly emphasised 'juche', approximately translated as 'self-reliance' (French 2007). It was the duty of Korea, guided by Kim, to take responsibility for its own destiny. Externally, as his centrally-planned and mismanaged economy faltered, he accepted more and more non-juche aid from his big neighbours. The USSR had helped

---

3. See 'What Really Happened' (26 Apr 1960).
4. See 'What Really Happened' (1950–2020).

liberate his country, while China had longer and deeper cultural and historic ties with the peninsula. Kim, who'd lived in China and in the USSR and spoke both Chinese and Russian (some said better than he spoke Korean), played his increasingly competitive benefactors against one another even as his rhetoric, for internal consumption, became more xenophobic (Oberdorfer).

As Cold War events unfolded in the years that followed, Kim came to view the Soviet Union as being weak in the confrontation with America, and therefore not a reliable source of support (Seth). Moscow obliged by cutting back on aid to Seoul. China remained a benefactor, but became less generous. The People's Republic of China recognised that Korea was not realistically threatened by anyone, despite Kim's increasingly strident rhetoric and increasing military expenditures. Requests from Kim to both Russia and China for help in developing nuclear weapons were rebuffed (J. Lee), especially after Kim provoked tensions with both Japans over maritime navigation and fishing rights. By the 1970s heavily-armed Korea's GDP was on a par with that of Bulgaria. It was able to feed and sustain itself, but just barely, and was almost universally ignored. Recent reports of a Korean nuclear weapons development effort are not credible.[5]

---

5. See 'What Really Happened' (1985–2006).

Chapter 23

China

The unexpected extent of the Soviet Army's August 1945 success against the Japanese in China was a major reason that Mao Zedong and the Chinese Communists came to power less than two years later. In turn, Mao's prompt success had major effects on the situation to his south in Indochina.

The Soviets swept through all of Manchuria and well into northern China, particularly into the highly important Beijing-Tianjin corridor. Stalin had promised Chiang Kai-shek that he would recognise Chiang's Nationalist government, but he did not oppose the Communists' People's Liberation Army (PLA) when they aided the Soviets against the Japanese in the final days of the war (Hsu 1995). So the Soviets captured Beijing, and the PLA Tianjin, while Chiang's Guomindang (GMD) Nationalist armies were no closer than 500 miles to the south (Map 8)

The PLA also positioned units around Nanjing and Shanghai to the south, so that they were able to take possession of those major cities without bloodshed when the Japanese surrendered. They also acquired major stores of Japanese weapons from those garrisons.

After the shooting stopped, Chiang sought US help to move his troops from their safe refuges in the south, up north, so they could take possession of the valuable lands and cities the Soviets had cleared of Japanese (Bernstein). The US attempted some airlifts and sealifts, but at every air and seaport, Soviet or PLA commanders denied them permission to land. Railways too were blocked (Yates). After seven months, the Soviets pulled out of the parts of China they had taken, leaving Mao's communist forces to take control in their wake (R. Bernstein). Thus in spring 1946, the Soviets also left behind mountains of weapons and materiel they had captured from the nearly 1.5 million Japanese, Menjiang and other puppet regime troops in Manchuria, North China and Korea. In Manchuria alone the Soviets unofficially transferred to the Communist PLA 925 planes, 360 tanks, 2,700 artillery pieces, 138,000 machine guns,

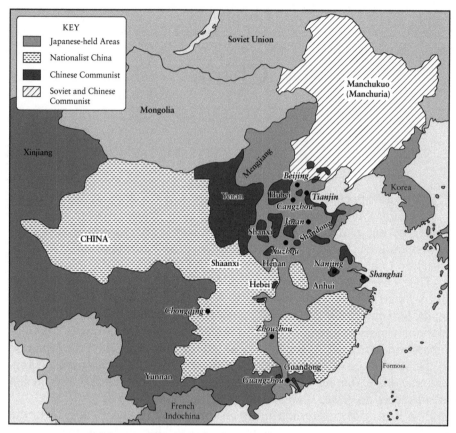

Map 8: China at the End of the Pacific War

and 300,000 rifles from surrendered Japanese units (House). Thousands of Japanese and Manchukuo POWs, with their expertise in use of these items, had also been induced to join the PLA (Gillen and Etter).

With a large and valuable base area to the north, a stronghold in the Shanghai-Nanjing area, and armament comparable to that of the GMD, the Communists abandoned the guerrilla warfare of former years, and went on the offensive with major field armies in mid-1946. Now, each side had several million troops (Lynch). Over the next 18 months, battles such as the Huaihai campaign were some of the largest in history as to troop numbers and geographic extent (Westad). The internally factious and corrupt GMD (Spence) scored only a few successes, and fewer after President Truman cut off further aid, not wishing to pour good money after bad (Lynch). The trend was clear. The Communists pushed Chiang

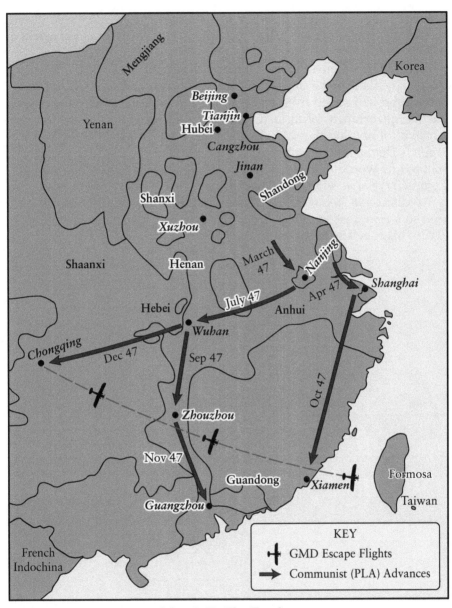

Map 9: To The Exodus

Kai-shek out of Central and Eastern China, chasing him into the southern interior to Chongqin, the wartime capital the Japanese had never reached (Map 9).

From there, Generalissimo Chiang Kai-shek and GMD loyalists escaped by plane to the island of Formosa (Taiwan), where they, and some troops who had sailed from south China ports, declared that theirs was still the government of all of China. Leaving resolution of the Taiwan problem for another day, Mao Zedong declared the establishment of the People's Democratic Republic of China in December 1947. He had never doubted he would be victorious, but he and his colleagues had thought it would take at least 5 years (Westad).[1]

As discussed below, the PLA's swiftly-moving tide of victory had been so strong that Mao had been able to render assistance even during 1947 to his comrade to the south, Ho Chi Minh.

---

1. See 'What Really Happened' (Aug 1945–Oct 1949).

Chapter 24

Revisiting Stalin's Far Eastern Actions

Stalin's actions at the end of the Pacific War were critical to the 1947 victory of the Chinese Communists over the Nationalists.[1] In August 1945 he had signed an agreement with Chiang Kai-shek to respect Chiang's legitimacy. Why then did Stalin renege a few weeks later? Preventing the transport of Nationalist armies into Manchuria and north China certainly seems contrary to Stalin's recognition of the GMD as China's legitimate government. But as President Truman well knew, the Soviet Union reneging on agreements, or squeezing very different interpretations out of them, was becoming the norm. For example, deals reached at Yalta about governance in Eastern Europe became a source of friction even before the war ended. In the Pacific theatre, Stalin had ignored his commitment to have a deal in place with Chiang Kai-shek before the Red Army invaded Manchuria. As a result of their Manchurian offensive, the Red Army sent more than 600,000 Japanese POWs to Siberia, where they held them long after the war. This imprisonment was contrary to the Potsdam Declaration's commitment that Japanese military personnel would be allowed to return home. Even the one time Stalin kept his commitment exactly (entering the war against Japan three months after VE Day) seemed deceptive because of differing dates the Russians had proffered to Truman, Marshall and others. In short, it was not unusual for Stalin to say one thing and do another.

Still, there were several specific factors that may have led Stalin to keep the troops of his 'ally' Chiang out of Manchuria and northern China. The Red Army had hauled forty divisions of troops and equipment from Europe to the Far East. Then they fought the Japanese for a month

---

1. See 'What Really Happened' (1 Oct 1949).

through 'impassable' mountains, deserts and swamps and sometimes in drenching monsoons. As a result, the Soviets could maintain that their stunningly rapid defeat of the Kwantung and much of the China Expeditionary Armies of the Japanese had precipitated the end of the war. Yet the three million or so Nationalist troops had spent much of the war, and all of that crucial final month of it, comfortably in their south China bases. The GMD did not launch a general offensive in concert with their Soviet ally to help free their own motherland. The Communist PLA had done so. It seemed to many senior Russians that the Nationalists were content to let Russian and Chinese Communists die clearing out the Japanese, so Chiang's well-fed and well-rested boys could come in after the shooting stopped. Stalin noted that after he learned about the PLA in action against the Japanese, he was more impressed with their abilities than he had previously been. So the attitude from Moscow may have been along the lines of 'When we leave, you guys can sort it out, but we're not going to help a bunch of bystanders against our comrades in arms'.

At least in their own telling, the Russians had played a key role in China, Korea and Japan in ending the war. It is not surprising then that they pushed back at US attempts to help Chiang Kai-shek adjust the chess pieces on the board before the Chinese contest resumed. There may have been a few more factors, too. Stalin was irritated at the pushback he was getting from the US and UK on those Eastern European issues (Spector). Also, the US had not invited the USSR to attend truce talks between Mao Zedong and Chiang Kai-shek immediately after the war. It would have been logical to include the Soviets, given their relationships with both the CCP and the GMD, and their presence in a major portion of China. But US Ambassador to China Patrick Hurley was a fervent anti-communist and there is no record that he even considered inviting the Russians to the talks he put together in Chongqin right after the Japanese surrender.

How different could things have been? If Stalin had not stymied Chiang and if the GMD had been able to relocate hundreds of thousands of soldiers into Manchuria, Beijing and elsewhere, and if the PLA had not beaten Chiang to Tianjin, Nanjing and Shanghai, then the resumed Chinese civil war might have evolved differently. Admittedly, saying that 'if two armies had started from different positions, the war would have been different' is about as profound as saying, 'If Mary had gotten more votes than Charlie she would have won the election'. But in this case, even if the US had inserted 500,000 or so GMD troops into various North China and Manchurian locations, it is unlikely that this would

158

have done more than delay Mao's victory by a year or two. One can imagine, for example, a couple of years of intermittent or back-and-forth fighting between the PLA and GMD for control of Manchurian cities such as Shenyang and Changchun. Coastal Shandong and adjacent provinces such as Shanxi and Henan could also have seen a military tug of war for a few years. Perhaps Beijing and Shanghai could have been held by the Nationalists for several years.

But the Communists very likely would have prevailed even if they had not kept the initial geographic advantage they had at the end of the war with Japan. The land reform of the Communists in rural areas and their increasingly effective organisation of workers in the cities won more and more support over time. Meanwhile, the corruption, economic mismanagement and stifling of dissent by the GMD government lost the Nationalists support among the masses (Westad). Significantly worsening the economic conditions for Chinese citizens under the Nationalists was the disproportionate expenditure on the military. Observers like George Marshall could see clearly that the situation was not long sustainable, and told Chiang and other Nationalists that. But they did not believe it, until they were holed up in Taiwan (Shaw).

So on the reasonable assumption that the US would not itself have undertaken a large armed intervention on behalf of the Nationalists, it is a good bet that Mao Zedong would have prevailed anyway, proclaiming the People's Republic somewhat later. In 1946 Mao himself had been comfortable predicting that it would take until 1955 for his forces to prevail; some of his colleagues thought it would be 1965 (Hooten).

Chapter 25

The United States, 1948

The end of the US occupation of Japan in 1948 was the logical transition point for Douglas MacArthur.[1] In announcing his retirement in February from a long career of service in uniform, he said he was eager to begin the next phase of his life, whatever that might prove to be.

President Truman accepted MacArthur's resignation with a terse statement of gratitude for the general's many years of military service. Actually, Truman would have preferred that MacArthur stay just where he was, in Tokyo, as far away from the Republican Presidential primaries as possible. 'I should have fired the sonofabitch when I had the chance,' he recorded in his diary. Truman had concerns about running against either of two five-star Army generals (Truman and Ferrell 1980). In 1948, Dwight Eisenhower was genuinely not interested, but MacArthur was. Mac came home to a hero's welcome in March, which surely contributed to his beating Thomas Dewey and Harold Stassen in the Wisconsin Republican primary in early April. That, and the fact that Mac was himself from Wisconsin. In addition to letting everyone know how he had almost single-handedly won the war against Japan, MacArthur also pontificated about how the Truman White House had lost China to the Communists. In just two years after the defeat of Japan, inept US policy enabled Mao Zedong's ragtag troops to usurp the internationally recognised government of Chiang Kai-shek, and consign hundreds of millions of Chinese to life under Godless communism. This would not have happened if American policy reflected a sufficient understanding of the Oriental world, said the five-star Oriental expert.

However, by the time of the New Jersey and Pennsylvania contests later that month, the inability of Supreme Commander and Shogun

---

1. See 'What Really Happened' (Apr 1951).

MacArthur to transform himself into Candidate MacArthur was becoming obvious. No longer able to control the press as his military staff had long done for him, MacArthur was ill at ease with big-city political reporters asking 'impertinent' and unscripted questions about economics and social welfare issues. It was in Pennsylvania's capital city, Harrisburg, where the old soldier shot himself in the foot. After a speech, a reporter asked MacArthur about his role in violently destroying the 'Bonus Army' camp during the Depression. This was an encampment of 40,000 First World War veterans and their families who had massed in Washington DC in 1932. Because of the Depression, they were seeking to obtain immediately the veterans' compensation Congress had promised would be paid to them in 1945 (James). MacArthur had led troops into the encampment with fixed bayonets and firing tear-gas canisters. The troops, supported by cavalry and battle tanks made a violent sweep through the camp. At least one infant died and dozens of veterans were injured in the melee (Leary).

'What do you say', the reporter asked the General, 'to those who maintain that you grossly exceeded Secretary Hurley's orders in dispersing the Bonus Army?' The indirect phrasing of the question suggested that the reporter was not necessarily looking to criticise the General, but might have welcomed the kind of 'turn it around' answer a seasoned politician would have had at the ready. But instead of taking the opportunity to cast himself as a dutiful soldier obeying civilian orders, the Imperial MacArthur let loose with 'that was a bunch of disorderly slackers and Communist sympathisers; anyone with any sense would have kept their families out of harm's way. Of course, I did everything I could to ensure safety, but the only troops placed at my disposal were green and clearly insufficiently trained for such situations.'

He was oblivious to this self-inflicted wound. He had spent decades essentially saying whatever he wanted and then letting lower-ranked officers deflect the pushback. He had come to believe that any pronouncements he made were just shy of divine revelation and that all sentient beings should accept them as such. The idea that it would be offensive to call veterans who had helped win the First World War 'disorderly slackers' who lacked 'any sense' apparently never occurred to him. Nor did it occur to him that trying to protect his spotlessness by blaming his troops for his leadership failure would not be widely applauded. (Unlike some public figures of the modern era who live on a fact-free diet, regularly spouting things they clearly know are untrue, but not caring a whit, MacArthur seemingly believed that what he said was indeed the Truth, because He would not have said it if it weren't.

In contrast to some more recent characters, Mac truly was supremely confident in his superiority.)

By the time MacArthur next spoke to the press two days later in Trenton NJ, the pack had smelled blood in the water: 'People have said that you were negligent right after Pearl Harbor' began the reporter,

> You knew about the Japs' sneak attack for eight hours before they also attacked the Philippines, but you, as senior military commander in the Philippines took no steps to protect your planes at Clark Field. Critics say your negligence let the Japs destroy most of your air force on the ground. Is this the kind of leadership you are offering the American people?'

MacArthur may never have had his infallibility as a military leader called into question like this, and certainly never by a mere civilian, just a reporter at that. Those who witnessed the exchange say that the 6ft-tall MacArthur attempted to assert his superior rank by looking as far down at the reporter as he could. Ralph Hayes, the 6ft 3in reporter with a linebacker's build, had himself been a GI in the 27th Infantry Division, with the extremely hazardous job of manning a flamethrower on Saipan, Tinian and Okinawa. He was not remotely intimidated by the general whom many soldiers called 'Dugout Doug', referring to the months MacArthur spent safely ensconced deep in a tunnel on Corregidor while his troops fought off the Japanese. Hayes calmly stared right back at His Imperiousness. The general then violated again the first rule of leadership ('a commander is responsible for all his unit does or fails to do'): he blamed his subordinates (Generals Brereton and Sutherland): 'Those under me failed to keep me properly informed of the situation and of their preparations,' he said.

Difficult to believe as it may be today, there was a time when politicians suffered consequences if they insulted segments of the citizenry, or if they tried to escape criticism by consistently blaming someone else. As quickly as it had arisen, the MacArthur boomlet petered out. Long before the mere forty-two convention delegates pledged to him cast their votes at the Republican National Convention Douglas MacArthur had accepted a directorship at Remington Rand. From this post he reminisced about past glories, and opined about current and potential future military and foreign policy issues, upon all of which he recognised himself as an expert. A relieved Truman recorded in his diary, 'And so the old soldier fades away.'

As it turned out, the 1948 Presidential campaign paid little attention to China at all. Republican nominee Thomas Dewey, along with most pundits, believed that Truman did not stand a chance of winning after the Democratic Party split into three factions, with the breakaway Dixiecrats and Progressives each nominating their own candidate. So Dewey campaigned on platitudes, seeking to win just by not making a mistake. Truman campaigned vigorously, but with the primary focus on domestic issues such as the evident recovery from the 1947 recession, and the shortcomings of the Republican-controlled 'do-nothing' Congress. On the rare occasions when foreign policy came up, Truman could point proudly to his Truman Doctrine of providing aid to countries such as Greece and Turkey to help them resist Soviet expansionism. He could also point to the Berlin Airlift whereby the US and the UK were overcoming (literally) an attempted Soviet blockade of West Berlin. Truman's interest, and that of most of his listeners, was primarily in Europe, but when asked about China he noted that the US had provided, from 1941 to 1947, far more financial and material aid to the Chinese Nationalists than to any other government fighting communism. The translation of course was: 'Chiang and his cronies blew it, but not for lack of American aid.' When the related topic of Indochina came up, Truman was happy to point out that America was providing military aid to the Bao Dai government of Vietnam to aid them in fighting the Viet Minh communist insurgency. As discussed later, this anti-communist assistance also supported France's efforts to retain some control over its Indochina colonies, but Truman glossed over that aspect. China was not an issue of any importance in the 1948 election of Truman. It played a much greater role in Truman's presidency after that.

PART III:
PACIFIC WAR AFTERMATH –
SOUTHEAST ASIA

Chapter 26

Vietnam, 1945–1946

For those who consume history in twenty-five words or less (e.g. 'Feeling oppressed in 1776, thirteen American colonies broke from England to fulfil their manifest destiny as a Great Power'), the decades-long, multi-sided Chinese war, with Communists, Nationalists, warlords, bandits and Japanese all fighting one another, is hard to comprehend. So are the millennia of turmoil in Southeast Asia, with the rising and falling of regional empires. It is far easier to just identify good guys and help them. But it wasn't that simple in Indochina.

The Vietnamese people, based in the Red River Delta to the south of China, have been repeatedly invaded by their Chinese neighbours; in one case, the Chinese stayed for a thousand years. In turn, over the centuries the Vietnamese were themselves frequently an expansive power, pushing south and encroaching on their neighbours in Southeast Asia. So were the Thais to the west. In between were the Laotian and Cambodian peoples, who also had expansive periods like the Khmer Empire that left behind the ruins of Angkor Wat. But more often the Lao and Cambodian peoples had been battered and squeezed by their more powerful neighbours to either side (Karnow). The Vietnamese, ethnically related to the Chinese, and the Lao and Cambodians related to Indians, all clashed with the region's mosaic of original inhabitants such as the Muong, Tai and many others, who met the same fate as aboriginal peoples worldwide – the survivors were marginalised. Thus when the French began their exploitation in the 1800s, they called most of these diverse indigenous people 'Montagnards', referring to the mountainous lands to which many had been relegated by the dominant cultures over the centuries.

Even within the modern territory of the two Vietnamese states (nearly a thousand miles from north to south, with a combined area a bit greater than New Mexico, or of Great Britain plus Ireland) there were important ethnic, cultural and political differences between the two national poles, the Red River valley of the north, and the Mekong River in the south. The Chinese who began farming in the Red River Delta 5,000 years ago established a strong culture of communally maintaining the flood-and-drought prone water system. This area has long been very densely populated (Hammer).

Eight hundred or so miles to the south (equivalent to the distance from Portland Oregon to Los Angeles California, or London to Rome), the climate is warmer and wetter, and rice growing is easier. The Mekong River is less flood-prone and its delta is capable of producing much more rice per acre. Relatively recently, in the 1700s, Vietnamese from the north wrested control of this area from the Khmer (Cambodian) residents. The Mekong delta's population still includes a minority of Khmers and others whose ancestry is closer to India and Indonesia than to China. The traditional culture in the south was more influenced by Hindu and Buddhist thought than Confucian, and with less need for communal work to manage their highly productive farms. The population density was perhaps a tenth of that in the north, and there was often enough rice for export (Filippelli).

During the latter half of the nineteenth century, France took control of the lands of the Vietnamese, which at that point comprised three entities – Tonkin in the north around the Red River and its delta, largely mountainous Annam in the middle, and Cochin China based on the Mekong and its delta in the south. The three entities were ruled by an Emperor centrally based in Hue, but that centralised control was a recent (1802) development. The Vietnamese states had frequently been at odds with one another (Hammer). While allowing the Vietnamese Emperor to retain his throne, the French made Tonkin and Annam 'protectorates', and designated Cochin China as a colony. By the late 1800s, France also came to control the Kingdom of Cambodia plus the three regions that then constituted Laos. All these lands became French Indochina (Map 10).

Thirty per cent larger than France in area, and with 23 million people compared to France's 40 million, Indochina was the richest and most important of France's possessions. Indochina before the Second World War was the world's third largest rice exporter, with important exports also of rubber and timber. Its mountains (mostly those in the north adjacent to China) also had iron, tin, manganese, zinc, tungsten and phosphate (Hammer).

It also had a key location. During the later 1930s, Vietnam's ports and its roads into southern China had served as a supply line for war materials to help the Chinese in their war with the Japanese. When France fell to the Germans in 1940, the Japanese (allied to Germany) pressured

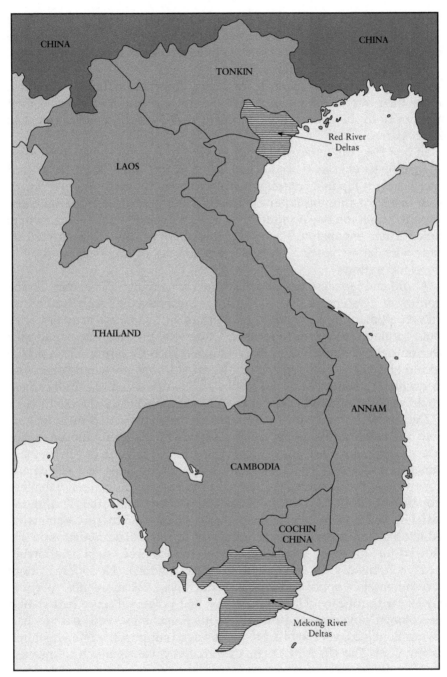

Map 10: French Indochina

the Vichy government of defeated France to stop allowing resupply of China through Vietnam. Vichy agreed, but in September 1940 the Japanese moved some troops into Indochina 'to monitor the situation' (i.e the French agreement to cut off supplies to China).

The Japanese let the French colonial authorities continue governing, under their overall supervision. The Europeans who had asserted their superiority to the Indochinese people were now seen as subservient to other Asians.

In late 1941 the Japanese began moving more troops into Indochina, ostensibly to ensure that the Chinese did not cross the border and interfere with Japan's commandeering rice, rubber and other resources from there. Positioning Japanese troops in Vietnam, and Imperial Navy ships at Cam Ranh Bay on southern Vietnam's coast, would also facilitate their further expansion. Protesting these moves, the US restricted its trade with Japan, cutting off important sources of iron, steel and oil to the island nation.

Additional Japanese troops arrived in Vietnam on 6 December. On the morning of 7 December 1941, the Japanese presented the French authorities with an ultimatum. If they did not interfere with Japanese activities, they could continue to govern Indochina. Otherwise, the Japanese would take over outright. By agreeing to these terms, French Governor General Jean Decoux knew he was freeing up many Japanese troops who would otherwise be needed to control Indochina. But he also believed the Indochinese would be better off staying under at least ostensible French governance.

Decoux was correct in that Japanese forces not needed in Indochina were therefore available for action elsewhere. It began the next day, 8 December, as Japanese forces deploying from Cam Ranh Bay in Vietnam launched attacks on Thailand, Malaya, the Philippines and elsewhere. Nonetheless the Japanese kept 35,000 troops in Indochina. Japanese propaganda about Asia for the Asians began soon thereafter. During the next few years, Admiral Decoux sought to counter that by somewhat reducing the repressive aspects of the French colonial administration. He allowed for improved education for the Indochinese (such as allowing their own history to be taught in their schools). He offered more government job opportunities for Indochinese, at more nearly equal pay as for Europeans. Unlike other colonial powers, France had staffed the colonial government primarily with Frenchmen. Few natives had government jobs, yet they had to pay taxes to support the French-staffed government. The effect of Decoux's initiatives was as much to increase the Vietnamese thirst for independence as to foster their good feelings toward the French (Hammer).

By March 1945, France was liberated and the Vichy government had disappeared. The Japanese could no longer count on the cooperation of the Vichy-aligned Decoux administration. Some French officials were beginning to openly align themselves with de Gaulle's Free French movement, the enemy of the Axis (Marr). French attitudes were likely to become even more resistant as British and American armies approached from the west through Burma and the east from the Philippines. In a swift move on 9 March, the Japanese removed the uncertainty about continued French cooperation. They deposed the French colonial authorities, imprisoning them along with all of the French and Indochinese colonial troops. Indochina was no longer even ostensibly under French governance, a fact not lost on the Indochinese peoples.

Within days of this Japanese coup, Emperor Bao Dai, whom the French had allowed to continue in a largely ceremonial office, declared the protectorates of Tonkin and Annam to be independent from France. The kings of neighbouring Cambodia and Laos did likewise (Hammer). Under the circumstances, these declarations had no practical effect.

Later that year, a few days after the Japanese surrender, a handful of French officials parachuted into Vietnam, some near Hanoi, some near Saigon. They included the newly-appointed Commissioners for Northern and for Southern Indochina. None were welcomed by the Vietnamese. Some were turned over to the Japanese (who were defeated globally but still effectively in power locally). Only a few of these Frenchmen survived their reception; none had any effect in restoring the presence of French colonial government (Hammer).

The communist-dominated League for the Independence of Vietnam, also known as the Viet Minh, had worked throughout the war against imperialism, both French and Japanese. During the war, Viet Minh guerrilla actions had limited success, mostly in Tonkin in the north. But in August-September 1945 as Japanese rule crumbled, the Viet Minh leader Ho Chi Minh took immediate advantage of the absence of the French colonial government. From Tonkin's major city Hanoi, he declared the independence of the Democratic People's Republic of Vietnam (Karnow). By proclaiming that this new state included all three Vietnamese regions (Tonkin, Annam and Cochin China) he was seeking to harness Vietnamese nationalism to counter the regional divisions the French colonial administration had emphasised (Hammer). In lifting some language from America's Declaration of Independence, Ho sought to gain US support for his nationalism. But the declaration went virtually unrecognised by the Viet Minh's political opponents, which included numerous anti-French, non-communist nationalist groups. In the north, the Viet Minh faced opposition from the Chinese-backed Dong Minh Hoi coalition, and the Vietnamese Nationalist Party (VNQDD), aligned with Chiang Kai-shek's Guomindang (Harrison). There was even armed opposition from militias affiliated with two Catholic bishops in Tonkin.

Ho Chi Minh's Viet Minh had even less influence in the south than in the north. In Cochin China, they were opposed by the non-communist United National Front, which had been involved in violent anti-French demonstrations in the south at the same time Ho Chi Minh was declaring his independent republic from Hanoi (Hammer). The Viet Minh in the south had opposition also from the Cao Dai, a politico-religious sect based in Tay Ninh near the Cambodian border. The Viet Minh had propagandised against the Cao Dai as being Japanese collaborators. The Cao Dai militia numbered perhaps 10,000, with weaponry in part provided by the surrendering Japanese, and they clashed with Viet Minh units in the Cochin China countryside. In the weeks after the Japanese surrender announcement, the Viet Minh in Cochin China disarmed some of their nationalist rivals, but fought inconclusively against the Cao Dai militia and the troops of another sect, the Hoa Hao.

Ho Chi Minh's Declaration of Independence was essentially ignored also by the outside forces that were moving into Indochina to take the official surrender of the Japanese. This despite Ho Chi Minh persuading Emperor Bao Dai to abdicate in favour of his govern-ment (Hammer). The former Emperor would become an advisor to the new government.

Under the terms of the Potsdam Declaration, Japanese forces in southern Indochina (below the 16th Parallel) were to surrender to the British, who'd borne the brunt of the fighting in Southeast Asia. So British troops, and a few French, arrived in Saigon in Cochin China a few weeks after the Japanese Emperor's surrender. The British took the surrender of the Japanese there. The fact that the French presence was negligible was not lost on the Vietnamese. Ho Chi Minh believed that if his forces could demonstrate their control throughout Vietnam, the British would recognise his new government and thereby keep the French out. However, the British re-armed the French soldiers who'd been imprisoned by the Japanese and for several weeks there were bloody clashes between the Viet Minh and British (mostly British Colonial) and French troops for control of Saigon (Gettleman). A few weeks behind the British, fresh French troops arrived. Through the end of the year and into January 1946, the British and French, sometimes also using Japanese troops, fought scattered engagements with the Viet Minh, gradually pushing them out of the area of Saigon and other major cities (Rosie).

172

For northern Vietnam, above the 16th Parallel, the Potsdam Declaration had demonstrated more concern for logistical expediency than for the region's deep history of enmity for the Chinese. It called for the Japanese forces in Tonkin and northern Annam to surrender to the Nationalist Chinese. Accordingly, in September 1945, 200,000 of Chiang Kai-shek's GMD troops moved south from neighbouring Yunnan Province into Tonkin to disarm the Japanese (Karnow). This did not represent an obvious improvement for the Vietnamese quality of life. The Chinese troops acted as much like occupiers as liberators, abusing civilians throughout Tonkin. They also busied themselves dismantling Vietnamese fortifications along the border with China (Hammer). Nor would they allow the return of the several thousand French troops who had escaped the Japanese coup by fleeing into China.

Still hoping for international recognition, in October Ho Chi Minh had promised nationwide elections in December, later postponed to January 1946. He also wooed the rival nationalist groups the Dong Minh Hoi and VNQDD, telling them they would be assured seats in the planned National Assembly. But setting up an independent democracy was clearly impossible as long as the French were violently 'mopping up' resistance in the south, and the Chinese were treating the people of the north about as well as they had treated them in past centuries of domination. The Japanese had dominated Vietnam for five years; the French for about a hundred. But the last time the Chinese entered Vietnam they had stayed for a thousand years (Miller and Wainstock). Moreover, since getting rid of the Chinese in 938, the Vietnamese had repelled repeated invasion attempts from their northern neighbour (Cima). Given this long history, the Viet Minh leader Ho Chi Minh was understandably eager to get Chiang Kai-shek's troops out as fast as possible, especially because of their current brutish behaviour toward the Vietnamese (Karnow).

If he could not rid all of his country of all foreigners right away, at least he could get the Chinese out, even if that meant dealing with the French. So in early 1946 he made a deal with the French whereby the Nationalist Chinese troops would leave northern Vietnam by the end of March 1946, and 25,000 French and French colonial troops would enter Tonkin for five years (Karnow). France agreed to once again allow the Nationalist Chinese to use the northern port of Haiphong and the railway to the north (thus ensuring they would have a supply line for materiel to use in their war, this time against the Communist Chinese instead of the Japanese). France also agreed to recognise Tonkin as a 'free state' within the planned worldwide French Union (the replacement for the pre-war 'French Empire'). As to the south, Ho agreed that there should

173

be a referendum by the people of Cochin China on whether they should become part of Ho's Hanoi-based Democratic Republic. (The former entity, Annam, now being split between these northern and southern occupation zones.) Faced with argument on this deal from his colleagues, Ho is said to have retorted that he would rather sniff French excrement for five years than eat the Chinese kind for a thousand (Karnow).

Then the French, he might have said, handed him an extra whiff later that same year. In negotiations about what a 'free state within the French Union' meant, it became clear to the Viet Minh that the French wanted to retain essential control of the primary governmental functions through the appointment of French 'advisors' throughout the 'free' Vietnamese government. Although this would look a little different from the pre-war setup, it was substantially the same in Viet Minh eyes.

The French wanted to emphasise differences within Vietnam so that they could keep it as divided as possible, lest a Vietnam truly unified from the Red River to the Mekong pose a danger to its smaller Cambodian and Laotian neighbours. To that end, the French also proposed that several of the minority groups in Vietnam be granted their own autonomous state. The French wanted to maintain particular control in Cochin China, where French businesses had their most significant investments, like the extensive rubber plantations owned by Michelin east of Saigon (Hammer).

For their part, the Viet Minh wanted Cochin China to be an integral part of Vietnam not just for nationalistic but also for practical economic reasons. The southern part of Vietnam produced 40 per cent of all of Indochina's revenue, especially in rice and rubber. The rice exports were crucial to feeding the northern population, while the excess labour in the north could move to the south and help increase rice production. The north could also supply coal and other minerals (Hammer).

In June 1946, even while the 'free state' issue was being negotiated, the French recognised the Cochin China Republic, with a Provisional Government appointed by the French. It was claimed to be a free and independent entity (albeit with more than a few strings attached). The Tonkin-based Viet Minh took this as a repudiation of the French commitment to hold a referendum on Cochin China's potential unification with northern Vietnam (Hammer).

The events of mid-1946 reflected not so much the French government intentionally reversing itself as it did the government's speaking with several voices. This may be hard for some readers to imagine, but national governments sometimes do not act in a coordinated or consistent manner. Paris politics at the time were in post-war turmoil, with rapidly-changing Cabinets sending conflicting signals; moreover, the colonial authorities in the field did not always follow guidance from the capital, even when they knew what it was. A major theme of French actions was that reasserting at least some control of colonies such as Indochina was essential to restoring French national pride. Charles De Gaulle, out of government at the time but still influential, believed that retaining control of the possessions which France had 'opened to civilisation' was critical to France remaining a great power (Hammer). (This despite Vietnamese civilisation predating that of France by several millennia.) Adding to French sentiment to hold on to Indochina were rumblings elsewhere in its Empire. Morocco, Algeria, Tunisia and Madagascar had also become restive. In Algeria, for example, there had been a violent clash between police and supporters of independence at a parade celebrating the end of the World War (Horne). While many French leaders realised the end of the colonial era was at hand, and that France could not long remain as the colonial master of Indochina, they believed that it should be France who would magnanimously grant these backward peoples the boon of independence (Miller and Wainstock).

Even while the future status of Cochin China was unclear, by early summer 1946 French troops were arriving in Tonkin and the Chinese were leaving. The French faced armed opposition, now not from the communist Viet Minh but from some of the non-communist nationalist groups, the VNQDD and Dong Minh Hoi. Abiding by their agreement to allow the French troops in, the Viet Minh helped them disarm the dissidents, thus helping to cement the power of the Viet Minh. By September 1946, Ho Chi Minh and his top general Vo Nguyen Giap had 60,000 reasonably well-equipped troops and thousands more irregulars (Hammer). If they didn't welcome the returning French, at least at this point, they did not shoot at them, often.

The French asserted control of customs at the major port of Haiphong and the right to tax French properties in Tonkin. The Viet Minh protested that this violated the deal which Ho Chi Minh had made earlier that year. In November, the French seized a ship carrying supplies for the Viet Minh. In the port, Viet Minh troops fired on the French. The French retaliated massively against not just Vietnamese troops but also against civilians throughout the port area. Several thousand people died (Hammer).

The fighting continued to escalate, with additional French troops flowing into several northern ports, and the Viet Minh attacking everywhere they could with all they had. By mid-December 1946 there was full-scale fighting throughout Tonkin (Hammer). The French blamed the Viet Minh for starting the violence; the Viet Minh blamed the French for not honouring the accord they had reached earlier in the year. Ho Chi Minh now rejected the 'free state within the French Union' concept and called for complete independence for all of Vietnam. On this, the non-communist nationalist groups such as the VNQDD could agree, and now aligned themselves with the Viet Minh.

Ignoring the noise from the north, French High Commissioner Admiral Georges d'Argenlieu installed a new government for the Republic of Cochin China. These were appointees who favoured separation of Cochin China from the rest of Vietnam. D'Argenlieu declared martial law throughout the rest of Vietnam (Hammer).

Chapter 27

Vietnam and the French, 1947–1948

As 1947 began, much of the fighting was taking place in the north, around Hanoi and its nearby port Haiphong (Miller and Wainstock). The French held the cities, but the Viet Minh held their own in the countryside. The Viet Minh leadership had fled Hanoi and were operating out of northern Tonkin. Their troops had some weapons acquired from the Japanese after the surrender. Increasingly, the Viet Minh were also obtaining weapons from Chinese sources (Hammer).

In the south, Viet Minh control was limited even in the rural areas. They faced stiff opposition from the two indigenous religious sects, the Cao Dai and Hoa Hao, each of which had militias with 10,000–15,000 troops (partly armed courtesy of the surrendering Japanese). The Viet Minh had alienated these groups during the Japanese occupation by propagandising against them as collaborators (Hammer). Also in and around Saigon the 3,000 well-armed members of the Binh Xuyen criminal organisation limited Viet Minh presence (Miller and Wainstock).

Emile Bollaert replaced d'Argenlieu as High Commissioner and sent emissaries to negotiate with Ho Chi Minh, but the terms the French insisted on essentially amounted to a Viet Minh surrender. The French brought in more troops and fighting continued; by April 1947, the French had 115,000 troops in Vietnam. After a visit there, the French Minister of War stated 'the greater part of the country remains in the hands of the Viet Minh. I do not think we should undertake the conquest of Vietnam. It would require an expeditionary corps of 500,000 men' (Hammer).

The French were too strong to be defeated by the Viet Minh, but not strong enough to defeat them. They sought a non-military option, turning to the former Emperor, Bao Dai, who then lived in Hong Kong.

They thought he could rally diverse groups to support him, and that he would then be a compliant figurehead for continued French control. The French were right about the first premise, but wrong on the second. There were long negotiations throughout the rainy season in the north while the fighting slowed to a muddy crawl. But Bao Dai held out for true independence for all Vietnamese.

After the rains abated in October 1947, the French launched Operation Lea, a major campaign against Viet Minh base areas in the north, near the Chinese border (Davidson). The French hoped to bring an end to the war before Mao Zedong's imminent victory in China made increased Chinese assistance to the Viet Minh possible (Miller and Wainstock). Other external events also prompted the French commander, Jean Valluy, to seek a swift resolution: he was under pressure from Paris, where the greater priority was on rebuilding France itself. And in Madagascar a bloody Malagasay uprising for independence had begun to divert troops away from Indochina (Leymarie).

The French massed over 12,000 troops – airborne, infantry, armour, artillery, even amphibious assault troops. The plan called for an airborne drop on 7 October 1947 right onto Viet Minh HQ at Bac Kan, to be supported by ground forces approaching from the north-east after skirting the Chinese border on the road up from Hanoi. An amphibious force would attack from the south-west after advancing up the Red River. Had it come off as planned, it might have ended the war, especially if they had captured or killed Ho Chi Minh and the Viet Minh leadership, which they almost succeeded in doing. Alerted by agents, Ho and his colleagues escaped, but apparently just barely; the paratroopers found Ho's paperwork for that day still on his desk. The other attacking columns were delayed. By the time they arrived days later, many of the communist troops had successfully withdrawn (Finch). In the overall month-long operation, the French did kill or capture Viet Minh, and they did disrupt their supply lines to China, but while the campaign was a setback for the communists, it was nothing like a war-winning victory for the French (Logevall).

More than offsetting the Viet Minh losses in Operation Lea, however, was the assistance that Mao's People's Liberation Army (PLA) was already providing to them. Though the PLA was still engaged in its struggle with Chiang Kai-shek, the Communists had maintained some operational base areas in far south-west China near the Vietnam border since the time of the war with the Japanese. In 1947 Mao Zedong was already allowing Ho Chi Minh's troops to use these areas as sanctuaries from the French (Westad).

True, there had been centuries of enmity between China and Vietnam. Nevertheless several hundred Vietnamese communists, including Ho Chi Minh, Vo Nguyen Giap and Pham Van Dong, had fought for a time alongside their comrade Chinese Communists against the Japanese in China (Miller and Wainstock). With the Japanese imperialists gone, communist solidarity helped prompt Mao's assistance to the Viet Minh against the French imperialists.

Indeed, Chinese-Vietnamese interactions increased even as Mao's PLA was completing its victory over Chiang's Nationalists in late 1947.[1] In the last months of that civil war, as noted previously, 30,000 of Chiang Kai-shek's GMD troops fled from south-west China into Vietnam. Even though the French and the GMD were both fighting communist enemies, the French nevertheless disarmed and interned the GMD troops (Westad). To some extent, this may have been payback: in March 1945, several thousand French troops had fled from the Japanese coup in Vietnam into GMD-controlled China. The GMD had interned them, even though they were allies in fighting the Japanese (Fall). In turn, this action may have reflected Chiang's lingering annoyance with French behaviour in 1940. In an attempt to prevent the Japanese from fully occupying Indochina, the French had acceded to Japan's demand to stop allowing war material for Chiang's fight against the Japanese to land in Haiphong and pass through Tonkin into China (Hammer).

Now in 1947 the French internment of GMD troops may also have been largely a matter of staying out of someone else's fight. The French had no inclination to antagonise the soon-to-be victorious Chinese Communists. That was a wise course of action: in addition to the materiel aid and shelter he was already providing, Mao Zedong was seriously considering sending his PLA troops into Vietnam. If France had aided Mao's enemy by aiding and sheltering those Nationalist GMD troops, Mao could well have directed his troops to actively assist the Viet Minh against the French (Westad). Thus France avoided provoking greater Chinese Communist involvement in Indochina. Nevertheless, by taking 30,000 GMD troops out of action, the French helped the Chinese Communists, and enabled them to more readily assist the Viet Minh in their fight against the French. This was not the last time there was a no-win situation in Southeast Asia.

As Mao Zedong was chasing Chiang's Nationalists off the mainland and establishing the People's Republic of China in December 1947, France continued to press Bao Dai to lead a government of a united Vietnam that

1. See 'What Really Happened' (1 Oct 1949).

would be an alternative to the communist-led regime in Tonkin. Partly in light of the failure of Operation Lea to crush the Viet Minh, and the potential increase in Chinese Communist assistance to them, Bao Dai agreed to a deal in December 1947, reluctantly. He signed a compact in which France recognised him as the legitimate ruler of all Vietnam. His government was to have autonomy, but not complete independence. Bao Dai saw this as merely a first small step and continued for months seeking a pledge of full independence. Many French considered this limited autonomy as already granting too much, but the threat of major Chinese Communist assistance to the Viet Minh prompted Paris to seek to transform a colonial war into an effort to aid a freedom-loving government of an independent nation in fighting communist aggression (Karnow).

As Vietnamese Head of State, Bao Dai appointed General Nguyen Van Xuan to be Prime Minister. This government was still widely viewed as a puppet of the French, and Bao Dai and Nguyen Van Xuan had difficulty staffing it with well-qualified people willing to serve. The result was that the Xuan government was highly ineffective in executing its limited responsibilities. From its inception in early 1948 on, corruption further diminished public support, even while Ho Chi Minh's government in the north was demonstrating effectiveness in such critical internal matters as maintaining the dykes, diversifying agriculture to protect against failure of the rice crop, lowering rents and increasing industrial output (Hammer).

Because the Communist victory in China made holding Indochina more difficult, the French also sought US aid. French representatives emphasised their view that Indochina was not a colonial war, but a front in the emerging Cold War (Logevall). The French told the Americans that they could not hang on alone against communism in Indochina (Karnow). Between the lines, the French said they might have to withdraw and hand the whole problem to the US, much as Great Britain had done the previous year in regard to the communist insurgency in Greece.

This was not the first time the US had dealt with the issue of Indochina: the Japanese 'takeover' of French Indochina after the fall of France in 1940 had been the proximate cause for the US trade embargo against Japan. This embargo in turn was one of the actions that led to the Japanese attack on Pearl Harbor (Miller and Wainstock). In early 1945, America's sometimes contradictory thinking became manifest: the OSS (precursor to the CIA) had a small operation in Tonkin which sought to aid the Viet Minh in their fight against the Japanese (and their struggle for Vietnamese independence). But the State Department in the same timeframe sought to assist the French in Indochina, largely for the sake of restoring French prestige in Europe. By April 1945, after the Japanese had completely taken over Indochina from the Vichy French, FDR approved airdropping supplies to the French Resistance in Vietnam (Miller and Wainstock). In his last months, FDR seemed to be overcoming some of his anti-colonial predelictions in favour of assisting the restoration of France as a world power, and especially as an anchor of Western European defence. This mixed thinking about Indochina became an American habit for many years.

Thus in early 1948, Mao Zedong's December 1947 victory in China was changing the dynamics of the war in Indochina. As Bernard Fall, the French chronicler of the Indochina conflict wrote: 'The arrival of the Chinese Communists on the Vietnam border . . . doomed all chances of French victory' (Fall). The Viet Minh leader was among the first to recognise the People's Republic of China, and Mao's government promptly reciprocated. The USSR also recognised Ho Chi Minh's government. Although the Viet Minh had previously touted itself as primarily a nationalist movement, it was becoming clear to outside observers that it was first and foremost a communist one. Ho Chi Minh travelled to Beijing to congratulate Mao Zedong, and to ask for assistance in his struggle. Although Josef Stalin was titular head of world communism, his attention was more on European affairs, and he left Asian matters to Mao (Radchenko 2012). Stalin did, however, promise to resupply Mao with weapons and materiel to replace whatever Mao might provide to Ho Chi Minh (Logevall). With this assurance, the Chinese agreed to assist the Viet Minh. This was, as noted earlier, partly driven by communist solidarity. But it was more driven by China's self-interest. As China's leaders have for many centuries, Mao wanted a friendly, and not very powerful, neighbour on his south-west border. He certainly did not want a Vietnam dominated by France or the US. So just a few months after the end of his fight with Chiang, Mao was not only providing weapons and other materiel to the Viet Minh, but also armed PLA advisors embedded with the Viet Minh fighters down to the battalion level. Before the end of the year, small PLA units were in combat (Westad).

Ho Chi Minh and his top general Vo Nguyen Giap had known for some time that the US might someday overcome its reluctance to get involved in a colonial war. Just as the French in 1947 had sought to end the war before their adversary got outside help, now the Viet Minh sought to end the war before the French could get major US assistance (Fall). Now with Chinese help, Giap rapidly built up his troop strength. Soon after the Chinese civil war ended, Giap had about 250,000 Viet

Minh troops (Karnow). Using bases in China along the Vietnam border, and with the help of the PLA, he formed five combat divisions and trained them for conventional large-unit warfare, rather than the small-unit guerrilla actions that had previously been their mainstay.

Giap took these large formations back into Vietnam and by September 1948 had inflicted a series of significant defeats on French positions in north-east Tonkin near the China-Vietnam border at Lang Son, Cao Bang, Dong Khe and Thai Nguyen[2] (Map 11).

The French lost over 6,000 troops and a small mountain of weapons, munitions and supplies. This constituted France's greatest colonial defeat since Quebec 200 years before (Schulzinger). By clearing the French from the border area with China, Giap had not only hurt the French, but had also widened his access to supply lines from China (Karnow).

By the last months of 1948, therefore, the impact of Mao Zedong's victory was becoming evident through the increasing Chinese-assisted effectiveness of the Viet Minh against the French. The French considered large-scale intervention by the Chinese themselves to be a very real, very worrisome possibility. France brought in new military leadership to turn things around in Vietnam. They also renewed their appeals for US aid (Logevall).

Immediately after the Second World War, the US had no appetite for getting involved in a colonial war. During the war against the Japanese, Ho Chi Minh had emphasised his nationalism and downplayed his communism. Accordingly, as noted above, he had gotten some assistance from the American OSS (Miller and Wainstock). For the first couple of years after Ho Chi Minh began fighting the French, America's competing antipathies toward colonialism and toward communism stayed roughly in balance. This kept the US out of the Indochina matter. The fall of China to communism in late 1947, and Ho Chi Minh's more explicit identification as a communist, changed that balance. After that, Washington became increasingly concerned about a potential Red tide sweeping through Southeast Asia, and beyond. The US came to view France's war as being against communist aggression in Indochina, and therefore as being in the US interest. The State Department began talking about the geopolitical impacts if communists were to sweep Southeast Asia. State Department officials such as Dean Acheson and Dean Rusk saw Vietnam as a bulwark against communism; US policymakers were beginning to overcome their distaste for colonialism (Karnow). Dean

---

2. See What Really Happened (Sep-Oct 1950).

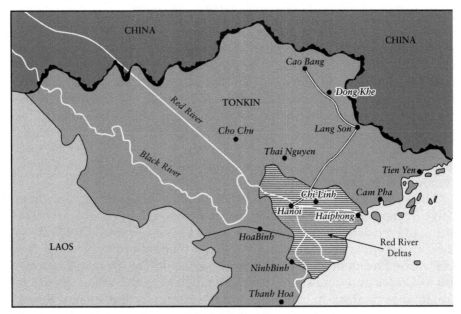

Map 11: Tonkin

Acheson said, 'Should the Chinese Communist regime lend itself to the aims of Soviet Russian imperialism and attempt to engage in aggression against China's neighbours, we and other countries of the United Nations would be confronted by a situation violative of the principles of the UN charter and threatening international peace and security' (Hammer).

The President's National Security Council, with the concurrence of the military's Joint Chiefs of Staff, recommended that the US take all practicable measures to prevent further communist expansion, lest everything from Japan to Australia to India 'go under'. The military chiefs in the Pentagon were very concerned that China might send troops into Vietnam (Schulzinger), as indeed were their French counterparts (Miller and Wainstock). American defence officials also noted that the war in Indochina was a drain on France (Finch). This was jeopardising her ability to contribute to European defence (Karnow), a commitment Paris had made explicitly in signing the 1948 Treaty of Brussels establishing a European defence pact, the precursor to NATO (Ismay).

Indeed, these Southeast Asian developments were occurring at a critical time in Europe. The Berlin Airlift began in late June 1948 in response to Russian attempts to cut West Berlin off from the West (Miller). President Truman's firm response in keeping West Berlin provisioned by an unprecedented airlift demonstrated Western resolve to push back against Soviet pressure in Europe. But with so much of East Asia (China, Korea and North Japan) under communist rule, and with pressure continuing in Southeast Asia, the President saw a need to push back in Indochina. Just the previous year Truman had made containment of communism a foundation of American foreign policy. In the words of the Truman Doctrine, it was 'the policy of the United States to support free peoples who are resisting attempted subjugation by armed minorities or by outside pressures' (Truman). Already by 1948, US economic aid and military supplies and advisors were beginning to help defeat the communists in Greece (Woodhouse).

Thus both European and Asian geopolitical considerations helped drive Truman toward a decision to send assistance to Indochina. The string of French defeats at the hands of the Chinese-trained Viet Minh in the China-Vietnam border area was the proximate stimulus in September 1948.[3] The Presidential election was also a factor. The Truman Doctrine, aid to Greece and the Berlin Airlift had lately helped Truman overcome the attempt by some to blame his administration for the 'loss' of Korea, North Japan and most recently of China (as if these were America's to lose). Now, military aid to Indochina to help those nations resist communist subjugation enhanced his domestic political standing. His opponent Thomas Dewey had little to say on foreign affairs, hoping that domestic economic issues would defeat Truman. They would not.

In October 1948, Truman unveiled the Pentalateral Mutual Assistance Pact, involving the US, France, Vietnam, Laos and Cambodia. In defence of the freedom and independence of the three Indochina nations, the US (and France) pledged substantial amounts of military aid (GPO).[4] Truman took pains to cast the war against the Viet Minh as being fought by the Vietnamese National Army under Bao Dai's government. He portrayed France as the former colonial power now seeking to guarantee Vietnam's freedom as a member of the French Union. Truman did not mention that the Vietnamese National Army was only then being formed, under French auspices, and that initially it would provide only garrison troops to free up French combat troops for active operations against the Communists. Officially, the US weapons and equipment were to go to the Bao Dai government to equip their troops. But in practice, much

3. See 'What Really Happened' (30 Jun 1950).
4. See 'What Really Happened' (Sep 1950).

of the materiel quickly flowed through to the French units doing the fighting.

It was important that the US be seen as helping Vietnam secure its freedom, rather than helping the French regain their position as colonial masters of Indochina. The State Department agreed on the need for strong containment action, but various officials were lukewarm about backing Bao Dai. They were concerned that he was another Chiang Kai-shek, to whom there was less than met the eye. There was concern that the former Emperor, former Advisor to Ho Chi Minh, and now Head of State under French auspices lacked the commitment and leadership to motivate his people to resist communist propaganda and pressure (Karnow). One State Department consultant, Raymond Fosdick, argued against the US backing Bao Dai at all. If the US stayed out of the fight, he suggested that America could eventually exploit Ho Chi Minh's nationalism to keep a Viet Minh-led Vietnam out of China's orbit. The US, he envisioned, could leverage 'the fundamental antipathy of the Indochinese for the Chinese' (Karnow). Fosdick's advice was ignored. But as we'll see, the idea of tapping into millennia of anti-Chinese hatred became valuable years later in South Vietnam.

The French had made Bao Dai head of state, but had limited his power and that of his Prime Minister Nguyen Van Xuan. The Truman administration realised that the French needed to do more to remove the colonial taint. The State Department pressed the French and Bao Dai to hold free elections for a truly independent Republic of Vietnam. As a nationalist, irked by being labelled a puppet of the French, Bao Dai was in favour of full freedom for Vietnam (Logevall). His appointed Prime Minister, Nguyen Van Xuan, a former general in the French colonial forces, also endorsed the importance and urgency of elections. In January 1949 Xuan declared that he was not himself interested in being a candidate, but he directed the government to prepare for nationwide elections scheduled for January of 1950. The US offered its assistance in making these preparations.

As noted above, the string of defeats along the northern border in September and October 1948 prompted the French to bring in new military leadership (Karnow). In December 1948,[5] General Jean de Lattre de Tassigny, distinguished commander of Free French forces in the Second World War, was diverted from his planned posting to the

---

5. See 'What Really Happened' (Dec 1950).

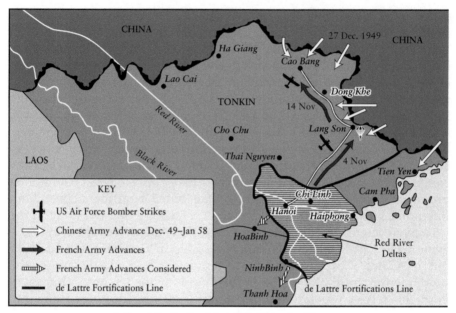

Map 12: Indochina War Early Phase

Western Union Defense Organisation (precursor to NATO). His new job was to command the French forces in Indochina and also to serve as High Commissioner. He emphasised from the beginning of his assignment that France's role was a disinterested one, and that the independence and freedom of Indochina were the goal. He maintained that he was fighting a war against communism, not a war for colonialism (Miller and Wainstock). With abundant US weapons and supplies now arriving, de Lattre immediately set to fortifying the French positions in the Red River Delta region at the heart of Tonkin. The 'De Lattre Line' consisted of hundreds of blockhouses, obstacles, fortifications, artillery firebases and other defences intended to keep the Viet Minh away from population and economic centres such as Hanoi and Haiphong (Filippelli) (Map 12).

Chapter 28

Vietnam and China, 1949

While denouncing US 'imperialist' aid to France and its 'puppet' Bao Dai regime, the Viet Minh also received an influx of outside assistance, from their neighbour to the north. The Chinese were sending weapons and advisors into Vietnam; the 300,000 Chinese troops positioned in Guangxi province near the Vietnam border were staying put, so far (Logevall). With the advisors came advice. Chinese General Lo Guipo advised Giap to capitalise on his September (1948) success in clearing the border region by attacking the French around the Red River Delta. This comported with Giap's desire to conclude the war against the French before the US got more heavily involved.

In early 1949 the Viet Minh took on the French at Vinh Yen north-west of Hanoi, at Haiphong, and at Nam Dinh, south-east of Hanoi.[1] The De Lattre Line of fortifications proved porous in a few places, but the French general also proved resourceful. His use of firepower, especially from the air, was decisive. This campaign marked the debut of US-supplied napalm (jellied gasoline). It was dropped from aircraft and had horrendous and devastating effects on massed Viet Minh troops in the open (Filipelli).

When the smoke cleared in mid-1949, the robustly US-equipped French and Vietnamese troops had inflicted disastrous losses on the Viet Minh in each of their three attempts to break into the delta. In acknowledging that he had overreached himself, Giap also blamed some of his field commanders for lack of sufficient fighting spirit (Fall). Not known is whether Giap expressed resentment of his Chinese advisor, Lo Guipo, who had pushed him to attack the delta fortifications. Nor can we know whether de Lattre's fortifications and generalship

---

1. See 'What Really Happened' (Early 1951).

would have been sufficient to repulse Giap's attacks had it not been for the massive US aid the French had received in early 1949. What we do know is this: with the help of US-supplied weaponry, munitions, air and ground transportation assets, General de Lattre shredded Giap's five combat divisions. Each one had suffered at least 40 per cent casualties and all had ceased to be effective fighting units.

And it was not just materiel the French had from the Americans. They also had US observers and coordinators in a Military Assistance and Advisory Group (MAAG). The Americans were non-combatants and were officially in the country at the request of the Bao Dai/Xuan government. Their job was to work with the French, and coordinate the use of the materiel aid which the US was providing ('to the Vietnam National Army'). In the civilian realm, there were also Americans providing advice on the conduct of the elections planned for early 1950.

Among the advisors were US Army veterans of 'Merrill's Marauders' the distinguished Ranger-type unit that fought in the jungles of the China-Burma-India theatre during the Second World War. One such was Colonel Charles Hunter, who had a well-justified reputation for toughness and leadership from his days in the Burmese jungle (CMH). Hunter was an advisor attached to the French headquarters, and de Lattre respected his advice.

The French staff officers were developing plans to follow up their successful defences of the Red River Delta. One option de Lattre's staff formulated was a major thrust from within the fortified Hanoi area back up to the north, to recapture the posts along the Chinese border lost to the Viet Minh the previous year. Another option was a strike to the south-west, toward Hoa Binh. The objective would be to cut an important Viet Minh supply route for transporting rice from south of the delta to their troops to the north (Filipelli).

The French also knew that Hoa Binh and the surrounding hill country was the home of the Muong ethnic group, one of several minorities who had been pushed out of the flatlands in previous ages by the Vietnamese migrating in from the north. The continuing enmity of the Muong for the Vietnamese led them to be friendly to the French. So by securing the Muong homeland against the Viet Minh, the French might gain increased support and local militia troops from the Muong. General de Lattre initially rejected the northward thrust, seeing it as a potential repeat of the unsuccessful Operation Lea two years previous in 1947. He opted instead to plan a thrust to Hoa Binh, for the value it offered in gaining Muong support and cutting off rice supplies to Ho Chi Minh. It also offered the opportunity for the large 'set-piece' European-type battle which French military doctrine saw as key to winning any war (Filipelli).[2]

As instructed, the American Colonel Hunter kept his superiors in Tokyo and Washington informed of French thinking. In August 1949, they asked him to try to adjust French plans. Senior US officials believed that a French thrust deeper into central Tonkin toward Hoa Binh could appear too 'colonialist'. Moreover, the attempt to exploit the outcast Muong group against the majority Vietnamese, another classic colonialist 'divide and conquer' gambit, was unlikely to help win over support from the many Vietnamese farmers of the Red River Delta. Instead, US officials in Tokyo advocated a prompt French thrust north toward Lang Son and the north-east border area to take back the lost positions. (Map 12)

Re-establishing French positions along the Vietnam-China border would begin to cut the Viet Minh off from their Chinese masters and provisioners. That would enable Vietnamese matters eventually to be settled primarily by the Vietnamese. Such a 'cordon sanitaire' approach, imperfect though it might be, would be more in keeping with the Truman administration's policy of containment of communism. Moreover, the time to move was right away, before Giap could rebuild those Viet Minh fighting units that were shattered in his mid-1949 attacks on the De Lattre Line.

Pursuant to his orders, Colonel Hunter conveyed to de Lattre's staff the strong US preference for swift French action back into the border area. As instructed, he intimated that US aid would continue to increase substantially for a thrust north to the border, but not for a French thrust toward Hoa Binh with its implications of colonialist exploitation of one ethnic group against another. Colonel Hunter, a thoroughly professional and accomplished soldier, followed orders. But he later expressed his misgivings in his personal journal: 'Not at all sure that heading towards China now is a good idea. Perhaps I shouldn't have tried so hard to change de L's mind.'

It is not clear how much influence the US 'suggestion' had on de Lattre's apparent change of mind and decision to head north instead of west. His successful defence of the Red River Delta was already bringing an increased flow of US aid, which he realised he could put to good use in a push to the north, avoiding the mistakes his predecessor had made in 1947. It was de Lattre himself who'd pitched to the Americans that the defence of Vietnam was critical to protecting all of Southeast

---

2. See 'What Really Happened' (Jun 1951–Feb 1952).

Asia, and indeed South and Southwest Asia and even Africa from Communism (Filipelli). He had also pointed out to the Americans that loss of Southeast Asia would not just be a geopolitical problem but also one of resources, such as rice, timber, rubber, tin and others. Remember, he'd said, the resources of Southeast Asia were a major cause of the Japanese expansion and war, and those resources were still economically important (Logevall).

The French commander knew that going back north to Lang Son would interdict a supply route from China in operation since antiquity. The strategically logical thing for the French to do after that would be to advance north-west along the border area to cut off more of the routes that were keeping the Viet Minh supplied with Chinese weapons and munitions. And de Lattre knew the time was ripe to do this, while the Viet Minh were reportedly recuperating. De Lattre also knew that morale was high among his nearly 200,000-strong force, who were a rich mix of French Foreign Legionnaires and African and other colonial troops, plus units of Indochinese ethnic minorities such as the Muong and the T'ai, along with increasingly well-trained units of the Vietnamese National Army (which Bao Dai had obligingly placed under his operational control).

It may be that General de Lattre allowed the Americans to persuade him to embrace the audacity for which his countrymen are famous. But what would ensure his success, he mused, would be increased air support, for both combat and transport. For that, he told the Americans in late August 1949, he looked to the US. His valiant troops would fight on the rugged terrain and thick forests of northern Tonkin, but abundant and prompt firepower from above, which the US could provide, would give them the edge they'd need this time to overcome the defensive advantages the Viet Minh would have.

Seeking such direct US military involvement was in a sense a straightforward effort to assemble appropriate military resources for an identified objective. It was also geopolitically crafty. The US 'persuaded' him to reclaim key positions; but if it was to be more decisive than Operation Lea, de Lattre pointed out, he would need additional airpower. By thus forcing the Americans to put some of their own skin in the game, he was protecting his Gallic behind from any potential future American second-guessing about the operation.

Elsewhere in the world, in September 1949, the US Air Force reported to President Truman that the Soviets had detonated their first nuclear weapon, several years sooner than the US had expected (Burr). The

French request for US air support reached Truman about the same time. This confluence of events caused the White House and Pentagon some concern. The idea circulated in Pentagon corridors that the timing of the Soviet blast was a signal to deter any American consideration of getting involved in Indochina. That notion faded (sometimes a coincidence is just that), but the inverse idea gained acceptance: now that the US no longer held the nuclear monopoly, it could not look intimidated by communist power. So America could not now fail to support its allies at a critical time in resistance to communist subversion. For the record, French commander de Lattre had worked through his Vietnamese counterpart to have the Bao Dai/Xuan government make the request to the US for air support.

Truman made no secret of his September 1949 Indochina decision. He authorised the US Air Force and the US Navy to fly missions in support of Vietnamese (and French) operations in Indochina. But neither did he make a major announcement of it. When the newspapers picked up on it, which they soon did, the White House cast the move as the logical progression of previous commitments of assistance in a conflict the President had previously determined to be strategically important to US interests. Against the background of the unexpectedly early loss of the nuclear monopoly, Congressional leaders kept silent. They did not want any criticism of the President's action to appear like a retreat from confronting the international communist threat.[3]

At the Pentagon, Joint Chiefs of Staff Chairman Omar Bradley made inquiries to the Far East Command in Tokyo about the likelihood of US airpower prompting the Chinese to commit troops into Vietnam. MacArthur's successor in the Far East Command was Lieutenant General Ned Almond. His chief of intelligence, a holdover from MacArthur's time, was Major General Charles Willoughby. Informed by Willoughby, Almond assured Bradley that Mao Zedong was uninterested in Vietnam and would not intervene in the war.[4] The Tokyo command assured Bradley that Mao was focused only on finishing off Chiang Kai-shek by attacking Taiwan. (As noted above, Mao had by then put the conquest of Taiwan on hold. He repositioned about 300,000 of his PLA troops he'd been planning to use for an invasion of Taiwan. He moved them near the Vietnam border.) Not for the first time, the Navy did not share the Army's view. Vice Admiral Arthur Struble, the Deputy Chief of

---

3. See 'What Really Happened' (1951–54).
4. See 'What Really Happened' (Aug–Oct 1950).

Naval Operations, considered a Chinese move into Vietnam a distinct possibility (Miller and Wainstock).

Following Truman's directive, the Pentagon assigned USAF B-29s from Clark Air Base in the Philippines to support the Bao Dai government (and their French allies) in Indochina. Likewise, the Navy positioned two carriers of the Seventh Fleet in the Gulf of Tonkin to provide naval airpower support.

With French, Vietnamese and American assets in place, de Lattre launched his late October 1949 campaign to take Lang Son for the fourth time. (The French had been forced out of the town by the Vietnamese in 1885, by the Japanese in 1940, and by the Viet Minh in 1948.) But never before had the French possessed the tools and techniques available to General de Lattre. In rapid succession, USAF B-29s bombed Viet Minh concentrations in and around the town. French paratroopers, delivered in US planes, then overran them. Reinforcements and resupply arrived quickly by air even before the Viet Minh could regroup for counter-attacks. When they did, French and US aircraft dropped enough explosives and napalm to inflict further heavy casualties on the Viet Minh. Meanwhile, a French armoured column headed north on Highway 1 from Hanoi. The column included several companies of American-made 'Rome Plows' (made by the Rome Plow company of Georgia) embedded with the armour units. With armour-protected cabs, these were large bulldozers equipped with heavy, sharp front blades designed to help clear trees and other roadside vegetation where it encroached close to the road and provided hiding places for Viet Minh ambushers (Starry). The powerful dozers could also clear obstacles or damaged vehicles from the road.[5]

Overhead, the column had carrier-based A-1 Skyraiders and brand new jet-powered F-9 Panthers on call. These ground-attack aircraft broke up several ambushes before they happened, and put an end to several others along the 80 miles between Hanoi and Lang Son. The armoured column got through almost unscathed. By 4 November, Lang Son was once again under French/Vietnamese National Army control, and firmly so. De Lattre brought reinforcements and resupply in overland, suffering only minimal losses en route. An important supply line to the Viet Minh from China was blocked.

De Lattre sensed that the Viet Minh were reeling from the punishment they'd suffered in trying to break into the delta, and now from the pounding they were taking around Lang Son. He was far from reckless, but he

---

5. See 'What Really Happened' (1967–1971).

understood the value of time and he pushed his staff and commanders to prepare carefully, but move swiftly. He made sure his American liaisons, such as Colonel Hunter and his staff, knew how much he appreciated the highly effective combat air support the US was providing. In well over a hundred sorties, no US aircraft were lost or even badly damaged by ground fire. De Lattre also expressed appreciation for the excellent logistical assistance the Americans were providing, and he looked forward, he said, to even greater efforts as his campaign advanced.

Which it did. The next objective was Cao Bang, 80 miles to the north-west and nexus of another major supply route from China. The French (and Foreign Legion, and Colonial, and some Vietnamese National Army) forces advanced quickly, parachuting from American-made planes, riding in American-made trucks, protected by American-made tanks, and watched over by American-piloted fighter bombers. By mid-November 1949, Cao Bang was back under French control, as was Dong Khe on Route 4 between them.

The fighting around the small town of Dong Khe near the China border yielded several prisoners, one of particular interest. Another former Merrill's Marauder was Major Fred Lyons (CMH). In 1949 he was an American liaison officer with the French at Dong Khe. With the help of some knowledge of the Mandarin language from his days with Merrill's Marauders, he determined that one of the POWs the French had captured was a Chinese PLA officer. It appeared that there were PLA advisors working with Viet Minh units down to the company level. This information was forwarded to the Intelligence section at Far East Command in Tokyo, but got no further. That was because the Intelligence chief, General Willoughby, already 'knew' that the PLA was focusing on Taiwan, and that it therefore had no interest in Vietnam. This was the position he had previously stated. He now had no interest in facts on the ground that did not fit the 'truth' as he had previously briefed it to his superiors.

Willoughby was not the only one ignoring the available information. Two months previous, the Chinese Foreign Minister Zhou Enlai had told the UN that 'Vietnam is China's neighbour . . . The Chinese people cannot but be concerned about a solution of the Vietnam question'. Lest that be too ambiguous for Western ears, the Chinese used neutral-country diplomats to warn that in safeguarding China's national security, they would intervene in Vietnam. President Truman interpreted the communication as 'a bald attempt to blackmail the UN', and dismissed it (Offner).[6]

---

6. See 'What Really Happened' (20 Aug 1950).

In late December, there were a few days of increased enemy probes of the French defences at Cao Bang. The French expected an attack in force to follow. They were right, but were surprised by who launched it. On 27 December 1949, a regimental-sized unit attacked the most northerly fort protecting Cao Bang. Forced out, the French defenders nevertheless took half a dozen prisoners with them.

'All these guys just looked different. Maybe it was their uniforms, or the way they handled themselves', said the French sergeant who delivered his prisoners to the French HQ in Cao Bang. They seemed different because they were Chinese, members of a PLA line division, not advisors embedded with Viet Minh units. The same day, Lang Son came under attack, also by at least a regimental-sized unit. It soon emerged that this too was a PLA formation. Red China had entered the war, with its own 'boots on the ground', perhaps a lot of them.

General Willoughby at Far East Command dismissed the reports of Chinese troop units, because this new information contradicted what he had previously stated as fact.[7] At considerable professional risk, Colonel Hunter on the ground at Cao Bang explained to Willoughby that several dozen enemy casualties bore uniform markings indicating they were members of the 'Black Flag' Army. The original Black Flag Army consisted of Chinese fighting units who had fought alongside the Vietnamese against the French in Vietnam in the late 1800s (Forbes and Henley). Hunter knew this history and tried to explain it to his superior. But Willoughby was mentally impregnable. 'His mind is made up,' Hunter is reported to have said of Willoughby, 'he refuses to be confused by the facts.'

When Joint Chiefs Chairman Bradley first heard about the major Chinese troop involvement–from his French counterpart – the second thing he said was 'get me Ned Almond', the Far East commander in Tokyo. Although known as the 'GI's General, and normally operating in a calm, managerial style, five-star General Bradley had relieved many a senior commander during the World War, and three-star General Almond presumably knew that (D'Este). Bradley directed Almond to immediately prepare a full assessment of the Chinese involvement and to formulate potential courses of action in response. 'And I don't want Willoughby's fingerprints anywhere near the intel', he told Almond. Bradley said later that he recalled MacArthur's comment about Willoughby during

---

7. See 'What Really Happened' (25 Oct 1950).

the Second World War: 'There have been three great intelligence officers in history. Mine is not one of them' (Frank 2007).

The Chinese Communists overran all the French positions at Cao Bang, Dong Khe, Lang Son, and along Colonial Route 4 paralleling the Vietnam-China border (Map 12).[8] There were terrible losses of French and Vietnamese National Army personnel and equipment. Hastily-organised US air sorties from the Philippines and from carriers off the coast supported the retreats of the survivors. French and American aerial reconnaissance indicated masses of troops streaming in from China into Cao Bang and across the Munan Pass into Lang Son. Even if Washington had authorised attacking these formations, sufficient air assets were not available to try to interdict these forces in addition to trying to cover the French retreat.

By 1 January 1950, de Lattre and his surviving troops were back within the De Lattre Line around the Red River Delta. He had suffered well over 10,000 casualties including the loss of many of his most elite, the paratroopers. He'd also lost much of the heavy weapons and other materiel. Although he had seemingly nearly beaten the Viet Minh, he now faced a new, potentially much more numerous and dangerous enemy. The indications were that most if not all of those 300,000 Chinese PLA troops which General Willoughby had earlier insisted were not massing on the Chinese borderlands, now truly were not there – they had gone across the border and were now in northern Vietnam.

Mao Zedong may well have been concerned about his neighbours, but much less for their sake, or for the sake of international communist solidarity than for China's own sake. As had been the case for millennia, if China couldn't have Vietnam for its own, the next best was to have it weak and compliant. A strong, independent Vietnam supported by France and the US was clearly not in Communist China's interest. And in those last months of 1949, it had appeared that the French and the Americans might crush the Viet Minh and open the way to just such a Vietnam that was no friend of China.

Also, the national elections slated in Vietnam for the last week of January 1950 were a threat. The UN had dispatched a multinational team of election supervisors and poll watchers. The Bao Dai/Xuan government had declared that they would recognise the results of all those election races throughout Vietnam that the UN determined were fair. Prime Minister Xuan had affirmed that if districts fairly elected communists or

---

8. See 'What Really Happened' (Nov 1950) and (Mar 1979).

pro-communist representatives, those representatives would be seated in the National Assembly. The government was essentially daring the Viet Minh to interfere with the elections.

The 1949 battlefield losses of the Viet Minh would take years to recover from militarily. The looming elections could do the communist cause irreparable damage politically. And the Americans' increasing involvement in air power and other combat support was a bad sign. An independent Vietnam with ties to France was undesirable; Vietnam with ties to the US was intolerable.

The politburo in Beijing understood that sending PLA troops en masse into Vietnam against the French could stimulate the US to send troops into Vietnam. But their assessment of the correlation of forces as of late 1949 was that the US had neither the troop strength nor the will to attack China itself. Nor did Beijing fear the US use of nuclear weapons, now that Moscow had them too. As for the US helping Chiang Kai-shek stage a comeback to the mainland, that was a possibility. But the Politburo believed that even with US naval and air support Chiang Kai-shek's Taiwan-based GMD troops would be no match for the PLA troops still in position opposite Taiwan, waiting for his attempted return. So the Beijing politburo believed that the importance of preventing the rise of a strong Western-allied Vietnam outweighed the risk of direct or indirect action by the US against China itself.

As hundreds of thousands of Chinese troops poured into Vietnam, their objective was not obvious to the French or the Americans. They could disrupt voting in parts of Tonkin, but the nationwide elections would proceed nevertheless. Would the Chinese attempt to evict the French entirely from Tonkin? Or from all of Vietnam down to and past Saigon? Were the pro-French governments in Laos and Cambodia safe? De Lattre's headquarters in Hanoi did not panic, but 'heightened concern' does not quite describe it either.

The French government made it clear to the Truman administration that they were at their limit. They had neither the funds nor the troops to substantially reinforce their Vietnam presence. Bao Dai's Vietnamese National Army was not yet a fully capable fighting force. The Chinese masses posed an imminent threat to at least the Red River Delta, Hanoi and Haiphong, and perhaps beyond. The Vietnamese, the French said, needed additional outside help to protect their freedom from communist aggression.

Chapter 29

Vietnam and the UN, 1950

The French government requested an immediate UN Security Council meeting, which convened on 8 January 1950. France made the case that their troops were in Vietnam at the request of the legitimate government of the independent state of Vietnam. Bao Dai's government was not a member of the UN, but his representative made it known to the council that they agreed with France's position. France further stated that their military actions were not in pursuit of colonial domination, but were intended to protect the Bao Dai government from armed communist subversion. The French ambassador said that the invasion of Vietnam by the Chinese PLA constituted international armed aggression and as such warranted UN action.

The US concurred, adding that the US was supporting the Bao Dai government in close coordination with French operations. Western involvement in Vietnam, the US said, was in support of the recognised government of that nation, and was intended to allow that government to proceed with national development as a free and independent state. The US ambassador cited the upcoming nationwide elections in Vietnam as an example of that national development. By contrast, the US and French both argued, Chinese armed involvement in Vietnam (though it was a pattern dating back millennia) was unacceptable meddling in the affairs of a sovereign state. In response to this, China's Zhou Enlai in Beijing released a statement that 'The Chinese people will not tolerate foreign aggression and will not stand aside should the imperialists wantonly invade territory of our neighbour' (Coker).

Not everyone bought the distinction between the roles of the Western vs. the Chinese militaries in Vietnam, but there were other factors in play. For example, one of the UN Security Council's non-permanent members at the time was India, clearly not an advocate of colonial power. But her antipathy to China and its communist regime counted for more. Another non-permanent Security Council member at the time was Yugoslavia. Its leader, Josep Tito, was a communist who might be expected to feel solidarity with Mao Zedong and Ho Chi Minh. But in 1948 Tito had broken with the world communist movement as directed from Moscow and was intent on charting his own course (Perovic). As a result, with the abstention of Yugoslavia, the Security Council adopted a resolution calling for the cessation of hostilities and the withdrawal of the invading troops. It also called upon all member states to render every assistance to the United Nations in the execution of the resolution (Millet). The vote came on 9 January 1950.[1]

Note that one of the five permanent seats on the UN Security Council belongs to China (the other permanent members are the US, UK, France and the USSR), and any permanent member can veto any council resolution. But in 1950 the China seat was occupied by Chiang's Nationalist government. Although they had taken up residence on Taiwan, Chiang's Nationalists still claimed to be the legitimate government of all of China. Unsurprisingly, China (Taiwan) supported the UN condemnation of China (Beijing). The USSR, another permanent member, could also have vetoed the resolution, and probably would have if they'd been at the meeting. But the Soviets had just that month begun a boycott of the UN Security Council over the very issue of seating the Beijing regime rather than that of Taiwan (Zickel). Stalin later claimed the USSR skipped the key 1950 Security Council vote deliberately, so as to help get the US dragged into a hopeless contest with China. 'America cannot cope with China having at its disposal large armed forces,' he claimed to have said at the time. He further claimed that this US entanglement would distract the Americans while giving the Soviet Union time to regain strength and tighten its control of Eastern Europe (Zubok).[2]

Following the adoption of the resolution, the US and other member states indicated they would respond to the UN's call, and would assist the Vietnamese to expel the invading Chinese so that the sovereign State of Vietnam could pursue an independent course of development without unwanted outside intrusion.

Certainly, the Chinese troops were an unwanted intrusion for Bao Dai. But it is not clear whether Ho Chi Minh wanted them either. Beijing's official position was that the members of this modern 'Black Flag' Army were all volunteers, prepared to fight in Vietnam against

---

1. See 'What Really Happened' (25 Jun 1950).
2. See 'What Really Happened' (27 Jun 1950 (1)).

her Western enemies, just as their predecessors had voluntarily done in the 1800s.[3] Beijing glossed over whether Ho Chi Minh had requested the help. It later became known that Mao and Stalin had agreed that China would send troops into Vietnam, and thereby risk US retaliation, if there were an existential threat to the Viet Minh (Miller and Wainstock). The two communist leaders decided that the defeats the Viet Minh experienced in late 1949 met that criterion, whether Ho Chi Minh concurred or not.

With the United Nations calling upon member states to use military force to assist Vietnam, President Truman took the US across the line he had refrained from crossing until then. He directed the Joint Chiefs of Staff to immediately increase air combat support to the French and Vietnamese forces, and to deploy, as soon as possible, such ground forces as necessary to counter the Chinese Communist threat to Vietnam.

Speaking to his advisors just after he learned of the invasion by China, he said 'If we let (them) down, the communists will keep right on going and swallow up piece of Asia after another. If we were to let Asia go, the Near East would collapse and there's no telling what would happen to Europe' (Leffler).

The message Truman sent to Congress was not a request for a formal declaration of war. The US President asserted that the UN Treaty obligated America to respond to the Security Council's call for armed action (Friedman).[4] Constitutional scholars then and to this day have argued the point, but Congress responded with an authorisation for the President to take the military action in Tonkin and elsewhere in Vietnam that he already had under way. What came to be called the Tonkin Resolution had broad bipartisan support.[5] The resolution authorised the President to provide military assistance to any Southeast Asian nation under threat of communist aggression (Schulzinger).

Truman later wrote that he saw the Chinese Communists acting 'just as Hitler, Mussolini and the Japanese had ten, fifteen, and twenty years earlier'. He felt that if the invasion went unopposed, 'communist leaders would be emboldened to override nations closer to our own shores. If the Communists were permitted to force their way in . . . without opposition from the free world, no small nation would have the courage to resist threat and aggression by stronger Communist neighbours.' He believed that fighting the invasion was essential to the

---

3. See 'What Really Happened' (8 Aug 1950).
4. See 'What Really Happened' (27 Jun 1950 (2)).
5. See 'What Really Happened' (7 Aug 1964).

American goal of the global containment of communism (Truman and Ferrell).

While the Pentagon prepared movement orders for ground units, Truman also ordered elements of the US Navy's Seventh Fleet to take up station in the Taiwan Strait between Taiwan and mainland China (Coker). Publicly, this was to protect the Nationalists on Taiwan from an attack from the Communists. Not so publicly, its intent was to dissuade Chiang Kai-shek from attempting a potentially disastrous invasion of the mainland. One war at a time was enough.

The US Far East Command at the time had four combat divisions in Japan: the 1st Cavalry Division, and the 7th, 24th and 25th Infantry Divisions (Stewart). The Joint Chiefs directed Ned Almond's Far East Command to dispatch two of those four immediately to the war zone. The 24th and 25th Infantry Divisions received that mission; lead elements of the 25th were aboard transports heading for the fighting within 10 days (PIO). The remaining divisions, the 7th Infantry and the 1st Cavalry, along with other US military assets in Japan (Marines, Air Force and Navy), went on heightened alert. The Japanese Self Defense Forces also ratcheted up their readiness and their watchfulness toward Hokkaido and Korea. One war at a time was enough.

The Pentagon also directed the 2nd Infantry Division stationed at Fort Lewis in Washington State to deploy to the war zone; the division completed its move within five weeks (Gough). By that time, the rest of the 25th Infantry Division and much of the 24th had arrived from Japan. The 3rd Infantry Division arrived from Georgia five weeks after the 2nd Division (Gough). Additional combat and support units (artillery, aviation, engineers, transport, communications, medical, etc.) also headed overseas along with the necessary headquarters units for directing an army in the field. The 1st Provisional Marine Brigade sailed from California within 10 days of the UN Resolution, and a full Marine division and Marine Air Wing were on their way in five weeks (Giusti).

Thus, by 1 March 1950 US Army and Marine Corps forces on the ground in Vietnam amounted to three-plus divisions, with additional combat and support units for a total of over 125,000 personnel. In that era, the ratio of combat division personnel to personnel in combat support units was about 1 to 1.5 – for every 100 fighting men forming 'the tip of the spear', there were about 150 other soldiers (including quite a number of women) in the war zone supporting them. They ensured that the fighting men had all the supplies and equipment, all the communications, the transportation and fuel, all the medical care and so on that they needed to fight effectively wherever they were needed (Eliot; Leighton and Coakley). Two more divisions arrived during March.

In January, as soon as American forces started moving toward Vietnam from Japan and the continental US, the Pentagon developed an overall domestic mobilisation plan and submitted it to Truman on 20 January 1950. The Active Army at the time consisted of roughly 600,000 personnel, with a total of ten combat divisions, nominally 15,000 men each (Coker). Of the six stateside divisions, two were going to Vietnam as quickly as transport could get them there. Of the four in Japan, two were heading for Vietnam. In light of the communist positions in North Japan, Korea and China, the Pentagon did not want to further deplete the remaining US forces in Japan. In fact the Pentagon recommended that as soon as feasible additional troops should deploy to Japan from the US to backfill those sent to Vietnam.

Nor did the Army want to deplete the four divisions remaining in the US; they were designated for potential deployment in the event of a general emergency – e.g. if the Russians attacked Western Europe (Gough). Nor should there be any depletion of the 80,000 garrison troops stationed in Germany and elsewhere in Europe. War with the Chinese was enough, but the US had to be ready to deal with the Russians in Europe if they stirred. So great was the concern about Russian troublemaking that the US took steps to demonstrate its resolve and capability to meet its European defence commitments: in the 15 months after the UN resolution, the US sent four combat divisions to Europe as more troops were mobilised (Gough).

Thus the early 1950 deployment to Vietnam of about four Army divisions and one of Marines was all the US military could manage with the existing active-duty troops. But more were certainly needed. The size of the increasing Chinese force in Vietnam was still unknown, but estimates were in the range of 250,000–300,000 troops (plus perhaps 300,000 Viet Minh troops). The French had 180,000 well-trained, well-equipped and well-led but exhausted troops, and France said that replacements would not be forthcoming (Miller and Wainstock). Other UN member states signalled their intent to send troops. These included Great Britain, Australia, New Zealand, Canada, Thailand and the Philippines. The participation by the United Kingdom was a matter of some debate in London. 'We didn't fight to keep India. Why should we fight to help France keep Indochina?' ran one argument. But against that was the extended 'domino' mantra that the Indochina war was not about French colonialism but about preventing the Red tide from toppling dominoes all the way, perhaps, to Melbourne and Wellington (Logevall).

In the end, Commonwealth solidarity won out. Troops from the British Commonwealth and from other UN members would be geopolitically important, but their numbers were not likely to exceed 40,000–50,000 or so. (As predicted, 18 months later the troop levels in the UN Command from these other allies peaked at just over 59,000, mostly from the British Commonwealth (USFK).) Pentagon planners recognised that the great bulk of troops for this war would have to be American.

To counter the Chinese incursion, the Joint Chiefs believed the need would be for a minimum of 400,000 US Army troops and 50,000 Marines in Vietnam, with additional Air Force personnel in and near Vietnam and naval assets offshore. Clearly, the Army and the Marine Corps would have to expand, through a combination of increasing draft calls, extension of the period of military service, and activation of the various reserve components.[6]

Accordingly, on 24 January, President Truman authorised the armed services to activate their reserves, e.g. Army Reserve and Army National Guard units, as needed. He also requested Congressional authorisation to increase the size of the active-duty components of the services. Further, he asked Congress to expand conscription. Since 1948 there had been a draft law on the books, obliging young men to register. But the peacetime military had needed to induct only some thousands of draftees in 1948 and 1949 (Flynn). What Truman envisioned was on the order of a million draftees. In the current era, when even trivial actions can take years to work their way through the labyrinths of the legislative and executive branches, it is stunning to consider the swift actions these branches took in 1950 in regard to America's fight against communism. Within 10 days of the UN Resolutions, the US Congress approved Truman's recommendations for an expanded active military and for extended conscription (Gough).

There was strong, although not universal, Congressional and public support for the President's actions. The 'subjugation' by the communists not only of Eastern Europe, but also of Korea, northern Japan and China was a great concern to many Americans. A Gallup poll in early February 1950 indicated that a majority of Americans had only a vague idea of where Vietnam was (many confused it with Thailand or Burma), nor did they know virtually anything about its history or culture. What they did know was that, as one respondent put it, 'a bunch of godless

---

6. See 'What Really Happened' (Jul 1951 and Apr 1968).

ACTIVE/RESERVE/GUARD: AMERICA'S ARMED FORCES

Supplementing the full-time active duty units of each of the armed services are a series of part-time reserve units (Army Reserve, Navy Reserve etc.). These are staffed by citizen-soldiers who report for military training about 30 days each year. Parallel to these federally-controlled reserve organisations are the fifty-four National Guard organisations of the states and territories. These modern descendants of the colonial militias are also primarily staffed by part-time citizen soldiers. In normal circumstances these units are under the control of their respective Governors, who can use them to assist in domestic emergencies such as natural disasters and civil disturbances. However, in wartime the President can and typically does call National Guard units to Federal service and deploy them not only outside their home state, but overseas as needed. (Stuckey and Pistorius).

---

commies were trying to take over yet another country and by God we have to put a stop to it'.

The hundreds of thousands of troops to be sent into harm's way clearly indicated a major national commitment of Americans' sons and brothers and husbands. But even the associated two-and-a-half-fold expansion of the Army to 1,500,000 personnel would be no comparison to the 8,000,000 troops in the Second World War army (the largest part of the 12,000,000 Americans in uniform in 1945). Also, the draft age population in 1950 was about 10 per cent larger than it had been during the last war (Census Bureau). Therefore the manpower demands of this war did not strain the nation's economic capacity, nor its social fabric. The Truman administration had been clear that the nation needed to go to war and that its purpose was to stop the advance of communism. The secondary purpose was to help the Vietnamese people, a population the average American had likely never heard of, nor given a thought to, a few years previous. But in a similar vein, US troops had fought and died in the Second World War to stop the advance of the Axis powers, and incidentally to free Polynesians, Indonesians, Burmese, Moroccans, Tunisians, Libyans and others with whom the average American previously had little knowledge of. For now, the American public supported the war.

US public and Congressional support, and indeed support in other nations, solidified. Newsreels (short news programmes typically shown in movie theatres before the feature film) showed the spectacle of thousands of Vietnamese queueing up to vote during the last week of January 1950. Prime Minister Xuan (with help from US and French advisors) had organised an efficient election process, and UN inspectors were on hand throughout the nation to ensure a minimum of fraud. The Viet Minh and the Chinese did not allow election officials to enter villages under their control in northern Tonkin, but successful voting went on throughout the Red River Delta, and throughout Annam and Cochin China.

There were over a dozen parties contending, but the ticket headed by Nguyen Van Tam, with Phan Hay Quat as his running mate, was the decisive winner. Educated in France, Nguyen had been fighting communists since before the Second World War. The Viet Minh had killed two of his sons (Logevall). Not only was he a committed nationalist; he also understood that the power of nationalism did not come from educated elites, but from the people in the fields and on the streets. As he said to an American journalist, 'The most important thing is winning the village populations over to our cause. Our nationalist fervour must match that of the Viet Minh' (Logevall). A teacher by background, Nguyen Van Tam had first made a name for himself as a French-appointed District Chief in the Mekong delta where he decisively suppressed dissidents and subversives in the early 1940s. More recently, as chief of police in Saigon, he developed an effective intelligence network that enabled him to root out cells of Viet Minh terrorists. He thus established a reasonable degree of security within Saigon (Bodard). His running mate Phan Hay Quat was a medical doctor, a nationalist and an ardent anti-communist (Corfield). In the early 1940s he had founded the New Vietnam Party (Tucker) and in the late 1940s served in several Bao Dai ministries.

Both Nguyen Van Tam and Phan Hay Quat campaigned stressing the importance of Vietnam being truly independent, prudently accepting help from the West in the short term but never reverting to Chinese control. They stressed the virtues of Vietnamese culture, emphasising, especially to their southern audiences, Buddhist/Hindu communalism rather than Chinese-style Confucian authoritarianism. They exploited the resentment caused by the Viet Minh's tactics of intimidation and conscription. To their northern audiences the candidates charged that the Viet Minh's mismanagement of food distribution in late 1945 had caused another wave of famine in the aftermath of the Red River flooding. This followed a disastrous famine in late 1944–early 1945 that perhaps killed more than one million people (Gunn). The candidates also decried the persecution and assassination of Catholics that the Viet Minh had carried out (Miller and Wainstock). They promised to end the corruption which Bao Dai's cronies had perpetrated. Candidate Nguyen knew that success against the Communists required not just winning military battles, but also earning the trust of the people and winning their hearts and minds.

The Vietnamese Nationalist Party (VNQDD) ran National Assembly candidates in central Vietnam. This Tonkin-based socialist party had collaborated with the Communists against the French in previous years, but after the Second World War Ho Chi Minh fought them as murderously as he fought the French (Logevall). The weakened party, never strong in central or southern Vietnam, fared poorly in the elections. A stridently anti-French nationalist named Ngo Dinh Diem ran for President under the banner of the Can Lao (Labour Revolutionary) Party. He received support from his Catholic coreligionists concentrated in the north. But his disdain for Buddhists and for the Cao Dai and Hoa Hao religious sects of the south severely limited his vote totals. He won a seat in the Assembly, but only two other members of his party did so, far from enough to have any influence on the government.[7]

The election results as tallied in early February 1950 were decisive enough that polling in the Viet Minh-obstructed districts in the northern border areas could not have changed the outcome. The party of Nguyen Van Tam and Phan Hay Quat won a clear majority of seats. Head of State Bao Dai accordingly requested that Nguyen Van Tam serve as prime minister and form a government. With Phan Hay Quat as his deputy, Nguyen assembled a government of respected figures, including some from smaller parties. With Bao Dai remaining in his largely ceremonial role, and a broad-based government of competence, Nguyen was at the head of a national government that had strong public support throughout Vietnam. He was determined to run his government in a way that maintained and strengthened this support while also ridding his country of the threat of communist domination. He affirmed the promise by former Prime Minister Xuan that any representatives winning fair elections in Viet Minh-controlled areas could take their seats in the National Assembly whenever such elections were held. However, the idea of elections involving competing candidates was not one the Viet Minh, nor certainly their Chinese colleagues, cared to consider.

---

7. See 'What Really Happened' (Oct 1955).

In the US in February 1950, Senator Joseph McCarthy launched a campaign against what he claimed were hundreds of communists embedded in the US government itself (Griffith). He charged that subversive elements within the US government had (somehow) led to Mao Zedong's defeat of Chiang Kai-shek, and subsequently to the Chinese Communists' 'invasion' of their much smaller neighbour (McCarthy). His claims rested on no evidence, but many people were willing to overlook that technicality. (As we in the current era know, fact-free assertions and groundless hyperbolic exaggerations are not merely tolerated but may be qualifications for high office.) Later that year, the arrests of Harry Gold, David Greenglass and Julius and Ethel Rosenberg as communist spies who stole American atomic secrets added to the public support for fighting communism (Miller and Wainstock).

Call-ups of reserve units were proceeding and draft calls were ramping up. The Pentagon recommended to President Truman that Matthew Ridgway command the expanded Military Assistance Command Vietnam (MACV). A highly-decorated airborne commander of the Second World War, Ridgway had spent tours of duty in China and in the Philippines before that war. After 1945, he served as a military staffer at the United Nations. He therefore had knowledge of his enemy and his war zone, and had also worked with military officials from the other nations that would be participating in the UN force. Most important, he had the leadership credentials to take control of a tough situation and turn it around.[8]

The President concurred in his advisors' recommendation and appointed Ridgway to lead the US forces in Vietnam. Then, the French government gracefully prevented an awkward issue of international command by notifying the UN Security Council and the US that they believed a US commander should lead the overall UN Command Vietnam (UNCV). This was a politically wise step, further removing the colonial taint from this 'war against Communist aggression'. It also helped the US avoid the domestic uneasiness that would have arisen if US forces had been under a French commander in Vietnam.

With the concurrence of the UN, the President then appointed Ridgway (newly promoted to four-star general rank) to command the UNCV. As commander specifically of the US forces, Truman then appointed Lieutenant General James Van Fleet, who had recently led the US military assistance mission helping the Greek government defeat communist insurgents. Truman praised Van Fleet as a great war-winning general (Coker).

---

8. See 'What Really Happened' (Apr 1951).

Chapter 30

Vietnam and the US, 1950–1952

Less than five years after the end of its deadliest foreign conflict, the US was rapidly mobilising for another. There was not the same air of outraged patriotism that had spurred enlistments after Pearl Harbor. Instead, it was a grimmer, more realistic, 'Here we go again' attitude at the wartime enlistment stations, which took in several hundred thousand recruits in 1950–1 (Gough).

The severe defence cuts after the Second World War had shrunk the Navy to about 10 per cent of its peak size (US Navy) and the Army to about 7 per cent (R. Miller). For this new war in Asia the military grew back rapidly. Within twelve months of the UN Resolutions the Army had 18 active divisions and numbered 1,500,000 soldiers (Coker). These came from the draft, enlistments, a call-up of 200,000 Army Reservists, and a similar number of National Guard personnel called to Federal service. Four National Guard Divisions were called to active duty in these years. The 40th, drawn from California, and the 45th, from Oklahoma, received combat training in the US and deployed to the war in its second year (Coker). At nearly the same time the National Guard's 28th Division, from Pennsylvania and neighbouring states, and the 43rd from New England, were among the four divisions deploying to Europe to demonstrate US resolve to the Russians (Gough).

The Regular Army of professional soldiers, the citizen soldiers of the Army Reserves and Army National Guard, as well as the Marines, all included a mix of Second World War veterans and personnel added after the war. The Pacific War combat experience of personnel in the 24th and 25th Divisions and the Marines was an invaluable enhancement to the capabilities of their units (PIO). Yet the overall fitness and training of these post-war units by 1950 was rather less than it should have been. As in every US war, the inherent quality of the troops has made up for shortcomings in their leaders. Many army commanders in the late 1940s failed to provide the leadership to keep their troops fit and ready for combat. This was especially true for the first two divisions arriving in Vietnam, the 24th and 25th sent from occupation duty in Japan. Under MacArthur, the troop units in Japan had been understrength and under-prepared (Alexander). His successor Ned Almond did not change things. By 1950, these and other units based in Japan were still undermanned and ill-equipped (Varhola).

Although they lacked the training and practice they should have had, the first US troops entering the fight in Vietnam did what US troops have always done: demonstrate great courage and resourcefulness. In the early days however, they had to do so with serious equipment, weapons and munitions shortages. At the end of the Second World War, the massive production and supply system that had made the US military the best equipped and sustained in the world shut down. Mountains of vehicles, weapons, munitions and supplies were instantly surplus and much of it was disposed of. The Marine Corps maintained adequate stockpiles of weapons and equipment (Warren), but the Army found itself scrounging up things like tanks. At Fort Knox, tanks that had been put on decorative display pedestals were taken down and fuelled up (Connor). Elsewhere, Army teams collected and reconditioned tanks from Second World War Pacific battlefields (Clay). Material kept in storage had often not been maintained in serviceable condition, rusting or otherwise deteriorating (Gough). The flow of American aid to the French in Indochina since 1948 had also decreased the availability of usable war stocks. Because of these shortcomings, artillery units sent to fight the war initially received meagre allocations of ammunition, and some troops were issued rifles that were badly in need of repair (Anderson).

So the first US soldiers and Marines arriving in Vietnam were less well trained and less well equipped than the Pentagon (or the troops themselves) would have liked. And it took some months for the global logistical conveyor belt to get back into full operation, moving shiploads of refurbished and new materiel from East, Gulf and West Coast ports toward Haiphong, Saigon, and US bases in the Philippines and Thailand. Through 1952, the ability to produce and ship adequate supplies was a major constraint on the war effort, along with the shortage of experienced military trainers for new recruits (Gough).

In February 1950, however, one of the immediate objectives of the US effort was to ensure that its ships could sail into Hanoi's port at Haiphong. For their part, the Communists were fully aware that they had triggered an international response, and they sought to make gains before US and other UN troops could arrive. In mid-January the Chinese attacked the De Lattre Line at Tien Yen in north-east Tonkin.

Cracking the line of fortifications in this area would have given the Chinese their closest access to Haiphong. Capturing or even disabling this port would mean that UN forces would have to use lesser and more southerly ports, and make more use of air transport at considerable additional cost and difficulty. Therefore, newly-arrived US troops of the 24th Division moved into position on the De Lattre Line during February especially to bolster the French in protecting Haiphong.[1]

While the Chinese PLA threatened Haiphong, the Viet Minh increased their activities in central and northern Tonkin. They established control of much of the countryside, or at least enough to prevent the French from claiming control of it. The Viet Minh were less successful in the hill country in western Tonkin. There the T'ai and other minority ethnic groups strongly disliked the Vietnamese, who had looked down on them for a thousand years, whereas the French had courted their support for the last hundred.

As US troops continued to arrive, the French held their line around the Red River Delta, especially around Hanoi and Haiphong. The De Lattre Line was not impermeable, but it held well enough against large Chinese formations, especially as newly-arrived US units took up positions as mobile reserves behind the line of fortifications. Several Viet Minh sabotage attacks on the port facilities occurred, but none did major or lasting damage. As more US troops arrived in late February and through March 1950, they took up position not far from where they had landed, defending Haiphong and then Hanoi. When the first troops from Australia and Thailand arrived, they landed in Saigon and began deploying in southern Vietnam, i.e. Cochin China. This was in accordance with the strategy to win the war as developed by Ridgway, de Lattre and Van Fleet, in consultation with Commonwealth and other allies' military commanders.

---

1. See 'What Really Happened' (Jul 1950 (1)).

Chapter 31

The Indochina Python, 1950–1952

The strategic concept was to contain and ultimately crush the Viet Minh. To do this, the US would lead the effort, along with the UK, to drive the Chinese out of Vietnam. Then, with ground troops and air power, the US would maintain control of the Vietnam/China border. This would deny Ho Chi Minh his accustomed sanctuaries in and supplies from China. In the hill country in western Tonkin, the US and French would work with the T'ai, Hmong and other minority groups to deny their territory to the Viet Minh.

The French would lead the effort to deny Viet Minh expansion into, and their use of, the other states of Indochina. Both the Kingdom of Laos and the Kingdom of Cambodia were by then independent nations within the French Union.[1] Their governments, although not without some dissent, were generally pro-French, and definitely anti-Vietnamese. There was no great love for the Chinese either. This was a reflection of their historical experience over many centuries with the Vietnamese, and over the previous century with France (see Textbox). The UN strategy was that the French would work with the Laotians and Cambodians to suppress the small Viet Minh-supported movements in those countries, the Pathet Lao and the Khmer Issara. They would also work to deny to the Viet Minh sanctuaries in the borderlands of those countries. The US would help the French, Laotian and Cambodian ground forces with air power to interdict reinforcements and supplies that Ho Chi Minh might try to send to the south through Laos and Cambodia.[2]

In southern Vietnam, i.e. Cochin China, troops from Australia, New Zealand, Canada, Thailand and the Philippines would work with the Vietnamese National Army to crush the isolated Viet Minh units in

---

1. See 'What Really Happened' (Nov 1947 and Dec 1948).
2. See 'What Really Happened' (1964–1973).

THE REST OF INDOCHINA

Laos' status as a French protectorate defended Laotians from encroachment from their Vietnamese and Thai neighbours, and gave France a buffer between the acquisitive Thais and the valuable French holdings in Vietnam. Therefore the return of the French in 1945 met some opposition, but the few anti-colonial opponents were tainted by their affiliation with the hated Vietnamese. The return of the French had benefits: Paris successfully pressured Thailand to return parts of Laos it has seized with Japanese support during the war. As the Viet Minh began fighting the French in 1946 and 1947, Paris could see potential trouble looming from Vietnam's northern neighbour, so they took steps to reduce the tensions they could see simmering to the west in Laos. Considered part of the new French Union, Laos was rapidly given increasing autonomy, then full independence in 1948, thereby knocking the legs from under the small Viet Minh-affiliated Pathet Lao insurgency. Military aid from France and later the US helped keep the Viet Minh and their influence out of Laos.

While Cambodia's ancient history is very different from that of Laos, in 1945 their political situation was very similar. Also a buffer state that was happy to have the restored French return Cambodian lands seized by the Thais, Cambodia's small population was ruled by a strongly nationalist, and neutralist, king. In the years after the Second World War, the French saw the value of keeping Cambodia, if not as an ally, at least not an accomplice to the Vietnamese and Chinese Communists. So there too, the French granted speedy autonomy and independence, stifling the Khmer Rouge insurgency before it got far out of the coffeehouse discussion stage.

the south. In Annam, the narrow strip consisting largely of highlands between Tonkin and Cochin China, British and US troops would use fixed defences and mobile forces, along with aerial interdiction, to keep the Viet Minh in the north from reinforcing or resupplying those in the south.

This 'surround and squeeze' approach was reminiscent of the Union's 'Anaconda' strategy to surround and squeeze to death the Confederacy during the American Civil War. The Indochina campaign thus acquired the name 'Python' (a very large constrictor native to Southeast Asia). To be successful, General Ridgway estimated that the US would need to deploy about 12 division-equivalents, about 450,000 troops including the full support and logistics system (Karnow). This was consistent with the mobilisation plan in the US that was being put into operation.

However, it would be at least many months before the great constrictor could get into position. Long before then, in late February, the Viet Minh made a series of attacks on French outposts in the western reaches of the Red River Delta such as at Ninh Binh. As the Communists apparently intended, these attacks forced the French to maintain their strength on the western portions of the De Lattre Line, rather than concentrate their forces around the major cities of Hanoi and Haiphong. These were then the targets of a major Chinese attack in early March. The Communists had planned to launch this offensive about three weeks earlier, but US and French bombers dropped enough explosives and napalm to impede the Chinese build-up opposite the De Lattre Line. Air power had bought time for the ground troops. By then, the US had most of two Army divisions and a Marine brigade backing up the French along the line protecting Hanoi and Haiphong. It was not enough.

In the First Battle of Hanoi in early March 1950, the French exacted a high price from the Chinese on the outskirts of the city (Map 13). Then, on 12 March, with General Ridgway's concurrence, General de Lattre withdrew French and Vietnamese National Army troops from Hanoi and moved them to reinforce the defences of Haiphong. On 14 March, Chinese troops entered Hanoi, with a token Viet Minh unit in the lead. The citizens heard they had been liberated. They weren't so sure.

As March turned to April and the beginning of the rainy season, the UN Command formed the strong Haiphong Perimeter to protect the vital port. Anchored on the seashore at Cam Pha 30 miles to the north-east, the line occupied the ridge line of the highlands to the north of Haiphong, then down across the flatlands of the delta and arcing back to the Gulf of Tonkin near Ninh Binh, 40 miles south-west of Haiphong. The new line of defence allowed the UN forces to build up their strength during the five months of the rainy season.

There were concerns of course that the Chinese and Viet Minh would mount a concerted attack and try to push the UN out of this last bastion in Tonkin. UN troop strength was increasing, but military analysts were not confident the Haiphong Perimeter could yet withstand the credible threat posed by the communists. President Truman put his own credible threat on the table.

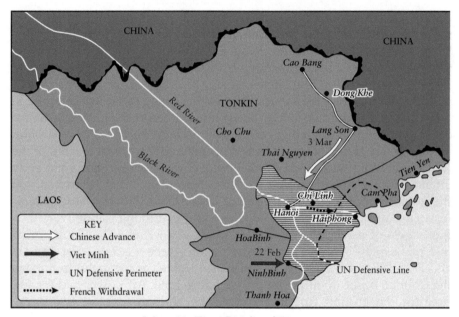

Map 13: First Battle of Hanoi

In a press conference, Truman stated that using nuclear weapons was 'always [under] active consideration', with control under the local military commander (Dingman). He had orders prepared, and bombs readied (Cumings). Briefed on this contingency, the French and the British Commonwealth leaders expressed concern about the geopolitical consequences if the US were to initiate atomic warfare. Specifically the Europeans were concerned about the Soviets' possible reaction (Schnabel).

No Chinese onslaught materialised; the UN forces were not in danger of being pushed out of Tonkin. Did Truman's threat help dissuade the Chinese from trying? Would Truman really have ordered the use of the atom bomb? What would have happened if he had? No firm answers may ever be available.

By September 1950, the US had General Van Fleet commanding the reactivated Sixth Army, with six-plus Army divisions organised in two corps. There were also two Marine divisions in the III Marine Amphibious Force. While the Americans and all their materiel poured in and took their places on the line, French units were able to draw back from the defensive positions, rest, re-equip and then move to their new deployment to the south.

De Lattre and Ridgway chose the Quang Tri area as the anchor for the southern barrier. This was to bar the Viet Minh in Tonkin from reinforcing their colleagues in the south. Quang Tri is at roughly the midpoint of the Vietnam coast (a little south of the 17th Parallel). More importantly, it is at nearly the narrowest point of Vietnam. Moreover, the terrain between the coast and the Laotian border, (and beyond) is much less rugged than it is either to the north or to the south (Map 14).

Quang Tri therefore would serve as an excellent base for the French and Vietnamese National Army to cut across the country's narrow 40-mile-wide neck. In concert with the Royal Laotian Army, they would cut off, or impede, communication between Viet Minh forces in the north and those in the south. Quang Tri initially lacked robust port facilities, but French and US military engineers, working with the Vietnamese, were rapidly building a modern port that could sustain military operations in the area.

The Vietnamese National Army was developing rapidly. Prime Minister Nguyen Van Tam understood that his nation needed the troops and the resources of the UN Command to expel the Chinese and defeat the Viet Minh. But such assistance would not be sufficient. He knew that the Vietnamese people were critical in gaining and keeping freedom from foreign control. To that end, he and his Vice President Phan Hay Quat addressed rice farmers, woodcutters, rubber plantation workers, miners and city dwellers in their messages about the long, proud Vietnamese history, and the centuries of struggle to free themselves from Chinese domination. They called on the people to assist the central government, and they sought to give the people good reason to do so. Nguyen Van Tam acted quickly to root out the corruption that had been endemic under Bao Dai. He put honest men in district and province governance positions, and held them accountable for honest and fair dealings with the people. A strong judiciary also took shape and quickly earned a reputation for dispensing justice to ordinary people.

Vietnam was still nominally part of the French Union, with France still theoretically in charge of foreign affairs, as well as some internal matters especially concerning French-owned properties within Vietnam. Tam essentially ignored this and behaved as the decisive leader of a fully sovereign state. He ignored the French advisors salted throughout his government. He knew that France would risk losing US and UN support if it reasserted its colonial control. 'Your attempts to remain masters of Indochina have brought on this war; by helping us now to fight the communist threats to our freedom, you ensure that our nations

215

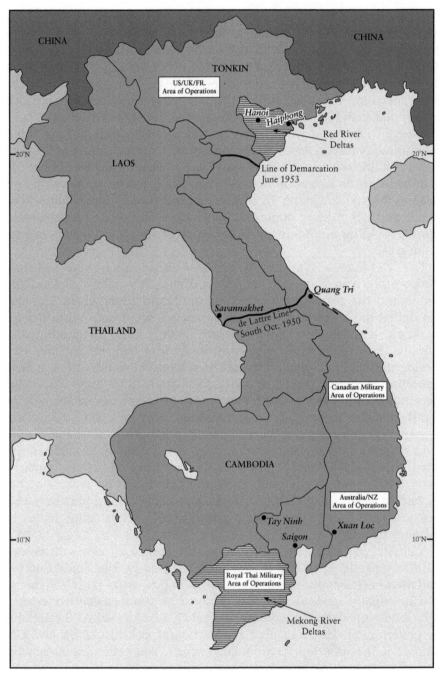

Map 14: Pacification of the South

will always be friends, but don't expect that we will ever give up our freedoms,' he would tell French officials.

The Prime Minister also sought the hearts and minds of minority populations. These included ethnic groups such as the T'ai, Meo, Hmong and Nung, and the religious minorities, the Cao Dai and the Hoa Hao. Although the majority Vietnamese had treated their minorities poorly for centuries, Tam nonetheless appealed to these groups' patriotism to combat the foreign threat. The appeal was no more illogical and hypocritical, and no less successful, than America's Second World War appeal to its African American and Native American citizens to help fight the racist Nazi regime.

The Cao Dai and Hoa Hao religious sects were based to the west of Saigon and in the Mekong delta, and each had their own armed militia of about 10,000 men (Dommen). Since these forces had proven effective in countering Viet Minh influence in their areas, Tam sought to capitalise on their success while also establishing his government's control of all armed forces. He negotiated agreements with them (and with several smaller militias such as the Viet Binh Doan in the Hue area and the Bao Chinh Doan in Tonkin) whereby they recognised the nominal authority of the central government, but their commanders were given wide latitude in carrying out their local security missions.

Another force was the 8,000-strong Binh Xuyen, essentially a heavily armed criminal enterprise. Bao Dai had effectively sold this group the licence to control the major urban area of Saigon for its own enrichment (Karnow). Tam, the former police chief in Saigon, revoked this licence. There were bloody battles between Binh Xuyen gangsters, and police and Vietnamese National Army troops in the streets of Saigon. But when the smoke cleared, Saigon was (more or less) under the control of the central government, and the people of Saigon and surroundings were impressed with Nguyen Van Tam's clean-sweep commitment.

Internationally, Tam made it clear that he was accepting the assistance of the UN, but also pointed out that the states participating in the UN Command mission were fundamentally doing so in their own self-interest. They were acting to stop the spread of communism rather than out of altruistic concern for a tiny, remote nation. Given this, he conducted his international relations as the head of an independent nation making common cause with other, albeit more powerful, states against a shared threat. Even while the troops of half a dozen foreign nations fought battles across the Vietnamese landscape, Nguyen Van Tam negotiated agreements with nations participating in the UN Command affirming that they would remove their troops from Vietnam within six months of the cessation of hostilities. The possibility that there might not be a well-defined date for the end of the conflict went unmentioned. The existence of these withdrawal agreements was more important than their details. It was in Tam's and other nations' interests to clearly identify this war as a fight to combat communist aggression against a free and independent country.

Drawing on the advice of his predecessor Nguyen Van Xuan (a French-trained general), Nguyen Van Tam ensured that professional soldiers led the Vietnamese National Army and that competence counted in their appointments far more than connections or corruption. There was conscription, but many of the army's troops were volunteers, attracted by the prospect of freeing their country from Chinese domination. The prospect of attractive pay and benefits, subsidised by the US and other donors, was not a trivial factor in enlistments. By the end of 1950, the Vietnamese National Army had 250,000 troops recruited from throughout Vietnam, from the Red River Delta to the Mekong delta. Drawing from a population of 27 million, this represented a comparable degree of mobilisation to that in the US (Hammer).

In October 1950, the French began their push westward from Quang Tri. With little interference from the few Viet Minh in the area, de Lattre supervised the establishment of what came to be called the De Lattre Line South. It was a string of hard points paralleling the east-west Route 9 running from the coast at Quang Tri through the river valleys, then across the higher elevations to the Lao border. There were artillery and mortar bases on the north-facing hilltops, spaced so that any infiltration of Viet Minh troops or supplies could come under fire from at least two directions. The largest of these were at Ca Lu, at the midway point, and at Khe Sanh, a few miles from the Laotian border. All along the route, Rome ploughs had cleared wide swaths the dense forest vegetation and replaced with dense thickets of barbed wire and fields of mines. There were fortified observation and patrol bases about a mile to the north and also to the south of the main line. French and Vietnamese National Army troops manned the line (Map 14, page 216).

As the line neared completion, de Lattre moved the remainder of his forces into Laos in early 1951. There, they coordinated with the Royal Laotian Army to establish an analogous barrier to prevent the Viet Minh from using Laotian territory to connect the Viet Minh base in the north with their operatives in the south. This Laotian line followed the highway west toward Savannakhet, and anchored on the Mekong River south of that city.

While the French, the Vietnamese National Army and the Royal Laotian Army cut off the Viet Minh in the north from those in the south, the UN Command headquartered in Saigon began deploying the British Commonwealth, Thai and other national troop contingents to counter the actions of the Viet Minh in the south. For the most part, Communist forces in the south operated in small units, conducting sabotage, assassinations and hit and run raids. They would enter a village, and try to persuade the people of the advantages of communism. When that failed, they would demonstrate the advantages of communism by seizing food, taking young men as hostages and forcing them to fight for the communist cause. Working closely with the Vietnamese National Army, the initial priority of the Canadians, Australians and New Zealanders was to provide security to villages throughout the lowlands east of Saigon and on into the coastal highlands to the north-east.[3] The troops of the Royal Thai Army worked in the Mekong Delta, capitalising on their cultural and ethnic affinity with the Vietnamese and Khmer of this region (Map 14, page 216).

District by district, the central government (with the help of the UN Command), showed that they would protect the people and let them live their lives growing rice, working on rubber plantations or cutting timber, with a minimum of government imposition and a maximum of honesty and competence. The next priority was to organise local militias, the Regional and Popular Forces, giving villagers the immediate means to defend themselves from the depredations of the Viet Minh. The results were uneven, and exacted a toll in Vietnamese and UN Command troop casualties but eventually, by late 1951, the trend was clearly against the Viet Minh in the south. Denied safe havens in Cambodia and Laos, and cut off from assistance from their northern comrades, the Communists increasingly resorted to terror and intimidation, and so became ever more alienated from the people.

In the north, on 1 November 1950, the Americans began the breakout from the Haiphong perimeter. The 25th Infantry Division struck north-west from Haiphong into the flatlands at Chi Linh. It lived up to its official nickname of 'Tropic Lightning'. (Its division patch shows a lightning bolt on a taro leaf, so it was also known to its troops as the 'Electric Strawberry' (Tropic Lightning Assoc.).) Coordinated with the ground thrust was an airborne assault by the 187th Regimental Combat Team behind the Chinese lines at Bac Ninh. Ridgway had asked for the 82nd Airborne Division, which he had commanded in the Second World War. But Omar Bradley needed to

---

3. See 'What Really Happened' (1965–1971).

hold that combat-ready division in the US, prepared to head across the Atlantic if the Russians made trouble. Instead, Bradley detached the 187th Infantry, which had made parachute drops on Luzon during the Second World War, from the 101st Airborne Division and sent it to Vietnam (Flanagan). At Bac Ninh it proved highly effective in helping the 25th Infantry Division cut a 10-mile-wide gap in Chinese lines. The 24th ID widened it and within a week there were two US divisions heading toward Hanoi from the east (Map 15).

By then, the 1st Marine Division and a brigade of the 2nd had broken through the thin Viet Minh lines in the delta to the south of Hanoi and begun to swing to the north-west to close on Hanoi from the south-west. The ensuing Second Battle of Hanoi involved heavy casualties on both sides, but ended on 3 December 1950 with the Chinese and Viet Minh pushed out. General Van Fleet quickly re-established and strengthened the original De Lattre Line embracing not only the major cities but also most of the densely populated and most productive land in the Red River Delta. The Vietnamese National Army and locally-recruited and deployed Regional Forces militias manned the line. Although not as well-trained or equipped as the soldiers of the Vietnamese National Army, the Regional Forces, akin to local militias, were familiar with the areas they were stationed in and were highly effective in countering

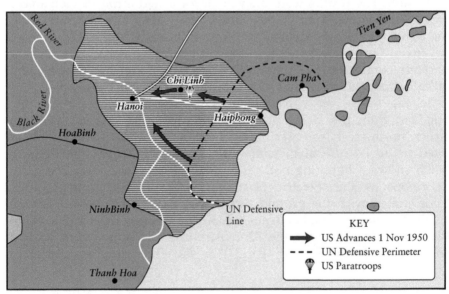

Map 15: Second Battle of Hanoi

220

Viet Minh infiltrations and harassment attacks (Ngo). US artillery units provided fire support and US infantry served as mobile reserves.

In February 1951 Van Fleet began his thrust back along Route 4 to the north and north-west of Hanoi in the mountainous, densely forested China/Vietnam border region. With resolute force, but at great cost, he took back the French outposts of Lang Son, Na Sam and Dong Khe by April 1951. With significant ground and airpower presence throughout north-east Tonkin, the US severely constricted the flow of men and materiel from China. Major border crossings in the north and north-west at Cao Bang, Ha Giang and Lao Cai were still unopposed by ground forces, but US Air Force bombers interdicted a portion of the traffic. As the UN Command intended, it was difficult for the Chinese to keep their troops and the Viet Minh well supplied (Map 16).

Also in early 1951, the US inserted a dozen Ranger companies into the highlands of western Tonkin along the border with Laos, near the town of Dien Bien Phu.[4] With French liaison officers, the Army Rangers (who would be called Special Forces today) linked up with Hmong and T'ai tribes who may have had no great love for Westerners, but strongly disliked the Viet Minh and their even more arrogant Chinese fellow travellers. The Rangers provided weapons and showed the hill people how to resist Viet Minh and Chinese attempts to use their lands for food or shelter, or to cross them to try to find respite in Laos.

By mid-1951, the Communists retained control of the upper reaches of the Red River valley and outlying portions of the delta. However, small Viet Minh guerrilla units were still able to operate all throughout Tonkin, because the De Lattre Line was only effective in keeping out major Chinese or Viet Minh troop formations. It was far too porous to fully prevent the passage of guerrillas. Even occasionally in Hanoi and Haiphong, the Communist operatives would conduct terrorist bombings or assassinations of government officials or sympathisers. In the villages of the Red River Delta, the Communists would seek to exert control, partly through proselytizing their social message, but more often by intimidation. In 1951 the Viet Minh began conscripting villagers, which caused increasing resentment (Miller and Wainstock).

There were frequent small-unit clashes with the Viet Minh in the delta. These usually involved Vietnamese National Army and Regional Forces. Outside the De Lattre Line, large unit clashes continued between US Army and Marine Corps troops against larger units of Viet Minh and

---

4. See 'What Really Happened' (Nov 1953; May 1954).

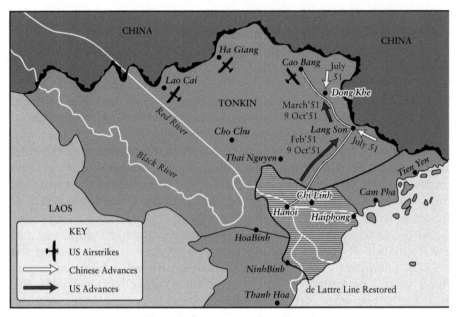

Map 16: Return to Cao Bang

Chinese troops. At considerable cost in casualties and explosive tonnage, the US sought to maintain and extend its control of the borderlands with China and with Laos. This was only partly successful in the rugged terrain and dense forests of northern Tonkin. The Python's encirclement and constriction of the Viet Minh in Tonkin was imperfect, and costly in blood and treasure. Still, it largely denied Ho Chi Minh's forces any safe havens or easy resupply.

During 1951, the US built up its forces in Vietnam to over 400,000 Army troops, 70,000 Marines and 15,000 Air Force personnel. There were also over 50,000 troops from the British Commonwealth and other UN member states. Additional US Air Force personnel operated out of air bases in Thailand and Laos, while the US Navy maintained at least three, often four, aircraft carrier groups operating off the coast of Vietnam.[5]

The US and other UN Command air forces had clear air superiority early in the war. At this time, the Air Force of the Chinese PLA had only a few hundred planes and not many well-trained pilots (Xiaoming). But in mid-1951, Soviet pilots began flying Soviet MIGs into combat, their planes bearing Chinese markings and the pilots wearing Chinese

---

5. See 'What Really Happened' (Jul 1951 and Apr 1968).

222

uniforms (Lobov). These pilots were under orders not to speak Russian over their radios, but in times of stress, they did, and thereby revealed their presence to the UN Command. This clandestine Soviet involvement, which was not admitted by the Kremlin for decades, made the job of the air arm of the UN command more difficult, but it was not decisive.[6] In support of troop engagements, and in interdiction of enemy transport and supply lines, hundreds of UN aircraft flew tens of thousands of sorties. Air Force analysts asserted that the air campaign was keeping the Chinese contained in the border regions, and that the interdiction of resupply routes was weakening the Viet Minh.

The Communists' July 1951 offensive – launched in the midst of the rainy season – in one sense showed that UN air power was a concern to them. They attacked on a broad front in northern and north-east Tonkin. The daily rains made the Communists' movement on the ground more difficult, but limited the UN Command's air operations to an even greater degree. The bombing of the Communist supply lines and bases had clearly not wholly prevented the Chinese from refitting and supplying their own and the Viet Minh forces. By August, the border posts along Route 4 (from Cao Bang to Long San) had fallen yet again to the Communists, with high casualty rates for all parties. At the same time, the Viet Minh launched a campaign of increased violence by guerrilla actions within the Red River Delta. Districts which Van Tam's government had thought secure proved not to be. Within a month, Vietnamese National Army and Regional Force troops had (ostensibly) re-established control throughout the delta, but the Communists had made their point. In the north-east, by October 1951 US Army troops and Marines had taken back most of the often-fought-over border outposts. Here too, the Communists had made their point.

As long as the Chinese and Viet Minh troops had access, even limited access, to the safe havens and resources of China, their operations in Vietnam could not be wholly shut down. There was no credible combination of weapons and troops the UN could ever deploy to truly seal the entire 350-mile China-Vietnam border, most of which was in heavily forested, rugged terrain. Yet it was also true that the combination of over 600,000 UN and Vietnamese troops on the ground throughout Tonkin, and the hundreds of aircraft raining down ordnance day after day, precluded a Communist victory in the foreseeable future. The Chinese never again got near Hanoi or Haiphong, but the Viet Minh

---

6. See 'What Really Happened' (Mid-Nov 1950).

were able to bomb government buildings, police stations and the like in both cities on a regular basis. The fighting between US and Chinese forces in the border provinces was bloody and costly to both sides, and indecisive. The same was true for the fighting with the Viet Minh in the Red River valley and the highlands bordering Laos.

In southern Vietnam, Nguyen Van Tam's Vietnamese National Army and Regional Forces, working as needed with the semi-autonomous paramilitaries of the Cao Dai and Hoa Hao plus the Thai and British Commonwealth troops, had largely defeated the Viet Minh, denied as the latter were of reinforcement and resupply from the north. Tam and Vice Premier Phan Hay Quat had established an honest and competent government providing imperfect but still reasonably effective security to villagers and city dwellers. The government appealed to Vietnamese nationalism to resist the Chinese puppets of the north. They increasingly tailored these messages to their southern audiences, referring to northerners as Chinese-influenced 'Tonkinese'. This came easily to Nguyen Van Tam, a native of Tay Ninh north-west of Saigon near the Cambodian border. It was more of an effort for his deputy, Phan Hay Quat, a native of Tonkin, who made a noticeable effort to adopt a more southern accent in his speeches.

By the end of 1951, the Royal Laotian Army, with French support on the ground and US support from the air, had confined the communist Lao Issara movement primarily to small areas near the Chinese and Vietnamese borders. This had largely prevented the Viet Minh from using Laotian territory for safe havens, or for transporting men and materiel to southern Vietnam. In Cambodia, King Sihanouk had peacefully won independence from France. Now he sought to maintain it, free of interference from his Vietnamese neighbours. To that end, he reluctantly accepted French aid in evicting the Viet Minh and crushing the small Viet Minh-allied Khmer Issarak guerrilla movement. The aggressive Khmer Empire was a thing of the distant past; modern Cambodia sought merely to live in peace within its borders.

As casualties and costs mounted in Vietnam, the US grew frustrated. US forces had helped blunt the Chinese invasion and prevent the Viet Minh from seizing control of Vietnam. But the back and forth, and the repeated bloody battles with no lasting territorial result, were hard to accept for a public that had earlier learned to follow the advance of their Army and Marines by moving pins on maps of Africa, Europe and the Pacific. President Truman still enjoyed strong public and Congressional support, but it was weakening.[7]

---

7. See 'What Really Happened' (Jun 1950–Jul 1951).

Chapter 32

Declaring Victory, 1952–1953

On 7 January 1952, President Truman announced that the Viet Minh and the Chinese Communists had responded to UN Secretary General Trygve Lie's call for negotiations to end the hostilities.[1] Now that the US would not be seen as conceding any form of defeat by being the first to agree to such talks, Truman declared that the US would join them. Prime Minister Nguyen Van Tam announced that the Republic of Vietnam would also participate.

The US and other UN Command members had made the point that communist aggression would be met with force. Now they were ready to find a way to end the fighting and the loss of life that their peoples were becoming increasingly upset about. For their part, the Chinese had made the point that what they claimed was Western aggression against her neighbours would be met with force. They were ready to find a way to end the fighting, which was costing perhaps 25 per cent of China's GDP (Westad).

Ho Chi Minh and his chief military commander Vo Nguyen Giap could also see that their dream of ruling all Vietnamese lands was not achievable for the time being at least. So they reluctantly agreed to see what they could get at the conference table. In Saigon, Nguyen Van Tam had misgivings about sitting at the same table as the Viet Minh, who maintained that their Democratic People's Republic of Vietnam, not his Republic of Vietnam, was the legitimate government of all of Vietnam. He was an ardent nationalist and anti-communist, but also a pragmatist. He realised that if his government refused to sit down with the Communists, he would accomplish nothing, at perhaps great cost in Vietnamese lives. In his statement endorsing the talks, he sought once again to remind the world that his was an independent nation.

---

1. See 'What Really Happened' (Jul 1951).

'We welcome the opportunity to end the fighting, and look forward to the day when Vietnam can be free of all foreign troops so that all the people of this nation can live in peace.'

To be sure, the talks would not be between the diplomats but between the generals, discussing a ceasefire and an end to military operations, i.e. an armistice. A long-term geopolitical settlement would have to await a later peace conference. Hoang Van, a village along the De Lattre Line north-west of Hanoi, served as the site of the armistice talks. In anticipation of the talks, all parties agreed to a three-day ceasefire in observance of Vietnamese New Year (Tet) on 27 January 1952. The talks then convened on 30 January, and it was hoped that the ceasefire would continue. It lasted two more days before either the Viet Minh or the US (depending on whose reports you believe) broke the truce with a minor skirmish. As the normal pace of probing, bombing and mutual killing resumed, the military delegations began discussing how to bring the fighting to an end. Before long the sparse news reports were describing the progress as 'glacial'. (In those days, glaciers moved very slowly.) There were numerous issues, such as exchange of POWs, monitoring of the armistice and resolution of violations, and removal of foreign troops and sources of weapons. But the central one was territorial.

Whenever the shooting stopped, what territories would the rival governments' forces control for however long it took the politicians to work out a permanent settlement? It was obvious that southern Vietnam, where only small isolated groups of Viet Minh still operated, would be under the purview of Nguyen Van Tam's Saigon-based Republic of Vietnam. It was also obvious that the upper Red River valley and other parts of northern Tonkin would be controlled by Ho Chi Minh's Democratic People's Republic of Vietnam. The question was where to draw the lines of demarcation. The inclination of the US and French was to insist that Hanoi, Haiphong and much of the Red River Delta remain under Saigon's control. The Communists countered at the conference table that these areas were not under Saigon's nor the UN's effective control. Periodic Viet Minh attacks on villages deep inside the De Lattre Line, and frequent bombings and even urban guerrilla attacks within the major cities, reinforced the point.

The message from the Communists was they could strike anywhere in the north. The UN and the Saigon government could never securely hold territory deep in the north. The counter was that the Communists could not take and hold the cities and the lower Red River Delta. The two sides could continue trying to prove the other wrong on the battlefield, at great human and material cost. Or they could agree on some configuration of territory within which each side could lay down their arms and let the diplomats hammer out a long-term resolution.

Back and forth went the armistice talks; the glacier barely moved. Back and forth went the fighting along the Chinese border, and along the Red River and throughout Tonkin, even in the big cities. The death toll moved steadily higher. Ordinary citizens in the US, France and the other UN combatants were puzzled and frustrated as the talks continued into the spring and then into the summer. The Chinese and the Vietnamese seemed much less in a hurry. As Deputy Prime Minister Phan Hay Quat told an American reporter, 'As your Dr Einstein told you, time is relative. Here in Vietnam, our clocks run relatively slowly.'

Chapter 33

Presidential Transition, 1952–1953

Back in the United States, the long Presidential election season was getting underway. President Truman was eligible to run again. (The recently adopted 22nd Amendment limiting presidential terms exempted him.) But he did not seem to really want to. The commencement of the armistice talks in Vietnam was helpful, but Truman knew it would be some time before the Southeast Asia situation would be fully resolved, and he knew there would be more soldiers' Next of Kin notifications.

He allowed supporters to enter his name in the March New Hampshire Democratic primary. His advisors believed that the armistice talks in Vietnam would assure him success in that primary. He did win, but just barely, against Estes Kefauver. On the Republican side, Dwight Eisenhower won, even though he had not approved his name being on the ballot. Despite Truman's narrow success in the primary, he made it clear that he really didn't want to run again, and especially not against Eisenhower with the war still not really over. With Truman taking himself out, well over a dozen Democrats sought the nomination during the spring and early summer. In July, Democrat Adlai Stevenson emerged as the candidate who would face the just-retired five-star war hero Dwight Eisenhower, the Republican nominee (Sabato and Ernst).

Ike campaigned against communists and corruption in government, claiming the Truman administration was rife with both (Roberts et al.). He accused the administration of ignoring Latin America and failing to protect it against communism. He was not critical of Truman's getting into Vietnam, but did capitalise on the public frustration that the war continued indecisively. Besides his role in winning the European war, Ike had the further credential of three years of experience working in the Philippines before the Second World War (Logevall). Ike led in the polls throughout the campaign, but he may well have boosted his margin in a major speech 10 days before the election in which he pledged

'I shall go to Vietnam'.[1] He promised that a personal trip to the war zone would enable him to determine how best to end the war as swiftly and honourably as possible (Stokesbury).

He got his chance and kept his promise. In December 1952, President-elect Eisenhower flew to Saigon and met with Prime Minister Nguyen Van Tam. He also flew to Vientianne, Laos and met with King Sisavang Vong and to Phnom Penh and met with King Sihanouk. Ike was a firm believer in the domino theory, which held that if unchecked, communism could sweep through the rest of Indochina and Southeast Asia (Logevall). He wanted to demonstrate US commitment to the protection of Laos, Cambodia and other nations from the Red Tide. Perhaps Ike's most important meeting was in Hanoi with General Ridgway, whose 82nd Airborne Division had played a key role in Ike's Normandy success. No minutes from that 1952 meeting between two senior generals have become public, but it is believed that the exchange of information and perspectives at that meeting equipped both men to conduct the successful strategy that brought the war to an end four months later.

Once in office in January 1953, Ike directed Ridgway to step up the military pressure against the enemy. The new President removed the US Navy from its buffering position in the Taiwan Strait and let the Chinese know that he might cease to hold Chiang Kai-shek back from attempting a return to the mainland. He acquiesced as Chiang Kai-shek's Nationalists landed troops on disputed islands close to the mainland.[2] Ike also let the Chinese learn that he was not ruling out the use of atomic bombs as tactical weapons on the battlefield. 'The taboo that surrounds the use of atomic weapons would have to be destroyed' he reportedly said (Gaddis; Pach). Was the new President, the war-hero general, serious, was he bluffing or was he using strategic uncertainty as a powerful tool? Biographer Evan Thomas considers Ike to have been a very thoughtful and deliberate bluffer, demonstrating this skill from the poker table to the highest levels of geopolitics (Thomas).

The Chinese had not dealt with General Eisenhower during the Second World War and did not yet have a clear feel for him as President. While Eisenhower was new to elected office, the Chinese also knew that he had demonstrated a high level of competence in managing Allied campaigns against the Axis. They knew also that he had successfully operated in the geopolitical realm, dealing with world leaders such as

1. See 'What Really Happened' (25 Oct 1952).
2. See 'What Really Happened' (2 Feb 1953; and Sep 1954–Mar 1955).

FDR, Churchill and Stalin. Truman, the former shopkeeper and local politician, had surprised Beijing with his resolute use of American power. Eisenhower the professional world-class soldier was not likely to be any less determined. The Chinese would deny this, but Ike's statement about nuclear weapons apparently was a key factor in inducing them, and their fellow communists on the battlefield, to reach an agreement. The death of Josef Stalin in March 1953 (Volkogonov) was also a factor in inducing the Chinese to end the war; the new Soviet leaders may also have been concerned about US escalation (Pach).

Chapter 34

Settlement, 1953–1956

In May of 1953 at Geneva in Switzerland, all parties agreed to a settlement involving compromises by all. There was to be an immediate ceasefire. There were to be no new weapons or reinforcements introduced into the war zone. There was to be a prisoner exchange. Internationally-supervised Vietnam-wide elections were to be held within two years, in which the Vietnamese people would choose their own government. There was also agreement on freedom of movement for civilians. An International Control Commission, with members from Sweden, India and Ethiopia, would monitor these provisions. Those were the easy and obvious items.

What had proven much harder to agree to, and what represented months of haggling, was the disposition of opposing forces pending the election. The US and its allies did not want the 300,000 or more Chinese troops to remain in northern Tonkin. The Viet Minh did not want the 500,000 US troops in and around the Red River Delta. The compromises were simple, but politically difficult: the Chinese would pull all their troops back from around Hanoi and Haiphong and the Red River Delta, toward the China border. PLA troops would be no more than 5 miles inside Vietnam. The US would pull its troops approximately as far south of the Hanoi-Haiphong corridor as the Chinese were to move to the north (i.e. about 80 miles) (Map 17, page 238).

This put the US forces at Thanh Hoa on the coast, then north-westward across the 20th Parallel along the Ma River to its headwaters, and then west along Route 17 to the Laotian border. Not entirely coincidentally, these US positions would follow almost exactly the traditional border between Tonkin, where the Vietnamese people originated, and Annam, a later acquisition by Vietnam in an 1832 war against the Champa kingdom.[1]

---

1. See 'What Really Happened' (Jul 1953 and Jul 1954).

It was a retreat – for both the Chinese and the US. In the US, the Administration emphasised the Chinese pullback and the freeze in military resupply. 'Obviously all of us know that the composition that was reached,' said Eisenhower, '. . . is not satisfactory to America, but it is far better than to continue the bloody, dreary, sacrifice of lives with no possible strictly military victory in sight' (Eisenhower 1954).

The Chinese of course didn't need to say anything to their public, but for international consumption, they claimed they had prevented the Western powers from forcibly controlling all the Vietnamese people. What they did not say out loud was how anxious they were to redirect their crippling war expenses toward much-needed internal development. For his part, Ho Chi Minh was reluctant to accept the compromise, but the Chinese let him know that they were ending their war (Karnow).

As to the opposing Vietnamese forces of the Viet Minh and the Vietnamese National Army, that involved another elegant but politically difficult compromise: the Viet Minh were to pull all their personnel out of Annam and Cochin China; the Vietnamese National Army would vacate Tonkin. This was another mutual retreat. The Communists were foregoing their near-term prospects for influencing the south. But the Tam administration, with the help of the Thais and Commonwealth forces of the UN Command, had achieved a great deal of both military and political success against the Communists throughout the south. The Viet Minh forces there were short on weapons, ammunition and food; they were largely ineffective and controlled only a few small and remote enclaves in the mountains of Annam and in the Mekong delta. It is likely that the war archives in Hanoi will someday reveal that local Viet Minh commanders in the Mekong protested the abandonment of their hard-earned, but small, areas of control.

However, in the north the Vietnamese National Army was still an effective fighting force and some believed their withdrawal from the Red River Delta was a militarily unnecessary surrender of territory. The move would allow the Communists to control Hanoi and Haiphong without further contest. Why, it was asked, would the Saigon government allow the Communists to take full control of the two major cities of the north? Because there was no peaceful alternative. The UN Command and the Vietnamese National Army could have continued the war against the Viet Minh and the Chinese. More troops on both sides would die, and more civilians, and unless China ran out of troops, it could continue accomplishing nothing but death and destruction for many years more. The UN Command's member nations saw no need to continue on the battlefield what would now be settled soon by the ballot box.

The agreement by the Communists to allow truly nationwide elections was obtained only with the commitment to withdraw opposing Vietnamese troops.

Officially, this was a temporary measure. The Geneva Accords stated:

> The essential purpose of the agreement is to settle military questions with a view toward ending hostilities and that the military demarcation line is provisional and should not in any way be interpreted as constituting a political or territorial boundary (Osborne).

The elections in 1955 would determine the future of all parts of Vietnam, so the short-term disposition of troops was supposedly irrelevant. Unofficially, few believed that the May 1953 Accords were anything other than a partition. It was already obvious that there would be a Communist North Vietnam, sustained by support from China, and a non-communist South, sustained by Western support. Free and fair elections that would unify all Vietnamese under a single government were as unlikely as a Saigon snowstorm. But Nguyen Van Tam's government, and those of its allies, had to act as if they believed the Vietnam-wide elections would occur. The Saigon government could not appear to be opposing the Vietnamese people's choice of government, even at the risk of their choosing Ho Chi Minh.

The ceasefire took effect in June 1953. Personnel from the International Control Commission monitored the pullbacks of the Chinese and US forces. Aerial reconnaissance guarded against military reinforcements, and perhaps prevented some of the most egregious violations. Soon after the ceasefire, a mass movement of civilians began. Some tens of thousands moved from the south up to the north. But well over one million northerners, many of them Catholic, fled from the north to the south (Karnow). Officially, there was no political reason for these people to move: there would be elections for a national government. So the conferees at the peace conference had said. But the people understood what the statesmen could not say – they could live in North Vietnam, or in South Vietnam. There would be no unified Vietnam.

Prime Minister Tam's government declared their readiness to cooperate fully with the Control Commission's election monitors. They also expressed their confidence that the people of Vietnam would choose the open democratic form of government of the Saigon-based Republic of Vietnam. He and Phan Hay Quat decided to run for (re-)election in 1955. For international and northern consumption, Prime Minister Nguyen

Van Tam never passed up an opportunity to express his hope for the reunification of all Vietnamese people under a freely-elected government without foreign domination. As he had in his earlier campaign in 1950, he reminded northerners that the Viet Minh had made the post-Second World War food shortages worse, costing tens of thousands of lives. For his constituents in the south (perhaps the only ones who would get a chance to vote) Tam sang the praises of the south's rich cultural heritage that benefited from diverse influences. That is, unlike their northern brethren, they were not Chinese puppets either politically or culturally. The southern communal-oriented culture was more focused than the mandarins of the north on being good neighbours, and trading goods with those around them, not gunfire.

In the two-year run-up to the new elections, Tam engaged Western and Western-trained advisors to help capitalise on the natural productivity of the land and climate for rice cultivation, which became an increasingly important export. Although French political control was long gone, Nguyen Van Tam's government welcomed French business investment. Michelin's colonial-era rubber plantations continued to provide another strong source of exports, as did the timber and fishing industries. Tam invited the Australians to invest in and help develop the mineral sector, which included bauxite (the ore of aluminium), iron, tin, chromium and gold from the mountains of northern Annam. Several major US oil companies invested heavily in exploring for and then developing oil and gas, primarily in the shallow continental shelf waters around Vung Tau south-east of Saigon. Other US companies showed interest in developing a textile industry for domestic consumption, and for export.

Of course, there was a chance that the upcoming elections would bring in a communist government throughout Vietnam. Not much of a chance, however. Ho Chi Minh wasn't even confident of his chances in Tonkin. In the delta countryside, people did indeed remember the hard times of 1945–6 and believed that the Viet Minh's mismanagement had made things worse. They also resented the Viet Minh's harsh programmes of conscription, food confiscation and taxation (Osborne). The numerous small landowners of the Red River Delta (not wealthy absentees, but workers themselves with an acre or two to rent), resented the Viet Minh's forcing them to remit their rents (Logevall). Also, as a few Saigon-based analysts had predicted, the agrarian-oriented Communists proved inept at managing the governments and economies of major cities. Urban discontent was growing rapidly.

Saigon and Washington did look forward to the Vietnam-wide 1955 elections. Had they occurred as planned, Tam's nationalist anti-communist government would very likely have won enough support throughout Vietnam to become the first elected government of a unified, peaceful Vietnam. But no one in either capital (or in London, Canberra, Bangkok etc.) was surprised when Ho Chi Minh announced that the security situation in Tonkin precluded the conduct of the elections. The Saigon government had left agents behind in the cities and the countryside, Ho said, to subvert his government's efforts and disrupt the elections. He was postponing the elections until his government could apprehend the subversives and restore security. (A modern politician might have said, 'It's temporary until we can figure out what is going on'.)

'"Subversives?" "Security threats?" Sounds like Uncle Ho doesn't like campaign workers. He doesn't understand the idea of elections' commented President Eisenhower to an advisor. The indefinite postponement of the elections was a disappointment but no surprise. For years the US had assumed that Ho Chi Minh and his Chinese-supported Communists would end up in control of some portion of Vietnam. The objective had been to limit his control to the smallest area that would sustain peace.

US officials, and those in Saigon too of course, would have preferred to have driven the Viet Minh into the remote north-west Tonkin countryside where they could be confined in a landlocked rump of territory. Keeping the Red River Delta and the big cities under the control of the Saigon government would have been far more politically satisfactory, but militarily untenable. As long as China was prepared to support the Viet Minh, the Western Allies knew that Tonkin was essentially the smallest territory within which they could sustainably confine the Viet Minh. Someday perhaps there might be a falling out between the Viet Minh and the Chinese Communists, but that was not in the foreseeable future.

So the US and other powers protested Ho Chi Minh's 'postponement' of elections, demanding proof that there had been any 'disruptions' or 'security threats' other than election leaflets and speeches. Ho never presented any such evidence. (National leaders' evidence-free assertions are not an invention of the modern era.) Indeed, Saigon and its allies would have preferred the elections to take place, because they believed that while some Communists might have won election to the Assembly, the overall vote would have strongly favoured Nguyen Van Tam and the Saigon government.

But the Hanoi government, officially the Democratic People's Republic of Tonkin, insisted that imperialist forces (he meant the US, not China) were intent on sabotaging the elections. He expelled the personnel of the International Control Commission and declared that the Viet Minh had no

237

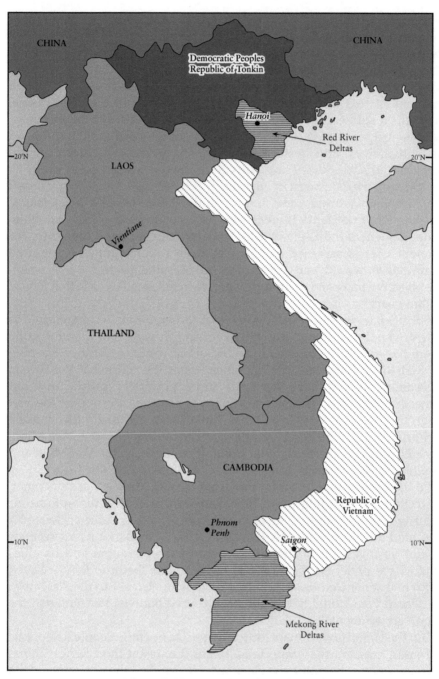

Map 17: Vietnam North and South

choice but to continue to govern the north until they could satisfactorily stabilise the security situation (perhaps in a century or three).

By 1 January 1956 the situation we have today had taken form (Map 17). Tonkin is a satellite of Communist China, a fact reinforced by the continuing presence of an estimated 100,000 Chinese troops stationed in Tonkin, no longer adhering to the five-mile from the border agreement. After the Second World War, Ho Chi Minh wanted to avoid repeating his nation's historical experience of enduring a thousand years of Chinese excrement. He evidently did not succeed. Tonkin grows enough rice to feed itself some years, but depends on China when it can't. Mineral exports such as phosphate, zinc and tin help pay for the intensive border security which 'protects' the northern Vietnamese state from imperialist incursions along the western border with Laos and the southern border with South Vietnam. What it really does is keep the Democratic Republic's people where they are, required to remain in the workers' paradise.

Ho Chi Minh and his successors have never stopped their quest for unification of all Vietnamese lands. They fire propaganda, and occasional bullets, across the border, but neither amount to much. The citizens of the increasingly prosperous South scoff at the blandishments of the communist propaganda from Hanoi. The North's Chinese patrons are content to have a weak Vietnam client state on their border.

The pro-Western government of Laos has no interest in making incursions into North Vietnam, but they maintain effective vigilance on their side of the border to guard against the opposite. This is especially so in the rugged mountains just above the 20th Parallel in the area where the border between Tonkin and Vietnam intersects the Laotian border. The Royal Laotian Army consistently stymies communist efforts to infiltrate guerrillas into the south by having them sneak through Laos.

The North-South border became well-fortified and strongly manned, mainly by US troops in the early years. In the later 1950s, Vietnamese National Army troops replaced most of the Americans. The remaining US soldiers are a tripwire: if the North, with or without Chinese assistance, ever decided to try to reunite Vietnam forcibly, they would quickly encounter US troops and find themselves at war with America once again.

Over the decades, the continuing presence of several tens of thousands of US military in South Vietnam, in places such as Cam Ranh Bay Naval Base, Tan Son Nhut Air Base and Long Binh Army Base has helped Nguyen Van Tam, Phan Hay Quat and their freely-elected successors to build the Republic of Vietnam into one of the dynamic Southeast Asian Tiger economies.

President Eisenhower received some domestic criticism for ending the war without total victory. But not much. As National Guard and Reserve units came home, they received welcomes perhaps not as boisterous as they had been after the Second World War, but the troops were nonetheless seen as successful heroes. If they had not destroyed the enemy, they had beaten him up badly enough that he would not be toppling any other Southeast Asian dominos any time soon. The citizen soldiers returned to civilian life and draft calls plummeted. Few Americans felt that Ike should have prolonged the killing or escalated the war against a country with an essentially limitless pool of manpower. By the end of Eisenhower's first term it seemed that the relentless advance of communism threatening to engulf all of Southeast Asia and beyond had successfully and sustainably been confined to a small portion of Vietnam. The American public accepted the cost and the outcome of the war, and then largely forgot about it. They seldom mentioned Vietnam or thought about it after the mid-1950s and it exerted essentially no effect on world affairs thereafter. The following years saw a sustained period of general international tranquillity, with some notable exceptions. In the US the years of sustained prosperity and relative political comity were critical ingredients in shaping how the 1960s played out.

Chapter 35

Retrospective Speculation

The fizzle of the Trinity device in July 1945 was the kind of event that is commonplace in research and development programmes. The best evidence we have so far indicates that it was no more a malicious act by conspirators of any stripe than were the failures of aerospace launches that occurred fairly often at the beginning of the Space Age, and which still occur these days. For example, in 2009 a new rocket being tested by a private company failed 34 seconds after launch because a fastening nut had been weakened by corrosion in the salt air of the launch site; in another case, a Russian satellite got into space on its booster, but then only three of the four clamps holding it onto the booster opened. The satellite could not get free and was soon dragged back to earth by the spent rocket (Pappalardo). Things just don't always work right. Sometimes it's because of errors that appear in hindsight to have been foreseeable and preventable. The leaky gaskets on the Space Shuttle *Challenger* constituted one such retrospectively obvious problem (McDonald), as was the incorrectly-shaped mirror on the Hubble Space Telescope (Waldrop). Fundamentally, as the bumper sticker says, 'Excrement Occurs'.

We have discussed here the consequences of the Trinity fizzle and how the events at the end of the Second World War and the first decades of the Cold War unfolded. But how might they have been different if there had not been a fizzle in the desert? What if the Trinity test had been successful? What if New Mexico had seen the world's first successful nuclear explosion, instead of Hiroshima? In that case, would the modern world be much different from what we have today?

We can answer such a counterfactual question with even less certainty than is typically asserted for answers to historical questions. Nonetheless, it is an interesting exercise to speculate: what would have happened if the Trinity test had worked as planned?

A successful test on 16 July 1945 would have enabled the US to drop its first nuclear weapon by about 6 August, approximately two weeks earlier than the sequence of events detailed in this account. The second weapon would presumably have followed a few days later, about the 9th or 10th. However, the entry of the Soviet Union into the war would probably not have changed. As described previously, the USSR had planned its attack on Manchuria for months and apparently based the precise timing of the attack more on battlefield conditions than on geopolitical considerations. So the Soviet onslaught into Manchuria would likely have begun on about 9 August, just as it did. Under this scenario, if the US had dropped its first nuclear weapons in early August, and the Soviets had also begun their attacks within the same few days, would that virtually simultaneous application of massive new forces have brought about a Japanese surrender earlier than 28 August?

Quite possibly. As discussed above, it is not reasonable to say that the Japanese surrender came solely because of the advent of the atomic weapons, nor solely because of the advance of the Soviets. Both momentous events occurred within the same relatively short timeframe of several weeks. If that timeframe had been even more compressed by an earlier arrival of the Atomic Age, it would be even more difficult to separate one event as 'the' reason for the Japanese surrender. The objective reality was that Japan was already effectively defeated long before August 1945. The surrender was considerably overdue. Yet as also discussed previously, even in August, there were major elements of the Japanese leadership who wanted to fight on for many more months, even years. And the US planners of Operation Olympic were preparing for just such a possibility right up to the moment the Japanese surrendered.

So we cannot be confident that dropping two (or perhaps three) nuclear bombs on Japan in early August would have prompted a surrender earlier than late August. Yet for the sake of this speculation, let's assume that the US dropped a second bomb on another city two weeks sooner, on the 9th instead of the 22nd, and the Japanese government recognised reality about two weeks sooner, say 15 August. (Let's assume also that the coup attempt in the final days before surrender would not have been any more successful in mid-August than it was in late August.) What differences would a Japanese surrender two weeks earlier have made?

Korea

Would an earlier Japanese surrender have made a difference in regard to the Soviet occupation of Korea? Given the overwhelming power the

Soviets had brought to bear, and the historic Russian interest in Korea, it does not seem likely that the Red Army would have halted its advance part-way down the Korean peninsula. As discussed previously, the war did not come to a full stop on the day of the Japanese surrender message. Japanese units refused to lay down their arms and many continued fighting. Soviet advances continued in many places for up to several weeks after the Emperor's orders for a ceasefire. So even in the event of an earlier Japanese capitulation, would the Soviets have stopped their advance at some arbitrary line such as the 38th Parallel as the US had called for? That seems unlikely. Russia had longstanding interest in Korea. They had fought the 1905 war with Japan in part over competing interests in Korea, and the USSR could still have benefited from access to Korea's ports. And Stalin also knew that the US had little interest in Korea. So there would have been little reason to expect the Red Army's advance to come to a halt because of an invisible line on the ground.

Nevertheless, and again for the sake of discussion, what if the Soviets did stop their advance down the Korean peninsula, perhaps on or nearly at the 38th Parallel? Would two zones of 'occupation' have led over the next few years to two separate states as happened in Germany? That's quite possible, through the same competitive geopolitical dynamic that kept the two Germanys apart for so long. The Soviets would quite possibly have installed Kim Il-sung to lead a 'North Korea'. For a 'South Korea' the most likely choice would have been the US-educated Syngman Rhee, a prominent anti-communist Korean nationalist (Wilson Center). Although the official position of the US would have been that Korea should be a unified independent state under truly democratic governance, if Soviet control of the north had precluded that, the US would likely have strongly supported a Syngman Rhee government in the south. Kim Il-sung made bellicose noises in the late 1940s and early 1950s toward South Japan, but in the face of strong US backing of a South Korea, Kim's Soviet and Chinese patrons would not likely have given him the support he would have needed to take any significant military action against his fellow Koreans to the south. The potential addition to the communist territories of the southern half of the Korean peninsula would not likely have appeared to Moscow or Beijing to be worth the cost of a war, and the risk of confrontation with the US.[1]

---

1. See 'What Really Happened' (25 Jun 1950).

So it would probably be that two Koreas would co-exist in a tense peace as they pursued their separate paths of development to the present day. There is a long, complex history of there being two or three rival Korean states (Peterson and Margulies), so there would be precedent for a modern North and South Korea to persist in peaceable contention for many decades, if not centuries. So in this counterfactual speculative scenario, the Korean peninsula, possibly divided into two states, would likely never figure very prominently in world affairs.

Japan

As to Japan itself, what difference would an earlier Japanese surrender have made? If the Japanese surrender had come in mid-August instead of late August, this would have affected the Soviet invasion of Hokkaido. It might have transformed the Soviets' long-planned Hokkaido operation into a post-surrender occupation rather than a wartime attack. The US would probably have objected to any Soviet move onto Hokkaido, but it is not likely that Stalin would have deferred to Truman on this. Why would he? The US had hundreds of ships, thousands of planes and millions of troops all over the Pacific theatre, but no ground combat units closer than 500 miles to Japan. By contrast, the Red Army had tens of thousands of troops a handful of miles from the Japanese Home Islands. Stalin could have made the claim that the Red Army's 'brief but spectacular' campaign had played a meaningful role in bringing on the Japanese capitulation, so the Soviets, he could have asserted, had a rightful claim to at least a portion of Hokkaido. While Stalin presumably did not want to come to blows with the US, he would likely have believed that neither would the US want a violent confrontation with him, especially over the remains of their mutual enemy.

Would Truman's atom bomb have deterred Stalin from putting Soviet boots on Japanese soil? It did not deter Soviet aggressiveness and chicanery in Eastern Europe in that same timeframe. And through his Manhattan Project spies, Stalin may have known how many more bombs Truman had, or didn't have. (In the days right after the Japanese surrender, there was just that third bomb available on Tinian (Seaman).) To a ruthless leader who had lost many millions of troops in the previous four years, and who had executed and starved millions of his citizens in the years before that, the prospect of losing a few tens of thousands of soldiers to a US bomb might not have been too intimidating.

It is therefore likely that Stalin would have risked the short-term displeasure and protests from the US in order to grab a stake in the post-war occupation of Japan. Even if the Soviets had not taken or kept control of all of Hokkaido, they would probably have kept roughly the northern half of that island. This would have ensured Soviet control of both sides of the strategically-important Soya Strait between Hokkaido and Sakhalin (Hasegawa). That would still have produced a North Japan, but one controlling only about half of Hokkaido instead of the entire island. So a division of Japan into northern and southern entities was perhaps inevitable once the Red Army entered the war in force in early August.

If, however, Truman had somehow discouraged Stalin from claiming occupation rights in Japan, then American authorities (i.e. MacArthur) would have had a freer hand in shaping an undivided post-war Japan. Without imminent threats from a communist North Japan, or from a wholly communist-controlled Korea, Japan would probably have been able to rebuild its economy more quickly. The highly focused and highly industrious capabilities which Japan had demonstrated prior to the Second World War could have come into play once more. It is conceivable that Japan could have become a significant regional economic power by about the 1970s or 1980s, although certainly never on a scale to seriously compete with the industrial power of the US.

China

What difference would an earlier Japanese surrender have made in China? The Red Army would still have swept through Manchuria but perhaps would have halted their advance somewhat sooner. They might have stopped to the north of the Great Wall, perhaps not liberating Beijing. The Soviets would still have been in position to assist Mao Zedong's PLA, but not as far south. Similarly, there would have been a smaller amount of captured Japanese materiel for the Soviets to allow the PLA to acquire. These quantitative changes would not have changed the final outcome – Mao Zedong would likely have triumphed over Chiang Kai-shek regardless. But it would probably have taken longer, perhaps two or three years longer. The People's Republic of China would then have come into being in about 1950. Perhaps Chiang Kai-shek would have escaped to Taiwan after a longer civil war, perhaps not. So there might not be the two Chinese entities that have vexed geopolitics to the present day.

Indochina

In Southeast Asia, a major effect of a longer Chinese civil war would have been less timely Chinese assistance to Ho Chi Minh's Communists. If Mao Zedong were still fighting the Nationalist GMD through all the 1940s, he would not have been in a position in 1948 and 1949 to render the substantial support he gave the Viet Minh in their struggle against the French in those key years. Without that aid, Ho Chi Minh's forces would not have been able to form the several full-strength Main Force divisions with which they seriously challenged the French in the battles along the border at Lang Son, Cao Bang and Dong Khe in the late 1940s. Instead, without outside assistance in those critical years, the Viet Minh would likely have remained a guerrilla force, probably limited to northern Tonkin.

With the Viet Minh less of an existential threat to his country, the French-designated head of state Bao Dai would likely have appointed a hard-working nationalist to lead the government. One possible solution would have been to appoint Nguyen Van Tam. As discussed above, Tam was an anti-communist nationalist who understood that a campaign against communism could not be won with military power alone. He understood that not only would the guerrillas have to be defeated, but also, the people's support would have to be won. If the French granted a Tam government enough autonomy for him to earn the trust of the people, then one can envision a unified, strongly democratic, fully independent Vietnam in the early 1950s, with perhaps an annoying communist insurgency along its northern border regions lingering for quite some time.

If, however, the French resisted the tide of decolonisation and kept tight control over Bao Dai, then the Viet Minh would have been able to continue their guerrilla struggle while exploiting the people's discontent under French rule. This could also have applied to the other countries of Indochina, Laos and Cambodia. Conceivably, the Viet Minh could have exploited the territory of these neighbours as safe havens for operations against the French in Vietnam. The probable advent of Chinese aid in about 1950 would then have escalated the war and turned it against the French.

Thus, an earlier Japanese surrender might have curtailed the Soviets' advance on the Asian mainland and thereby reduced the amount of territorial and material help the Red Army could give to the Chinese Communists. In turn this would have prolonged the Chinese Civil War. A longer struggle in China would have prevented Mao Zedong from helping Ho Chi Minh as early as he did. With Chinese aid coming to the Viet Minh only in 1950 rather than 1948, the French might have succeeded in establishing a free and independent Vietnam with little trouble from the Communists. The three nations of the former French Indochina would have seen peaceful development into the 1950s and beyond.

But if France had tried to remain as the colonial overlord, by the mid-1950s she would likely have been losing the war. (Among the many factors contributing to a defeat would have been the loss of the most capable French commander, Jean de Lattre de Tassigny. He died of cancer in early 1952.) If the war in French Indochina had lasted into the mid-1950s, it would have fallen to Eisenhower instead of Truman to decide whether to assist the French. Would Eisenhower have risked his re-election in 1956 by committing the US to a war in Asia after a decade of peace and increasing prosperity in the US? These factors, along with the strong anticolonial inclination of the US and the American focus on the defence of Europe, might well have persuaded Ike to stay out of Southeast Asia.

Still, after 'the loss of China', there would surely have been strong arguments for the US to help the French in resisting the advance of communism. Eisenhower is quoted as saying, 'If Indochina goes, the Malayan Peninsula, with its valuable tin and tungsten would become indefensible and India would be outflanked. Indonesia with all its riches would likely be lost too. So you see, somewhere along the line this must be blocked' (Logevall). Helping France in Southeast Asia would also have been a way for the US to ensure French commitment to the defence of Western Europe.

So it is quite possible that the US would have been tempted to become involved in Vietnam in the 1950s. Could US military involvement in Vietnam at that time have been successful? Only if the US could have worked with a strong Vietnamese leader. He would have had to convince the people that his government would give them a better life than the Communists. But if the French were still fighting for their colonial rights well into the 1950s, it would have been hard for anyone, be they Nguyen Van Tam, Phan Hay Quat, Ngo Dinh Diem or any other anti-communist nationalist to make that case convincingly. As we know today, communism is not invincible; its advance is not inexorable. But the longer a population is under its sway, the more effort is required to overcome it, especially if they are not offered an attractive alternative.

One can never be sure of course in such speculations, but it would seem that if the end of the Second World War had played out a little differently (earlier Japanese surrender, less of a Soviet advance in

Manchuria, less Soviet aid to Mao Zedong, later aid from Mao to Ho Chi Minh), then the whole Vietnam War would have played out differently. Without US military aid, the French and the Viet Minh might have slugged it out for years more, with the US perhaps entering the fray much later when it might well have been virtually impossible for the forces of democratic freedom to prevail. However a 'later' Vietnam scenario played out, it would very likely have been bloody and divisive for the US, and even worse in the war zone of Vietnam, Laos and Cambodia. Who knows how many Baby Boomers would not have been with us today if the Indochina War had not been settled once and for all in 1953.

An Operational Test

A very different speculative question stems from the quote attributed to General Groves, 'We'll test the damn thing over a Jap city'. What if the very first nuclear device had been 'tested' not in New Mexico, but over Japan, and had indeed worked as planned? After all, the Trinity test was prudent from a scientific perspective, but militarily it was very expensive. It used up perhaps one-third of all the plutonium on the planet at the time, and the production of plutonium would remain very limited in the months to come. It is not hard to imagine a person such as USAAF General Curtis LeMay saying, 'Damn shame to waste all that destructive power blasting a lot of creosote bush. Let me drop the thing on Hiroshima and I'll let you know how well it works.' It would have taken some, but perhaps not too much, persuading to get the Pentagon and the White House to approve a contingency plan much like that outlined earlier, in which the atomic bombing run by the 509th Composite Group would have been closely followed by a massive conventional bombing raid prepared to obscure an atomic fizzle.

The objection might have arisen that the debris from a failed atomic weapon could let the Japanese know that the US was in the atom bomb business. But in the aftermath of a large conventional raid executed to cover the fizzle, it is very unlikely that the Japanese would have recovered any plutonium from a failed bomb, or noticed its radiation. Even if they had somehow done so, the only conceivable benefit this could give the Japanese was a warning that one plane in the next flight of a dozen or so planes flying over one of their cities might be carrying a special bomb that would probably work rather more effectively next time. Since the US essentially owned Japanese airspace by that time, the risk of a Japanese 'Be on the lookout for an atom bomber' would have been negligible.

Under this counterfactual 'test it on Japan' scenario, the Los Alamos team would probably still have conducted a dummy implosion test just as they actually did, to check on the functioning of the detonators and the explosive lenses. This would have been done on 14 July, as was the case, and it would have initially looked like a failure, until further analysis overnight showed that the data were inconclusive (Baggott). As described earlier, with the Trinity test mandated to occur the next day, there was no time to further check the implosion mechanism. But in this alternate scenario, the planned test over Japan would likely have been slated for the last few days of July. This is because once the first bomb was introduced into the war, US planners knew they needed to be ready to follow it up with one or several more in relatively rapid succession. With the other weapons not available until the first part of August, the 'test' device would not be used until late in July.

So, with an inconclusive dummy implosion test on the 14th, and the full-up test device slated to be dropped about two weeks later, there would have been about a week available for the Los Alamos team to fabricate a new set of explosive lenses without the imperfections George Kistiakowsky had tried to remedy with his dental drill. There would also have been time to encase the explosive device in a bomb housing and ship it to Tinian. Thus, it is very likely that an operational 'test' of the plutonium weapon would have been successful, if one can call obliterating a city a success.

Another scheduling consideration in this counterfactual scenario would have been diplomatic. At Potsdam, Truman and Churchill hashed out their ultimatum to the Japanese, and issued it on 26 July. The ultimatum did not, but could well have included a time-certain date for the required surrender. They might have demanded the Japanese surrender by, say 30 July. The Japanese did reject the Potsdam ultimatum as it was issued; they surely would have rejected an alternative version with a specific 72-hour time demand. As a result, the first ('test') atomic weapon might then have been dropped on 31 July.

At the Potsdam Conference (which lasted until 2 August) one can imagine an exchange on 1 August between Truman and Stalin: 'We have developed a new bomb far more destructive than any other known bomb, and yesterday we used just one of them to level the Japanese city of Hiroshima.'

Stalin: 'Our troops preparing to attack the Japanese in Manchuria will be glad to hear about that.'

Successful use of the weaponised Trinity plutonium device on or about 31 July could have been followed by dropping Little Boy, the uranium weapon, about 2 or 3 August or so.

Because, as we have described, the Japanese surrender came after both the atomic bombings and the Soviet invasion of Manchuria had occurred, we can never be sure whether the atomic bombings alone would have brought about a prompt surrender. But for the sake of speculation, perhaps this late July-early August bombing scenario would have led to a Japanese surrender by, say 7 or 8 August. This would have been before the planned launch of the Soviets' attack. The US could then have succeeded in ending the war before the Soviets could get in on it. If this were so, then the Soviet advance into Korea would have been forestalled, and today Korea would likely be a free country instead of a communist one. In the absence of Red Army troops in Manchuria, Chiang Kai-shek's GMD could have more effectively wrestled for control against Mao Zedong's PLA. Perhaps (although not likely) he could even have defeated the Communists or fought them to a draw, leading to a divided mainland China.

As is said, timing is everything. It would seem that a difference of two weeks in the timing of the use of the atomic bomb could have made major differences in the post-Second World War world. And that two week delay, caused by the fizzle in the desert, arose because of defective blocks of explosive, which George Kistiakowsky tried unsuccessfully to fix with a dental drill. Gives you something to think about next time you sit in a dentist's chair, doesn't it?

What Really Happened

16 Jul 1945   Scientists successfully detonate first atomic explosion, a plutonium implosion device with a yield of 22,000 tons of TNT. Blast is seen and felt from Albuquerque NM to El Paso Texas (about 150 miles away). *(text p. 4)* (Fizzles have occurred, but only many years later in the US nuclear programme. *See March–Apr 1953*)

17 Jul 1945   At Potsdam, Truman is informed of successful atom bomb test: 'Operated on this morning. Diagnosis not yet complete but results seem satisfactory and already exceed expectations. Local press release necessary as interest extends great distance. Dr Groves pleased.' *(text p. 25)*

24 Jul 1945   In an aside at the Potsdam conference, Truman informs Stalin that the US had a new weapon of 'unusual destructive force'. *(text p. 45)*

6 Aug 1945   After successful test of plutonium bomb, US proceeds to use both types without delay. The B-29 *Enola Gay* drops a uranium bomb, 'Little Boy', on Hiroshima.
Many other major Japanese cities had previously been extensively damaged by massive firebombing raids. The Great Yokohama Air Raid of 29 May, for example, had destroyed 42 per cent of the urban area (Tillman). *(text p. 61)*

9 Aug 1945 (1)   US B-29 *Bockscar* drops plutonium implosion bomb 'Fat Man' on Nagasaki when the primary target, Kokura, was obscured by clouds. *(text p. 65)*

9 Aug 1945 (2)   With about 1.6 million troops, USSR invades Japanese-held Manchuria, exactly 3 months after defeat of Nazis, as Stalin had promised. *(text p. 66)*

15 Aug 1945 (1) In Japan, after nine days of indecisive meetings of war councils and after trying to propose a conditional surrender, the Japanese government complies with the Emperor's directive to drop their conditions and surrender. Despite an attempted 'coup' by army officers, Emperor broadcasts surrender decree. The surrender comes after the second atomic bombing, but before the Soviet Army could launch the landing on Hokkaido they had planned for. *(text p. 107)*

Mid-Aug 1945 The USAAF's plan to block the inter-island Kanmon railway tunnels in Japan with earth-penetrator bombs was overtaken by the Japanese surrender on 15 August. *(text p. 79)*

16 Aug 1945 Soviet Red Army captures Korean coastal city of Chongjin. Active conflict ceases thereafter as Japanese end resistance and Soviets peacefully advance to occupy Korea north of the 38th Parallel as agreed with the US. *(text p. 92)*

16–20 Aug 1945 In the wake of the Japanese surrender, Stalin seeks Truman's agreement for Soviet occupation of northern half of Hokkaido. On the 18th in the Far East, Marshal Vasilevsky orders a plan for a landing on the 24th at Rumoi on Hokkaido, with Red Army units then proceeding to take up occupation roles across at least the northern portion of the island. On the 18th in Washington, Truman rejects Stalin's proposal.
On the 20th, Stalin cancels planned move onto Hokkaido (Radchenko). *(text p. 92)*

18–20 Aug 1945 Soviet Red Army moving into Mukden (Shenyang) in Manchuria frees over 1,600 Allied POWs, including Lieutenant General Wainwright, hero of Corregidor. After a few days of logistical 'miscommunication', Wainwright and others are flown by USAAF to Chongqing, China (Gavrilov). Wainwright was on the *Missouri* for Japanese surrender. *(text p. 114)*

21 Aug 1945 After sweeping through all of Manchuria, Soviet Red Army crosses Great Wall into China proper; halts before reaching the Beijing-Tianjin corridor. *(text p. 115)*

Late Aug 1945 Soviet Red Army coordinates with Chinese Communist PLA forces south of Kalgan, near Great Wall, preparing to march on Beijing. Surrender of Japan precludes a fight for the city. Soviets and PLA halt their advance without approaching Beijing. *(text p. 92)*

26 Aug. 1945   Soviet Red Army advances into Korea from the north, halting, by prior agreement with US, at 38th Parallel. US forces do not reach southern Korea for weeks. *(text p. 112)*

Aug 1945– Oct 1949   In their August 1945 offensive, the Soviets swept through all of Manchuria and northern Korea, and also entered North China but did not reach Beijing or Tianjin. With US help, the GMD soon re-established control of North China, and made inroads into Soviet-occupied Manchuria. When the Soviets left, the Communist PLA was in control of most but not all of Manchuria, and were equipped with some Japanese materiel. From this substantial far-northern base Mao resumed his war against US-backed Chiang Kai-shek. Mao suffered reverses, but his greatest allies over the next several years were the arrogance, incompetence and corruption of Chiang and his commanders, which enabled the Communist armies to defeat the Nationalists, who fled to Taiwan. Mao declared the establishment of the People's Republic of China in October 1949. *(text p. 156)*

2 Sep 1945 Japan   Japan formally surrenders to Allied Powers on deck of battleship USS *Missouri* in Tokyo Bay. *(text p. 119)*

Sep 1945– Sep 1951   Allied occupation of Japan. US troops occupy all Japanese Home Islands. USSR occupies southern half of Sakhalin Island, along with the Kuril Islands. *(text p. 119)*

9 Sep 1945   In accordance with General Order #1 of 17 August 1945, US Army takes positions in the southern portion of Korea. US General Hodge takes surrender of Japanese forces there. Although not subject to US commander's authority, Soviets acted consistent with the General Order. On 26 August the Soviet Red Army had halted its advance from the north at the 38th Parallel line and had taken surrender of Japanese in the north.

The 38th Parallel was intended only as a convenient dividing line for the Japanese surrender, not as a permanent political boundary. *(text p. 114)*

6–10 Oct 1945   In China, the Japanese North China Area Army, in sole control of Beijing until arrival of US Marines on 6 October, formally surrenders to just-arrived Chinese Nationalist GMD on 10 October. *(text p. 112)*

1946–8   As established at the December 1945 Four-Power Moscow Conference, a US-Soviet Joint Commission for Korea seeks to determine composition of a Korea-wide Provisional Government that would work under a Trusteeship toward independence. Disagreements between US and USSR, and among Korean political factions, preclude agreement on government composition. 'Temporary' occupation zones become North and South Korea. *(text p. 149)*

1 May 1946 In Tokyo, large May Day protest; Japanese communists participate but play no major role. *(text p. 133)*

Nov 1947 France grants Laos quasi-independence in November 1947,
and and Cambodia in December 1948, 'within the French Union',
Dec 1948 while retaining effective control. Full independence comes in 1954. Viet Minh continue aid to communist Pathet Lao and Khmer Issarak movements in those countries. *(text p. 211)*

Oct 1948 USSR recognises Kim Il-sung as Premier of Pyongyang-based Democratic People's Republic of Korea, holding sway in the north. *(text p. 149)*

1 Oct 1949 In Beijing, Mao Zedong proclaims People's Republic of China *(Indochina p. 179) (Speculative p. 157)*

1950–2020 North Korean military numbers about 180,000, growing to about 2,000,000 by 2020. *(text p. 151)*

25 Jun 1950 North Korean leader Kim Il-sung, using a strong military force trained and equipped by the Soviet Union, invades South Korea. The same day, the UN Security Council meets and adopts, by a unanimous vote, with only Yugoslavia abstaining, a resolution demanding the withdrawal of the invading troops and calling on Member States to assist South Korea. *(text pp. 198, 243)*

Jun 1950– After North Korea invades South Korea in June, the fighting
Jul 1951 front reaches almost to the southern tip of the peninsula in September. On 15 September, an amphibious invasion by UN forces at Inchon, midway up the peninsula, enabled MacArthur to recover lost ground and invade the North, reaching almost to the border with China in October. China then intervenes and pushes the UN out of North Korea. By mid-1951 major north-south movement had ceased but fighting continued at roughly the line of the 38th Parallel, the pre-war demarcation of North from South. In July 1951 talks begin for an armistice, but fighting continues along the line of stalemate for two more years. *(text p. 224)*

27 Jun   UN Security Council condemns Korean invasion;
1950 (1)   recommends member states provide military assistance to
          South Korea. There is no Soviet veto because USSR continues
          its boycott in a dispute about seating the Beijing government.
          (text pp. 116, 198)

27 Jun 19 Truman orders US military into action in support of South
50 (2)   Korea. Truman states that without UN intervention in Korea,
          'communist leaders would be emboldened to override
          nations closer to our own shores . . . without opposition
          from the free world, no small nation would have the courage
          to resist threat and aggression by stronger communist
          neighbours'. Truman orders US Navy to take up position
          in the Taiwan Strait. This helps dissuade Beijing from
          attempting an invasion of Taiwan. The Communists' Taiwan
          invasion force is re-oriented as a Korean assistance force.
          (text p. 199)

30 Jun 1950 After North Korea attacks South Korea, and the US gets ready
          to fight communists in Northeast Asia, Truman announces
          the US would begin providing weapons and material to the
          French to help them fight communists in Southeast Asia.
          (text p. 184)

1950–4   Shortly after the outbreak of the Korean War, President
          Truman announces US financial assistance to France in their
          war in Indochina. From 1951 to 1954 the US gave or lent to
          the French equipment such as aircraft and ships, including
          an aircraft carrier. Officially, no US military personnel were
          involved in combat operations. Unofficially, several dozen
          US pilots flew combat missions in US aircraft painted with
          French markings to resupply French forces besieged at Dien
          Bien Phu. *(text p. 191)*

Jul 1950 (1) In Korea, elements of the US 24th Infantry Division, hurriedly
          flown in from Japan, with sometimes faulty or missing
          equipment and limited ammunition, are pushed back from
          Osan by advancing North Koreans. The remainder of the 24th,
          and elements of the 25th Infantry Division, along with South
          Korean forces, manage to establish the 'Pusan perimeter', a
          firm defensive line in the south-east corner of the peninsula
          around the port of Pusan. The line holds until US forces
          under the command of Douglas MacArthur conduct a daring

amphibious attack behind enemy's front lines at Inchon Korea on 15 September. US forces are subsequently able to break out of the perimeter and push the North Koreans out of South Korea. *(Indochina text p. 209)*

Jul 1950 (2) Japanese Parliament authorises establishment of 75,000-man army, dubbed 'National Police Reserve'. Seventy years later, Japan's population has grown about 50 per cent, but its Self Defense Force has grown by over 330 per cent, to 250,000. *(text p. 144)*

Aug– Oct 1950 US forces push North Koreans out of South Korea, then keep pushing them north toward border with China. MacArthur, confident of imminent conquest of North Korea, assures Washington that Chinese would not intervene. *(text p. 191)*

8 Aug 1950 China's Mao Zedong redirects the forces of the PLA slated for an imminent invasion of Taiwan. Instead, they will be designated as the North East Frontier Volunteer Army, ready for deployment into Korea. *(text p. 199)*

20 Aug 1950 China's Foreign Minister Zhou Enlai tells the UN 'Korea is China's neighbour . . . The Chinese people cannot but be concerned about a solution of the Korean question' (Stokesbury). *(text p. 193)*

Sep 1950 In the wake of the outbreak of the Korean War, France, the US, Vietnam, Laos and Cambodia agree to a Pentalateral Mutual Assistance Pact. The US would provide assistance to the others to guard against Communist aggression in Southeast Asia. *(text p. 184)*

Sep– Oct 1950 In northern Vietnam, the communist Viet Minh capture Lai Khê, Đông Khê, Cao Bằng, and Lạng Sơn, in Tonkin border-lands with China, inflicting heavy French losses.*(text p. 182)*

25 Oct 1950 South Korean units advancing toward the North Korea/ China border are attacked by Chinese Communist troops. MacArthur and his intel chief, Charles Willoughby, dismiss reports of presence of Chinese troops. *(text p. 194)*

Nov 1950 Several hundred thousand Chinese Communist troops pour into North Korea and attack US and other UN forces. *(text p. 195)*

Mid-Nov 1950 Over Korea, Soviet pilots in Chinese uniforms and flying Soviet MIG fighters bearing Chinese markings enter air combat. Although lapses into Russian in their radio communication revealed their presence, the USSR never admitted their presence. *(text p. 223)*

Dec 1950   French General Jean de Lattre de Tassigny assigned to head the Indochina war effort. Stabilises French positions by building fortified line protecting Hanoi and Red River Delta. *(text p. 185)*

Early 1951   Viet Minh's Vo Nguyen Giap makes three large-scale attacks on French positions north-west of Hanoi, north of Haiphong, and south of Hanoi. None were successful. *(text p. 187)*

Apr 1951   President Truman relieves MacArthur of command after he challenges Truman on war policy. Truman appoints Matthew Ridgway to succeed MacArthur in command of UN forces. MacArthur addresses Congress and says, 'Old soldiers never die, they just fade away'. MacArthur hopes to be given the 1952 Republican nomination without campaigning. Instead, he gets the Chairmanship of Remington Rand. *(text pp. 161, 206)*

Jun 1951–   In northern Vietnam, General De Lattre clears most Viet
Feb 1952   Minh from Red River Delta, then seeks to expand security perimeter with capture of Hoa Binh to the south-west. French take Hoa Binh in November 1951 but are unable to hold their logistical and support lines against heavy, continuous Viet Minh pressure. French pull out of Hoa Binh and back toward Hanoi in February 1952, having inflicted losses on the Viet Minh, but sustaining substantial losses themselves. *(text p. 189)*

Jul 1951   US troop strength at the peak of the Korean War is about
and Apr   350,000; at the peak of the Vietnam War in 1968 it is about
1968   540,000. *(text pp. 202, 222)*

Jul 1951   Korean peace talks begin, with continued back-and-forth fighting between Communist forces and those of sixteen United Nations member states. *(text p. 226)*

Sep 1951 (2) Treaty of San Francisco ends occupation of Japan and restores Japanese sovereignty. US-Japan Security Treaty provides for basing of US forces in Japan. *(text p. 142)*

25 Oct 1952 Campaigning for President, Dwight Eisenhower pledges 'I will go to Korea' to determine how best to end the war. *(text p. 230)*

2 Feb 1953 Newly-inaugurated President Eisenhower reveals that using nuclear weapons to end the Korean War is under consideration. He lifts US naval blockade in Straits of

Taiwan, enabling Nationalists on Taiwan to put pressure on mainland Communists (which they do 18 months later by landing 75,000 troops on disputed islands of Quemoy and Matsu close to mainland). *(text p. 230)*

Mar–
Apr 1953

Two uranium implosion devices are tested in Nevada. Both 'fizzle', producing about 200 tons' (0.2 kilotons') yield. *(text p. 60)*

27 Jul 1953

Korean War armistice freezes battle lines in place, almost exactly along the pre-war line, the 38th Parallel. Dividing line is demarcated by a 2.5-mile wide demilitarised zone. In August, South Korea and US sign a Mutual Defense Treaty under which US forces remain stationed in South Korea to the present day. Their presence near the DMZ is a tripwire. If the North were to invade again, they would immediately encounter American troops, and would be at war with the US. *(text p. 233)*

Nov 1953

After repeated back-and-forth fighting in Tonkin, Viet Minh put pressure on French by attacking Laos. To stem Viet Minh advances into Laos, French fortify Dien Bien Phu in a valley near Laotian border. US provides the French with limited material assistance. *(text p. 221)*

May 1954

Using artillery on the high ground overlooking the French-held Dien Bien Phu valley, the Viet Minh cut off French use of their airstrip for resupply or evacuation. Massed troops overrun French positions all around the valley floor, leading to the decisive French defeat that ends the First Indochina War. *(text p. 221)*

Jul 1954

In Geneva, France and Viet Minh agree to 'temporary' partition of Vietnam, pending 1956 elections. Dividing line, roughly the 17th Parallel, approximately bisects Vietnam a few miles north of Quang Tri, with a mile-wide Demilitarised Zone. *(text p. 233)*

Sep 1954–
Mar 1955

Chinese Communists and Nationalists skirmish over Quemoy and Matsu, disputed islands off mainland coast. US Secretary of State Dulles says that US is considering use of atomic weapons against China. *(text p. 230)*

Oct 1955

In South Vietnam, Prime Minister Ngo Dinh Diem is dissatisfied with Geneva agreements; he wrests control of government and forecloses reunification elections.

Vietnamese communists increase guerrilla warfare in South Vietnam. *(text p. 205)*

26 Apr 1960   Repatriated to Korea in 1945 from the US, Syngman Rhee rapidly rises to Presidency of (South) Korea, with US backing. Rhee governs with a heavy hand through three presidential terms that included invasion by North Korea. After the armistice, the South's economy recovered slowly, not helped by Rhee's repressive measures. Shortly after he was elected a fourth time, students and others vehemently protested the autocracy and corruption. Rhee was forced to resign and flee the country to exile in US. Although there is a Korean community in Annandale VA, there is no record he ever spent time there. *(text p. 151)*

7 Aug 1964   President Johnson informs Congress that North Vietnamese patrol boats had fired on US Navy ships in international waters in the Gulf of Tonkin. In a bipartisan vote, Congress authorises him to take any steps necessary to retaliate and maintain international peace and security in Southeast Asia. This Gulf of Tonkin Resolution was the legal basis for US prosecution of the Vietnam War. *(text p. 199)*

1965–71   Australia and New Zealand send army, air force and naval units into combat in the Vietnam War, operating in the lowlands east of Saigon in Bien Hoa, Phuoc Tuy and Long Khanh provinces. Peak personnel strength was about 8,500. *(text p. 219)*

1967–71   Land Clearing Companies of the US Army Engineers use powerful armoured bulldozers with heavy, sharp plough blades made by the Rome Plow Co. of Georgia to clear swaths of jungle vegetation from the sides of important roads in Vietnam, to deny close-in hiding places for Viet Cong to ambush military traffic. *(text pp. 192)*

1968–2010   From 1968 to 2010 Japan has the world's second largest economy; China is #2 after 2010. *(text p. 146)*

Mar 1979   Communist China and Communist Vietnam go to war. In 1978 Vietnam had invaded Cambodia, toppled the genocidal Khmer Rouge regime of Pol Pot and remained in occupation. To dissuade Vietnam from such aggression, China invaded northern Vietnam with over 200,000 troops, briefly occupying border outposts including Lang Son, Cao Bang and Lao Cai. Both sides claimed victory. *(text p. 195)*

1964–73   Throughout the US-Vietnam war, North Vietnam extensively uses safe areas in Laos and Cambodia, and a well-developed 'road' network, the Ho Chi Minh trail, to channel troops and material from the North into South Vietnam.

The French defeat in the First Indochina War ended all French support for the Royal Laotian government, allowing the communist Pathet Lao to take control of portions of Laotian territory, enabling the Vietnamese Communists to use Laotian territory as sanctuaries and supply routes. In Cambodia, the Vietnamese Communists exploited King Sihanouk's 'neutralist' stance, and in concert with the local communists, the Khmer Rouge, used Cambodian territory as safe havens and for transport of supplies from North Vietnam and Laos, and from communist bloc ships using the port of Sihanoukville. Aware he was aiding the communists, King Sihanouk felt too weak to resist the Vietnamese. *(text p. 211)*

1985–2006   After the USSR and China refused help in developing nuclear weapons, North Korea undertakes its own programme, producing a sub-kiloton plutonium nuclear device in 2006. In 2017 the North claims their latest test was of a thermonuclear device. *(text p. 152)*

References Cited

Accinelli, R. (1996), *Crisis and Commitment: United States Policy toward Taiwan, 1950-1955*. The University of North Carolina Press.

Agnew, H. and Schreiber, R. (1998), *Norris E. Bradbury 1909–1996: A Biographical Memoir* (PDF). National Academies Press.

Akamatsu, P. (1972), *Meiji 1868: Revolution and Counter-Revolution in Japan*. Harper & Row.

Allen, R. (1960) *Korea's Syngman Rhee: An Unauthorised Portrait*. https://biography.yourdictionary.com/syngman-rhee

Allen, T. and Polmar, N. (1995), *Codename Downfall. The Secret Plan to Invade Japan - And Why Truman Dropped the Bomb*. Simon and Schuster.

Alexander, B. (1986), *Korea. The First War We Lost*. Hippocrene Books.

AmEx (American Experience) (1999), *MacArthur*. WGBH/Public Broadcasting System.

Anderson, W. (2000), *Memoir. Korean War Educator* http://www.koreanwar-educator.org/memoirs/anderson_william/index.htm#Defective

Andrew, C. and Gordievsky, O. (1990), *KGB: The Inside Story of Its Foreign Operations from Lenin to Gorbachev*. New York: Harper Collins.

Aspray, W. (1987), *An Interview with CHARLES CRITCHFIELD OH 134 on 29 May 1987*. Charles Babbage Institute. The Center for the History of Information Processing, University of Minnesota. https://conservancy.umn.edu/bitstream/handle/11299/107233/oh134cc.pdf

Atomic Archive (a) undated. Jumbo. http://www.atomicarchive.com/History/trinity/jumbo.shtml

Atomic Archive (b) undated. The Potsdam Declaration. http://www.atomicarchive.com/History/mp/p5s10.shtml

Atomic Heritage Foundation 2014. Plutonium. https://www.atomicheritage.org/history/plutonium

Atomic Heritage Foundation 2014a. Project Silverplate. https://www.atomicheritage.org/history/project-silverplate

Baggott, J. (2010), *The First War of Physics*. Pegasus Books.

Bartlit, N and Yalman, R. (2016), *Japanese Mass Suicides*. Atomic Heritage Foundation. Atomicheritage.org

Bergamini, D. (1971), *Japan's Imperial Conspiracy*. William Morrow and Company, Inc.

Bernstein, R. (2014), *China 1945: Mao's Revolution and America's Fateful Choice*. Alfred Knopf.

Bird, K. and Sherwin, J. (2007), *American Prometheus. Triumph and Tragedy of J. Robert Oppenheimer*. Knopf Doubleday.

Bodard, L. (1967), *The Quicksand War. Prelude to Vietnam*. Little, Brown Publ.

Boffey, P. (31 January 1969), 'The Hornig Years: Did LBJ Neglect His Science Advisor?' (PDF). *Science* 163 (3866): 453–8.

Bowen, L. (1959), *Project Silverplate 1943–1946. The History of Air Force Participation in the Atomic Energy Programme, 1943–1953 Vol. I*. US Air Force, Air University Historical Liaison Office.

Brians, P. (1987), *Nuclear Holocausts: Atomic War in Fiction, 1895-1984*. Kent State University Press, https://brians.wsu.edu/2016/11/16/nuclear-holocausts-atomic-war-in-fiction-3/

Brooks, L. (1968), *Behind Japan's Surrender. The Secret Struggle to End an Empire*. Carpe Veritas Books.

Burr, W. (2009), *U.S. Intelligence and the Detection of the First Soviet Nuclear Test, September 1949*. National Security Archive, George Washington University.

Buruma, I. (2003), *Inventing Japan*. The Modern Library.

Buruma, I. (2013), *Year Zero. A History of 1945*. Penguin Press.

Buzo, A. (2016), *The Making of Modern Korea*. Routledge.

Caprio, M. (2009), *Radical Assimilation under Wartime Conditions. Japanese Assimilation Policies in Colonial Korea, 1910-1945*. University of Washington Press.

Census Bureau (US) (1975), *Historical Statistics of the United States, Colonial Times to 1970*.

Central Intelligence Agency (2014), *World Factbook*. Government Printing Office.

CMH (Center of Military History) (1990) *Merrill's Marauders February - May 1944*. CMH Pub 100-4. Superintendent of Documents, U.S. Government Printing Office, http://www.history.army.mil/books/wwii/marauders/marauders-fw.htm

Chandler, D. (23 August 1999), 'Cambodia's ruthless dictator cheated justice, dying before he could answer for the atrocities committed during his unrelenting quest to create a rural Utopia.' *TIME* 154: 7.

Chang, K. (1946), *Last Chance in Manchuria: The Diary of Chang Kia-Ngau*. Hoover Press, 1989.

Chen, C. (2008), *Preparations for Invasion of Japan 14 Jul 1945 - 9 Aug 1945*. World War II Database. http://WWIIdb.com/battle_spec. php?battle_id=54

Cima, R. (ed.) (1987), *Vietnam: A Country Study*. Library of Congress.

Clay, B. (2003), *The Forgotten War: America in Korea, 1950–1953*. Naval Institute Press.

Coker, K. (2013), *U.S. Army Reserve Mobilisation for the Korean War*. US Army Reserve Command.

Combined Chiefs (1944), *Papers and Minutes of Meetings Octagon Conference*. Office, US Secretary of the Combined Chiefs of Staff. US Joint Chiefs of Staff.

Connor, A. (1992), *The Armor Debacle in Korea, 1950: Implications For Today*. US Army War College.

Corfield, J. (2013), *Historical Dictionary of Ho Chi Minh City*. Anthem Press.

Coster-Mullen, J. (2012), *Atom Bombs: The Top Secret Inside Story of Little Boy and Fat Man*. John Coster-Mullen.

Cressman, R. (1999), *The Official Chronology of the U.S. Navy in World War II*. Contemporary History Branch Naval Historical Center. http://www. ibiblio.org/hyperwar/USN/USN-Chron/USN-Chron-1945.html

Cully, G. (2020), *Operation Silverplate*. Cybermodeller Online https:// www.cybermodeler.com/history/silverpl/silverpl.shtml

Cumings, B. (2005), *Korea's Place in the Sun: A Modern History*. W. W. Norton & Company.

Davidson, P. (1988), *Vietnam at War: The History, 1946–1975*. Presidio Press.

Department of the Army (US) (1966), *The Campaigns of MacArthur in the Pacific*. Reports of General MacArthur.

Department of Energy (US) (2) (undated), *Espionage and The Manhattan Project (1940-1945)*. Office of History and Heritage Resources https://www.osti.gov/opennet/manhattan-project-history/ Events/1942-1945/espionage.htm

Department of State (US) (2) (undated), *Occupation and Reconstruction of Japan 1945-52*. Office of the Historian.

D'Este, C. (1995), *Patton: A Genius For War*. HarperCollins.

Dickson, D (1956), *Oscar Seborer*. Office Memorandum, Los Alamos National Lab 17 September. ,https://int.nyt.com/data/documenthelper/6627-seborer documents/9253f3b83621d52313bf/optimized/full.pdf#page=1

Dingman, R. (1988), 'Atomic Diplomacy During the Korean War', *International Security* 13 (3): 50–91. doi:10.2307/2538736. JSTOR 2538736

Dobbs, M. (2012), *Six Months in 1945*. Alfred Knopf.

Dommen, A. (2001), *The Indochinese Experience of the French and the Americans*. Indiana University Press.

Dower, J. (1999), *Embracing Defeat: Japan in the Wake of World War II*. W. W. Norton & Company.

Dryburgh, M. (2000), *North China and Japanese Expansion 1933–1937: Regional Power and the National Interest*. Routledge Curzon.

Ealey, M. (2006), *As World War II Entered Its Final Stages the Belligerent Powers Committed One Heinous Act After Another*. History News Network George Mason University. http://historynewsnetwork.org/article/22336

Eddy, M. (14 February 2020), 'New meaning in looking at bombing of Dresden', *New York Times*.

Eisenhower, D. (1954), *Address at Springfield IL 19 August*. Eisenhower Presidential Library https://www.eisenhowerlibrary.gov/eisenhowers/quotes#War

Eliot, G. (5 August 1951), 'Troops In a Division Include Both Service and Combat Men', *Toledo Blade*.

Elliott, K. (2011), *Remember when 'made in Japan' meant cheap junk?* https://www.dpreview.com/forums/post/40113485

Fall, B. (1961), *Street Without Joy. The French Debacle in Indochina*. Stackpole.

Farmelo, G. (2013), *Churchill's Bomb: How The United States Overtook Britain in the First Nuclear Arms Race*. Basic Books.

Federal Bureau of Investigation, US (undated), *Duquesne Spy Ring. Famous Cases and Criminals*. https://www.fbi.gov/history/famous-cases/duquesne-spy-ring

Ferrell, R. (1994), *Choosing Truman: The Democratic Convention of 1944*. University of Missouri Press.

Filipelli, R. (undated), *Vietnam Notebook*. www.parallelnarratives.com

Finch, M. (2014), 'Forgotten Battles: Operation Léa, Oct-Nov 1947: A wild gamble at finishing the Indochina War?', *Defence-In-Depth*, King's College UK. https://defenceindepth.co/2014/11/27/operation-lea-oct-nov-1947-a-wild-gamble-at-finishing-the-indochina-war/

Flanagan, E. (1997), *The Rakkasans: The Combat History of the 187th Airborne Infantry*. Random House Publishing Group.

Flynn, G. (1993), *The Draft, 1940–1973*. University Press of Kansas.

Forbes, A. and Henley, D. (2012), *Vietnam Past and Present: The North*. Cognoscenti Books.

Frank, R. (1999), *Downfall. The End of the Imperial Japanese Empire*. Random House.

Frank, R. (2007), *MacArthur*. Palgrave Macmillan.

French, Paul (2007), *North Korea: The Paranoid Peninsula – A Modern History*. Zed Books.

Friedman, G. (29 March 2011), 'What Happened to the American Declaration of War?', *Geopolitical Weekly*.

Gaddis, J. (2005), *The Cold War. A New History*. Penguin Books.

Gavrilov, V. (5 September 2005), 'Saving General Wainwright', *Sputniknews* https://sputniknews.com/analysis/2005090541306298/

Gettleman, M. (1959), *Vietnam*. Fawcett.

Giangreco, D. (2009), *Hell to Pay: Operation Downfall and the Invasion of Japan, 1945–1947*. Naval Institute Press.

Gillen, D. and Etter, C. (1983), 'Staying On: Japanese Soldiers and Civilians in China, 1945-1949', *The Journal of Asian Studies* 42:3.

Giusti, E. (1951), *Mobilisation of the Marine Corps Reserve in the Korean Conflict 1950-51*. Headquarters U.S. Marine Corps.

Glantz, D. (1983), *August Storm: The Soviet 1945 Strategic Offensive in Manchuria*. US Army Command and General Staff College Ft. Leavenworth Combat Studies Institute.

Gough, T. (1987), *U.S. Army Mobilisation and Logistics in the Korean War*. US Army Center of Military History.

Government Printing Office (1957), *Mutual Security Appropriations for 1958: Hearings Before the Subcommittee of the Committee on Appropriations*, House of Representatives, Eighty-fifth Congress.

Grey, A. (April 1951), 'The Thirty Eighth Parallel', *Foreign Affairs*.

Griffith, R. (1970), *The Politics of Fear: Joseph R. McCarthy and the Senate*. University of Massachusetts Press.

Groves, L. (1945), Memorandum for the Secretary of War from General L. R. Groves, 'Atomic Fission Bombs,' April 23, 1945, Manhattan Engineer District. The Atomic Bomb and the End of World War II National Security Archive https://nsarchive2.gwu.edu//NSAEBB/NSAEBB162/

Groves, L. (1962), *Now It Can Be Told*. Harper.

Gunn, G. (January 2011), 'The Great Vietnamese Famine of 1944-45 Revisited', *The Asia-Pacific Journal: Japan Focus*.

Hahn, O. and Strassmann, F. (1939), 'On the detection and characteristics of the alkaline earth metals formed by irradiation of uranium with neutrons', *Naturwissenschaften* Vol. 27, No. 1, 11–15.

Halberstam, D. (2007), *The Coldest Winter: America and the Korean War*. Hyperion.

Hammer, E. (1954), *The Struggle For Indochina*. Stanford University Press.

Harrison, J. (1989), *The Endless War: Vietnam's Struggle for Independence*. Columbia University Press.

Hasegawa, T. (2005), *Racing the Enemy. Stalin, Truman and the Surrender of Japan*. Belknap Harvard Press.

Hastings, M. (2009), *Retribution: The Battle For Japan 1944-45*. Alfred A Knopf.

Hastings, M. (2012), *Inferno: The World At War 1939-1945*. Alfred A Knopf.

Heiser, J. (1974), *Vietnam Studies Logistic Support*. Center for Military History.

Heinrichs, W. and Gallicchio, M. (2017), *Implacable Foes*. Oxford University Press.

Hillsborough, Romulus (2005), *Shinsengumi: The Shogun's Last Samurai Corps*. Tuttle Publishing.

Hirshon, S. (2002), *General Patton : A Soldier's Life*. Harper Perennial.

Hoddeson, L., Henriksen, P., Meade, R. and Westfall, C. (1993), *Critical Assembly: A Technical History of Los Alamos During the Oppenheimer Years, 1943–1945*. Cambridge University Press.

Holloway, D. (1994), *Stalin and the Bomb*. Yale University Press.

Horne, A. (1978), *A Savage War of Peace. Algeria 1954-1962*. Viking Press.

Hornig, Lili (2011), Interview for Voices of the Manhattan Project. Atomic Heritage Foundation https://www.manhattanprojectvoices.org/oral-histories/lilli-hornigs-interview

Hornfischer, J. (2017), *The Fleet at Flood Tide*. Penguin Random House.

House, J. (2012), *A Military History of the Cold War, 1944-1962*. University of Oklahoma Press.

Hoyt, E. (1989), *Japan's War: The Great Pacific Conflict*. Cooper Square Press.

Hsu, I. (1951), 'Allied Council for Japan', *The Far Eastern Quarterly* 10:2.

Hsu, I. (1995), *The Rise of Modern China*. Oxford University Press.

Huber, D. (1988), *Pastel: Deception in the Invasion of Japan*. Combat Studies Institute US Army Command and General Staff College.

Irish, A. (2009), *Hokkaido: A History of Ethnic Transition and Development on Japan's Northern Island*. MacFarland & Co.

Ismay, H. (undated), *Origins of the North Atlantic Treaty*. NATO Archives. http://www.nato.int/archives/1st5years/chapters/1.htm#f

James, D. (1970), *The Years of MacArthur. Volume 1, 1880–1941*. Houghton Mifflin.

Joint Chiefs of Staff (1945), *General Order #1 For Surrender Of Imperial Japanese Forces*. https://en.wikisource.org/wiki/General_Order_No._1

Karnow, S. (1983), *Vietnam: A History*. Viking Press.

Kemp, R. (2012), *The End of Manhattan: How the Gas Centrifuge Changed the Quest for Nuclear Weapons. Technology and Culture*. DOI: 10.1353/tech.2012.0046. https://www.researchgate.net/publication/236766581

Kim, D. (2014), *The History of Korea*. ABC-CLIO.

Klehr, H. and Haynes, J. (September 2019), 'On the Trail of a Fourth Soviet Spy at Los Alamos', *Studies in Intelligence* Vol. 63, No. 3; https://www.cia.gov/library/center-for-the-study-of-intelligence/csi-publications/csi-studies/studies/vol-63-no-3/pdfs/Fourth-Soviet-Spy-LosAlamos.pdf

Ko, S. (28 October 2009), 'Ma marks anniversary of historic battle on Kinmen', *Taipei Times*.

Koschmann, V. (1996), *Revolution and Subjectivity in Post-war Japan.* University of Chicago Press.

La Forte, R. (2000), 'World War II-Far East' in Vance, J., *Encyclopedia of Prisoners of War and Internment.* ABC-CLIO.

Lallanilla, M. (2014), 'Hiroshima, Nagasaki & the First Atomic Bombs', *Live Science.* https://www.livescience.com/45509-hiroshima-nagasaki-atomic-bomb.html

Lankov, A. (2002), *From Stalin to Kim Il Sung.* Hurst & Co.

Lankov, A. (2013), *The Real North Korea.* Oxford University Press.

Leary, W. (ed.) (2001), *MacArthur and the American Century: A Reader.* University of Nebraska Press.

Leckie, R. (1962), *Conflict: The History of the Korean War 1950-1953.* G. P. Putnam's Sons.

Lee-Jae Bong (2009), 'U.S. Deployment of Nuclear Weapons in 1950s South Korea & North Korea's Nuclear Development: Toward the Denuclearization of the Korean Peninsula', *Asia-Pacific Journal* Vol 7, Issue 8, No 3.

Leffler, M. (1992), *A Preponderance of Power: National Security, the Truman Administration, and the Cold War.* Stanford University Press.

Leighton, R. and Coakley, R. (1955), *United States Army in World War II. Global Logistics and Strategy: 1940-1943.* Office of the Chief of Military History, Department of the Army.

Leymarie, P. (1997), 'Deafening silence on a horrifying repression', *Le Monde diplomatique.* https://mondediplo.com/1997/03/02madagascar

Lin, B. (1965), *Build a People's Army of a New Type. Long Live the Victory of People's War!.* Foreign Languages Press.

Lobov, G. (1991), *Black Spots of History: In the Skies of North Korea.* JPRS Report, JPRS-UAC-91-003.

Logevall F. (2012), *Embers of War: The Fall of an Empire and the Making of America's Vietnam.* Random House.

Lynch, M. (2010), *Chinese Civil War 1945-1949.* Essential Histories. Osprey Publishing.

Lyons, F. (1945), *Merrill's Marauders In Burma.* Ex-CBI Roundup. http://www.cbi-theater.com/marauders/marauders.html

Maddox, L. (1995), *Weapons for Victory: The Hiroshima Decision Fifty Years Later*. University of Missouri Press.

Maga, T. (2001), *Judgment at Tokyo: The Japanese War Crimes Trials*. University Press of Kentucky.

Matray, J. (1998), *Korea's Partition: Soviet-American Pursuit of Reunification 1945-48*. Mt. Holyoke Press.

McCarthy, J. (1951), *Major Speeches and Debates of Senator Joe McCarthy Delivered in the United States Senate, 1950–1951*. Gordon Press.

McDonald, A. and Hansen, J. (2012), *Truth, Lies, and O-Rings: Inside the Space Shuttle Challenger Disaster*. University Press of Florida

Miller, R. (1998), *To Save a City: The Berlin Airlift, 1948–1949*. US Government Printing Office, 1998-433-155/92107

Miller, R. and Wainstock, D. (2014), *Indochina and Vietnam: The Thirty Five Year War 1940-1975*. Enigma Books.

Millett, A. (2000), *The Korean War, Vol. 1*. University of Nebraska Press.

Morris, S. Jr. (2014), *Supreme Commander: MacArthur's Triumph in Japan*. Harper Collins.

Morton, L. (1953), *The Fall of the Philippines*. U.S. Army Center of Military History.

Nahm, A. and Hoare, J. (undated), *Kim Gyu-sik*. Wilson Center Digital Archive. https://digitalarchive.wilsoncenter.org/resource/modern-korean-history-portal/kim-gyu-sik

National Diet Library (2013), *Tokuda Kyuichi. Portraits of Modern Japanese Historical Figures*. http://www.ndl.go.jp/portrait/e/datas/407.html?cat=129 per cent20Tokuda, per cent20Kyuichi/

National Security Archives (undated), *Hull/Seaman Transcript 13 July 1945*. National Security Archives Gwu.edu.

Ngo, Q. (1978), *Territorial Forces*. U.S. Army Center of Military History.

Navy History and Heritage Command (2017), *Typhoons and Hurricanes: Pacific Typhoon at Okinawa, October 1945*. https://www.history.navy.mil/research/library/online-reading-room/title-list-alphabetically/p/pacific-typhoon-october-1945.html

Nohlen, D., Grotz, F. and Hartmann, C. (2001), *Elections in Asia: A data handbook, Volume II*. Oxford University Press.

New York Times (26 January 2013), 'Donald Hornig, Last to See First A-Bomb, Dies at 92'.

Nichols, K. (1987), *The Road to Trinity: A Personal Account of How America's Nuclear Policies Were Made*. William Morrow.

NuclearFiles.org (undated), *Transcript of phone conversation, Senator Harry Truman and Secretary of War Henry Stimson, June 17, 1943*.

Nuclear Weapon Archive (undated), *The 100 Ton Test*. http://nuclearweaponarchive.org/Usa/Tests/Trinity.html

Oberdorfer, D. (1997), *The Two Koreas: A Contemporary History*. Addison Wesley.

Offner, A. (2002), *Another Such Victory: President Truman and the Cold War, 1945–1953*. Stanford University Press.

Oliver, R., (1954), *Syngman Rhee: The Man behind the Myth*. https://biography.yourdictionary.com/syngman-rhee

Osborne, M. (2013), *Southeast Asia: An Introductory History*. Allen and Unwin.

Pace, E. (15 November 1993), 'Sanzo Nosaka, 101, Communist in Japan Ejected by the Party'. *New York Times*.

Pach, C. (ed.) (2015), *American President: Dwight Eisenhower*. Miller Center University of Virginia.

Paine, L. (2013), *The Sea and Civilisation*. Alfred Knopf.

Pappalardo, J. (October 2019), '10 Rocket Launch Failures That Changed History', *Popular Mechanics*.

Park, J. (2009), *In Search for Democracy: The Korean Provisional Government*. Wesleyan University. https://wesscholar.wesleyan.edu

Pennington, D. (2006), *Dien Bien Phu: A Battle Assessment*. MilitaryHistoryOnline.com

Perovic, J. (2007), 'The Tito–Stalin Split: A Reassessment in Light of New Evidence', *Journal of Cold War Studies* (Spring) 9#2: 32–63.

Peterson, M. and Margulies, P. (2009), *A Brief History of Korea*. Infobase Publishing.

Public Broadcasting System (undated), *American Experience: MacArthur and the Japanese Occupation*.

Public Information Office (undated), *Tropic Lightning: A History of the 25th Infantry Division*.

Radchenko, S. (2012), *The Soviet Union and Asia 1940s-1960s*. Slavic-Eurasian Research Center.

Radchenko, S. (5 August 2015), 'Did Hiroshima Save Japan From Soviet Occupation?, *Foreign Policy*. https://foreignpolicy.com/2015/08/05/stalin_japan_hiroshima_occupation_hokkaido/

Rafalko, F. (undated), *Counter-Intelligence in WWII*. Federation of American Scientists.

Record, J. (1996), 'Vietnam in Retrospect; Could We Have Won?', *Parameters, Journal of the U.S. Army War College*.

Rhodes, R. (1986), *The Making of the Atomic Bomb*. Simon and Schuster.

Roberts, R., Hammond, S. and Sulfaro, V. (2012), *Presidential Campaigns, Slogans, Issues, and Platforms: The Complete Encyclopedia*. ABC-CLIO.

Rosie, G. (1970), *The British in Vietnam*. Panther Books

Ross, Russell R. (ed.) (1987), *Cambodia: A Country Study*. GPO for the Library of Congress.

Rusk, D. (1991), *As I Saw It: A Secretary of State's Memoirs*. Tauris.

Russell, R. (1997), *Project HULA: Secret Soviet-American Cooperation In The War Against Japan*. Naval Historical Center, Department of Navy.

Sabato, L. and Ernst, H. (2006), 'Presidential Election 1952', *Encyclopedia of American Political Parties and Elections*. Facts on File.

Savada, A. (ed.) (1994), *Laos: A Country Study*. Library of Congress .

Saxe, W. (2006), 'Arming The Soviets', *COLUMBIA The Magazine of Northwest History* Vol. 20, No. 2 http://www.washingtonhistory.org/files/library/summer-2006-saxe.pdf

Scalapino, R. (1967), *The Japanese Communist Movement: 1920-1966*. Cambridge University Press.

Schnabel, J. (1992), *United States Army in the Korean War Policy and Direction the First Year*. U.S. Army Center of Military History.

Schulzinger, R. (1997), *A Time For War: The United States and Vietnam 1941-1975*. Oxford University Press.

Seaman, L. (1945), *Memo, 13 Aug 1945 Discussion with General John Hull, re: Availability of Additional Bombs. The Atomic Bomb and the End of World War II*. https://nsarchive2.gwu.edu//NSAEBB/NSAEBB162/72.pdf

Seig, L. (6 April 2007), 'Historians battle over Okinawa WWII mass suicides', *Reuters In Depth* April 6. https://www.reuters.com/article/us-japan-history-okinawa/historians-battle-over-okinawa-WWII-mass-suicides-idUST29175620070406

Selden, M. (undated), 'A Forgotten Holocaust: US Bombing Strategy, the Destruction of Japanese Cities and the American Way of War from World War II to Iraq', *Asia-Pacific Journal: Japan Focus*.

Seth, M. (2010), *A Concise History of Modern Korea*. Rowman and Littlefield.

Shaw, H. (1960), *The US Marines in North China 1945-49*. Historical Branch, HQ US Marine Corps.https://web.archive.org/web/20130322034516/http://www.scuttlebuttsmallchow.com/northchina.html

Sheehan, N. (2009), *A Fiery Peace in a Cold War. Bernard Schriever and the Ultimate Weapon*. Random House.

Shulimson, J. (undated), *The Marine War: III MAF in Vietnam 1965-1971*. U.S. Marine Corps Historical Center.

Smith, J. (2012), *Eisenhower in War and Peace*. Random House.

Spector, R. (2007), *In the Ruins of Empire*. Random House.

Spence, Jonathan D. (1999), *The Search for Modern China*. W.W. Norton and Company.

Stalin, J. (1945), *Draft Message from Joseph Stalin to Harry S. Truman, August 17, 1945*, History and Public Policy Programme Digital Archive https://digitalarchive.wilsoncenter.org/document/122330

Starry, D. (1978), *Mounted Combat in Vietnam* (PDF). Vietnam Studies. Washington, DC: Department of the Army.

Stepanovich, I. (1945), *Reporting on the plan of operation of the 87th rifle corps to the island of Hokkaido and the southern part of the islands of the Kurile chain*. Wilson Center Digital Archive. http://digitalarchive.wilsoncenter.org/document/122335

Stewart, R. (2005), *American Military History Volume II: The United States Army in a Global Era, 1917–2003*. Department of the Army.

Stokesbury, J. (1990), *A Short History of the Korean War*. Harper Perennial.

Strand, W. (2004), 'Opening The Hermit Kingdom', *History Today* 54:1.

Strategic Bombing Survey (US) (1946), *The Effects Of Strategic Bombing On Japan's War Economy*. US Government Printing Office.

Stuckey, J. and Pistorious, J. (1985), 'Mobilisation for the Vietnam War: A Political and Military Catastrophe', *Parameters, Journal of the US Army War College*.

Sublette, C. (2002), *Operation Upshot Knothole*. Nuclear Weapon Archive. http://www.nuclearweaponarchive.org/Usa/Tests/Upshotk.html

Takaki, R. (1995), *Hiroshima: Why America Dropped The Atomic Bomb*. Little Brown & Co.

Takemura, Masayuki and Moroi, Takafumi (2004), 'Mortality Estimation by Causes of Death Due to the 1923 Kanto Earthquake', *Journal of Japan Association for Earthquake Engineering* 4(4): 21–45.

Taylor, D. (28 June 2016), 'The Inside Story of How a Nazi Plot to Sabotage the U.S. War Effort Was Foiled', *Smithsonian Magazine*. https://www.smithsonianmag.com/history/inside-story-how-nazi-plot-sabotage-us-war-effort-was-foiled-180959594/

Teague, P. (2016), *The Soviet Invasion of Manchuria and the Kwangtung Army*. Amazon Digital Services.

Thomas, E. (2013), *Ike's Bluff: President Eisenhower's Secret Battle to Save the World*. Back Bay Books.

Tillman, B. (2014), *D-Day Encyclopedia*. Regnery History Publishers.

Treaty of Peace With Japan 1945. Argentina, Australia, etc. https://treaties.un.org/doc/Publication/UNTS/Volume per cent20136/volume-136-I-1832-English.pdf

Tropic Lightning Association (1970), *Vietnam 1970: The US 25th Infantry Division*.

Truman, H. (1945), *Notes on the Potsdam Conference, July 17-30, 1945*. President's Secretary's File, Truman Papers. Harry S. Truman Library and Museum. http://www.trumanlibrary.org/whistlestop/study_collections/bomb/large/documents

Truman, H. (1945), *Statement by the President Announcing the Use of the A-Bomb at Hiroshima*.

Truman, H. (1947), *Address To US Congress 12 March*. https://www.ourdocuments.gov/doc.php?flash=false&doc=81&page=transcript

Truman, H. and Ferrell, R. (1980), *The Autobiography of Harry S. Truman*. University Press of Colorado.

Tucker, S. (2011), *The Encyclopedia of the Vietnam War: A Political, Social, and Military History*. ABC-CLIO.

Turnbull, S. (2003), *Genghis Khan and the Mongol Conquests, 1190–1400*. Taylor & Francis.

US Army (2014), *Army Command Policy AR 600-20*. HQ Department of the Army. https://cascom.army.mil/s_staff/EO/AR_600-20.pdf

US Forces Korea (2015), *United Nations Command*. usfk.mil.

US Marine Corps (1986), *The Soviet Army Offensive: Manchuria, 1945*. Combat Studies Center.

US Navy (2017), *US Ship Force Levels*. Naval History and Heritage Command. https://www.history.navy.mil/research/histories/ship-histories/us-ship-force-levels.html#1945

US Strategic Bombing Survey (1946), *The Effects Of Strategic Bombing On Japan's War Economy*. US Government Printing Office.

Varhola, M. (2000), *Fire and Ice: The Korean War, 1950–1953*. Da Capo Press.

Vasilevsky, A. (1945), *Order of 18 August 1945 to Commander of 1st Far Eastern Front*. Wilson Archives http://digitalarchive.wilsoncenter.org/document/122332

Vogel, S. (2008), *The Pentagon: A History*. Random House.

Volkogonov, D. (1999), *Autopsy for an Empire*. The Free Press.

Waldrop, M. (17 August 1990), 'Hubble: The Case of the Single-Point Failure', *Science Magazine* 249 (4970): 735–6.

Warren, J. (2005), *American Spartans: The U.S. Marines*. Simon & Schuster.

Watry, D. (2014), *Diplomacy at the Brink: Eisenhower, Churchill, and Eden in the Cold War*. Louisiana State University Press.

Weinberg, G. (1994), *The World At Arms*. Cambridge University Press.

Westad, O. (2003), *Decisive Encounters: The Chinese Civil War 1946-1950*. Stanford University Press.

Williams, J. (16 July 2016), 'How typhoons at the end of World War II swamped U.S. ships and nearly saved Japan from defeat', *Washington Post*.https://www.washingtonpost.com/news/capital-weather-gang/wp/2015/07/16/how-typhoons-at-the-end-of-world-war-ii-swamped-u-s-ships-and-nearly-saved-japan-from-defeat/

Wilson Center (undated), *Syngman Rhee. The Cold War Files.* Cold War International History Project. https://www.wilsoncenter.org/programme/cold-war-international-history-project

Woodhouse, C. (2002), *The Struggle for Greece 1941–1949.* Hurst & Company.

Woodward, L. (1971), *History of World War II - British Foreign Policy in World War II.* Her Majesty's Stationery Office.

World Nuclear Association (2017), *Military Warheads as a Source of Nuclear Fuel.* https://www.world-nuclear.org/information-library/nuclear-fuel-cycle/uranium-resources/military-warheads-as-a-source-of-nuclear-fuel.aspx

Xiaoming, Z. (2002), 'China, the Soviet Union, and the Korean War: From an Abortive Air War Plan to a Wartime Relationship', *Journal of Conflict Studies.* Gregg Centre for the Study of War and Society.

Yates, W. (1983), *Chiang Kai-shek, the United States and the Fall of the Kuomintang Regime.* US Army War College, Carlisle Barracks. https://apps.dtic.mil/dtic/tr/fulltext/u2/a132000.pdf

Yumashev, I. (1945), *Report to Aleksandr Vasilevsky, August 19, 1945.* History and Public Policy Programme Digital Archive, Library of Congress, Manuscript Division, Dmitriĭ Antonovich Volkogonov papers. https://digitalarchive.wilsoncenter.org/document/122335.

Zaloga, S. (2002), *The Kremlin's Nuclear Sword: The Rise and Fall of Russia's Strategic Nuclear Forces.* Smithsonian Books.

Zickel, R. (1991), *Soviet Union.* Claitors Publishers.

Zubok, V. (2007), *A Failed Empire: The Soviet Union in the Cold War From Stalin to Gorbachev.* UNC Press.

Index